COVET

ELLA JAMES

Note: This book explores topics including addiction and abuse. If you are extra sensitive to those things, please be aware and take care of yourself.

Love, Ella

For my family—blood and chosen. But most especially my kids.
May you always overcome.

COVET

VERB   COV·ET   \ ˈKƏ-VƏT \

1: to wish for earnestly
2: to desire what belongs to another

PART I

PROLOGUE

FINLEY

January 31, 1998

"Tell me again about the prince and princess?"

Mummy smiled down at me, her face crisscrossed by shadows from the halo of wildflowers on her head.

"What kind of story would you like, dear?"

I let go of her hand, skipping down the dirt path and then twirling, my dress puffing out around me. "The one with rainbow dolphins!"

My own halo wobbled. I reached up to steady it. Mummy smiled—a *really* happy smile that made my tummy feel warm.

"Rainbow dolphins it will be, then."

I held out my hand for hers, and we strolled down the grassy hillside. Overhead, the kingbirds cawed. Down below, at the bottom of the winding path, the ocean spread before us like a great, glittering blanket.

"It was a cloudy day," Mummy murmured, "with clouds that

foretold stormy weather. Perhaps a bit like this day. And it was the princess's birthday."

"Like mine!"

"A bit like your birthday." Her lips curved slightly, showing me the dimple that I sometimes liked to touch. "This princess, with the red hair and the angel kiss on her big toe, and the gemstone staff for herding sheep, she woke up on that morning *needing* to see dolphins. It was what she wanted most for her seventh birthday—to see the lovely glitter rainbow dolphins that would jump right by the royal island's coastline. They only swam about on the best sorts of days."

I smiled. "Like our dolphins here?"

"Just like those—only showing themselves to the best people."

"Like us?" I grinned, and Mummy nodded gamely.

"Quite. So, the princess asked her mother for a special treat —to go out on a magic boat and call the rainbow dolphins. The queen wasn't sure at first if it would happen. The king had quite a few old, stodgy rules, and sometimes frowned on ventures such as that. But the queen and the princess wanted to go very much, and so they made it happen. They put on their crowns—" I smiled proudly— "and after the princess's royal birthday celebration, they made their way down to the ocean for their expedition, wearing their finest clothes and in the finest of spirits. They knew they would see the rainbow dolphins.

"They arrive there at the docks and get on their boat. They're going to get off, but there's the prince! Prince Declan. He was at the birthday party at the café a bit before, but he stayed late, gobbling all the cake. He has a sweet tooth, you'll remember."

"Oh, yes." I giggled.

"The queen pulls back up to the dock and Prince Declan hops in, and he and the princess exchange smiles, as best friends do. She says, 'I'm glad you're here,' and he says, 'Oh, of course. I would never dream of missing rainbow glitter dolphins on your birthday.' So they set off, with their hats on—"

"What was everyone wearing?"

Mummy smiles, touching the skirt of her lilac dress. "Well, the queen wore a long, quite regal-looking purple gown. The princess wore her green gown with glitter and sequins. And Prince Declan wore blue."

"Is blue his favorite color?"

"I believe it is."

I stored that detail in my mind as the path flattened, tall grass fluttering around us. A cloud shifted in front of the sun. I looked up, and then out at the ocean—gray now, with more whitecaps and a slightly brownish tint in some spots.

"Mummy, what if there's not time before the storm comes?"

"Oh—we'll be fast. Gammy said she saw the dolphins earlier. We'll go and be back straight away."

Mummy's mouth was pinched now as she looked out at the harbor.

"So they went on their boat ride," I reminded her. "What did the prince say?"

"About what, my dear?"

"What did he say to the princess?"

"He...sang songs." She smiled.

"He did?"

"Of course. The royal birthday songs."

"What sort of royal birthday songs?"

Ocean sounds filled my ears—the slosh of water lapping at the island's rocky ledge, the spray of waves clapping against the dock—and comfort filled me as we stepped onto one of the arms of Calshot Harbor's semi-circle dock. To me, it always looked like two arms wrapped around a big, round basket—a pretend basket, of course—the hands almost meeting, but not quite. The dock's arms jutted from the island's ledge into the open sea, and through the small space where they didn't quite meet, boats would pass into the shelter from the waves, docking along the inside of the arms.

Calshot Harbor was the only safe port at Tristan, and not a big or fancy one. Big ships couldn't dock at our island at all. They'd anchor out a bit, and if someone wanted to visit, they'd have to hop into a dinghy.

Mummy told me that many other islands had beaches made of soft sand, where people would lie about in swimming suits, frolicking in the sun and wading in the water. Not our Tristan. It rose from the sea, a great behemoth chunk of brownish rock, its edges cliffs where the waves beat and currents raged, its center a cloud-swathed volcano. We had a mere patch or two of rock-strewn sand, and no one ever passed time there.

My Gammy always said Tristan was another world away, and I sensed that was true.

I'd heard tell of when the volcano erupted in 1961, and everyone was whisked away to England. How the Englanders thought we Tristan folk would gladly stay, but we came rushing back to sea as soon as the volcano settled down again. Perhaps it *was* another world away, but I didn't know who wouldn't love our island, with its cool winds and tingling fog, the cozy wool and sweet sheep, and the peak with smatterings of winter snow, and fishing boats and lobsters, and our cottages with lovely tin roofs. Surely it was the rest of the world that was really losing out, and not we proud and happy islanders.

Today a few boats waited at the dock, including our old skiff. We passed by a few men drinking ale and laughing, gathered 'round a bucket. I clutched Mummy's hand. She smiled down at me, slowing as we reached our wee wooden boat.

"How did it get here?"

Mummy winked, and I knew the answer: Gammy.

Mum got in first and then took my hand to help me in. She

held the orange life vest as I threaded my arms through the holes. It was cool and damp around my neck, smelling of salt water and mildew. I wrapped my hands around it, squeezing slightly as Mummy fussed with the snap of hers. When a piece of plastic broke off, she tossed it in the floor and shrugged.

"Only when you're big like Mummy," she said, shaking her finger.

"I'll swim like a mermaid then!"

A ray of sunlight peeked through the gray clouds. I remember reaching for my halo, thinking Mum and I would need to take them off and set them in the boat's belly with her discarded vest. Just as she leaned away, there he was.

My father's skin was sun-darkened, his blond hair just one shade shy of brown, as if someone had rubbed dirt in it. From his perch there on the dock, he scowled down on us, and my stomach flipped like a frightened fish.

"What the hell is this then?"

I could see the redness in his eyes, the meanness all about his mouth, and I felt scared for Mummy.

"We're going to find the dolphins! It's my birthday!"

He glowered down at me, and I noticed the stains on his tee shirt.

"We'll be back quite soon," Mummy said. Her tone was tight and careful, a bit nice and a bit like she might perhaps be ready for a row. "We can talk then," she offered softly.

Daddy stepped into the little wooden skiff. It rocked with his weight, water sloshing up on one side. "I don't think so." He sat down on the bench beside Mummy, folding his large arms. "I believe I'll go." He glared at Mummy like an angry villain. "Wouldn't want to miss the *fun*."

Unshed tears made my eyes ache. I swallowed hard and looked down at my sandal-clad feet. Mustn't cry in front of Daddy. Mummy told me many times: no tears except when I was alone or with just her or Gammy. This was different, though. This was my birthday.

"Only Mummy!"

Daddy's blood-shot blue eyes popped wide at my shriek.

"So you want to get out of the boat, then?" he snarled.

Tears spilled down my cheeks. "It was a Mummy-Finley affair!"

"Not anymore. Let's go," he said to Mummy, flicking his hand at her. She jumped up to start the motor. She did whatever Daddy asked; she always gave him what he wanted. Who could blame her? When she didn't, bad things happened.

I wiped at my eyes and wondered, as I often did, why Daddy was this way. I'd seen the other daddies. They were different. Holly's daddy always held her Mum's umbrella when it rained, and Dorothy's daddy liked to ride Dot on his back. My daddy rarely looked at me, and when he did, I knew I was in for it.

As soon as we got off into the waves, the rain began—fat, cold drops that hurt my forehead.

Mummy said, "Let's turn back, Pete."

"I don't think so. I want Fin to see the dolphins."

Fin was what he often called me, despite me not liking it.

"I don't like the rain," I whimpered.

"Toughen up!" Daddy laughed, but it was too loud, making Mummy wince. Mummy steered along the eastern coastline, where the island's rocky ledge stretched up toward the clouds.

I held onto my little wooden bench, pressing my legs together as the boat bounced over the waves. The rain beat down against the skiff, making a low roar. I saw Mummy's mouth pinch. She looked tiny on the bench beside Daddy. She touched her battered flower halo, looking like she thought she should perhaps remove it, but I suppose she didn't want to. Anna's mum had pinned it into her hair. She caught me staring, pulled a towel from her bag, and passed it my way. I took it, gladly covering myself.

Under the towel's blue and white stripes, I let my tears fall. I drew my legs up, feeling warmer, and I hoped the dolphins would come quickly so we could return to shore.

We hadn't seen Daddy in a bit—not even at my birthday party in the village's café. I hoped when we docked, he would disappear again. My mummy never smiled when he was with us, and I didn't either.

The skiff jolted. My tummy pitched, and I peeked out from underneath the towel. Wow—the waves had gotten big. One sloshed right into the boat with us, landing on Mummy's lap. My throat felt tight and pinched as she frowned at her pretty dress. I saw her fist tighten around the steering wheel.

"I'm turning back. With her," she said to Daddy, shaking her head as if to say that for me, this weather was too dangerous.

"Just a bit more. I'll say when to stop, not you."

My heart was pounding, and my throat felt stuck. When Mummy turned the wheel despite him, Daddy grabbed her arm and twisted.

"Stop it, Peter!"

"You want me to stop, we'll talk about something!"

She wriggled free of his grasp. "No, we won't! Not now!"

Water spilled over the skiff's low, wooden walls, a shock of cold soaking my towel and chilling my feet. Another wave splashed Mummy's dress, and I started to cry.

"I want to go back—please!"

"Hush, you!" Daddy turned to Mummy, his face deep red. A bolt of lightning streaked behind him. "I want to talk about him," he sneered. "Charlie Carnegie."

"Peter!"

Water sloshed into Daddy's face, and in that moment, Mummy got us fully turned back toward the harbor. Daddy growled, shoving his hair out of his eyes. Then he stood and tossed Mummy over the bench. He turned the boat around, and I fell in its flat, wooden belly, clutching Mummy's legs. I'd been in storms before, but not one like this.

"Daddy!"

His eyes seared Mummy. "Charlie and Declan! Who is *Declan?*"

"He's a prince!"

My Daddy bellowed, the sound so harsh it took a bit for me to realize he was laughing. Not the nice sort. His face twisted as rain pummeled us. He wiped his hair out of his face again, and then looked down at Mummy.

"I should fucking kill you for this."

Horror seared me like a lightning bolt. Surely he wouldn't do that! I hugged Mummy's knees for dear life. Water splashed over the skiff's sides, covering my legs. Father Russo said that when he's frightened, he prays.

I moved a hand from Mummy's leg to cross myself, which is how the Ave Maria begins, and that's when Daddy snatched her up.

"No!"

The blow came so fast that when I drew my hand away from my mouth, I felt shocked to see the blood there. Still more water rolled over the boat's side, so much I choked on it. Daddy had Mummy by her long, red hair, her head against his lap, her arms curled at her sides. I clutched her skirt, and Mummy kicked at me gently.

"Get away!"

Her words seemed like a line from a horrible story. I felt dragged down by my dress and tried to pull at it, realizing that the water now rose to my elbows. Thunder clapped, and Daddy wrapped his hand around my mummy's throat.

"NO!"

I threw myself at him. The boat stalled, the front jutting up then slamming down atop the waves, as I clawed Daddy's arms and Mummy writhed beside me. Lightning snapped across the sky, and thunder boomed, and Daddy jumped up, making the boat pitch as he dragged Mummy to her feet and screamed, "So tell me, trollop! Tell me about *Carnegie*! Is he going to save you? Can he save you now?"

Mummy tried to sink into the bottom of the boat beside me, but she couldn't. Daddy held her shoulders. Another cold wave sloshed into the boat, smacking me so hard I choked and couldn't get my breath. When I came to, I saw Daddy's hands on Mummy's shoulders, holding Mummy's head into the waves.

Hatred that was cold as ice surged through me. I hit his back with all my might, and Daddy whirled toward me. I shoved his arm, and as he grabbed at me, I remembered something Mummy said—about the one thing that could hurt a man. So I drove my head into his crotch. The feeling as he tipped over the skiff's side was one of swallowing a brick. When Mummy rose up, still gasping violently, my attention snapped to her: the blue hue of her lips, the blood that flowed from one of her eyes. Her gaze careened around the boat, and then she made a high-pitched sound.

"PETE! Oh, Pete! *Christ on the cross!*"

I tried to tell her, tried to tell her that I hadn't meant to push him over. But Mummy shrieked and cried, and when a pale hand thrust out of the murky cauldron of the sea, she screamed again and turned to me. "Stay here, Finley! Do not move!"

The skiff rocked mightily as she jumped out. Water rushed in. I saw a flash of red—my Mummy's pretty hair—then a dash of yellow as a whitecap stole her halo. And then nothing. Nothing.

Nothing.

ONE
DECLAN

April 2018

Smoke seeps from my lips, drifting out over the boat rail like a curl of fog. Tonight, the water's placid, an inky black with smears of pastel starlight. Out here in the middle of the Atlantic, the sky at night is more glitter than darkness. Hazy swaths of purple, peach, and green sky twinkle with diamond-bright stars, their reflection gleaming on the curve of wave that runs alongside the boat.

I curl my hand around my cigarette and bring it to my mouth again.

I'm standing atop the cargo ship's flat hull, hidden from most vantage points by the twenty-foot-tall boxy structure just behind me: the navigation post and captain's quarters. At this hour, both are likely empty. The crew is down below deck, playing poker. Still, I turn the cherry toward my palm.

Better to stay hidden.

That's been my game since I boarded *Miss Aquarius* back in Cape Town: wear my cap low, keep my mouth shut, and help out where I'm needed till I reach my destination.

I close my eyes on a long drag and lean against the railing. That'll be tomorrow. Fuck.

I finish off the smoke and light another one.

It's fucking cold out here. My T-shirt's not enough, even with jeans. South of the equator, we're headed into fall—in early April. Strange stuff. I swallow hard and look down at the deck under my feet. Then I cast my gaze up to the sky and fill my lungs with salty air.

When I feel something in my hand, I look down, finding a line of ash in my palm. I bring the Marlboro to my lips and take the last drag with shaking fingers before pinching the cherry out.

I should go below deck. Play some solitaire in my cabin. Instead I light a third smoke, and, with my free hand, rub my arms. Even after just a few months off, they're smaller than I'm used to, making me feel like someone else.

Laughter trills into the quiet, voices rising as footfall thuds inside the stairwell to my left. Before I can turn toward the sea, figures spill onto the deck. I whirl around, snuffing my smoke out against the rail. Then I turn the other way, aiming to sneak around the navigation post, but there's a loud "Hey, man."

I turn slowly. Half a dozen guys are lined up in some kind of formation, making a semi-circle between the stairwell they just came out of and me.

I nod, meeting the eyes of the one who spoke. Kevin is his name. I think. He's only an inch or two shorter than me, with blue eyes and close-cropped brown hair. He's one of the Americans on board.

I step toward the stairwell, but Kevin catches my arm. "Hang on a sec. We wanna talk to you."

I hear another say, "We barely know you," at the same time as a third—not an American, judging by his accent—is saying, "been six days."

I nod. Hold up a hand. "George," I say, as I step between two of them.

"That's the thing, though," he sneers. "We don't think it is."

"No?" I look behind me.

They're all grinning. "Hell no."

"We been watching."

"We've got an idea about you."

My stomach pitches as a hand claps my shoulder.

"You can tell us."

"We know you're not George."

One dude jerks a thumb at the captain. "You know Bo, don't you? He's the cap'n. No good lying to the captain."

Bo steps closer. He's older than most of the crew members, but still young. If I had to guess, I'd say no older than forty-five. He's wearing khaki-looking shorts and a stained Costa tee. "I know what your papers say. But take your hat off, mate, and help me win a wager."

I shake my head, stepping backward toward the stairwell. "Night, guys."

"I told you it's not him." Someone's in the stairwell, lighting a cigar. He grins around it.

At that same time, I lose my hat. I spin around and snatch it back, glaring at the fucker who took it. His eyes widen at the clear view of my face.

Gasps chorus around us.

"Holy shit."

"I fuckin' told you, Bo!"

The one in the stairwell spreads his arms, chuckling as he blocks me.

"That's some damn good camo, brother. I need something, though, before you get to pass."

He holds a slip of paper out, and the men gather around.

"Homer Carnegie on our boat, we're gonna need some autographs..."

I fake a grin and take the paper. Six thousand miles from Boston, and I'm fucking outed.

* * *

Finley

I clutch the bottle to my chest and cross myself. Then I shut my eyes, bring my arm back, and throw it hard over the cliff's edge. With my eyes shut, I picture its trajectory as it plummets toward the ocean. I inhale, feeling dizzy as birds caw above my head, and far below me, waves break on the rocks.

Vloeiende Trane, these cliffs are called; it means "cascading tears" in Afrikaans. The highest peak is two hundred meters above the ocean's ragged waves. Midway between the cliff-top and the sea, water pours out of the rock in three long streams that look like tears from further out.

Standing atop Vloeiende Trane, the white caps look no bigger than a fingernail, the ocean's swirling cauldron just a gentle dappling of greens and blues.

Deceptive.

I wipe my eyes and fold my arms over my chest. *I won't throw another bottle,* I promise myself as I step toward the cliffs' edge. I search the waves for a flash of glass, for something that will give me satisfaction, but of course, I see nothing.

That's the point, though, isn't it? Throwing letter-stuffed bottles into the void. It's like a prayer. That's its magic. Still, it hurts to know no one will ever read my words. I wipe my face again and whisper, "Give me courage."

I lick my lips and stand with my eyes closed, thinking of Mum. It's something that I almost never do, because I can't bear it. Today, though, I can't seem to help myself.

When my eyes feel puffy and hot, I walk back across the stony plane that forms this small plateau and look down at the field below, its tall grass pressed flat by the wind. At the edge of the field, a cottage. Beyond that, the village valley—an expanse of lush, green grass framed by the cliffs that form the border of the island.

Three gravel roads stripe the valley where the village lies. Scattered along them are sixty-seven cottages, topped by roofs of thatch or brightly colored tin. My gaze runs over the island's few landmarks: the yellow roof of the café, the bare dirt of the base-ball field, the green roof of the clinic near the village's east side.

The church's small, white steeple looks thin as a toothpick from here. I squint, but I can barely make out the blue tin roof of my dear friend Anna's house. I lift my hand to my eyes and stretch my thumb out sideways, and the village disappears—the whole world, gone.

Climbing down the plateau's steep side into the field behind Gammy's house takes half an hour. I move carefully without a harness, slow and steady in the warm glare of the sun, until my soles press into soft grass.

The wind-flattened field—Gammy's backyard—is big and round, hemmed in on one side by the dirt path that leads from the lower slopes of the volcano down to the village, and on the other by the rocky cliffs that overlook the ocean.

Before she passed, we built a table from wood scraps and set it near the field's center. I climb onto it and peer up at the sky. Early autumn now, its blue is almost violent. Today, for once, there are no clouds except some wispy tendrils behind me, wreathing the volcano's peak.

I watch the kingbirds fly, swooping off the cliffs and out of sight, and my heart aches for Gammy. She would have righted my course. Gammy would have told me to say "no" when I was asked. Probably "hell no," I admit. My stomach knots.

I shift my gaze to the cottage, to the stone kiln beside it and the blue sky spread above it, and the cliffs that rise out of the grass beside it. I inhale the salty air and tell myself *just stop*. Now is not the time for despair. Gammy would tell me to keep focused. There are options yet.

I swipe the hair out of my face and carefully re-braid it as my shoulders tingle from the sun's heat. When my damp shirt has dried in the breeze, I get up and walk to the kiln.

There's a small door on the front and two shelves in its slightly rounded belly, where I set my pieces. I haven't done enough of this lately. I'm not even sure I retrieved my last load. I open the door and find indeed I didn't. Two hunter green bowls and a thin, black vase with golden flecks wait inside. I gather them carefully into my arms and follow the stone path to the cottage's front door.

When I first moved in with Gammy, I called this the Hobbit cottage. She didn't know, of course—I wasn't speaking—but it reminded me of a Hobbit's house: the south side built into a hill; one small, round window punched into the grass; the rounded, dark wood door and beige stone facade in front; a thatched roof tilting low; chimes affixed to several spots; and a flower garden growing wild about the stoop.

The door opens with the old, familiar creak. I step into the tidy living area. I run my hand over the well-worn armchair and try to look at it through his eyes. The green and blue rug—woven by my great-grandmother—that's spread across the cement floor. The slouching navy love seat, with its tiny, beige polka dots. The boxy TV on a tiny cedar table in one corner. The wild banana plant dominating the other. Grandma's needlework adorns one wall. A fern hangs in a basket near the TV. The wall to my right, which divides the living room and kitchen, sports a horizontal bookcase.

It smells like rose and lemon here, and the lovely musk of aging paperbacks. I rip my eyes from the bookshelf and walk into the kitchen. Small and standard, I suppose, with a pale blue laminate countertop, a small, round table; some wall-mounted shelves; and a wooden cabinet/pantry in one corner. Wallpaper in a faded, fruit basket pattern adorns the walls.

I scrub my arms and hands with the same lemon pumice soap I use to get the clay grit off after I finish a new piece, and then unpack the bags of food I brought before my hike. I arrange apples, pears, and peaches in a small, wooden bowl and leave a shrink-wrapped loaf of friendship bread atop a matching wooden platter. I check the refrigerator again, as if the eggs, butter, chicken, duck, and various sauces I left there a few hours ago might have walked away. They didn't.

I line jam along the wall beside the sink, double-check the seal on three bags of homemade potato chips, and check the pantry for the pasta, canned goods, Pop-Tarts, and bags of popcorn I already know are there. I re-fold the towel on the oven —Home Sweet Home it says, in faded blue script—and drift back through the living room, picturing him walking down the short hall to the first door on the right, which I'll leave slightly ajar.

It was my mum's room, but when my parents passed, it became mine. It has one window, covered with a lace curtain and facing the ocean. When I was young, it held a full-sized bed, a bookcase, a dresser, and a rocking chair. Now I've moved the bookcase into Gammy's old room, where I store my pottery and package it for shipment on occasions when I sell a piece.

I step in front of the vertical, wall-mounted mirror by the

dresser and peer at myself. Still no wrinkles, no more freckles than I've ever had. I don't look older than twenty despite my twenty-seven years. I pull my hair down from its tie and spread the long, rust-colored locks around my face. I blink my yellow-brown eyes, purse my lips, and study my cheekbones...the smooth skin of my throat and collarbones.

Will I look like an islander to him? Or just a woman?

I laugh. Does it matter? I suppose that shall depend on what I choose to do. The mere notion of that possibility brings about a need for smelling salts, so I move on from the mirror and my thoughts, stepping into the en suite washroom to pull open the curtains.

I look out at the vast, gray sea and smooth blue sky, and I try to imagine any other life for myself than the one I have. Could I have been happy here? *If Mum had lived.* The answer floats up from my bones, a truth too potent to quash.

The sea breeze slaps against the windowpanes and whistles through the thatched roof as I tidy up. Will our cottage be comfortable to him, or will this place appear pitifully lacking? The pristine American homes I've seen were all in magazines or movies, so I'm not sure they were the regular sort. Then again, neither is he. As my mum's stories alluded, he's more king than commoner.

I set my favorite eucalyptus bath crystals on the table by the claw-footed tub and arrange lavender fizzies in a wee bowl. These things were mine, once—but they haven't been for a while. Anyway, I don't mind sharing.

I stroll back into the bedroom, leaving a pack of Doublemint on the night table. I step over to the dresser and reach for the framed photo of Mum and me, twin flower halos on our twin red heads...but then I draw my hand away. I can't say precisely why, but it seems important that I leave it in its place, that I let her stay here—perhaps especially now.

Another spin through the house with the duster, and I call it ready. I linger in the living room, my chest aching and my head too light. On a whim, I turn back to the bedroom. I fetch a small bottle of rose water from the top drawer and spray the living area, tucking it into my pocket as I go.

TWO
DECLAN

I press the power button on my phone and squint at the bright light.

2:49 AM.

I stuff the phone under my pillow, roll onto my side. A bolt of pain sears my right shoulder, sending me onto my back again. Dammit. I've gotta quit forgetting that. Left side it is. Except the left side has me facing the door to my matchbox-sized stateroom. There's a little window on it.

There's no paps here, asshat.

I made headlines in November, but nobody besides my team at Red Sox headquarters and a bunch of folks in white coats know the worst of it. I've been out of the press since the TMZ video shit, in no small part because the Sox have taken care of me. I try to find some comfort in that. I think about my agent, Aarons; my publicist, Sherie. Even the Sox board was more than generous with me, more than forgiving.

Instead of making me feel better, remembering everyone's kindness makes my throat knot up. I run a hand back through my hair and tug until my eyes stop stinging. Nothing's fucking wrong. It's always this way, I remind myself. I fold my knees up toward my chest and cover my eyes. I just need to sleep. Even an hour or two would help. A nap before breakfast...

After my identity was revealed, the ship's cook demanded to know what I wanted for my last breakfast on board, and he's now planning to cook omelets starting at six. He wants me there while he cooks—"to make sure I get it just the way you like it." The chief navigator and the captain plan to join us in the kitchen. After that, more autographs. And pictures with the crew.

Fuck me.

I don't know what to tell them. "No" makes me sound like a dick, and "yes" means I'll end up trending on Twitter.

I sit up and rub the shoulder. Useless. Without my usual concoction keeping me numb, the fucker hurts every time I breathe. My Sox trainers pushed for surgery before this trip, but my med team pushed back. Of course they did.

I lie back down and shut my eyes and focus on my breathing. In and out...and in and out. Behind my eyelids, I see sunlight stretched in gold webs on the sand and on the underside of waves.

My phone's alarm wakes me at 6:05 after one snooze. I throw some clothes on, climb the stairs on legs that shake, and step onto the deck, stopping as a soft breeze feathers my hair back. Fog settled sometime overnight, blanketing the ocean in a haze that's tinted sepia by the rising sun. It's so thick I can barely see beyond the deck's rail.

I know I should haul ass to the dining room, but we're close to the island now. I can't resist climbing up onto the deck atop the nav post. The damp stairs squeak under my shoes as I hasten my steps. The stair rail is cool under my palm. I step onto the upper deck, feeling my pulse quicken at the thought of being here again. At that moment, a breeze pushes the fog aside, revealing a sight that I haven't seen since I was six: Tristan da Cunha—a massive chunk of dark brown rock that rises to a cloud-swathed peak.

Of all the islands in the world, this one is the most remote—the most isolated patch of land where humans live. These thirty-eight square miles of land are 1,700 miles from South Africa and 2,000 miles from South America. With no airport and no safe harbor for large ships, no GPS or cell phone towers, people here live cut off from the world. Mail comes every two to three months, the birth of a baby is a rare occasion, and if someone has a medical emergency, it's flag down one of the fishing vessels or cargo ships that travel back and forth from Cape Town to Antarctica and back, and hope it's headed *back*.

My throat tightens as I squint at the island, searching the grassy valley at the foot of the volcano for cottages that I don't see from here. Somewhere, maybe on the other side, there's a little village. If the guidebooks are to be believed, there are just a dozen or so shy of three hundred people—fishermen and farmers, mostly descended from a handful of British.

I remember them packed in their church, their heads all bowed in prayer, some cheeks wet with tears. I can see the women clutching rosaries, the men pulling on jackets and stepping into boats. I remember the lights at night as boats arrived and departed. Each time they came back empty handed, more tears.

Despite the circumstances, Dad and I were welcomed right into the fold. I remember helping an old lady knead the dough for bread while my father went out in a boat and helped search. I remember all the misty rain. I shut my eyes, seeing Dad's face when he stepped back onto the dock for the last time. His eyes were closed, but hers were open. That's what I remember most. This little girl wrapped up in blankets, with a dirty, sunken face and ropes of tangled red hair. And weird eyes.

I remember how they stood out in her pale, grimy face. Unlike all the other eyes I saw, hers hadn't leaked with tears. They seemed as depthless as the sea itself, and hot, almost like brownish-yellow fire. I think they stuck with me because I couldn't pinpoint the emotion in them. Not for years.

A gull caws, bringing me back to the moment. I can hear the swish of waves against the boat, can feel the wet fog on my face.

I did it. I'm back here. I laugh. Genius or crazy?

I don't have time to decide before someone slaps my back. I turn around and give the captain a smile. For the next hour, I'm Homer Carnegie—household name. I tell myself to buck the fuck up, try to act like the record-breaking Red Sox pitcher they expect. I sign everything from baseballs to a woman's sports bra, telling jokes and answering a bunch of questions while the chef serves me two omelets I can't taste.

"Thanks, man. Real good."

I sign his apron, listen to someone's account of a record I broke last summer. When I can, I steal away to have a smoke and hide my shaking hands.

I close my eyes and try to feel the warm sun on my face, but all I feel is pressure in my throat and chest, behind my eyes.

"Hey, dawg." I look up and find one of the crew lighting his own smoke. I think his name is Chris. He's kind of short and wiry, with brown hair hidden beneath a gray beanie. He's another one of the American crew members. "Just want to tell you thanks. My kid loves the Sox. He's gonna be so happy when he sees that ball."

"Yeah—no problem, man."

"If you don't mind my asking...whatcha doing way out here, in the middle of the ocean?"

I smile tightly. "Here with the Carnegie Foundation. We're laying new phone lines. Maybe internet, too, if we can find a way to make it work."

He nods once. "Riding back to Cape Town with us?"

"Yeah."

"Damn, that's eleven weeks. I'm surprised you can be gone that long. Aren't things firing up?"

I guess this guy's an actual fan. I shrug. "I'll miss some, but it's a one-time thing."

He nods. "Yeah. It's cool you're doing what you're doing. It was nice to meet you." He holds his hand out. I shake it, squeezing harder than I have to so he can't feel my fingers shaking. "You're an idol to so many. Don't forget it."

I give him a small smile and a nod, and, thankfully, he turns and goes downstairs.

I spend the next half hour packing up and helping haul wooden crates—full of supplies provided by the foundation—to the boat's ledge. From there, they'll be lowered in an elevator type of apparatus that's hooked onto the boat's side, and eased into a boat from Tristan.

Since the island's coastline is mostly rocky cliffs, with just one tiny harbor, ships dock out about three hundred yards, and islanders come out in small boats to get visitors like myself.

Morning crawls toward noon. The fog burns off, and I can see the island more clearly. Is that a seal? Fuck, there's a bunch of seals or sea lions on the cliffs. I reach for my phone, snapping a few shots. I remember those guys.

Finally, I spot the smaller boat—a nickel-sized brown dot moving from the island toward *Miss Aquarius*. The crew shuffles around me. I step closer to the rail, stopped short by a hard lump in my throat.

Meanwhile, two crewmembers go overboard on rope ladders

to attach the smaller boat from Tristan to the side of this one. After that, the crates are slowly lowered.

I fill out some departure forms, toss my pack over my shoulder, and move to the boat's edge, where my gaze falls down a rope ladder to the waiting boat. It's pretty small, maybe even smaller than a cabin cruiser—the smallest of all yachts—and looks like it's powered by a single motor on the back. I'm watching two guys strap down the crates when the captain's voice startles me.

"Pack off," he says. "We'll lower it. Just climb down and you'll be on your way."

Then I'm over the boat's side, clinging to the ladder as I inhale salt and brine and the scent of wet rope. I can feel the dim sun on my shoulders, the boat's slight rocking underneath my boots. One rung at a time, and I can see the sea shifting between my moving feet. Then I step into the boat and turn to greet my island escorts—two ordinary-looking, middle-aged men in ordinary, working-class clothes. One—in a pair of oil-smudged coveralls—reaches to shake my hand as the other tips his ball cap.

"Homer Carnegie," the hat-tipper says, as the hand-shaker says, "I'm Rob."

"Mark," the one with the cap says. "You got everything?" His face is creased with sun-lines, and his pale brown eyes are kind.

"Once you're here, you're here to stay," Rob chuckles.

I nod. "Good for it."

Rob nods to the wooden bench behind me. "Have a seat."

I sit, the motor rumbles, and we're off.

The sea looks like a sheet of black glass as we zip over it. A fine spray arches up on each side of the boat, dotting my arms and cheeks with cool water. The breeze lifts my hair off my head as we move along the island's rocky coast.

I look up at the grassy cliffs with eyes that sting. From down here on the surface of the water, I can't see the valley that covers most of one side of the island; Tristan da Cunha simply looks like grass-covered cliffs that stretch to an unseen plateau.

I'm wondering where the boat will land when its nose points slightly inland, toward the cliffs, and I see...yeah, that's penguins. A bunch of little dudes on a low-lying, flatter-looking rockface, hopping up and down and doing penguin shit. As we pass by, I swear one looks right at me. A cold sweat flushes my skin, but I shake my head and laugh and rub my hands together.

I'll feel better by the time I leave this place, if everything goes right. Until then, penguins.

We curve around the island's edge, and finally I see it—Edinburgh of the Seven Seas, the long name of the little village I remember.

From here, it looks like a smattering of brightly colored buildings in the shadow of a mountain. Fuck—it looks like almost nothing.

I wrap a hand around the top of my pack, take a deep breath. I rub my forehead. Christ.

We're headed toward the jagged shoreline, which has dipped down lower, rising only ten or fifteen above the crashing waves. I tighten my grip on my pack and try to look alive when Mark glances at me.

Soon the motor's noise softens, the boat slows slightly, its nose tipping up, and I see we're coming up on the strange dock—two lines of cement jutting outward from the shore like two arms forming an almost-circle. Waves crash into them, shooting toward the sky in a wall of frothy white. As we edge closer, spray slaps my cheeks. I push a hand back through my now-wet hair and smile as my escorts grin back at me.

As we idle into the gap between the arms of the dock, the waves beneath the boat smooth out some, so we're bobbing lightly. I can hear birds caw above us, smell the thick, salty air. A wave hits the dock behind us, and I see a flash of rainbow just ahead of the boat. I'm looking at it when I notice people standing at the shoreline—blurry figures through my wet eyelashes. They're clearly here to greet us. To greet me.

Fuck, I'm really here again. And suddenly I feel like I can breathe.

THREE
FINLEY

I see him coming up the hill from Calshot Harbor like Richard the Lionheart, trailed by half the island.

I'm the watcher—Miss Alice's eyes and ears outside the kitchen. I turn and hurry down the backside of the hill, toward Middle Lane, where the café sits half a mile down, between the Smiths' house and the Crenshaws'. My arms swing with my long, fast strides as I pass homes with wreaths and flags that weren't there yesterday.

On our island, Carnegie is a holy name. Has been since his father, Charles Carnegie, wandered off a ship bound for Antarctica in 1988 and failed to step back on before the ship's departure from Tristan. He was here almost three months before leaving on another ship, not to return for seven more years. But his resources came in his stead. Crates of medical supplies, books, food, and other goods started arriving a few months after Charles departed, and in 1991, his famous family's foundation upped the ante even further with a million-dollar donation for updated farm equipment.

We got a new schoolhouse in 1992; in 1993, a new medical

clinic was built. Carnegie Foundation dollars have helped lure three fulltime school teachers to Tristan—and, of course, Doctor. Before Dr. Daniels arrived four years ago, the island had only transient physicians. Prior to those, my grandmother and Mrs. Petunia White cared for sick people, Uncle Ollie for the unwell animals. Before Charles Carnegie and his pocket-book, children here stopped attending school at age sixteen. Now we're in class until twenty. For those eighteen-year-olds who are eligible, there are scholarships to schools abroad for university.

The last time a Carnegie stepped foot on the island was in 1998, when Charles and his young son visited, ostensibly to look in on their wealthy family's charitable endeavor.

When Declan began playing baseball for the Red Sox—about the time Doctor arrived here, I believe—the island was star-struck. The few times the Red Sox have played and we could get the signal, a group gathered to cheer him on at the café. When they heard this past September that the foundation was sending a crate of signed baseballs, they were quite beside themselves. Then the shipment was delayed. When word came, around Christmas, that "Homer" would be bringing them himself, no one believed it.

The day Mayor Acton got Declan Carnegie's travel applica-tion, people gathered at the pub and nearly drained the bar dry. When I got his medical records, it was as good as confirmed.

We Tristanians have been busy in the last week. Drew Hollis smoothed the packed dirt of Upper, Middle, and Lower lanes with a tractor; flowers were planted in every last window box; front doors were re-painted; two homes got new roofing; the café was redecorated; the barber shop stayed open an extra hour each day to accommodate the many who wished to get hair cuts; the island's twelve vehicles—four rusty Land Rovers, five pick-up trucks, and three Broncos—were washed and cleaned. Fresh crawfish were caught, meat pie was made, beef was marinated, and lamb was stuffed—but not yet sliced.

Miss Alice, the café's chef, didn't want to cut the lamb until she knew Declan had stepped foot on the island. Couldn't have it drying out.

I'm panting slightly when I shove through the café's teal door. My friend Holly looks up from where she's setting a table, and Dot laughs from a corner where she's watering a plant.

"You look a mess," she says.

I sniff and march past them into the kitchen.

"Slice the lamb, Miss Alice! The Carnegie has arrived!"

She smiles from underneath her hair net, blue eyes twinkling in her lined face. "I'll get to it," she says gamely. She turns to a counter bearing four platters of lamb, and I watch her slice for a moment, marveling at how quickly she works. I hope I'm that dexterous when I'm ninety.

I walk back into the dining room, which is buzzing with activity. If one half of the village is escorting him here, the other half is waiting for him. Rachel, Maura, and Blair—all clad in Sunday best and lacy aprons—wave their arms, herding the stampede, while Holly stands behind the largest chair at an empty table, fussing with the ribbons tied to the end of her blonde braids. She's wearing her favorite candy-apple-red dress and red lipstick, and I'd wager she's got those inserts in her bra. Holly's flat as a boy, but she's got something that resembles cleavage peeking from behind her dress's neckline. She gives me a panicked wave, and I laugh. Holly's single, and she loves celebrities. At least she thinks she does. No one here would really know.

As I wave back, our friend Dot comes to stand beside her. She's wearing a white dress that makes her lovely skin look deeper olive. Her dark hair is piled atop her head—perhaps a bit extravagant for the occasion, but she looks none the worse for it.

"Finley!" She gestures up and down her body as her eyes

bulge, and I gather she's not pleased with my wardrobe choice. I step closer to her. "I'm headed to the slopes right after this." Which makes my blue jeans, boots, and flowing green blouse perfectly appropriate.

"Your hair!"

I run my hand over my ponytail as more familiar faces arrive, almost everyone dressed in Sox gear. Babies wear hand-painted onesies, kids homemade sport jerseys. Old Mr. Button has his face painted—God spare him.

I try to spy the guest of honor as more people cram inside, but it's bedlam. Villagers crowd 'round the café's eight tables and then line the walls, their bodies heating up the air and scenting it with ghastly quantities of perfume.

I spy Anna, my dearest friend, on the other side of the room. She's wearing a navy dress with a pink hydrangea print, and wee Kayti is draped over her shoulder in a pale pink onesie. Anna slides into a spot behind the coat rack to the right of the door, and I start toward her, swimming through the sea of elbows and shoulders.

I smile in greeting as I squeeze past Mrs. Dillon, whom I'll need to speak to after the gathering is over, to see if she'd like me to show Declan Carnegie to the house. I'm maneuvering through the crowd when Anna shifts Kayti in her arms, turning her around to face me. Kayti blinks her big, blue eyes, and I grin, pausing mid-step to make a silly face at my goddaughter.

I'm sticking my tongue out when it happens—something hard and warm bumps my shoulder. I turn and blink at one Declan Carnegie.

That first glance drives the breath out of my lungs. I know it's him because his face is unfamiliar; there's no such thing as a stranger on Tristan. At the same time, I feel as if it can't be him. If he was quite so stunning, surely I'd have heard.

His hair is chestnut brown: rich and dark, with streaks of

burnished gold. Stubble lines his hard jaw, drawing my gaze to his thick lips, then to his nose—strong and straight—and at last to his eyes. It takes me a moment to note their color—sea blue—because the set of them, above those high cheekbones and under strong, thick brows, is so disarming.

He looks like a warrior. Like a king. He's tall and large, with hulking shoulders, smooth, tanned skin, an air of confidence and ease.

Privilege, I almost murmur.

Then I feel his hand on my shoulder. "Sorry." He smiles, revealing dimples and a set of sparkling white teeth.

My breath is hung up in my throat. I swallow and croak, "Quite all right."

It's work to tear my eyes from his, but somehow I manage. Time trips back to normal speed as I near Anna and wee Kayti. Anna's arm wraps around my back. Her pink lips smirk. I laugh, too, only half aware of how the volume in the café has grown louder. By the time I have the wherewithal to turn around, facing the table Dot and Holly claimed for Declan, he's standing beside it with his arm around Sara Hollis. She looks bewitched as she stares up at his statuesque face.

"Shockingly gorgeous," Anna murmurs.

Her husband, Freddy, nuzzles her hair and pulls a mock frown. "Is that right?"

We all laugh, and I'm supposed to help serve lamb, so I stroke Kayti's pudgy cheek, smooth her silky black hair, and blow Anna a kiss before turning toward the kitchen.

"Watch your step," she calls, and I shoot her a wicked look.

The kitchen is hot enough to make me sweat in my jeans and boots. As soon as I step in, Miss Alice smiles at me and holds a plate out.

"Take this to him, Finley. I think you should be the one. His dear father cared so for your mum, you know."

Hank Smith is standing at my elbow. I look up at him, and he winks.

"Rawr."

I roll my eyes. "I'm not the one, you are."

"Go on, dear. Before it cools." Miss Alice waves toward the door.

I take the plate, but as I walk through the doorway, Dot appears.

I thrust the plate toward her. "Take his food, Dot."

Her hazel eyes widen. "Oooh, is this for him?"

I nod, and she grins wide enough to hurt.

"Okay." She sounds breathless. I watch from the wall just outside the kitchen as Dot serves Declan his plate. The way she smiles and preens. The way he smirks and winks. My body warms just watching his big shoulders shift, seeing flashes of his white teeth. When he smiles, he looks like a playboy prince. When he frowns, a pirate.

And you're ridiculous.

As if he can hear my thoughts, his gaze rises to meet mine. Our gazes lock, and for that moment, nothing's on his face; his features freeze as if he's been hexed, and I feel like I'm looking through his eyes into the heart of him.

I can't breathe, can't even move my throat to swallow. Dot touches his elbow, and his eyes are ripped away from mine.

My heart hammers. My stomach flips. I don't want to stand here anymore. I suck in, tucking my elbows to my sides, and try to sidle through the crowd as quickly as I can.

When I reach the café's door, I push through carefully. Outside, I find the smooth, dirt street cloaked in strange silence. The green Land Rover is parked near the door—for him, I'm sure. Being the least rusty of our vehicles, it's reserved for foreign dignitaries and other honored guests. God forbid they should have to walk a mile or two.

I walk quickly down Middle Lane, looking at nothing but my own two feet. As I follow Upper Lane toward Gammy's cottage, my heart feels as if a stone's become lodged in my belly.

What did you think, Finley? What did you think he would look like? Who did you think he would be?

I wipe my eyes and fetch the bags I stashed beside the kiln at Gammy's house. When Mrs. Dillon doesn't find me at the café, she'll show Declan here. She has the key. It was never necessary for me to show him inside. I just...wanted to. But now I have no interest. Now I've seen him.

FOUR

DECLAN

"It's a pretty good life." I smile at the little blue-haired lady who's been standing by my table for five minutes. She's clutching a cane that's got a dog's face carved up top.

"But aren't you worried about being injured?" She shakes her head. "Those balls are thrown so fast."

"I'm good at dodging them." I flash her another smile that falters at the corners.

Her son, a big, burly guy standing behind her, pats her shoulder.

"I think it's time we get on, Mum."

"Quite right, Johnny." She smiles over her shoulder, and I hold out an index card bearing my pen-scrawled signature. "Don't forget this."

She smiles, and Johnny leads her to a group of four other white-haired ladies. I toss back the last of my Guinness and turn to the girl beside me.

"I'm gonna step outside for just a second. Hold my seat?" I wink, and Dorothy beams. "Of course."

But on the way outside, I'm stopped by a young mom and her son—this one grade-school-aged. He wants a baseball signed. I take some time for him. A few more steps toward the door, and an older man stops me. He's wearing a plaid flat cap, his face sporting the deepest grooves I've ever seen. He sticks his hand out.

"Seymour, sir."

I shake it. I can never tell how hard to go with old guys. Better to go too hard than too soft, I think, so I do that, hoping I don't crush his hand.

"Nice to meet ya, Seymour."

His lips twitch at the corners. "You're my favorite." His voice warbles.

"Is that right?"

He nods once. "Used to be my wife's, too."

I know better than to ask about the wife, and sure enough, Seymour tells me she passed on three years ago.

"She spotted you when you were just a rookie. Said, 'That one'll be a record-breaker.'"

I give him what I hope is a kind-looking smile. "Thanks for telling me that."

He shakes his head then clears his throat. I run a hand back through my hair. "I just wanted to greet you," he tells me, in that halting way that very elderly folks have. When I feel sure he's finished speaking, I nod.

"Thank you. Looking forward to spending time here again."

I get out the door, but kids are outside. These are older kids—teenagers. I see them notice me in a sort of domino effect: one then two then three, now eight, and finally a hush falls over the group. Some look down, a few grin, and one girl's jaw drops right before her cheeks flush.

I can't help laughing. "C'mon, guys. You're making me self-conscious."

That's all it takes to break the ice. The youth of Tristan da Cunha crowd around to see my iPhone, begging me to show them videos of other Sox players, pleading for me to sign their clothes and, in one case, a hand.

The look in their eyes...especially the guys. It's pretty sweet at first, but soon I feel like I can't breathe. They all talk fast and loudly, desperate to impress—to impress *me*. Their questions never end, and that's okay, except my hands are shaking now. My throat is dry. My head is pounding.

By the time a brown-haired woman in a pale pink pants suit walks up, my eyelid is twitching.

"Homer? Hi—I'm Mrs. Dillon, hospitality coordinator for the island. I'm here to help you escape," she teases, in a soft, low voice.

Thank fuck she's pretty low key, because her appearance heralds another half hour of on-air time. We get into a green Land Rover and she drives me down the road, onto another little road, and up the foothills to a little Hobbit cottage tucked into a grassy hill, under a sky of storm clouds. Inside, she shows me everything, even opening the freezer and trying out the faucet in the bathtub. I appreciate her hospitality, but when she leaves, I lock the door.

Back in the bedroom, I open my bag, fumble past some folded clothes, and snatch out one of two oversized ibuprofen bottles I've got rolled up in two editions of *ESPN Magazine*.

I wrap my fist around it, feeling lightheaded at the clattering sound it makes. Still, I walk around the house again, checking things out. I open a few windows so I can listen to the rain when it comes.

I'm okay, I tell myself. Sweat prickles along my hairline as I look down at the bottle. I want to take the top off, but not yet. If I see the shit inside, sometimes it's too hard to hold off. I'm not due for another mini-dose of subs for two more hours. With that taper and the Valium one, I'm allowed to take a little extra—but I don't. I didn't bring much extra. Don't want room to fuck up.

So far, knowing what will happen if I cave to either craving has been enough to keep me straight. If I blow through the subs or the Valium all at once, the post-acute withdrawal will be worse than it is now—and on the island, there's no getting more of either drug.

I poke through the fridge and pantry, but I don't think I can eat, so I step onto the patio behind the house and watch the clouds gather and burst. I lean my back against the wall and shut my eyes and feel my body tremble.

You're okay. This is the best place for you. Good things coming.

Back inside, I force myself to eat an apple, drink some water.

The rain is really coming down now, bringing darkness early. Good. I lie on the too-soft bed and stare up at the ceiling. I laugh softly.

Here I am.

Just a few steps and I'm in the bathroom, running the faucet of the claw-footed tub.

Another few minutes and I'm sinking into a pile of minty-smelling bubbles.

I squeeze the ibuprofen bottle in my hand and grit my teeth. My chest feels hot and tight. I dry my hand off on a towel, twist the top off...peer inside. It's the tiny Ziploc bag of papery amber fragments that gets my blood pumping: the Suboxone strips, cut into micro-doses. My hand shakes as I work the baggie's zip-seal open. I just want to touch one of the strips. Sometimes a fake-out like that helps...something to chill me out.

I stick my fingertip into the baggie. It's no bigger than a business card. I feel the strips. So many of them. My jaw aches as I clench it against the urge to stuff a dozen of the little fucking triangles under my tongue.

I'm not the praying kind, but I send one up.

Help me. *Please.*

Then I lean my head against the bathtub's rim and breathe.

* * *

Finley

Carrying a bleating lamb down a muddy trail in the midst of a storm is quite a challenge. I couldn't do it if I didn't know the trail by heart. But I do, and so we're making it.

The sky is black as night and pouring buckets, with rolling clouds that move and shift so quickly they seem supernatural. Wind blows sheets of rain across the valley out below me, turning all the dirt paths mud. Another strong gust makes me wobble, but I dig my heels into the squishy ground, wrap my little lambie baby closer, and lean my head back slightly so my jacket hood falls lower over my forehead—and I keep going. Slow and steady wins the race.

I'm shivering as I tuck the wool blanket around my bundle. I found the ewe who birthed her dead near the feed troughs, with this wee one bleating in the grass. I helped her feed from another ewe for a bit, but when the lightning started up in earnest, I knew it was time to head downhill.

I've got some ewe colostrum in the freezer at Grammy's house. Also a thermal blanket. I wish I had stored those things down at the clinic, but...I didn't. I'll be dropping by and knocking, politely asking him if I might rummage through his freezer.

I cuddle Baby closer as I reach the ridge of rocks near Gammy's cottage, over which I see the blurry lights of the settlement. With careful footwork, I make it past the stones, down the steepest part of the path, and into view of the house.

I see light through the windows. I hope that means he's awake. It isn't late, only about seven, although the storm has caused dark's curtain to fall early.

"Almost there," I murmur, blinking rain out of my eyes.

Baby bleats in reply, and I feel her rooting at my arm as I clomp through the mucky grass around the cottage. I shift her weight so I can work the key into the door. Then I remember I'll need to knock.

I raise my hand and knock three times, loud and steady. Then I shut my eyes and steel myself for that face. Jesus, Mary, and Joseph—but that face. I've never seen a man so handsome. If I'm being honest, I didn't realize one existed. That he's Declan Carnegie...well, it makes my heart sore. For so many reasons.

I paste a polite smile on my face and wait, my heart tap-dancing.

C'mon, Carnegie. I know you're in there.

I look around the stoop, searching for mud tracks or other signs of life, but all I see are my own boot-prints and shadows.

Perhaps he's not here. Perhaps someone took him home for dinner or he's at the pub. A fellow like him—probably the pub. Dot is pouring him drinks, and Holly's giving him that odd look I saw her give another tourist recently; she said it's called a duck face. Dot and Holly are both young and unencumbered. Maybe he'll sweep one of them away, across the ocean and—

Sod off, Finley.

I knock again, a wee bit louder. Maybe he can't hear over the monsoon. Baby bleats, and after yet another minute, I knock as if I'd like to beat the door down. When it remains shut, I chew my lip and push my key into the lock and slowly turn the doorknob.

"Declan?"

Saying his name into the dark crevice between door and door-jamb makes my throat feel like it's closing up. But Baby bleats again, and I'm not sure what choice I have. She needs warmth and sustenance. Wee ones must eat quite a lot quite quickly after birth. We've already lost a bit of ground on our walk.

I push the door open and, finding the living room dark, step inside.

"Declan?"

I should shout, but I can't seem to speak above a murmur. I'm shivering as I glance down the hall. The bedroom door appears cracked, just as I left it. The place feels still. Likely it's unoccupied.

"Declan?" Loudly this time. When I hear nothing, I release a long breath.

He's not here, and why would he be? The entire island wants to take him home. They're likely stuffing him with milk tarts.

I kick my sopping boots off gently by the door, wriggle out of my dripping coat, and creep into the kitchen. I grab a few colostrum bottles from the freezer, plunk them in a pot atop the stove. While they thaw, I'll get some blankets from my old bedroom.

I move quietly down the hall, as if he might pop up at any moment. If he did, we could be stranded here together. *Lunacy.* How disappointing that I'm such a base creature. One fine-looking male specimen, and it's farewell to Godly morals and good sense.

In the bedroom, I find the quilt a wee bit wrinkled, and I wonder if indeed he was here. Surely I'd have left it tidier than that. I move toward the bathroom, Baby squirming in my arms now.

"Shh," I murmur. "Just a moment and I'll get you fed, dear."

I want to dry her off and get her wrapped more tightly. Then the bottle will be thawed, and I can feed her underneath the awning on the patio so I won't be inside should he return. After that, it's down the road and to the Patches for me. When it pours like this, the flocks end up stranded on the foothills near the fields where we grow potatoes and graze cattle, afraid of the flowing gulches, mired in the mud, or caught in flash floods. Since Uncle Ollie hurt his back last year, it's been my job to tend them.

I step into the bathroom, my head filled with such thoughts, and stop dead in my tracks.

Stone the cows!

He's in the tub.

I gape down at him, sprawled out in a bubble bath. His dark head rests against the tub's rim, exposing his thick, tanned throat. His eyes are shut, so he can't see me as I blink down at his massive shoulders, round biceps, and thick, hair-dusted forearms.

One big fist is locked around...a bottle? As I squint, he shifts his shoulder, wincing like he's had a long day at the nets and needs a good soak.

What in the name of the Blessed Mother?

He rubs at the shoulder, shifting his big body underneath the cloak of bubbles, and I see his thick pectoral—

"BAAAAAAAAH!"

Baby bleats, I jump, and Declan jolts up in a slosh of bubbles. He looks stunned, confused, then horror-stricken as his gaze falls to the bubbles.

"FUCK!" He bats at his lap, sloshing water all about. Then he jumps up, slapping at the water's surface, yelling, "FUCK! FUCK! Aghh, *goddamn it...*"

I'm gaping at his bubble-covered bum when his hand connects with the tub's side instead of the bubbles, making a sharp, metal sound that sets my heart racing.

"I'm sorry," I manage.

He leans lower, shoveling water from the tub onto the floor.

Then he steps onto the rug, his massive body dripping bubbles. He mutters something, spins away from me. "FUCK!"

I step back. His backside...it's so *muscular*. Quite unreal, really. He turns sideways, facing the wall, his arms drawn up about his head, and I can see his—

Don't look!

I make a noise—something like "whoawhoa"—and he whirls toward me, looking murderous. "And who the fuck are you?"

MALE PARTS! Not for long, merely an instant before my gaze leaps to his furious face. But I can feel my own cheeks burning.

"I'm sorry. I came to get—"

"How the hell did you get in here?"

"This was my Gam— err, my grandmother's home."

His face is pure fury: that lovely mouth pulled taut, his brows drawn down, his ocean-blue eyes narrowed with contempt.

"Your grandmother used to live here, so you thought you could let yourself inside, wander around, then into the *bathroom*, without *knocking*?"

I take another step back. I'm not looking down, but I can sense the size of it in my periphery, the way it simply hangs there, dripping bubbles on the floor.

"I'm terribly sorry. I didn't mean—what I mean to convey is, I thought you weren't home."

He steps forward. "You knew I was staying here? And you still barged in?"

My neck and cheeks are burning, suddenly with irritation. "I knocked quite a lot and called for you. You didn't answer."

"What kind of person lets herself into a house where she knows someone else is staying? Even if the person isn't home? Is that how you do things here? No regard for other people's privacy?"

Anger stiffens my spine. "Absolutely not. I required something I could only get here. Frozen milk for her." I hold up Baby, who bleats woefully, as if on cue.

Declan tilts his head, then makes a show of looking around the bathroom, as if to point out there's no milk in the bathroom.

I grit my molars. "I had no clue you were here. As I said, I knocked—"

"I was asleep."

"I knocked loudly on the front door, *many* times."

"And then you let yourself in."

"Hardly novel!" I'm surprised by the edge in my voice, more surprised to find that I feel angry and not frightened when his face tightens. "I knocked many times, as is the proper custom universally. When no one answered, I came in to get something essential. Is that a crime where you hail from?"

"Yeah." His mouth twists. "It's called breaking and entering."

"I didn't *break* anything. And it's *my* house!"

He gives a little shake of his head. "There are Peeping Tom laws, too."

"Excuse me?"

His mouth twists in a devilish smirk.

Shame sweeps through me as I realize what he means, followed by sheer outrage. "I didn't know you were here! And I'm not *peeping* at anything."

He shifts his stance, lifting his brows as he attempts to draw my eyes downward.

"You're...horrid." The ache in my chest blooms like a wound. All these years, since *Prince Declan*—

Baby bleats. I cradle her closer. "If it weren't for me, you wouldn't even have a place to stay."

"You don't think so?"

"What, because your last name is Carnegie?" I see a smirk lift his lips, and it makes want to pop him. "You think you're so vitally important? Do you think we owe you something? No one asked you to come!"

"Actually, Mayor Acton begged me to visit."

"Well he's deluded! Baseball is an awful sport. I don't find you impressive in the slightest!"

"No?" He looks down at himself. My eyes dip down on reflex —only for an instant before I jerk my gaze back to his face.

"You're a pig!"

"And you're in heat." He arches his thick brows, as if to challenge me.

"That is absolutely vile."

He shrugs. "You should own it. You may think baseball is boring, but you're not bored by this bat." A tight grin rounds his cheeks, and I struggle to use words.

"That's repulsive as well as completely untrue. As it happens, I'm repelled by knob-heads."

His eyes narrow. "I don't think so." He points to his chest, and I glance down in horror. I can see the hard points of my nipples through my blouse.

Stricken beyond coherence, I whirl and fly into the kitchen, where I start tossing frozen milk bottles into a canvas bag. Baby bleats her hunger. I'm shaking with fury.

"Rushing out?" I hear him say behind me.

"Jump off a cliff!"

"I don't think so. Not yet, anyway." I hear a sigh-like sound. "Why don't you sit down there for a minute? We can start this over."

I whirl. "Sod off!"

I hate myself for how my eyes peruse his body—clad now in a towel—before I brush past him, setting Baby on the floor so I can jerk my boots and coat on.

I feel him watching from the doorway between den and

kitchen. When I'm dressed to go, I grab a blanket off the couch, scoop Baby up, and grab my bag.

"Try to stay dry," he calls.

I stick up my middle finger as I stomp out the door and into the storm once more.

FIVE
FINLEY

When I awaken, curled on my side with Baby cuddled near my chest, I see sunlight streaming through the blinds into the clinic's main room—but a glance outside reveals it's streaking through more dark clouds. The radio confirms what I can tell by looking at the sky: more rain expected. When I step outside to urge Baby to go poo in the grass, I can feel it in the air—a kind of pause. The air feels too still between breezes, too heavy as it tosses my hair.

Lower Lane is fairly sunken, just a muddy river lined by dripping houses. Someone drives by—Father Barnard, I believe. The tires of his Jeep spray mud. I gather Baby back inside and spend the morning feeding her and working out a sort of diaper.

"What am I to do with you?" I smile down at her.

She prances over to the waiting area and back to our bed, tossing her head back, as if to make me laugh. I'm doing just that when a knock sounds at the door.

"Mmm? And who could this be?"

Baby stands beside me as I pull the door open, revealing Anna and wee Kayti. "Well, hello there."

"Oh, my shoes!"

Anna's Mary Janes are caked in mud.

"Oh no. It's a river out there, and more coming, I hear."

"Right monsoon."

I smile at Kayti. "Hello, lovely."

"Are you going to let us in?"

"Of course, but—"

"What is that thing?"

I follow Anna's wide eyes to my fuzzy comrade. "Baby?"

"You let a lamb into the clinic?"

I shrug. "She's an orphan, needed frozen milk. Did we have a well check this morning?"

Anna laughs. "I'm supposed to be the one with mum brain, Finley!"

"You were in the morning, before Wills and Doris?"

She waves Kayti's hand at me. "I need a vaccine! So the tourists don't kill me with their horrid germs!"

"Ugh—speaking of."

I roll a football from a basket in the corner across the rug. As Baby trots after it, I lead Anna and Kayti to the birth and baby room, where I tell Anna what happened with the Carnegie and check Kayti over. Well, not *all* of what happened. I leave out the part about his bull-sized male parts. And my own parts. I can't bear repeating it.

"I think he dropped a soda bottle in the tub. Some sort of bottle."

Anna shakes her head, frowning.

"He was a right knob-head, that's the primary point of my story. Spoiled, entitled, rude. The worst sort."

"Disappointing, but perhaps I'm not surprised," she says. "I saw him."

"Meaning?" I ask as I press on Kayti's belly.

"Well, he is uncommonly easy on the eyes. You know how that can go to one's head a bit at times."

I check under Kayti's diaper, and then Anna re-fastens the Velcro. "I wouldn't know."

"Oh, c'mon. You've always been one of the pretty girls, Fin-Fin."

"Not so." I take a bit to listen to Kayti's heart then pull the stethoscope away from her pudgy chest and smile. "Sounds healthy to me."

Anna smiles. "On to the fun now?"

I nod. While I prep the syringe, Anna asks, "Are you missing Doctor?"

I grab a swab of numbing lotion. "I think not so terribly."

"That's good. Does he call often?"

"Every few days, unless there's something to discuss. I'm holding up quite well, though. I know how to get along without him." I wince. "Okay, Kayti, it's that time. Ready to give those lungs a workout?"

I clean her fat thigh with an alcohol wipe and rub numbing lotion over that spot.

"I'll make it quick, okay?"

I do just that, but there are many tears, so many Anna rushes out with Kayti so she needn't see my evil face longer than necessary.

"I'm sorry, Kayti! Have a nicer day now!" I call out behind them.

After they leave, I offer Baby another bottle and try to keep my mind away from *him*.

What does it matter if he's a lout? What has he to do with me? There is something, of course, but...that's no matter. It's hardly my only option.

I think of other things, like what the night will bring for me. I didn't check the slopes last night for wayward sheep; Baby was shivering so badly by time we neared the clinic, I felt I should stay put with her. Later, though, I'll have to leave her somewhere

—perhaps with Petunia White—and go and round them up before a mudslide gets them.

Baby guzzles four bottles between the time that Anna leaves and Wills arrives. I draw his blood without much incident; he's required growth hormone injections since he turned two, so he's accustomed to needles. After he leaves, Doris hobbles in and laughs at Baby in her cloth diaper.

"She looks more a mess than I do!"

Doris checks out fine despite her kidney disease. I help her down the muddy steps and into one of the community Broncos, driven by her daughter, May.

When the vehicle pulls away, I find I'm face to face with *him*.

The Carnegie stands in the mud pie that is Lower Lane, wearing a blank face and a black T-shirt. His dark hair is messy, his full lips turned down. From where I stand, some twenty meters away, he looks preternaturally large—like a cowboy ready for a showdown in some Western film.

I stare at him. Well, glare at him. Why is he taking up good space in Lower Lane? Why am I wasting my time looking at him?

Without another moment wasted, I march back inside the clinic.

Declan

After a stop at the café, confirming what I know in my bones— I'm fucked—I walk back to the house in a steady drizzle. The house that belongs to her, to Finley Evans—keeper of the clinic keys. Tristan's one and only temporary doctor in the absence of the real one, who's gone on some kind of trip to Capetown.

I didn't sleep more than half an hour last night—not just because I dropped my whole stash into the tub and had no sleeping pills. I felt like shit when she left. Not just bad, but kind of surprised that I was such a fucking dick. And not to just anybody, either. I was a fuckface to this red-haired girl who might be *the* girl: Finley Evans.

It didn't take me long to poke around the house and confirm my suspicions. The gorgeous woman I lashed out at is the grown up version of the girl with the devastated eyes and dirty face. I found her name on the backside of a faded-looking apple magnet on the 'fridge, scrawled in sloppy kid print.

Maybe that makes sense, because when I first stepped into this place, it felt familiar, and I'm pretty sure the missing girl's grandmother was the one who let me help her knead the bread dough that time.

I step back into the house now, leaning back against the door for just a second before stripping off my shirt and shoes. I'm such a fucking moron. Chill-bumps pop up all over my body as I walk into the bedroom and lie face-down on the bed. Her bed.

I cover my head with a pillow and roll onto my side, curling my arms up to my chest. My neck and face feel hot. My eyes throb slightly from behind. I draw a deep breath in and hold it.

I can figure this shit out. I can. I rub my watery eyes. I just need to move. I think of running in the rain, but I don't know if I can. Everything's so fucking soggy.

I roll out of bed and do some jumping jacks. A hundred. Then three hundred sit-ups. Two hundred push-ups. I remember a few yoga poses, so I try those. Not enough. I need to get my heart rate a lot higher to feel relief.

I run around the house for half an hour, feeling like a fucking nut, before I sink into the tub again, rubbing at the film of dissolved pill residue around it.

Fuck.

I lean my head back, exhale slowly.

My arms are underwater. I lift my hands up through the bubbles and squint at my fingertips. Water ripples all around them. I close my fists, draw them back under.

I can run after the rain stops.

I kill some hours playing real card solitaire, sitting on a wooden stool under the awning over the back porch. The sound of waves crashing against the rocks behind the house should be a soothing one, but it makes me feel jumpy. Almost fearful.

Back inside, I pull on a shirt and force myself to eat some eggs. When it's five, I slide my phone into my pocket, grab an umbrella, and make my way down to the pub.

"What can I get you?" The old man behind the counter has to raise his voice so I can hear above the rain that's pelting the tin roof. He's smiling, though, as if I'm not the only asshole in the bar, the one who made him set his book down and put on his apron.

"Rusty Nail?" It's posed as a question because I don't know how familiar he is with mainstream drinks.

He gives me a small smile.

"Heavy on the scotch. Please."

"One Rusty Nail coming right up."

As he sticks an orange peel in the glass, a swell of noise punches in from behind us—low voices and a brief soundbite of driving rain. A few seconds later, all the other barstools fill up. Dude beside me takes his hat off, giving me a nod before he turns back to the guy beside him.

"Need more hands on deck," he's saying. "Cannot patch the roof and mend the fence and clear the road and fill the buckets at the church all with the same four or six hands."

The other chuckles. "Don't forget the good doctress."

"The clinic's leaking, too, but I heard she's out at the Patches. Sheep up there around the gulches as they do."

Their odd English accents are so thick I'm several seconds behind, translating in my head.

"Tireless, Finley."

My chest flares at the sound of her name. "Finley?"

They turn to me.

"I'm...uh, I think I'm renting her house?"

Their lined faces bend in confusion.

"Staying there," I correct. "At her grandmother's house." The older one's eyebrows jut up. "Oh. And so you are."

"Is it leaking as well?" the younger asks, shaking his head.

"Nah. It's been okay." My stomach tightens as I fish for information. "Is she—did I hear you say Finley is the doctor?"

The man beside me pushes wet curls out of his face. "She does many jobs. Shepherd. Nurse. Although with the good doctor in Cape Town, I suppose she's naturally his stand-in." He smiles. "And the livestock doctor. Too many caps, that one. She's got sheep stranded up the slopes. Probably a need for her here, or there will be fore the weather's blown by. Quite a shame no shepherd's as good as she is."

Something rises in my chest—a kind of brightness.

"She needs help? Another shepherd?"

He nods. "Two others help at times, but they're both occupied. One ill."

I frown. "Does she have dogs?"

Several men look up at me.

"You know...herding dogs?"

"She did," one says, "but Heath passed on. No more to be trained."

I nod, and toss back half my glass. Then, with the sting of whiskey still filling my throat, I say, "I've done some shepherding before."

SIX

FINLEY

Jesus, Mary, and Joseph.

I shut my eyes and inhale slowly. When I open them again, the view is still as bleak. I'm standing on one of the higher slopes out near the Patches, looking down the valley where we grow our food, where we corral the cattle. My view is framed by the hood of my rain coat, striped by gulches shining in the moonlight. Gulches growing wider as the rain pours. It's quite dark out, so the sheep scattered about the slopes below me are pale dots—scattered dots, because the herd has splintered...twice.

Patch Valley didn't have so many gulches prior to this past spring. Joe White used to take a group to work on erosion in the valleys, but he hurt his leg slipping on Upper Lane after a hail storm this past winter, and most of his former crew are feeling their years. I suppose it's time for someone else to take over stacking stones and sand bags.

For now, I've got to get these sheep into a herd again and drive them down the slopes onto the flat land at the bottom of the valley.

Took me the better part of an hour to walk the road from the village, on the island's northwest tip, over the Hillpiece and past Runaway Beach. The road petered out near the flat plane of the Patches, by the sea; from there I climbed the lower slopes to reach my charges.

First, I tried to lure them down along one of the wider gulches. I rattled a bucket of feed, calling like always. But it was raining too hard; got the feed soggy so it didn't rattle—and anyway, my wee fluffins wanted nothing to do with the gulch.

I miss Heathcliff, my canine companion. He would have them down the slope in two shakes of a lamb's tail.

I count heads and decide I'll start with the two small groups off to my right—closest to the Patches, and the ocean beyond. I'll walk the path I'm on and cut down around the outside of them. Then I'll drive them east, toward the next small group. After that, I'll climb up to where the gulch is narrower, drop back down, and herd that new group toward the next. I groan, realizing I'll be doing this all night if no one comes to help.

I asked Mayor Acton for help over the radio an hour ago, and he said he would send someone. Then my radio broke. Perhaps I'll have help, perhaps I won't. No more time to wait, though.

I kick the mud off my boots and glance back up above me at my pack, wrapped in a tarp and wedged under a rock up near the Triplets—three large boulders that serve as an island landmark. Then I start down the boot-worn path, moving carefully, my heels dug in to keep from slipping.

I'm farther downslope, picking my way over small rocks and using larger ones for balance, when I see something moving in the Patches, out beyond the scattered herd. I track the figure for a moment. Definitely human. Rather than drive the sheep solo, I turn my flashlight on and off a few times and perch on a rock to wait for help.

I watch as my companion flashes his or her light, too. When

he or she is close enough—it's a "he," I'm fairly certain—I analyze the person's gait to try to discern who.

Mike Green is long-legged, and wide up top. He's fifteen, but the nicest boy. He'll make a good shepherd one day. Or I suppose it could be Benny Smith. He's a bit of a chair-dweller, but occasionally he'll help if prodded. Mayor Acton is his uncle, so perhaps he was shook out of his chair.

I watch my helpmate hike until he reaches a stone-scattered ridge, disappears beneath an overhanging rock, and emerges on its other side, perhaps two meters over. When I realize who it is, I nearly faint dead away.

The Carnegie stops a few yards downhill, shielding his forehead with his large hand, so I can only see the lower half of his face: pale against the darkness, hard jaw dripping. He moves his hand, revealing wet-lashed eyes and stubble-covered cheeks, wide-boned above his hard-cut jaw. He looks like a sculpture— Michelangelo's fine marblework.

I look him up and down, stricken by his perfection—physically. Then I look into his somber eyes and give a sharp laugh. "How did you get lost up here?"

"What?"

"The village is that way." I point back across the valley where the Patches lie.

"I'm here to help you with the herding. Mac sent me."

I can't help but guffaw. "Did he find you at the pub? How many empties were beside him?"

His mouth tightens. "I know how to drive a herd."

"And I'm a Red Sox catcher."

"I do." He seems serious.

"Do you then?" I scoff. "With a nice doggie? What was it, a camp for foolish wealthy?"

His eyes widen, just a bit. I watch his gaze dip to his boots before it rises back to mine. "Listen—" His full lips twist, pensive. "I wanted to say I'm sorry for last night."

"You mean when you acted like a pig that's escaped the fences?"

His head bows a little lower. I can see his shoulders rise and fall. "Yeah."

"What?" I cup my hand around my ear. "Can't hear over the rain."

He looks up and says, "Yes." His voice is low and hard.

I watch as he adjusts the poncho over his head, shifts his broad shoulders, curls one of his fists. When I felt I've held him prostrate long enough to suit, I dismiss him with a wave. "You can go back to the village now."

His eyes flash, but the fire doesn't burn. "You need help."

"What I need is for a ship to come and carry you away."

His lips press into a thin line, and then he nods once, barely. "I acted badly and I'm sorry. It was...inexcusable."

"And yet you're here, seeking...forgiveness?"

"I heard you needed help."

"Quite a riot that you think that's what you're offering."

His mouth tightens, and I feel the buoyance of my own mean spirit. "Do you have a crook, then?"

His eyes roam the soaked grass around us. "I don't, but I can find one."

"Try that, then. I'll wait." I sit back on the rock, tucking my knees up to my chest and wrapping my arms around them. I've been wet for so long; my skin feels plastic-y and strange. Despite my jacket hood, rain leaks in and trickles down my scalp. There's nothing worse than being cold and wet.

Scratch that—there is: it's being cold and wet and stuck on a mountainside with someone you abhor.

The Carnegie roams the path that runs horizontally across the slope, and I laugh. He'll never find a stick up here. When he walks back toward me some five minutes later, I'm grinning in the dark. Until he holds out a crook.

"What is that?"

He grins, looking quite pleased with himself.

I stand. "Very well then. Let's see you use it."

"You want to help me gather, moving down into the valley?"

"I'll let you work solo a bit. Then I'll come in from the far side, there by the brush." I point to a fluffy smattering of bushes on the far side of the splintered herd, a bit downslope. While he's working, I'll hike up and grab my pack, move past the Triplets, and descend.

His dark brows do something funny—a twist between puzzled and amused. "Okay, boss."

He turns away from me, and I sit back on my rock. He's shed his poncho, for reasons I can't fathom. In the rain, his long-sleeved shirt clings to his muscled back and shoulders. I tell myself it's okay that my eyes are clinging, too. I'm not admiring *him*—only his form.

He circles out around the first cluster of sheep—ten or eleven white spots, maybe thirty meters downslope—the way a good dog would.

So he does know a bit about it.

Still, I don't think my lambs will move for him. Not for a stranger. They'll spook up the slope, or down at best.

A moment later, I watch, slack-jawed, as he herds them in a straight line across a smattering of boulders, over a dozen or so meters, driving toward the next cluster of sheep.

I clench my jaw and give a shake of my head. Lucky break there. He won't be able to move this larger group. No chance of that.

The Carnegie's a good stretch away now. I can hear his low voice, but I can't make out his words, although the rain has quieted down a bit. I watch in shock as he gathers the two small groups together. They move as one great splotch of white down the dark hillside.

What's he saying to them?

I get to my feet, and I want to move closer. I want to see what he's doing. What is it about him? Is it posture? Something about his footing? Was his mother part border collie? Makes fine sense, given he's a son of a bitch.

I'm holding my breath as he gets the sheep to move along beside him, gaping as he moves them down the slope a bit to where the gulch narrows. The way it stripes the landscape, he can't get them down into the valley without crossing it.

Let's see him try this! He steps out ahead of them, and then starts walking backward through the water. He doesn't stumble or slip once, and soon he's standing in the middle of the flowing gulch.

The flock won't follow. My fluffins will cross gulches when it's not raining, but when the runoff flows this swiftly, they won't move, even for me. They won't move unless there's two with crooks, coming at them from both directions.

Except...they do. My lead ram, Dumbledore, follows the Carnegie like a puppy. For a long moment, he's the only one swimming toward Declan. Seconds later, the rest follow, turning the gulch white in the moonlight, spilling up around the Carnegie into a spread of slanted pasture not fifteen meters from the final cluster.

What *is* this?

My head spins as he neatly gathers the flock and drives them down the slope-side in a wearing pattern, moving side-to-side behind them, making a soft sound that, from here, sounds like a throaty hum.

Mike and Benny can just barely move this flock, and that's with me assisting and no rain at all. The Carnegie herded them as well as I would have. I scowl at the splotch of white spreading over the dark grass. Maybe better.

I shake my head, hands on my hips. Of course he's good at this. He's likely good at everything, which is why he's not Declan but *the Carnegie*—a wicked, arrogant pig of a man.

I start up the slope to where my forgotten pack sits. By the time I've got it strapped to my back, the Overlord of Ewe has got the flock grazing a patch of grass deep in the valley. Streams of runoff from the slopes pool at the valley's center, then flow toward the Patches; beyond there, the gulches drain into the sea.

Operation Ewe must have taken fewer than forty minutes, and he never had to ask for my help.

I make my way down the hillside slowly, watching him move among the herd. He's a dark blot gliding through a sea of fluffy pale, blurred by the rain that won't stop falling. As I near him and see his large form more clearly, I'm surprised at how sparse and lithe his movements are.

Who is he?

A git. A self-enamored plonker of the highest order. Some people like to preen at all times. My mum used to call these people "showboats." That's what he is—a showboat. Quite a handsome showboat, I admit as I close the distance between us. He looks even better with his hair slicked back, pasted darkly to his forehead and his temples. Again, I think of pirates.

When I'm near enough for him to touch, he reaches for me, palm out, as if going for a handshake.

I draw my hand away, making my point. I'm burning to ask what trick he used, where he learned it. Instead, with just the briefest glance at him, I say, "You're free to go back to the village now."

SEVEN
DECLAN

Her head is down, so I can't see her face, and she can't see the grin I'm trying to hide.

"What did you think?" My mouth bends into a smirk as her eyes swing back to mine.

"Of what?" Oh, but she's frosty. So nonchalant.

I hold my crook up, wiggling my eyebrows. "My skill with the crook, of course."

Her poker face is on point. "It's quite lucky that you found that crook. Not so many trees up there."

I snort. "Not good at being wrong, huh?"

"What?"

"You thought I was full of shit."

"I simply didn't want to see your face again."

I bark a laugh.

"In any event, your work is done." She waves out toward the ocean, gleaming beyond the patchwork expanse of fields and pastures. I realize what she's really gesturing to is the road that runs along the cliffs, bridging the Patches and the village. Then she waves over her shoulder at me and starts up the hillside.

I give her a minute before following.

I was right—exertion helps. Being in this valley, in a stream-striped bowl of grass between the foothills—that helps, too. The fog at my feet, the mist on my skin—I feel...relief.

But I know it's temporary. I can't leave here, not until I get something worked out with her. Clonidine, if nothing else. I don't want to offer her much in the way of why, but somehow I've got to win her over.

The slope she's hiking up is steeper than the one we just came down. At its peak is an arc-shaped rock formation, rising up alongside several steeple-like spires. Off-the-cuff, I'd put this peak at maybe two thousand feet. Behind it and back some distance is the infamous volcano—formally known as Queen Mary's Peak. I can't see it for the clouds.

I shield my eyes from the rain and squint up at her. What's she doing anyway? Trying to escape me, or looking for more straggling sheep? I wonder what's on the other side of this peak; I don't know the landscape yet.

I decide she's probably heading to the high ground to have one more look around before she heads in for the night. Does she know more rain is coming?

I don't want to spook her, so I hang back as she climbs, keeping maybe forty yards between us. And I watch her. I watch the way she gathers her hair, braiding the loose strands even as she weaves around boulders and navigates the river-like runoff that's flowing down around the deeper gulches. I watch the way she hefts her pack up higher on her back, stopping for a second to do something with the strap.

When she reaches the top of the grassy slope and the bottom of the rockface that marks the peak, she leans her head back, as if tasting raindrops. Then she turns slightly to look over her shoulder, her face turned toward the Patches.

Looking for me?

Maybe.

I pull out the infrared binoculars Mac sent with me and watch as she flares red and yellow. That'll be my cover story when I catch her: I forgot to hand these off as promised. Hopefully I'll get to offer more apologies, maybe help her herd a few more sheep. As we walk back toward the Patches, I can broach my dark topic.

It's not a solid plan, but it's the best I can come up with. Of all fucking people, why does she have to be the stand-in for the doctor?

Serves you right for being a dickwad.

I follow her until she slows at the spot where the cliffside goes sharply vertical, pointing toward the archway and the spires. Then I close the distance between us, coming up on her as she pauses to shift her pack again.

"Hey...just me."

Finley whirls on me with wide eyes, wobbling back as she holds up her hands. "Why are you here?" Her voice is shrill and very English.

"Sorry." I hold out the binoculars. "Mac sent these with me. I forgot to pass them off down there." I wave down the hill as Finley reaches for them slowly. She grabs the binoculars and takes a hasty step back.

"You're not— Are you afraid of me?"

In the moonlight peeking through the clouds, I see her lips purse. Her pretty eyes are wide and wary. "Oh, of course not. I'm completely at ease. I have known you since we were wee ones in our nappies, after all."

Fuck. "I'm sorry." I run my hand back through my wet hair. "I..." I shake my head. "That was thoughtless."

"I always find it reassuring when someone follows me silently up a mountain after dark. So it's lovely you did that. Thanks for these." She holds up the binoculars. "Have a nice hike back now."

"Actually, I want to see the rocks up there. Is that a natural arch?" I point to the rock formation fifteen or twenty yards above us.

"It only looks that way. It is, in fact, a hologram."

I grin. "Someone's a smartass."

"Don't slip on the way down." She turns to go, and I move with her. "Wait."

She turns back to me. Rain starts falling harder again, and I watch her tighten her hood. "Yes?"

"Why'd you come up this way?"

"Why do you think?" Her voice is harsh—derisive.

"To look for more strays?"

"Clearly."

She sets off again, picking her way over the sheer rockface, moving slowly at times as she finds her hand- and footholds. I hum softly so she knows I'm still behind her, feeling like a fucker even as I know I can't turn back without her—without at least talking to her. If she won't help me, I'll be in the bed by tomorrow.

After she hoists herself up onto the small plateau where the archway and the spires are, she disappears behind the arch's left side.

Touché.

I shouldn't be surprised, though. Why would she want to spend time with me?

I lift myself onto the plateau and blink down at the slopes below us. Fuck, we're way up in the clouds now. From up here, the fields look postcard-sized, the six-foot-wide gulches like tiny trickles. I can barely make out the herd down near the mouth of the valley. The huts scattered all about the Patches look like soda cans. I'd say this is two thousand feet—easy.

I turn and look behind me, at the archway, which rises twenty-five or thirty feet above me, and at the area around it. The plateau looks no larger than a spacious great room, but the moon has gone behind the clouds again, and I can't see the space well.

"Finley?"

"Up here!"

I look up.

"Atop the archway."

I crane my neck, and sure enough, I think I see a shadow up there.

"What the fuck?"

"Don't try to climb it, *Homer*. You're quite a bit too large. The column might break. Just go back down." I hear her airy laugh. "Or I suppose if you're the foolish sort, you could attempt it."

The arch's "legs" are maybe three or four feet in diameter. They're grooved, and actually they look pretty sturdy. I chuckle as I wrap my arms and legs around one. Even as I get started, I know it's not a good idea, but...fuck...can't hurt to try. I'm a pretty fucking competent climber—I summited the Matterhorn, Kilimanjaro, and Denali in an off year before college—so I press forward, grapping for each divot for my hands and feet.

By the time I near the top of the thing, the rain has petered to a sprinkle, a little bit of moonlight is beaming through the clouds, and I'm sweating like a motherfucker. My foot is wedged into a crevice that doesn't feel quite steady, and my hand aches as it clings to a groove that's barely big enough for one finger. To get up to the top of the arch, I'll need to put all my weight on the unsteady nook under my left foot and grab something else with one of my hands.

Fuck me.

I grip my handhold tightly, even tucking my chin against the cold, wet stone, and find a spot that feels pretty decent for my right foot. Then, with my hand stretched up toward a notch in the stone, I shift my weight to my left foot and lunge.

The rock crumples so fast I don't have time to readjust my

grip. I slide halfway down the column, my palms getting sliced to shit as I grasp for another hold. My mind see-saws between plans to spread-eagle myself—in hopes of landing solid on the plateau—or go ahead and tuck, because odds are, when I hit the plateau, having fallen twenty or so feet, momentum's gonna make me roll on down the slope.

Then my fingers catch on something. Fuck—I've got a hold.

"Declan!" She's above me. "There's a metal bar! By your left hand—stretch up a bit—maybe three inches! There's a metal bar, you see it glinting? There's metal bars all in the arch for climbing! Just hang on until you get your footing!"

I straighten that hand, my right one shaking with the effort to hold on. I feel around where she said to, and my fingertips brush something hard and cool.

"That's it! Grab that!"

Gritting my teeth, I grab onto the little metal bar. *So that's how she climbed up without falling.*

"You've got to find another spot for your feet."

No shit, Sherlock. My arms scream; my right shoulder is blazing. I'm going to fall. I try to find a spot for my foot—*there's one*—but it crumples. I let my body dangle as she screams. When my legs are slightly bent and my soles feel parallel with the plateau, I relax and let go.

I land on the balls of my feet—the impact gets me mostly in the shins and ankles, making me yell out—and tuck into a roll. Then I spread out like a starfish to slow down. Rain hits me at a bunch of different angles as I tumble, gaining momentum. Something smashes into my cheek. *Shit fuck!* Stars float in my eyes, and then I'm on my back, the hard rain blurring everything. I'm laughing from adrenaline, even as it makes my face throb.

What a fucking idiot.

"I'm so sorry! Are you quite all right? I'm so—"

"*Shhh.*" I try to push myself up, but find I can't. Her hand is on my cheek.

"Jesus, Mary, and Joseph! Can you see me? Do you know where you are?"

Something in my chest aches. My right cheek feels like someone's stabbing it.

"Declan?"

I shift slowly onto my side. When nothing hurts too much, I push up on my arm and look around the flooded hillside. Her face swims in front of me—wide-eyed and a little fuzzy, like the hologram she mentioned before.

"I'm so horribly sorry!"

I try to swallow, but my throat feels locked up. I realize that's blood I'm tasting. There's a sharp sting in my cheek.

I spit some blood out. Finley gasps.

"Sorry." I rub my aching head, realizing that the cold at my back is the water running down the slope; I'm fucking soaked now.

"What's hurting? How can I help?"

I blink up at her just in time to see a vein of lightning spread behind her. "I'm okay."

Lightning streaks across the sky again, a spider web, followed by a clap of thunder so loud, I think I feel the rock below us tremble.

"Fuck."

"I'm so terribly sorry."

"That lightning," I rasp.

Her hand brushes my shoulder. "Can you get to your feet?"

I start to stand and feel her hands on my arm. I don't mean to toss her off. It's just...instinct.

I get to my feet and find her right in front of me. Lightning strikes again, illuminating her unhappy face. All around her, the rain-soaked landscape seems to pulse and writhe. Streams of runoff glisten as they flow down the slope across from ours. Muddy water gushes over our feet, on its way down to the valley, which sparkles like a lake.

Out to my right, beyond the flatland of the Patches, the ocean roils. The rain's falling so hard now, it beats on my neck and shoulders like a waterfall and casts a veil between Finley and me.

I move my arms and legs, testing things out. My right shoulder burns like a bitch, but that's normal. The rest of me feels...okay. "I'm fine," I half-shout over the rain.

"My apologies again," she shouts back. It's hard to see her face in the deluge, but she sounds sorry. Even concerned. "Do you need help to your vehicle?"

"Nah. You want a ride back?" I remember what I'm here for, and I have the fuckwit thought that maybe I can hype the injury and get the help I need without admitting my issue. *Addict.*

She gives a slight shake of her head, leaning in closer as she cups her hand around her forehead. "I've got to get to the other side of this peak. The volcano's that way, and there are likely some stragglers on its lowermost slopes." I watch her mouth tug into a frown. Then the rain picks up—it's painful on my aching head—and she leans toward me again. "I shouldn't have urged you to climb the arch!"

"Ehhh, I didn't have to."

"You were goaded."

"Still my choice." I gesture to myself, realizing as I do that my pants are so wet and clingy, she can probably see the outline of my junk. I tug on one of the pant legs, feeling like an asshole. "I'll go with you. We can leave together."

Thunder booms, and something heavy hits the ground beside us. Her eyes widen and her jaw drops as a chunk of rock rolls past us. A pretty big one.

"Fuck..."

"You've the mouth of a sailor."

"The sailor and the siren." I flash her a painful grin.

Her forehead rumples before she shakes her head.

I wave at the peak. "Lead the way, Siren."

For a moment, she looks unsure. I waggle my eyebrows, and her mouth tightens in what might be a small, reluctant smile, though I can't tell before she turns and starts to climb back up the slope. She goes so slowly, I'm pretty sure she's trying to be courteous—or insulting.

Even when we're elbow-to-elbow, she moves at a snail's pace. Our shoes slosh through the runoff, and she ducks her head, holding her jacket hood with one hand. When we're back up level with the plateau where I landed underneath the arch, she hefts her pack onto her back.

I put a hand on it. "Let me."

She snorts. "Did I just tumble down the slope?"

"No, but—"

"Thank you. Now proceeding."

I shake my head, immediately regretting it when struck with a bullet of pain, and follow her under the archway. She starts down the slope's back side; I stop to absorb the view. I can see the village off to the northwest: a few pinpricks of light beside the dark blanket of the sea. Pale pink clouds have covered up the moon, but even in the darkness, that huge volcano can't be missed; it looms over to our right, its wide base rising from the steep valley in front of us, its massive slope tilting up into a thick blanket of fog.

Thunder booms, reminding me that I should get my ass in gear. Half a second later, lightning splinters the sky, gleaming off Finley's raincoat. As if she can feel my gaze, she looks over her shoulder. I give what I hope looks like a friendly wave.

I'm at her side a minute later, watching my footing as we move through a sea of baseball-sized stones that make our descent tricky. A few times, Finley wobbles. Once, my hand darts out to grab her, but I manage to rein in the impulse. She seems prickly... or maybe it's prideful. Hell, maybe she just hates me. Better not to piss her off again—yet.

The rain falls harder than it has since I've been on the island, like someone in the sky is emptying a bucket over us. The water racing down the slope-side hits my ankles and my calves from behind—hard enough to threaten my balance—and as I step forward, I'm riding blind, because the moonlight's glaring off the runoff, making it impossible to gauge the angle of the slope.

Near the bottom, my foot comes down on a stone that rolls under my shoe. I pinwheel, and when I get my balance again, I find Finley smirking. Our eyes meet, and she arches her brows.

"That's how it's gonna be, huh?" I shout.

"Most definitely!"

I can't be sure that's what she said—the rain's too loud—but the tilt of her lips as good as confirms it.

"Siren." I grin.

That's the last thing I process before the sky rumbles, a few octaves too low and loud to be thunder, and the ground under my feet gives way.

EIGHT
FINLEY

It's like a film reel with a bit clipped from the middle. One moment, I'm working my way down the slope alongside the Carnegie, wondering what's making me feel squirmy: his gaze on my rear end or my own antsy self-consciousness. Then that thought is overlaid by a horrible rumble.

The next scene opens with me lying somewhere dark and *him* over me. I squint, and when I try to move my head, a thunderclap of pain bursts behind my eyes.

"Oww."

"Finley? Are you okay?"

Too loud.

I bring a hand to my face, surprised to find my arm feels weak and...heavy. And— "My head." My voice is scratchy, near inaudible, so I try to swallow, struggling while my throat remembers how to work. I crack my eyes open again and find his wide as he leans, dripping, over me.

I look around, and dread slams through me. It looks dark and...cave-like. My eyes are blurry, but I see the dark walls and ceiling in the dim light.

Tears fill my eyes as my throat tightens. *What happened?*

He moves slightly in my frame of vision, shifting away from me as he sits back on his heels. "There was a mudslide. Rockslide. I don't know." He blows a breath out. "Maybe an earthquake. When it happened, we got knocked off our feet. I grabbed you and took off down the hill, and...I don't know." He shakes his head, not meeting my eyes. "There was a fucking ton of rock. Like part of that peak fell. It came down so fucking fast. I threw you over my shoulder and just ran...until it got right on us."

"Where are we now?"

I sit up—or try to. I feel weak and strange, and can't seem to coordinate my limbs. He leans in and helps me. The cave spins slightly as I feel his hands on my upper arms. A cold sweat sweeps me, and I wonder if I'm going to be sick. "Where are we?"

I look around, my stomach churning. I don't recognize this place, and my head feels odd and foggy.

I watch as his mouth tightens. He shakes his head once. "I don't know."

I look around again, gauging the space. It's bigger than the living room at Gammy's house, but probably not as big as her living room plus kitchen. The walls are damp, the air smells dank as caves do, and the curved ceiling is not far overhead—maybe just six or seven feet above the cool stone floor. I hear the tinkling of water, likely from a stream, as most caves on the island are intersected by small rivulets of water.

"I don't think I understand. How did we get in here?"

He looks as confused as I feel. "I ducked underneath some rocks and—" he exhales, shaking his head— "into here."

I feel ill as he looks away, trying not to meet my eyes. "What's it like now outside?"

He blinks, and I know the truth by the roundness of his eyes, the stillness of his features. In the space between that look and his words, I turn my head and see a pile of rubble rising from the cool floor into the ceiling. It's perhaps a meter and a half away, this six-foot-tall rubble pile that's mud and grass and rock.

My stomach bottoms out as I look at it.

"Listen—don't be worried. I know it looks like we're blocked in, but I can get us out. You woke up pretty fast. I haven't had a chance to start, but I can get the rocks and mud moved quick."

I squeeze my eyes shut. My chest aches as if it's cracking.

"Does your head hurt? I think a rock hit you right here." His fingertip brushes my forehead, near my hairline, and I struggle not to recoil.

I nod, and despite my still-shut eyes, I feel his body brush mine. When I peek my eyes open, I see a swatch of his wet shirt; he's sitting right beside me...quite close. I feel him shift again and get the sense that he's moved back a bit.

"Talk to me." His voice is low and soft—a pleasing voice accompanying a pleasing physique.

A shudder ripples through me, then another. A trough of fear and horror makes me feel as if I'm sinking. *This cannot be happening. It cannot be.*

"Hey now...it's okay." He scoots closer—close enough that I can feel his knee brush my thigh. "Those rocks aren't that big. Just watch. I can get them moved in half an hour. Then we're outta here."

I press my lips together, inhale slowly through my nose. We will not get stuck here. I will not be stranded—*never again.* If he can't dig us out, the village will come for us.

I lift my head and find his face more earnest than I've ever seen it. Contrite, I hope. I raise my eyebrows, telling him with my face to sod off. His mouth twitches at the corners. *Message received.*

A few feet away, a familiar lantern flickers. It's set beside my pack, which looks lumpy and rumpled. "I see you took the liberty of going through my belongings."

He brings his palms together in a praying pose, raising his brows in a look of definite contrition, and gets up without a word.

The spineless knob.

I bring my knees up to my chest and wrap my arms around them. With my back to the rear of the cave, where I believe the stream is, I watch as the Carnegie walks to the rubble pile. Underneath his drenched clothes, his body looks impossibly chiseled. A bit like a superhero, actually. There's not a soft spot to be found on him, except the lump of clay between his ears.

He steps around the rubble pile, which I note again extends from floor to ceiling—signifying that the cave's mouth must be there in the ceiling's slant.

The opening is likely not large—I'd guess a meter or so, most. If it were bigger, I'd know of this place. Glancing around the area again, I decide it's more burrow than cave. I wonder if its entrance is masked by a tree or hidden beneath a crest of rock or grass, further disguising it from plain sight.

My throat cinches. I'm stuck in a burrow with Sheep Whisperer Carnegie.

He's now poking at the rocks near the top of the pile, causing several to thud to the floor. The dull sound echoes off the walls. Then he steps back, hands at his hips. He remains that way, unmoving for a few long moments before pacing back to me.

"Here's the thing, Siren. I'm not feeling a lot of water dripping through. But you can hear it raining out there, right?"

I look up at the ceiling. Now that he says so, I notice the low hum, but prior to now, I hadn't. I nod quickly, as if to say *of course.*

"That tells me one of two things: either there's a larger stone up top, blocking the rain, or it's a pile of smaller stones that's pretty thick."

My belly flip-flops.

"Don't worry. We can figure out which one is true, and we

can do it faster if you've got something like a long antennae or some tent joints in that pack of yours. I can use something long and straight to poke up through the rocks and see if I can tell where the pile-up seems to end. If it's stacked pretty thick above us, might make sense to wait till daylight to start digging. See if any sunlight can get through, and if so, where."

I shut my eyes and use some of the Lamaze breathing Anna and I learned for Kayti's birth. When I open them, he's crouched down just in front of me, rubbing a fingertip over the damp floor.

"What I'm hearing," I say sharply, "is you'd like me to sleep here inside this...burrow. With you."

His somber face transforms as his lips twitch into a tiny smile. "With me? You say that like it's a bad thing."

I snort. "Oh, I wonder why that is."

He shakes his head once. "Listen, Siren—I'm the one who's gonna dig you out of here. I just helped you heard a bunch of sheep, and then I saved you from ending up under a ton of rock. I was a dick the other night, but that was then, and it was a one-time thing. You caught me at a bad moment. From this point on, I'm your partner."

I can't help myself—I howl. "My partner!" My head is thrown back as I cackle evilly, trying to decide which of his comments is the most offensive. Is it the notion that I couldn't dig myself out, or his seeming assurance that I'll simply move on from what happened last night and be his "partner?" When I recover—my head is pounding—I find him standing with his big, thick arms folded in front of his chest, peering down his nose at me.

"My partner..." I throw my head back once more, wiping pretend tears from my eyes. "Quite the comedian, are we?"

His lips twitch in a smirk—or stifled smile—as he shakes his head. "I get the feeling that I'm not appreciated."

"How astute of you."

His mouth rounds into an "o" of mock offense. "I'm wounded."

"If only." His jaw drops even as he's laughing, and I aim an awful look his way. "I'm not your siren, so let's get that bit settled. We're not friends or family, therefore no pet names shall be required. Thirdly, I suspect what you are actually saying is you're worried that the pile of rocks may collapse, and if that happens wrongly, we'll be stuck here."

Cold sweat glimmers through me even as I go on in a steady voice. "I agree that seems a danger. Other things for you to know: I don't need you to dig me out." I hold my hands up. "I've got these, and they both work quite nicely." I tap my head. "This is full as well, and although I concur we should perhaps wait for some sunlight—and to see if rescuers arrive—before we poke the beast, and that means *technically* you and I agree, I don't want to be partners. I'm not forgetting how you behaved before because it's relevant to who you are."

He gives a low whistle that echoes through the burrow. "Ouch."

"I doubt quite a bit that anyone is ever honest with you, *Homer*." I hold up my hand, as if I'm pledging. "I will be. My hands work well enough, but I'd prefer you dig us out with yours while I sit back and think up a new knitting pattern. My service to you in return can be my honesty."

One of his cheeks curves, a dimple appearing near his mouth. "I've always been a fan of English accents. Got a couple friends from England. But yours is different. A little Scottish sounding, maybe a little bit of Welsh. I like the softness of it."

I roll my eyes. "I do so value your assessment." *A bit of Welsh; is he brainless?* "I'll do you the favor of not commenting on *your* accent."

Again, I'm rewarded by a widening of his eyes and a small part of his lips before he grins as if he's pleasantly surprised. "Are you insulting my accent?" He tilts his head, folding his arms again.

I smile back cheekily. "Not yours specifically."

"I think I get it. You're an American-hater."

"Whatever gave you that impression?"

His brows furrow. Then he shakes his head, smiling like he thinks I'm quite the rogue. "Could it be a lewd encounter with a shameless interloper?"

"Dammit, woman. What does a guy have to do to say he's sorry?"

I stretch my fingers out in front of me, peering critically down at the dirt under my nails. "Oh, I don't know. For behavior like that, it might take two or three apologies...especially when the offender has got the innocent party trapped inside a burrow."

He sighs as he crouches back down. "Last night was a shitty night for me. That's no excuse. I was a dick, and I regret it. You might not believe me, but that's not how I usually am. I'm...I don't know. Honestly, I'm kind of a nice guy."

I pick at my cuticle, and he gives a soft laugh. "C'mon, Finley." I look up to find his hand in his hair. That must be his nervous habit, and I find I like it. I like that he's nervous, that he feels sorry for his knob-headed behavior.

I like it enough that I say, "How about a deal? A sort of truce? I'll extend to you the benefit of the doubt as well as my prized honesty if you promise you'll improve quite a bit. Should you violate the truce's conditions, I reserve the right to exact revenge."

He grins, shaking his head. "What sort of revenge?"

"You should hope you never find out. We Tristanians know a lot of very odd things. I have ways to make you pay that you'd never expect."

When his brows rumple, I wiggle mine. "Have you ever smelled a yellow-arsed penguin's egg?"

He laughs at the name of my fictional penguin, and I find

myself smiling—an error that I quickly remedy. I purse my lips, looking at the floor so I'll avoid his too-familiar gaze. "Is that it, then? You truly want to wait here until daylight?"

He rubs his hands together, then exhales audibly, as if he's got the weight of the universe on his wide shoulders. "I could start digging now, but I'd rather know a little better what's up there above us."

"A night in the burrow, then."

He presses a palm against the floor, then looks up so our eyes meet. He doesn't speak or make a face, but simply stares at me—until I want to scoot away.

"Are you having a seizure?"

He laughs. "Jesus."

"Is not an expletive I tolerate."

One big hand covers his face before he gives me a pointed look. "You feel okay? Do you feel dizzy or sick?"

"I believe I'd know if I had a concussion. I'm the fill-in doctor after all."

His lips purse. *Bastard.* But he doesn't change his tone. "You think you can stand okay?"

Weren't we in reverse positions just a bit ago, when he rolled down the slope? I run my fingertips over my soaked pants leg, finding I don't want to look at him as I say, "Of course."

He's crouching too close for me to breathe properly, so I do stand and pace around a bit. I don't want to see that awful pile of rock and mud, so I wander toward the rear of the burrow, where I find a stream that's perhaps a foot and a half wide, burbling from a stone on one side of the cave and flowing across its back wall into the other side. I crouch down to examine its point of exit, hoping perhaps there's a hole there to another cave—one whose entrance isn't blocked—but no such luck.

I wonder if the water's good and dip my hand in like a ladle. It tastes fine, which means it's likely safe to drink. Exactly nothing on the island is polluted. We're so isolated, we are largely shielded from humanity's idiocy.

When I stand back up, the Carnegie is beside me—so close I flinch as he holds out a water bottle.

"Rifling through my bag again, are we?"

"Oh yeah. Pillaging the good stuff." He gives me a sidelong glance and a funny little look, as if he's humored by me. I have a long swallow of water and rub my fingers over my palm. My hands are prunes from being in the rain for so long. My head aches from where I hit it, and my body feels achy and sluggish.

I lock my gaze onto the stream and wonder when he's going to walk off.

"You can get a blanket from my bag," I tell him. "There should be two thin sleeping bags packed tightly near the bottom." I sometimes unzip them and use one as a mattress and the other as my blanket; since they're waterproof, I also sometimes sleep in one and use the other as a makeshift tent.

"Sounds good, Siren."

As he turns back toward the burrow's "front," where my pack is, I release a held breath. Best for him to stay as far away from me as possible. Of all the myriad things I need at present, friendship with a wicked American sports star isn't one of them. I'd go so far as to say it's at the very bottom of my list.

Why does he have to play faux nice guy now that we're stuck in here? I'm fair at assessing people, and I'm pretty sure he *isn't*— nice. I've not read much about him, but Holly sought out information on the world wide web, and read that he's a self-pleased playboy, dressing up for parties he attends with models on his arm. Besides the desperate plan that I'd considered, I'm not quite sure why I'd looked so forward to meeting him.

I take another long swallow from the bottle. How much do I have to drink before I'll need to relieve myself? That's sure to be barrels of fun.

I lean down and refill the bottle from the stream. When I cast my gaze over my shoulder, I see my "partner" spreading the bags out. I turn slowly around, scarcely breathing as I watch him from the shadows.

I glean nothing from his movements and his mannerisms—nothing but athleticism and perhaps a sort of masculine elegance. I can almost see him jumping four feet off the ground, his arm flung above his head to catch a fly ball. He looks like someone in one of Gammy's dog-eared travel magazines: a breathing mannequin with sinewy, deep-tanned limbs and freakishly squared shoulders. Of course, he's bigger than all that. Despite being lean, I'd say he's what you might call burly. More the chest and shoulders. He's built like a bull.

I feel nothing as I watch him move the bags about, spreading the green one out, with its top beside the cave's right wall and bottom pointing at the middle of the burrow. As I walk slowly over, he spreads the purple bag about three feet from that one.

Without ado, I sit on it, glancing at the rubble pile, which sounds as if it's dripping.

Not stuck, I remind myself. Not if rain is getting in. We can get out. If we're not out soon, most of the village will descend upon us. We'll be dug out in no time at all.

The Carnegie sits beside me on the green bag, and I can feel his gaze move over my face. I drop my gaze to my hands, now folded around the water bottle, then dart a glance back up to him.

I hate him. I hate it that I can't stop looking at him. I hate that when I do, I feel off-balance. It's the same unsteady feeling I get in nightmares, when I'm forever trapped inside the bottom of a boat.

Thunder booms above us. As his gaze flies to the rubble pile, I find mine hung up on the contours of his face. Truly, I've never seen a man that looks like him. His cheekbones seem a bit feline...

"You okay?"

I jump. Cover my face with my hand. "Fine." I hear the blood whoosh in between my ears and hate him, hate him, hate him.

"I...uh...thought I saw some clothes in your bag," he says quietly. "Want me to turn around and you can change?"

I shake my head, running my nails along the plastic bottle's grooves. I won't be here long enough to need dry clothes, and even if I did...

I stand slowly and look up at the ceiling, curved a mere two feet or so above my head. I walk to the rubble pile, where rain-drops and faint splotches of moonlight play over the cave's floor.

"Careful," he calls. "You don't want to touch that."

I swallow, refusing to look back as I hear him move toward me. I run my fingers over the rocks, my touch feather-light. They're mostly large stones, plus or minus the dimensions of a football—though near the bottom of the pile, one's more boulder, perhaps half a meter long. My gaze rests on a jagged piece of dark rock near the top. I run a fingertip over it. It looks like part of the archway we just climbed atop. I believe it is.

"Finley." His fingers wrap around my wrist.

I snatch it back.

"You move something wrong, the whole thing falls."

"Oh, is that how that works? What a pity. We could climb out."

He's quiet for a long time. I refuse to look at him as tension thickens between us.

"We could crawl out," he says quietly, "or we could get crushed." I turn my head in time to see him catch his lower lip between his teeth. "No way to tell."

Tears fill my eyes, and my cheeks and neck burn as I feel my pulse race. "You're saying we're trapped here."

I swing my hand out toward the rubble pile—the impulse born of panic and terror.

Nothing can prepare me for his hands snatching me by the

waist, for the ease with which he drags me toward the sleeping bags.

I buck against him, kicking my legs into the air. "Put me down!"

He sets me on my sleeping bag, and my heart beats so hard and fast my head spins. "Don't touch me!" My voice is plaintive. "Don't touch me again—so help me!"

He peers down at me, his face barren until I realize his cheek is sucked in on one side; he's bit down on it. "You can't take risks like that, Finley. Now is not the time to be impulsive. Trust me."

"Do you know when I would trust you?"

He blinks at me.

"*Never*. I would never trust you, never in a billion years would I trust you, Declan *Carnegie*. You are not the hero; you're the villain! I don't want to *know* you. I don't want to be trapped here with you! I want you to disappear, but if we're here come morning, you will dig us out and if you don't, then I will do whatever I please—do you understand?"

His jaw tightens, and I can see I've raised his hackles.

I lie down on my side, putting my back to him. "By the way—I've got a tracker in my pack, so someone will come find us soon. If you can't dig us out, my village will."

So don't you think of touching me again.

NINE
DECLAN

I grind my teeth against the square of gum, relishing the hit of flavor and slight burn. Eclipse Polar Ice. Had a sleeve of eight that I found in my pocket. I've chewed three since she told me to fuck off.

That was coming up on two hours ago. I know because I can't stop looking at my phone. Fucker's got ninety percent battery, and I've got it on the power-saver mode, but still, I need to leave it face-down and forget about it.

Eighteen minutes after midnight.

Sun will rise at seven.

On the list of my worst fuckups, where does this one rank, I wonder as I sit beside the stream. *Way below the biggest one,* a cruel voice whispers. I inhale slowly and rub my aching eyes. I can't think about that shit now.

I'd say this probably ranks below the time I was ninety feet under the ocean in the Maldives and lost my scuba tank. Earned myself a helicopter ride to a hyperbaric chamber. Below that...but probably above the Encierro three years ago, when I tried to jump up on a fountain in Pamplona to dodge a bull and ended up with nineteen stitches in my calf. Spent the Barcelona portion of that trip laid up, but being stuck inside a fucking cave is definitely worse. Siren's right—it's not even a cave; it's like a fucking rabbit burrow.

I blow my breath out slowly, inhale through my nose.

Never been a fan of being stuck places. Not since...I shake my head.

Once, when I was fourteen, the mast broke off of a sailboat Nate and I had taken out on Lake Constance. The motors blew a fuse, so we drifted around for half a day before another boater came up on us. I'm not sure if this is worse than that. Too soon to say.

I look over my shoulder at the lump of Finley's body in her sleeping bag. I'm pretty sure she's bullshitting about the "tracker." First, what is a tracker? She'd have to mean something with GPS, and that shit doesn't work out here.

I splash some water on my face and turn around to face her. Before she went to sleep, she disappeared behind the rock pile with her dry clothes, and I came here to sit beside the stream, hoping it might make her feel more comfortable. When she came back around the pile, she stood and stared at me a minute before sliding back into the bag.

I walked over to her, wanting to reassure her somehow, but woman seemed to read my mind. She said, "Just don't."

I think of her somber face as I scrub my own, rubbing my temples before heading back to the bags. I don't think she's awake. Hasn't moved in a while. She's curled on her side so tightly she looks almost kid-sized. I can't see her face, just a bunch of penny-red hair spread over a blow-up pillow.

What's this do to her, I wonder. How does she feel about being trapped? I don't know all that much about what happened while my dad and I were here last time; I was just six, and right after we left Tristan, he took me to Carogue, the boarding school where I grew up—so we didn't really ever talk about it. But I know when we arrived, she was lost at sea in a small boat she'd been in with her parents. When they found her, near the end of our visit, she was alone.

I shake my head, wondering why we didn't stay here longer that time. Normally, most visits last a few months because the ship that brought you doesn't come back by until then. I think Dad and I left on a different ship than the one we came in on. I don't know.

I knead my aching shoulder and slide into my bag. I don't sleep with my back to anyone, not even pint-sized redheaded sirens, so I'm on my side, facing her. I'm looking at her hair, watching her shoulders rise and fall under the sleeping bag as she breathes. I can't be sure, but I think maybe I can smell her. Something floral...roses, maybe.

Her hair looks soft. I lie there staring at it, thinking about touching it for what feels like eternity. I close my eyes and inhale the rose scent and let my mind drift, taking care to steer away from last time I was trapped somewhere. At what turns out to be 5:11, I break down and check my phone. After that, I set it down beside me, and Finley's hips shift in her bag. I lay my hand out on the ground between us, and finally, I fall asleep.

* * *

Finley

I don't want to laugh. In fact, I *refuse* to. But the Carnegie doesn't make it easy.

I awoke sweaty and breathless, my fists clenched—because in

the dream, I couldn't reach the boat's sides from under the bench, where I was huddled, and I needed something to hold onto. For the first few moments, that sensation—up and down, of being tossed by the waves—was so potent, I didn't notice where I was. Then I sat up, and I saw him.

The Carnegie has pulled off his shirt, and if I'm not mistaken, that's it tied about his head. And underneath it, smooshed against his dark hair, boots. He's set his boots atop his head and tied his shirt around them. He looks like some sort of clothes bin monster, though not really; with his physique, he can look like nothing except what he is—a sort of living, breathing *David*. Edit that: an arse whose flawless body is a temple, for baseball, I suppose. Deep grooves line his bare back. Shadows flit about his muscles. As he moves, poking something long and stick-like into the top of the rock pile, muscles in his shoulders ripple.

I divert my eyes, and that's when I notice my pack is open near the foot of the sleeping bags, and most of my belongings are strewn out.

"What the devil?"

He turns to me, and I straighten my spine. My gaze locks onto his hand. "I suppose you robbed my tent of one of its joints?"

He wipes at his forehead. "Poking through the rocks to see if I can get an idea of—"

"You didn't think to ask me?"

He blinks. "You were sleeping."

"You could have woken me."

"You're right. I could have."

"And?"

"I didn't."

I draw a deep breath. Press my lips together. Grit my molars. *Doesn't matter*, I tell myself. Very soon we will be out of here, and nothing about him will be relevant to me ever again. In a few weeks, he'll sail away, and that will be the end of him.

"Well, then. What have you found?"

"Just poking around."

"And?"

He lifts a shoulder in a sort of shrug. "I just want to mess around a little, see if I can get this joint through to a spot where it's not touching anything."

The tent's joint is near half a meter long. If he can't manage to poke it through...I inhale deeply.

He reaches into his pocket, tossing something my way. "Catch."

I scramble to snatch something small and flat before it hits the ground.

"My phone," he says. "You can turn it on with the button on the right side. It'll want a password. Put in one, one, one, nine, one, seven. Swipe your thumb across the screen until you see an app—a square that'll say 'Kindle.' There are books there. Find something to read and don't be worried. I won't move the rocks around unless I'm sure there's not much else on top of them." He taps his head, flashing me a grin. "And I've got a helmet."

A retort slams through my head—*Do you think I care?*" But it's too much, even for me in my present agitated state. Instead I say, "You're absurd."

"If absurd means genius."

"Most certainly not."

He laughs, holding the joint up. "I'm not looking like a genius over here? You sure?"

"I am absolutely certain."

He chuckles. "Go on, turn the phone on."

He feels he needs to distract me? Between glaring daggers at him, I feel around the side of the small, flat thing and press a button. Its screen lights up, revealing a picture that's so pristine, I can't help gaping at it. It's a sailboat in a harbor, and it's *stunning*.

"There's a circle at the bottom of the phone's front. Press the circle button." I do, and at the bottom of the screen appears a message: "Slide to unlock."

"Slide your thumb across the lock screen."

I try, but nothing happens.

"Ever used a touch screen?" He steps slightly toward me.

What's a touch screen?

"If you haven't, you want to drag the tip of your thumb over the screen. Not too hard, but hard enough."

I try again, and the phone reads: "Enter Passcode."

"Passcode is one, one, one, nine, one, seven."

I punch in the numbers, and I see another picture: this one of a group of grinning kids in Red Sox T-shirts.

"You got it?"

"Of course."

"If you don't see the Kindle square, swipe your thumb again and it'll be on the next page of the menu options."

I tilt the phone toward my face and peer down at it. The children pictured look so real. As if they're right here next to me. How very odd. What makes the photos so lifelike? I cast my gaze back up to the Carnegie, who's turned away from me with one hand outstretched toward the rubble pile.

"Warn me before you move things," I murmur.

"Will do."

I swallow and look back at the screen. One of the squares says "Photos." I want to press that and see what happens, but he didn't tell me to. I drag my thumb across the screen again, and all the boxes change. Now there's one that says "Kindle." I press it and look up again, in time to see him step to his left, pull the tent joint out, and poke around the rocks with it again.

"What are you finding?"

"What are you reading?" His voice is slightly strained. I watch the lantern light play on his back, making shadows as his muscles flex. I press my lips together.

Be careful.

"Why don't I help?" I murmur, chewing at my lip.

"Stay there. If something did fall, I'd need you to doctor me, yeah?"

I rub my lips together again, noticing they sting. I take some gloss from my pack and spread it over them, and then, when I look up to find him standing in the same place, I return to the phone. It asks for the passcode in again, but that's okay; I have a memory for numbers.

He moves around a bit, but I pay him no mind. I wonder why this little square is called "Kindle." Does it feature forbidden books, the sort of books one might burn?

I press a small, square cover that says *The Art of Power*, and then glance up because I think he murmured something.

"Everything all right then?" I call.

"Fine." He's got his arms raised to the ceiling right beside the rubble pile. As I look at him, I realize he's straining.

I jump up.

"Stay back!"

His arms are clearly braced against the ceiling right beside the rubble pile. "What happened?" I dash closer.

"Get back!"

As I step closer still, the ceiling caves in. It's a blur, a shout from him, and then he's lunging at me, dark rocks bouncing off his shoulders. I glimpse his face—wide-eyed and open-mouthed—before he sweeps me off my feet. I'm spirited away, my body pressed against his hard one as he tucks me to his chest and doesn't let me go until we're near the stream. When I look up, his head is down. Low panting fills my ears. He looks up, blinking through a streak of blood that's streaming from his forehead.

"You okay?" His eyes are intent on my face.

"You touched me." It's half laughed—hysteric-laughed—and in the darkness, I can see the strange look on his face. It's not a smile and not a frown, but something in between. I realize I can't tell for sure...because it's *pitch black dark.*

TEN
DECLAN

Her mouth lolls open and her eyes bug out like a deer in head-lights. Except of course, there's no light here. I don't know her well enough to know her tells, but I'm pretty sure she's close to crying. Something she does with her mouth after she closes it...

"Hey..." My hand's on her shoulder before I remember she said don't touch her. I move it off her and step back a little. "The lantern must have gotten hit. We're still okay."

She shakes her head once, covering her face with both hands.

"I stuck that joint into a spot it didn't fit, and that made things shift." I pop my jaw as I look down on her bowed head. "Listen, I'm still gonna dig us out. You want to sit down, get the lantern up and running again, and you can watch me?"

"I lied!"

"What?"

She lifts her head, her face a twisted mess. "I lied about the tracker. No one knows where we are!"

I let out a slow breath. "I knew that."

"You did?"

"There's no GPS out here, Siren."

She covers her face again, shaking her head. Then she looks up at me, her brows drawn together. "I was *scared*. Of being stuck in here with *you*." Her voice cracks on the word, and I feel something tighten at the base of my throat.

"Fuck." I blow a breath out. "I'm an ass, all right? Look—I know I was. I'm an ass sometimes—I try to be a nice guy—but that night, I was an ass. Nothing to do with you, just bullshit you walked in on. That shit's over now, though. Asshole's not my normal MO, like I said, and even if it was, you and me—this isn't normal stuff. We're stuck together in a fucking cave. What's good for you is good for me. We need each other."

Finley frowns up at me.

I give her a panty-melting smile, and her lips quirk just slightly at the corners. "Don't believe me, do you?"

"I'll believe it when I see it." She sighs.

"You don't think I can be a nice guy?" I smile again—*c'mon, sweetheart*—and she looks down at her feet.

"Nothing points to that fact, no." Her shoulders rise and sharply fall. "At any rate, I don't care that you're nice, as long as you can dig."

I laugh, despite the blood that's stinging my eye. "That right?"

She puts a hand on her hip. "Yes, that is so." She leans in closer. "In spite of that lovely helmet, something hit your head and now you're bleeding. Let me patch it up before you start round two."

I snicker as she walks past me and I lose sight of her in darkness. I hear her fuck with something and a couple seconds later, light floods our humble burrow. I can see the relief I feel mirrored on her face. I'm moving toward her when she turns toward the rubble pile and freezes.

Fuckkkk. In the lantern light, shit doesn't look so good. The pile was maybe the size of your average port-a-potty box last time.

It's double that size now, maybe even triple, and interspersed among a bunch of smaller stones are several rocks I think would qualify as boulders.

"It fills half the cave!"

I drag my gaze around our quarters. "Nah—a fourth at most."

She turns to face me, her mouth pressed into a thin line. I see tears in her eyes, even as she points to my sleeping bag. "Sit there."

I humor her, sitting cross-legged while she digs through her pack, pulling out a small, red first-aid box. She looks up and then scoots slightly back, as if she finds me too close for comfort.

I wipe the blood out of my eye—the thing is twitching now—and Finley leans in, squinting. I wait for her soft voice, almost lyrical in its lilting English accent. But she just peers up at my forehead, her face so close to mine that I can tell she's holding her breath. Finally, she leans back, her pretty face a mask.

"Are you hurt anywhere else?"

I shake my head—it's true, or at least I'm hurt nowhere new—and she presses her finger to my forehead, near the gash. Her frowning mouth is close enough that I could kiss it.

"This likely needs stitches. Since we have none, I'll just tape it very tightly."

As she moves again, reaching for something in her first-aid kit, I get another whiff of rose. I shut my eyes. With them closed, I notice I feel kind of dizzy. And kind of heavy in the forehead region. *Shit.*

"This will hurt," she says. I feel her words against my cheek and then a sting that's so intense my mouth and eyes water.

"Sorry," she murmurs.

And then I feel her warm breath blow across my forehead. I feel her shift her weight and murmur something I can't really hear before her finger's dabbing something on the wound.

"Clearly," she says, "you have quite a hard head."

"Quite." Despite myself, I struggle not to smirk.

I feel her hand brush my forehead before her fingers frame the gash, pushing on it so the edges pinch closer together. "Sorry." It's whispered so softly, I'm not sure I really heard it. She blows on it again, and then I feel her fingers bend so she can stretch something across the wound. It stings under the tape, but I don't mind. I like the sharp sensation. It's grounding, like pinching yourself.

When I open my eyes, I find I'm looking into hers. For a long moment, neither of us moves, and then she's up, brushing at the seat of her cotton shorts before she turns away from me, ever the skittish doe.

She's facing the new, larger rubble pile, one hand to her forehead as if she's shading her eyes from sun.

"Do you have a plan for where to start, or shall I come up with one?"

I get up—my joints have started aching—and stand by her. My gaze travels from her wavy hair down to her bare legs before resting where it should be: on the rock pile.

"If I push it from the bottom, I'm not sure what happens at the top. How much more might fall in when we make more space." I touch the bandage tapped to my head. "Only one way to find out. I can kick the rocks there at the middle." I gesture midway up the pile's height. "Everything will fall against that wall up there if I kick that way. If there's more up top, we'll see how much more."

"We keep doing that until it stops pouring in, and we see sunlight?" She looks worried.

"That's the plan."

Until we see sunlight or the withdrawal finally gets me. I'm not telling her that, though.

* * *

Finley

I watch the Carnegie as he examines our new, mammoth rock pile. I believe he hurt his shoulder when the stones fell on him last time. He's not moving his right arm quite freely as he runs his hand along the pile. He moves slowly and carefully, his shadow falling at odd angles on the walls as the battery-powered lantern flickers, mimicking a flame.

I'm holding my breath when he turns to me.

"I'm going to give it a good shove. See what happens. You ready, partner?" He gives me a smile that's likely meant to reassure, and I gnaw my lip.

"Surely it will work. There can't be too much up there..."

One of his cheeks lifts in something that looks like a twitch, though I think it may be his attempt to smile again. "Step back for me, Siren. Far back as you can."

For him.

I do as he asks, backing up to the sleeping bags. I grab the lantern; this time, if I have to rush back toward the stream, it's coming with me. As he looks back at me, I call, "Do be careful!"

"Always."

Then he kicks the rubble pile. The cave rumbles, and as he dives out of the way, more rocks come crashing in from above. As the dust settles, I see him tilt his head toward the ceiling.

"Still blocked. Take two," he calls.

I hug myself as I watch him move nimbly sideways, throwing his long leg out for a kick. When nothing happens, he kicks again, and that does the job; more rocks clatter to the floor in an ever-growing sea. They stop falling, and he stands again, looking up. When he's still for a moment, I hurry to join him.

"What is—"

He reaches his arms above his head, and I look up to see my first glimpse of the cave's mouth. It's small, as I assumed—perhaps one meter at most—and as I blink at it, I realize that I'm looking at a paler stone. There's a large, pale gray rock blocking our exit. The Carnegie positions himself below it, pushing upward with both palms, his biceps bulging as he strains against it...but to no avail.

My stomach somersaults.

He grits out a swear word.

"Sailor," I murmur—but he hears and flashes a quick smile.

"Fucking boulder." He pushes again, and I can see his chest pump with exertion.

"Will it give at all?"

His body trembles, his eyes shutting for a moment. Then he lowers his arms. "Might just need to re-approach it from another angle," he says, looking briefly at his feet.

As I peer up at it, he walks around me, nudging my arm gently as he does. The motion is so feather-light, I might have imagined it. I watch as he strides back to the stream, splashing water on his face and hair before he bends into a crouch, breathing perhaps a bit hard.

I'm not sure what to do with myself, and I'm feeling nearly faint with terror, so I join him, bending over and dipping my cupped hands into the stream for a drink.

When I straighten up again, he's looking at me, his head tilted sideways like my dog Heath used to when he saw something that puzzled him.

"How ya holding up, Siren?" he asks quietly.

"Better if you'd stop using that ridiculous name."

"Fin?"

"Never—if you value your life." Someone I loathe calls me that, and I dislike it intensely.

"Finny?"

"Of course not. I will warn you, though, I'm calling you 'the Carnegie' in my inner monologue." I don't mean to flash him a wicked smile. It just happens.

"The Carnegie?" His mouth opens. "That sounds like a villain name."

"So it does."

"Tell me, Finny. Do you have a hatchet in that bag of yours? Something I could use to chip away at the rim of the cave's mouth —the rim of rock around that stone? If I could get rid of some of that rock, I could maybe get my hand around the motherfucker."

By that, I assume he means the boulder.

I don't have a hatchet, but I have a hammer. I give it to him and fiddle with my broken radio while he starts hacking at the rim of the cave's mouth. I know for sure the radio is broken, but I keep toying with it anyway.

I feel as if I'm in a Hitchcock film, where everything is menacing and surreal. I'm locked in a nightmare, and the stranger out in front of me is all that's standing between me and utter isolation.

* * *

Declan

She's nervous. Not just because we're stuck here, but because of me, too. I saw her fucking with that broken radio last night before she fell asleep, and as I chip at the rim of rock around the mother-fucking boulder, I see her messing with it again. When she thinks I'm not looking, her gaze runs up and down my body. When I glance her way, it falls back to her lap.

The hammer she had in her bag is a wall hammer, the kind

that people use for climbing. One side is more flat, the other more pointed. Neither side is great for chipping rock, but the rim of the cave's mouth is sort of flaky, like slate, so I'm making a little bit of progress. I try not to think about how long it might take to chip away enough to move the stone that's got us trapped here.

Fuck, I'm getting lightheaded from not eating. Last night, I saw a couple of meal bars in her bag, and I know I should probably ask for one. Doesn't matter if I've got an appetite; gotta fuel up if I'm going to work. Right about the time my stomach growls, I hear the distinctive rip of a wrapper and look across the way to find her munching on one of said bars. A moment later, she's on her feet, coming to stand slightly behind me.

I turn to find her with her eyebrows arched, her delicate face soft with what looks a little bit like shyness.

"Would you like an Atkins bar? I had several stashed in my bag."

For a second, I'm just looking at her—trying to reconcile that soft voice and pretty face with all those smartass comments. Who is this woman? I like calling her "siren" because it gets a rise, but maybe she's more mermaid. The more I'm around her, the more I get the feeling that her temper masks a secret soft side. Something sort of like shyness.

I blink. "Yeah." She passes the bar to me. "Thanks."

She stands there looking at me for a minute. Then she crouches, rising with a stone in hand. It's flat with jagged-looking edges. As she looks at it, she murmurs something.

"Mmm?"

"It might have been a lightning strike." She holds the stone out. "I think this is from the arch. Look..." She turns the stone over, and something flashes on it. It's a metal bar, shaped like a giant staple. "Years back, someone welded these into the arch, so when the youth would climb it, there'd be safer handholds."

She looks back up at me with sad eyes. "They're most likely

searching for us as we speak." She holds the stone up. "I'm going to chip the rock with this—the bar part. Better than doing nothing."

"Yeah, for sure."

She takes a long step back. "Waiting to see how you're swinging, so I can stay out of the line of fire," she says softly.

"Sure thing." I cringe at how eager I sound. Something about her voice...I don't know. She's not the type that seems to need protecting, but I guess I want to, I realize as I swing the hammer. Shards of rock go flying, and a moment later, I feel her behind me.

"Back to back," she says. "I'll work on the other side of the rim."

I inhale slowly, telling myself it's okay for her to be behind me; I'm not asleep—or helpless. "Sounds good, Fin."

Silence shifts between us. When I look back at her, I see tears in her eyes.

ELEVEN
FINLEY

"Not a word about it." I wipe my eyes, glaring at him through my fingers.

He turns more fully toward me, giving me a searching look.

"I don't like being stuck in caves. And I well and truly hate to be called Fin, so never again, please. I'm not a crier, only cry when very tired or in a fury."

He lifts his brows, his handsome face gentle and kind despite those too-shrewd eyes that always see too much. "The kind of fury one might feel if one was stuck inside a cave and being called...you know?" He smiles.

"That kind exactly." I breathe deeply, wiping my eyes once more before I slam my rock into the ceiling.

"Fin doesn't feel right anyway," he says as he turns back around. "Think I'm gonna stick to Siren."

"That's absurd."

"How come?" he asks, striking the ceiling with a sharp rap.

"Well for one, I'm not a siren. You do realize it's a real thing, at least in Greek mythology?"

"A woman-bird. A temptress. Their songs lured sailors into shipwrecks."

"You're not a sailor, not except your shameful, depraved language. And neither is your ship wrecked."

He gives me a funny look over his shoulder. "Finny."

"What?"

"It's Finny or Siren."

"What, pray tell, is wrong with my name?"

His face splits into a grin. "Did you just say *pray tell*?"

"I did." I straighten my spine. "And you liked it. Now, get back to work."

He chuckles as he turns around, tapping the ceiling with the hammer. "Hear that?" He taps again.

"The tapping?"

He reaches his arm out, tapping in another spot. Then he taps the first again.

"That first one sounds a higher pitch."

He taps again.

"A bit more hollow than the other. I suppose that's good?"

He nods. "The cave's mouth might be thinner here." He switches the hammer into his left hand and slams it against the spot with a sharp *rap*.

And nothing happens. He strikes the wall repeatedly for half an hour, going at it from all angles, with both arms, later using rock and striking other spots—and nothing happens. Not a thing besides a few flakes of rock off here and there.

I check the watch I keep in my bag and find it's just past one o'clock in the afternoon.

"No one shouting for us," I murmur, as I peel open my half-eaten Atkins bar.

I get a pinch to stop my stomach growling, pass the rest to him.

"Not yet, Finny."

"I'm not Finny."

"Yes you are." He smiles at me as if we're lifelong friends. "You're very Finny."

"You're corny."

He wipes his brow with the back of his wrist, exhales so his shoulders seem to sink. "I'm going to try to swing a different way. See if that helps."

"Knock yourself out." I smirk, and he rubs at his forehead.

"I kind of want to," he confesses.

Over the next few hours, we make slow-but-steady progress, flaking shards of rock away each time we strike the cave's mouth. My muscles tremble and cry out in pain the more I use them.

I have hopes that if we chisel enough, larger chunks of rock will fall away...but that's not so. As night falls outside our wretched burrow, I feel like my throat is being squeezed.

While the Carnegie swings his strong arm for the millionth time, I eat the third segment of my Atkins bar and fetch another for him. I sit on one of the scattered rocks that used to be the rubble pile and beckon him over.

He rejects the bar with a shake of his head, then walks to the stream to splash his face. After that, he positions himself below the stone and tries again to push it. He strains until his veins are bulging and a sheen of sweat shines on his back and shoulders.

And still...nothing. The stone blocking our exit is a large one, seemingly larger than the mouth of our burrow.

When my arms ache too much for me to lift them without groaning, I rub my face, and he turns to me.

"How ya doing, Siren?"

"Your arms must be made of steel. Mine are screaming bloody murder."

"It's not comfortable." His face is serious and, I think, for the first time, perhaps a bit strained.

I squeeze my eyes shut, and then look up at the stone. "Do

you think we could hear if they came calling?"

I'm talking to myself, really, but he nods. "I think so. But it'd be better if I could get that fucking rock moved." My face must register my dislike of his language; he runs a hand back through his hair and has the good form to look sheepish. "Sorry."

"I'm growing used to it—your sailor's mouth."

He bends down to get his water bottle, and I watch him guzzle from it. He drinks so quickly, it runs down his chin and throat. As he wipes it with the back of his hand, his gaze rests on me again. "You Catholic? Grew up Catholic?"

"Everyone is Catholic here, cradle to grave."

He offers nothing of his own religious practices. I'd be surprised if he had any.

"Tell me something, Siren."

"What?" I'm still sitting, my right ankle on my left knee, folding my bar's wrapper into a small square.

He slams the hammer into the rock. "Anything." A beat of silence passes, and he glances at me with a little smirk. "What's the craziest thing that's happened here that you remember? Something that really shocked all you Catholics."

The answer comes quite easily to me. I feel my stomach dip, and I suppose my face must reflect...something. He lifts his brows; after a moment, he slaps his pants leg. "Oh—I think I heard about that. Can't believe she did that to her."

"What?" I'm stifling a smile.

"Oh, you know." He lifts his brows. "The *thing* she did."

"The thing?" I'm chuckling now, at his strangeness.

He nods once. "I know," he says sagely. "And I see why you don't want to talk about it."

"Oh, sod off."

"Isn't that a swear word for you English types?" He's grinning, and I roll my eyes because he looks so proud of himself.

I slip my folded Atkins wrapper into a pocket on the front of my sleep shorts and force my aching legs to stand. "Being near you is wearing on my morals." I say it lightly, but I cross myself discreetly as I walk around him.

He snorts, and for a while longer, we toil in silence, shards of rock flaking onto our shoes as we chip at the rim of the cave's mouth.

When it becomes impossible to lift my arms, I sit on a nearby mini-boulder, rubbing at my knotted shoulders and watching him swing the hammer. Sweat coats his neck and back, and stains the waistline of his battered khaki shorts. His shoulder rolls as he reaches around to rub his back. Then he glances back at me, pirate-swarthy with his dark scruff turned into a light beard, and his high cheekbones, and those lips...

"So tell me, what do Tristan girls like yourself do for entertainment when you've got some down time?"

I snort. "Down time?"

He turns around to face me, wiping his forehead. "Not much of that around here?"

"Nearly never."

"They were talking about you in the bar last night." He runs a hand back through his sweat-wet hair, which I wish looked even a bit off-putting, and my tummy dips in response to his words.

"And?"

He shrugs. "Just saying how you work with the animals and at the clinic."

"We all do different tasks. I'm no exception."

"That's not what I heard."

"You were hearing bits from Mac at the pub?" I bite my lip to hide a smirk.

He laughs. "Mac seemed all right."

I look down at my lap, flexing my cramping fingers. "Seeming all right's not his problem."

"How does that work, anyway?"

"How does what work?" I look up as he takes a small step toward me. My stomach jerks downward in a sort of flipping feeling.

"How much liquor do you have here on the island?"

"And can someone drain the bar dry?" I put my hand to my damp forehead, shutting my eyes briefly. "Yes, most certainly. It's happened before. The liquor comes on ships, of course, and only perhaps twice a year. If we run out, we're out, and we've had people get too glad about the bottle."

I hear his low chuckle. "Glad about the bottle."

"Well, that's what it is." I open my eyes to find him rubbing that shoulder.

"Guess so."

"I've never cared for it myself," I tell him.

"No?"

I shake my head. My father famously drained the island dry a multitude of times—until at last they banned him from the bar. And after that, he learned to pick the locks and take what he desired. "Never wanted to be one of those sorts."

"One of what sorts?" he says quietly.

I chew at my lip, trying to think of how to say it without mentioning my father. "I'm not sure I've ever wanted anything enough to lie and skirt the rules to get it. Not sure that I want to want something so desperately. Seems exhausting. A bit dangerous."

I watch as his features seem to soften, and he nods.

"How did we get on this?" I sigh, looking at the dark gray stone that's got us stuck here.

"I asked what you do for entertainment."

"Most of us don't court the bottle like Mac. For me, I knit on Saturdays with a few friends—on Saturday evenings. We celebrate occasions at the café or the Burger Joint. That's once or twice a month. And then there's things that come and go with seasons. Fishing and the factory—processing crab. Helping sort the mail when that comes. Every one of us wears many different caps, as I said. When I do get a bit of time," I offer, looking at my feet again, "I like to throw a bowl or two."

"Throw a bowl?"

I look up at him. "Clay-throwing. Pottery. Ceramic working. Throw a bowl, so...form it on the wheel. And then I fire it in the kiln and sometimes sell it."

"Here?"

I blink. "I apparate to London to throw clay and put it at the market."

I enjoy watching his face bend in surprise that morphs into amusement. "So we've got a smartass, and a wizard."

"I'm not any sort of arse." My lips twitch. "That's your place."

He grins broadly. "Touché."

"Merely honest."

"Hey—" He holds his hands up. "That was one night. One...*crummy* night."

"Bravo, Sailor."

"You stick around, you'll see that night's not representative of Declan Carnegie."

"Perhaps not, but I believe I've only met *the* Carnegie." When I feel my mouth trend upward at the corners, it feels as if someone's yanked the floor from under my feet. I tuck my mouth back down and try to frown, although I believe it comes out smirk-ish.

"There's that name again." He shakes his head as he walks backward toward the stream. "Not sure I know *the* Carnegie. I'm just Declan. Nice guy." He holds up the middle three of his fingers, as if he's making a pledge of sorts.

I scoff. "That's what you say."

He nods. "I do."

Then he's turned around, and I'm left looking at his back as he moves to the stream, where he kneels down and splashes his face.

My heart pitter-patters, as if something inside's cracked and now is leaking.

*　*　*

Declan

"Siren...stop."

She looks over her shoulder, wide-eyed, like I've just caught her doing something naughty.

I wipe my forehead, where my hair is dripping into my eyes. "You can't even lift your arm up straight."

"I can." She holds her chipping stone up, and my own shoulder aches with sympathetic pain.

"Go lie down. And in a few hours," I lie, "we can swap shifts."

She turns away from me, and then back toward me, lips pursed and her eyebrows drawn down. "Promise?" She looks sulky.

"That we'll switch shifts?" I nod. "We both need to get some rest so we can keep at this until we get it."

She exhales and nods once. Her hair's falling into her eyes, and her face sags with exhaustion.

"I'll wake you in five hours. Or six if that works better."

"Absolutely not. Three and a half at most." She gives me a pointed look I've come to recognize. I put one toe out of line, and those slightly scrunched eyebrows go full-on pissed off and her pert mouth pulls into a disapproving frown.

"Yes ma'am." I salute her. "Three and a half it is."

"And then it's your turn. I'm enforcing that," she says as she stalks past me.

"Do it."

I sift through the rubble quietly as she goes to sleep. When I'm sure she's out, I walk around what remains of the rock pile and sit on one of the larger stones with my back to her. I take a few deep breaths until the anxious hum that's buzzing through me eases just a little. Then I rub my head and eyes and knead the inside of my wrist—a pressure point that's supposed to help you keep from puking.

Fuck.

I run my hands back through my hair a few more times before I stand up, grab the hammer, and go at the cave's mouth like my life depends on it. Over the course of a few hours, I bring another three or four inches of stone crumbling down before my hands are shaking too bad to keep going and I'm seeing bursts of light behind my eyes.

Fuck this.

I wedge my palms against the boulder, bend my knees, and shove as hard as I can. I push until I feel my heartbeat in my eyebrows and I'm groaning at the pain from my shoulder. When Finley stirs, I drop into a crouch. I hold my head and feel my eyes sting.

Jesus.

I just need to lay down for a second. I walk to the sleeping bags, feeling my knees shake. They've been hurting kind of bad for the last few hours. The joints in my arms, too. I stop beside Finley, looking down at her as lantern light plays on her face.

When I ducked behind the slab of rock that hung over the cave's mouth, I didn't realize that there *was* a fucking cave. I just had to put us behind something, somewhere out of the rocks' way. About the time I realized we were fucked—I had wrapped myself around Finley and was getting smacked to shit by big rocks—one of my legs went into the hole. I tried to get my balance, and instead we fell through. While I was checking Finley over—she still wasn't moving, and I was scared she'd gotten hurt bad in the fall—rocks came pouring in. A few seconds later, it was a done deal.

I blow out a long, quiet breath. When I'm in my bag beside hers, I shut my eyes and let my chest pump, let my jaw clench, let my fingers knead my shoulder till my nails break the skin. I press my lips shut so I don't groan.

I just need to get some sleep. I scoot a little closer to her, close enough so I can smell that nice, flowery smell.

My heart's beating fast. I can do my meditative breathing till it isn't. I know how to do this shit. At some point I think I nod off. It's hard to tell for sure because I almost never sleep since starting the tapers, but I think this time it actually happens. Next time I check the watch that's lying between Finley and me on the cave's floor, it's almost an hour later, and almost two hours past the time I promised I'd wake her.

I get up quietly and move around in front of her. She's tossed her way out of the top half of the sleeping bag, and her T-shirt is jacked up over her breasts, giving me a view of her belly. For a long second, I can't tear my eyes away from it. Unlike most bellies I've seen these past few years, Finley's is soft and slightly rounded, protruding just a little bit over the top of her pajama shorts. I find myself smirking down at it. Nonconforming—that's what it is.

Fuck toned and tan, Finley's stomach is whiter than the moon, and it looks soft like women's thighs and asses can be when they're nice and thick. I have the strange impulse to run the back of my hand over it, see how soft she really is for someone so damn prickly.

I look up and down the sleeping bag a time or two, and then

back at that belly and her full breasts, hidden by the rumpled tee shirt, before I reach out and touch her shoulder.

"Siren?" I whisper it a time or two, smirking as I watch her face twitch and her balled-up hand lift up to rub her cheek. She cracks her brown eyes open, then gives me her signature glare.

"Good morning, darlin'."

She scowls, but it lacks its full force. She blinks around the burrow, seeming confused.

"You want to sleep some more?"

She yawns, balling her small self up. Her hand brushes her belly as she does, and she yanks the hemline of her shirt, as if she knows how hard I perved on her when she was sleeping. I give her a wink. Finley rolls her eyes and pushes up on her elbows.

She groans. "The ground. So...hard."

I nod.

"I hate it here." She shakes her head, and her long hair falls over her shoulders, covering her breasts until she uses something wrapped around her wrist to fasten it back.

I pass her a protein bar—one of only six left. "Fuel up. And wake me in an hour."

She gives me another troubled frown, but nods.

"Not a morning person?" I smile.

"It's not morning."

"Fair enough."

Shortly after I stretch out, she gets up without a glance my way. I watch discreetly as she works, going at it hard and feeling probably the same way I do—like every second we're in here makes it less likely we'll ever get out.

For a second, I consider getting up, but it's a minor miracle I slept before. If I can get a little more, I know I can get us out of here.

TWELVE
FINLEY

I realize while he dozes: there's something amiss with the Carnegie. I notice him stirring as I slam the hammer into the wall. I feel badly for interrupting his rest, and my arms ache so terribly that swinging the hammer brings tears to my eyes. So it seems sensible to take a break at the stream.

I don't like the dark rear of the cave, but I adore the running water. It may take them a bit to find us, but as long as we've got water, we can stay alive for quite some time. I run my fingers through it, and that's when I hear the sound. I spin around and find him upright, holding his head and breathing in such loud huffs, I hear it over the burbling stream.

"Declan?"

The name bursts from my lips unbidden, but it doesn't seem to reach him. I watch as he stretches out on his back, his hips twisting as one thick arm covers his face. From my angle back off to his right side, I can see his chest pump with his heavy breaths.

"Declan?" It feels strange on my tongue: such a knightly, masculine name...and somehow also delicate—almost pretty.

When he doesn't respond, I realize he must be dreaming.

A low moan reaches my ears, and my belly tightens. I stand slowly as he writhes and starts to pant. His hands fist in his dark hair, tugging, and a gentle crest of empathy swells in my chest. I walk quickly over to him, dropping down to my knees on the ground beside him.

"Declan. Hi there," I whisper. "It's Finley."

After a heartbeat's hesitation, I reach for his shoulder. At that moment, he bolts upright. For an instant, he looks aghast—all wide eyes and open mouth. Then his eyes fix on my face, and he appears to steady. "Siren?"

"You had a nightmare," I say gently.

He's up quickly, stalking toward the stream, where he drops to his knees and splashes his face. I watch as he kneels there, heavy breaths still pumping through his muscled back and shoulders.

Watching panic pass through his strong body kindles my own. For a frantic, airless breath, I'm clinging to the underside of a boat's seat, shivering in water that reaches my neck; the blood pounding between my ears is louder than the howling wind.

When he stands, I whirl away, realizing a beat too late that I'm standing by the sleeping bags with no apparent purpose save for watching him. My pulse gallops as I hear him moving toward me. In my periphery, I see him reaching for the pack. The crinkle of a wrapper lets me know he's grabbed a bar. I hear the crack and plastic thump of his hands opening a water bottle. Then he's moving toward the rubble pile without a glance my way.

Something heavy settles near the base of my throat. For a too-long moment as my eyes cling to his shoulders, I can't swallow. I decide to follow his lead, sitting on my bag with a bar, of which I take only a small bite.

The next time I look up, I don't see him. He steps out a moment later from behind the remnants of the rubble pile, his head back as he drinks from his bottle.

He seems more composed now. I know when he looks at me. He's very still for that one moment, making it feel like a greeting despite the lack of smile or wave. After that, he bends down for the hammer, his big body flickering in lantern light as he resumes his work.

When he seems lost in his own rhythm, I slide in behind him with my chipping stone. I can feel the heat of him, smell the musk of male sweat as his powerful movements bend the air around us.

"Not much done while you were dozing," I say as I swing the stone. "But a small bit."

"Good."

His voice is strange, and when our gazes tangle a bit later, I realize his eyes are strange as well. His are like no male's I've ever seen—fierce and expressive—but when they touch mine this time, they seem different. Troubled, I think.

"Declan?"

He pauses at his name, and when he turns to me, I see his silly, faux-stunned face. I can't help laughing. "Don't get too excited. I was bound to slip up sometime."

He smiles, though—a brilliant smile that makes me feel like I just swallowed sunlight.

I twist my face up and beckon him with my hand. "Come here. Closer."

He gives me a curious frown, but he moves nearer—near enough so I can smell his minty breath. I pull my flashlight from my pocket. When I shine it in his face, he flinches. I wait for his pupils to shrink, and when they don't, I zero in on one. He mutters something.

"Hush that foul mouth."

He chuckles softly as I watch his pupil shrink under the light —but just a wee bit. The other one behaves the same, shrinking only a smidgen in the light, as if something has happened to cause it to be dilated. I shut my own eyes for a moment, and he makes a soft sound.

"That bad, huh?"

I shake my head. "I feel badly that I let you sleep. I should have realized, with your head..." I gesture to my own forehead. "I think you've got a bit of a concussion."

His fingers play over the bandage. "Nah."

"I think so. I—"

"Listen, Siren, I've had a concussion. This is too much whiskey, no shut-eye, and being stuck inside a hole in the ground."

I chew my lip. "But your pupils—"

"Here." He holds his hand out, and I set the flashlight in his hand. He leans in so near that I hold my breath, and he shines light in both my eyes, making a low sound in his throat as he does.

"How small would you say they should get?" he asks.

"Very, if there's bright light. Near to pinprick."

"Well here we go. We're both concussed." He moves the light, and I shut my eyes to regain my equilibrium. "Yours didn't do that either. Probably because we're in a place with no natural light."

He steps slightly back, and I put my hands on my hips. "Can I trust your word, Carnegie?"

He lifts one of his brows. "Calling me a liar, Siren?"

I laugh. It slips out, and then, in my exhaustion, I forget what he asked, so there's this moment where I just stand there before I remember and shake my head. "Well, no. I'm just trying to do my due diligence."

I lift my brows at him, giving him the scolding look that's usually reserved for Mr. Braun, who likes to skip his diabetes medication.

Declan smiles like the Cheshire Cat.

"Your hair is all..." I wave my hand about my head.

He runs a palm back over his dark locks, and as he does, he makes another brows-scrunched face at me. "Question for you, Siren."

"Yes?" I realize after I say "yes" that I just answered to that silly nickname.

"Do I smell? Every time I get close, you hold your breath."

I purse my lips, and he shakes his head. "Damn."

"No." I sigh, feeling my cheeks warm. "It isn't that. It's that I can't find toothpaste. Usually I have some in my pack, but I could only locate the toothbrush..."

He reaches into his pocket—I note the mud stains on his khakis, which badly need a wash now—and then holds his hand out.

"Check it."

I frown at the square packet in his hand.

"Gum."

I take it, squinting at the unfamiliar label. "Eclipse."

"That work?"

"I'm not sure." I turn the package over and his hand comes over mine.

"Here..." He pulls out a sleeve from inside.

"I knew that," I say softly, even though I didn't. "I've seen one of these before. A tourist left the garbage."

He pops a wee, white square out of the sleeve and holds it out. "A token from a tourist."

I accept the thing, a bit bigger than a communion wafer, and set it in my mouth. He watches with his brows up as I bite—and nearly cry out. The flavor is so intense, it's almost violent.

I open my mouth to let some of the minty air out, and I find him smiling with a curious tilt. "Tell me you've had gum before, Siren."

"Of course. It's just...we get the Doublemint."

"That's what my old man swears by."

"This, though." I laugh. "This is...it's like mouthwash!"

He laughs, shaking his head. "I think it's time for some questions." He reaches for the hammer. "It'll make the work go faster."

"Questions? Of what sort?"

He looks over his shoulder at me. "Let's start with the gum. Are you telling me you've never had *any* gum except for Doublemint, or just that it's been mostly Doublemint?"

I scrunch my nose at him before scooping up my own stone. "How many sorts of gum have *you* had, Mr. Fortunate Sports Star?"

That gets another low laugh. "Sports star."

"When the shoe fits..."

His hammer slams into the rock. "I'm not sure that shoe fits."

I look down at his boots-clad feet. "I'm quite sure it's just your size."

"There are a bunch of different kinds of gum. In every country," he says as he assaults the wall.

"I assume you've been to all of them?" I tease.

"Not by a long shot."

"How many? Tell me, do you know how many there are total?"

His eyes meet mine over his shoulder. "Hundred and fifty?"

I shake my head, bashing my stone into the cave's wall. "Try one hundred ninety-five."

He gives a low whistle. We hit the wall at the same moment, sending shards of rock all which ways. He says, "I've been to thirty-one of them."

I shake my head at his back. Thirty-one countries. What must that be like—to have traveled so much? "Someone like you..." His family's funds must be near unlimited. He's been to university, began a career. Perhaps he's being groomed to take over his family's business in the longer run, and that's what's behind his visit to us.

"If you could go anywhere?" he prompts, cutting in on my thoughts.

I lick my lips as my heart beats more quickly. "I don't know." My tight throat makes my voice sound strange. "Perhaps to Oregon. Or California."

"Yeah?"

I get a good chunk of rock as I slam my stone into the rim again, and he says, "Nice one."

"Thank you. And I'm not sure..." I worry a bit, having revealed my real answer. I've long kept it secret—where I'd go if I were to flee—but I doubt the Carnegie would remember anyway, nor be consulted were I to go missing, so I carry on. "Perhaps I'd hate both places. But I've heard of redwoods. I've heard they're massive, and I've never seen a terribly tall tree. And California being sunny, with all the oranges and avocados, and the movie stars. San Francisco with the sailboats. I would like to see the beach in California. I've heard the sand is soft and warm, and people swim there in the ocean."

He turns to face me, his lips pressed together and his head angled as if he's puzzled. "You don't swim here?"

"Nearly never."

"No good beach?"

I shrug. "There are tiny spots of beach. The current's strong, though, and the sand is rocky. No one ever thinks to lounge about there. For the children, it's forbidden. Also, it's quite cloudy." It's almost always cloudy here.

"What's that like?" he asks, giving me his back again as he turns away.

"Wait a bit—you'll find out." I consider what he said, though. He's correct: chatting will help pass the time. "I don't think I can answer," I offer. "I've never been anywhere but here, and rain is part of life. It helps the crops grow."

Silence settles in around us, and we work as we have for the past however long it's been. I notice he's not hammering as quickly as he was in hours prior, but neither am I.

He starts humming, and I wonder at the tune until I hear his low voice. "What show?"

I look up to find him glancing at me over his shoulder.

"Come again?"

His face is fiercely handsome as he smiles before swinging the hammer. "What show is that song from?"

"I rarely watch the telly."

"Mm, so you don't know?" He flashes a smirk my way. "Ever heard of a show that rhymes with The Shady Hunch?"

I snicker. "What?"

He turns to me, dark brows arched skeptically. "*The Brady Bunch?*" He gives a low whistle. "You've never watched *The Brady Bunch?*"

"I've heard of it."

"Marsha, Marsha, Marsha," he says in a falsetto, and I shake my head.

Declan chuckles. "You're a tabula rasa, Siren."

"I know what that is. I do know my Locke."

"And I thought I was isolated growing up at a Swiss boarding school."

"You went to Swiss school?"

I watch his nape as he nods. His tricep flexes as he swings the hammer.

"Where was it located?"

"Near Geneva."

"Do you speak French, then?"

"I do."

"*Parlez-vous aussi Italien et Allemand?*"

He turns around to smirk at me. *"Oui, oui. Et vous parlez Francais."*

"Yes, I had several years of French, and for a year we had a tutor. I do believe you paid for it."

He shakes his head. "I didn't pay for it. I didn't even know we still brought stuff out to the island—" he falters, his gaze veering away from mine for just a moment— "until my cousin told me."

"Why Tristan?" I know the answer, of course, but I'm testing him to see if he does.

My heart pounds as he says, "My father came here as a young guy. Says he never forgot it."

The ache in my chest breaks like a wave, and pain drips through me. I remember Mummy as we walked to the post office. I remember how her face went dreamy when she thought no one was looking. I remember putting my hand to hers—to her hand that held the letter.

"What's that word mean, Mummy?"

"Which one, darling?"

I frowned, trying to remember what it looked like on paper. "Yearning."

She stopped and glanced around, and seeing no one, leaned in closer, speaking softly. "Dearest, did you read my letter?"

"Just the one bit. What does it mean?"

Her face softens, and I can see her thinking—trying to decide whether to tell me. "Yearning is when you want something, my darling...especially something you can't have."

"So, when you want something forbidden?"

"Yes, my dearest. It's a bit like forbidden."

THIRTEEN
FINLEY

When I was fifteen, someone phoned Gammy. I suppose the call must have come when I was lingering about, so she waited and returned it when I was at the summer dance.

I couldn't dance that afternoon, though—I remembered too well father twirling Mummy in our living room—the calm before the storm—so I picked up the end of my dress and walked slowly home—not to Gammy's house, but to my other home. The one that still sits empty by the cliffs.

And there I wrote my name in dust, and there I found the letters.

Dearest Hudson...

To My Darling Isla...

If they had a girl child, they would name her Finley. He thought it whimsical; she would be a sort of lovely mermaid. If the firstborn were a boy, he would be Declan—a family name in the Carnegie line.

Mummy called him Hudson because his favorite of his family's homes was there—a castle, he said, on the verdant bank beside the river. He'd told her he'd never cared for Charles, his given name; it was a hand-me-down from his father, who sent him to a place called *Le Carogue*.

He had refused a planned marriage since he'd arrived back in New York, he told her in one of the first letters. When could he come back and get her? He would make his father understand...

Mum refused to go without her mum. Hudson said he would send for Gammy, too, and buy her closetsful of gowns and a home of her own, with stacks of fine china and a mountain of silver.

Mummy wasn't sure that she could manage in America, even alongside him. He wrote her, "Here I am a king—and you would be my queen. There is nothing I can't give you, dearest."

He was wrong. He couldn't give my mother strength.

She didn't go. She urged him to marry as he'd planned, a better wife than she could hope to be, and in an effort to propel him toward that end, she let herself be married to Peter Evans, the last of the island's capable, unmarried males—a quiet, slightly younger boy who'd brought her a flower when her father died at sea.

When she told Hudson what she'd done, his letters halted for five months, and when at last he wrote again, he raged and railed. Henceforth, he wrote daily, begging her to annul the marriage if some unknown-to-me bit of information she'd conveyed to him in a previous letter was indeed true.

Finally, after a few months of such letters, one read simply, "Please take great care. If you would deliver in Cape Town, I could help with transport. For all three of you. Anything. I am always yours, Isla. Always, insensibly always..."

Another year, another creased, time-stained letter: "I developed the film, love. She is nothing short of magic." And on another line, one halfway down the page, "I did it. I can't say much for fear of breaking my own heart. Soon she'll be with child. If a son, Declan. If a daughter, my Isla."

I found the last letter hanging from the mouth of a wine bottle, having previously been tightly rolled.

My father likely found it shortly before my seventh birthday.

"I pray you're on your way here. He's gone mad! Finley & I must escape. There's no time for further correspondence. Hear me through the stars. I'm always yours, and you are always mine. Remember Rumi?"

And there was a poem there at the bottom, something heady and enchanting.

I took that letter with me, a cylinder I folded into an accordion and pressed against my palm, and at the moment I stepped back into Gammy's cottage, she was on the telephone, telling someone, "I understand—but she can't go. Finley is not a simple girl, but she is broken. She has never spoken since it happened. No, it's not. In Switzerland?" My Gammy laughed. "See if they will learn to read her mind, as I have, Charles. In the meantime, send her tutors."

I waited, still, until the call ended, and longer before making a sound. Gammy turned to me and smiled as if I wasn't mute, as if she'd merely been baking a pie. And from that day onward, I imagined Charles. Years later, I looked him up on the new Macintosh at the café, gotten, as were all our things of value, by a grant from the Carnegie Foundation.

I found a newspaper image of his wedding, and inside me, something swung open—a sort of locked door. Charles had a son, I found, and he had indeed named the boy Declan. I saw him as a young teen pictured on a sailboat—lovely eyes, a luscious mouth, and wild, dark hair befitting of a prince. Sadness blossomed like a flower in my heart.

That night at the dinner table, when I set my napkin down beside my empty plate, I opened my mouth, and I told Gammy I'd enjoyed the meal. Each night after, I lay on my back in the field under the cliffs where Vloeiende Trane flowed, and I whispered to the stars the poem Mummy had scrawled. Those final words she thought to send to sea.

Out beyond ideas of wrongdoing and rightdoing,
    there is a field. I'll meet you there.
    when the soul lies down in that grass,
    the world is too full to talk about.

I didn't know until I met Doctor, who had been to university, that the poem was longer. Longer than, by then, I cared to memorize —although I did learn some of it.

Out beyond ideas of wrongdoing and rightdoing,
    there is a field. I'll meet you there.
    when the soul lies down in that grass,
    the world is too full to talk about.
    Ideas, language, even the phrase "each other"
    doesn't make any sense.
    The breeze at dawn has secrets to tell you.
    Don't go back to sleep.
    You must ask for what you really want.
    Don't go back to sleep.
    People are going back and forth across the doorsill
    where the two worlds touch.
    The door is round and open.
    Don't go back to sleep.

It comes to my mind now because I think he is asleep—Declan. The prince who's not a prince. The man who, in some backward-bent world, might have been my brother, were that Mummy had been braver. Were that Charles and his son arrived the day before my seventh birthday, as, years later, I found they were scheduled to.

I watch him lying on his side now, having first eaten part of a bar and drank some water, and I wonder what he knows of me. What he remembers from his last trip here. What had his father told him as they traveled? Had they really planned to take us? How would they have spirited us away? Here on Tristan, if a married person wishes to leave the island, it requires spousal consent.

Here I am a king—and you would be my queen.

His voice cuts into my thoughts, saying a word I don't understand at first: "Nike?"

"Come again?" I tuck the hammer to my chest and step a bit closer to him.

He doesn't move from where he's lying, but he says, "You heard of Nike?"

"Oh—the shoes. Of course."

Just as I'm turning back toward the cave's mouth, he says, "George W. Bush?"

A small smile curves my mouth. "If you're tired, you should sleep."

"Is that a no, Siren?"

"I know history and politics. In fact, I believe he's number forty-three."

"What's a Macbook?" he asks from behind the hand rubbing his temples.

"Mac*intosh*," I murmur. Macbook. "Is it a computer?"

In the lantern light, I see his small smile. "Martha Stewart."

"The cookbook?"

"Yeah." His voice is low and quiet.

"Tired, Sailor?"

He shakes his head. "Shoulder needed a quick break."

"You're younger than me. One would think you would be able to keep up."

His brows crease as his shrewd eyes narrow, and my tummy backflips. "How do you know that, *pray tell?*"

I can't help giggling. Because I've no sense of decorum. Because I'm plebian and inexperienced and tired. Because I'm oh so tired. He looks up at me, and I put on my poker face.

"Everyone here knows your age, Carnegie. The island was obsessed long before you arrived."

"And now?" His mouth twists on one side.

"Now we've got you buried in a burrow. I'd say your stock has plummeted dramatically."

That earns me a soft chuckle.

I spend a moment looking at his face. From several meters away, in the gentle amber of the lantern light, his dark brows, wide cheekbones, and princely lips stand out the most. I run my gaze down his lovely form and then back up, and I wonder what his loved ones would think if they knew where he was tonight. What sort of people love him? Likely many...

"I suppose you're not so awful." The quiet words are blurted, but I can see them reach his ears. His mouth opens, and he gives a chuckle. "It's true," I continue. "I'd have never given you a chance prior to this...entrapment. But perhaps I do believe you weren't yourself that night."

He pushes up off the floor and gets to his feet, surprising me anew with his height as he strides toward me. He stops beside me, and for a breathless moment, I can feel his gaze caressing me despite my own eyes clinging to my feet. "Glad you're seeing reason now."

I hear the grin in his voice. I don't dare peek at his face until he bends to scoop my rock off the floor. His muscular back ripples as he bashes it against the wall. "So—we bros?"

I fold my aching arms, trying to stifle a smile. "I'm no one's bro."

"Buds?"

I snort. "I'll agree to be your friend. A proper friend and confidant, for the duration of our time here in the burrow."

He knocks my shoulder gently the next time he stops his swinging to get a gulp of water. A strange warmth spreads through me. For the first time, I feel grateful for his company.

* * *

Declan

Two days in, and I'm starting to learn her siren ways. I'm pretty fucking sure she's shy—or at least reserved. She doesn't like me zeroing in on her too much or asking her too many questions. I can get her talking if I don't seem over-interested. If I grin at her or nudge her arm with mine, woman's like a hermit crab. Goes right into her shell.

"You're pretty funny, you know that?"

We're sitting on what's left of the old rubble pile, and Finley's pulling a square of Atkins bar into a bunch of little pieces, having just insisted "it tastes different this way."

When I give her a smile, she draws her knees up to her chest and wraps her arm around them, one hand cupping the remnants of her bar, her damp hair curling over one shoulder.

"I'm not wrong. It does taste different with the insides pulled out." She pops a little piece into her mouth. "If nothing else, the texture's different."

"I guess so." I have the last bite of my own bar, which is sitting heavy in my stomach.

"You know you can eat more than me, right?" she asks. "You're what, twice as large as I am? I can go without a bit if need be. I doubt you can."

I make a cringy face, and Finley shakes her head. "Samesies."

That makes me laugh. "Pray tell me, where'd you come across 'samesies?'"

She shrugs, looking shy again. "One of my friends says it."

"Which one?" I drink some of my water, trying to ignore the churning in my stomach.

"Oh, you know. Anna." She rolls her eyes.

"Hey, now, let a guy make small talk."

"Anna is my dearest friend. She's married to Freddy, and they have a wee one, Kayti."

I smile when she says "wee one," and she shoots me a dark glare. "Let's avoid critiquing your American-isms, shall we?"

I stand up, stretching my sore-as-fuck back before bending down to grab the hammer. "Tell me what slang is gettin' your goat."

I hear her laughter behind me. For someone so prone to bossiness, she's got a nice, soft laugh that's what I think one might call a giggle.

"Gettin' your goat? Are you sure you aren't from Mississippi?"

Something tugs behind my breastbone. I rub at it before swinging the hammer again.

"Used to have a buddy from down in Texas."

For a moment, all the air is sucked out of the cave and I can't get a breath, but then she's smiling beside me, tucking her hair, which she just washed, into a bun atop her head. "Did he or she have goats there?"

"I don't know. It was a friend from Carogue," I manage.

But I realize I do know. I went to Nate's family's place a

couple times, and I never saw goats—although I guess that doesn't mean they didn't have some.

"Did he wear a cowboy hat?"

Another steady breath. "He did. He liked them Stetsons," I drawl.

"Did he speak like that? Do they speak improperly, as in caricature?"

"Texans?" I shrug. "Sometimes, for effect. Most of them know the difference, though."

I hear her make a soft, pained sound when she swings her arm, and I reach for her without thinking. She recoils, and I step back.

"Sorry." I rub my forehead, which is throbbing. *That was stupid.*

She folds her arms and gives me a look that's hung somewhere between a frown and a glare. "Was that a sneak attack?"

I shake my head, letting a breath out. "Used to locker rooms."

Her blank look lets me know she's got no clue what that means. "Have you ever seen a locker room?"

"I have—in the movie *Carrie.*"

That makes me laugh, which makes her glare. "Anyway." I bring my hands together. "Locker rooms are full of guys stretching and getting dressed, undressed, taping themselves up, just fucking around." I wince when she does; now I know what bothers her, and any swear word is on that list. "There's not a bunch of space that's yours. You want someone's attention, you just knock their shoulder or give them a swat."

"Is this your way of calling me a bro again?" Her mouth curves up into a smile that makes my dick hurt, and I shrug. "Too good to be my bro?"

"Of course." She rolls her eyes, and I frown at her right arm. "Where're you hurting?"

She rubs a strand of hair back off her forehead and says,

"Everywhere." Now that I'm looking closely, I realize she looks tired as hell.

I hold my own sore arm out, massaging the inside of my forearm with my free hand. "Is it more down here, or more up here?" I squeeze my triceps.

"There," she says softly.

"So stretch your arms above your head like this, right?" I stretch mine toward the ceiling, bending them so I don't touch it. "Keep your hand closed and reach back like you want to grab the back of your neck. Then with your other hand, lightly press the side of your elbow."

I demonstrate for her, feeling almost sick with joint pain as my triceps pull.

Finley shuts her eyes, looking relieved, and I resist an impulse to tweak her chin. When she looks at me again, her face is relaxed.

"Wow, that did help. Thank you."

"No problem."

"I suppose you're well versed in such things," she says, at the same moment I'm saying, "You want to use your other arm more, too, if you can."

She switches the rock to her left arm.

"Are you left-handed?" she asks.

"Little bit of both."

"You're ambidextrous?"

"Not really," I hedge.

"Well you're using mostly your left arm to swing the hammer."

"Trying to use both."

"Your right one hurts." After she says this, her gaze falls down to her shoes before it lifts back up to mine. "I'm right, aren't I?"

I roll the shoulder. "Pretty obvious?"

She nods. "I can tell it bothers you. I noticed you swing

mostly left-handed, although I don't remember hearing that about you—that you throw a baseball left-handed. And I would have, because we've got a lot of children who're lefties."

"Yeah, fucked up the shoulder."

Her brows draw together. "Is there no fix for that?"

"Oh, yeah. There's a fix."

"Why haven't you been fixed?" She gives me a no-shit look, and I can't move as a cold sweat hits me—at the word "fix."

I feel my teeth start to chatter, clamp my jaw shut as my shoulders tremble. *Jesus Christ.* My stomach churns. "Didn't get around to it yet."

"Before your trip here?" She looks skeptical—or maybe it's dissatisfied.

I nod. "Gonna try a few things when I get back."

"What's the story there?" With my weak, shaking arm, I start to hack at the wall again. I pause mid-swing, squeezing my eyes shut. What the fuck did she just ask me? *Story...*

"Story what?"

"What's the story of why you came here? What motivated your visit?"

Another cold sweat, and my legs feel weird and wobbly again. Fuck. My stomach rolls as I'm gripped by something like panic. *Just withdrawal*, I tell myself. I struggle to think as I grab a quick, desperate breath. "My cousin drops the shipment off..."

She nods. "Bryant. We see him perhaps twice a year. I didn't think of him as your cousin."

"Well, no." I give her a smile I hope doesn't look too strained. "You didn't know me."

Everything feels kind of echo-y as I focus my gaze on her.

"In any event, I've met Bryant a time or two, and once his girlfriend Mary. Did something happen to him?"

"No...but he was telling me about it. He mentioned how people wanted autographs." I shrug, feeling like a fucking moron as I struggle to find words. Finally I manage to add, "I wanted a break."

"Put another pin on your corkboard," she says. I frown before realizing what she means: add another destination to my travel log.

"Yeah, something like that."

"Is it all you'd dreamed of?" She waggles her eyebrows, and I turn my head so she can't see me quite as well.

"Oh yeah. Better." I glance back at her as I strike the wall again. "You ever read that book *Watership Down*—the one with rabbits?"

"I adore it."

I nod. "That's the kind of trip I really wanted. Get back close to nature. Underground. Just find a burrow, find a buddy. Bam. Vacation." I smile, and I feel it ease up—that dark, bad feeling that withdrawal brings on.

"Good and well, but I'm not your buddy, Carnegie."

"You're my buddy, Siren. When that fucker—" I point to the stone blocking our exit— "moves, and I get you out of here, you're going to admit we're buddies."

"I thought we were bros." She's smirking.

"How do you say this word...?" I spell avocado. Her mouth twists with a smile she kills by pressing her lips together, but she can't hide the way her eyes tilt at the corners.

"Avocado," she says softly.

I grin, because she's saying *ah-vo-cay-doh*.

"You spend your days throwing balls at grown men, partying with too many women to keep track of, and herding sheep pro bono. I'd say you're no authority on anything, Carnegie."

I laugh. "Herding sheep's not a good enough vocation for you?"

"Sheep herders are the worst sort. I hear they're perfectly unbearable."

I nod sagely. "I'm afraid I heard the same thing."

"How'd you learn that, anyway? Did they teach it at your pretty boy school?"

That makes me laugh again, which makes my head ache. "You calling me pretty?"

She shoots me a fuck-no look—one that's aimed mostly at my shorts, and I shake my head. "Hell no. I spent a couple summers in the Alps."

"As a shepherd?"

"As a sheep."

She smiles, and I "baaah," and her face falls, and she murmurs, "Baby."

"That your little fuzzy guy?"

"Fuzzy girl. I wonder if she's missing me." She slams her stone into the cave's mouth again, and her whole body seems to sag.

"I bet a lot of people miss you, Siren."

"Then where are they?" Tears flash in her eyes. She whirls, stalking over to the sleeping bags. I start toward her, and she flees toward the stream.

The cave is so small—burrow, whatever the fuck—I could be to her in a half-second, but I take my time getting a water bottle from her pack and cross the modest space between us slowly, giving her space.

When I get to her, she's sitting cross-legged by the little stream, her head bowed, one hand dangling into the water.

Even in the shadows, I can see she's got her jaw locked as I sit beside her.

"Where are they? Where *are* they?" She wipes her eyes, sniffling. "What happened? What if it wasn't a mudslide but an earthquake? Otherwise," her voice breaks, and she covers her face. "Otherwise, I feel they'd be here. I think they'd have found us. You said you merely ducked and we were in here. So we're close to surface level."

I catch myself wanting to scoot a little closer to her, so I lean the other way. "We were, that's true. I think we're still close to the surface. We can feel that little breeze around the rock—and even more since I can wobble it a little better, yeah?"

She nods, her mouth tight as she wipes at her eyes. We're not making great progress, but we've made enough so we can feel a little bit of fresh air sometimes.

"Another day or so—" God fucking help me— "I think I can get my hand between the cave's wall and that rock that's got us stuck."

She nods, and a tear glitters as it streaks down her cheek.

"Don't be worried, S. We've got this."

She sniffs, wiping her eyes again. "My name is Finley. Just so you know."

"I can't call you F, though," I tease. "Who wants an F?"

"You're insufferable." She stands up, tugging at her cotton shorts, and I look up at her.

"Too bad you're stuck with me."

She kicks my shoe, and then she marches off theatrically. I stay there for a second, splashing water on my neck.

It's true, what I said to her. Just another day or so until I get us out of here. And I can hold on that long. I fucking have to.

FOURTEEN
FINLEY

"Do you ever sleep?" I'm whispering, although I'm not sure why since it's just us and I know he's awake.

He's lying on his side. I'm facing him because I don't like sleeping with him at my back. I offered him the first sleep shift, because anxiety had me wound too tightly to try, but then I got this horrid headache, so I stretched out beside him, where I quickly realized he's not sleeping. He keeps breathing deeply and shifting about.

"Do you?" His low voice comes like something corporeal through the dark, and I find I'm grateful for it. I turned off the lantern when I stretched out here, although it frightens me to be entombed in darkness.

"A bit." I sigh, adjusting my hair band so my locks flow down my back instead of over my shoulder. I prop my cheek on my palm and blink at him. "I can sort of see you, even though there's no light."

I watch his lips twitch. "I can sort of see you, too."

"Tell me something, Declan Carnegie."

"What kind of something, Finley Evans?"

"You know my surname."

"Magnet at the house." His voice is a bit hoarse with what I presume is exhaustion. His head is propped on the small, plaid blanket I gave him to use as a pillow. I scoot a fraction closer to him, and our gazes lock like magnets. Something electric zips through me—a sort of boldness, borne perhaps of sheer stir-craziness.

"What are you scared of?" I murmur.

I feel him shift a bit as he props his elbow on the blanket and his cheek against his palm, peering down at me. "I bet you're wanting me to say bugs, aren't you? Or clowns."

"Why would I want that?"

"Oh, you know. Big dude scared of a little bug."

"Or a child's entertainer?" I smile, because it would be a bit funny.

He gives me an I-told-you-so look. "I'm not scared of bugs. Clowns don't really wind me up either. I'll tell you what I'm scared of."

I lift my brows.

"Other than clocks. I fucking hate cuckoo clocks."

I laugh. "You hate cuckoo clocks?"

"Have you ever seen one?"

"The sort that open up and something totters out?"

He nods. "Those things will knock you on your ass."

"They jump out at you?"

"Not literally. I'm talking figuratively."

I can't hold back a giggle. "So...they startle you?"

"They startle everyone," he says in righteous tones. "Who wants that? Some fucking mouse or chiseled wood Pied Piper shit just bounces out and the clock does that loud *gong* noise. Hey, fuck you, it's eight o'clock, did you just shit your pants?"

I laugh so hard, I roll about and wind up on my back, where I'm faced with the ceiling.

"What's your other thing?" I whisper tightly. "You said other than clocks..."

"Nu-uh. Now you owe me. Tell me one of yours and I'll tell you my big one."

I heave a deep sigh. "Only really one big fear here, and I'm afraid I couldn't share it. I'm quite off my rocker, not the funny sort of off. Just off."

"Oh, c'mon, you *can't* not tell me after that. It's..." He reaches for the watch I keep between us, pressing the light-up button to make its screen turn faintly blue. "It's two fifty-one in the morning. We're stuck in a fucking cave—"

"A burrow," I correct.

"We're stuck in a rabbit burrow. You've got a phobia that makes you sound off your rocker. I'm thinking fear of panty hose or terrified of cutlery. I want something really good here."

He yawns behind his hand, still giving me a pointed look, and I scrunch my nose. "You're making me feel anxious as you speak."

"What is it, Siren? I gave you clocks. What do you have for me?"

I squeeze my eyes shut. Fold an arm around myself inside my sleeping bag. "It's not the funny sort, nor will you necessarily find it novel. You're going to be sorely disappointed."

"No? Well that's okay." His voice is soft and kind, and at that moment, I decide I'll go through with it. I exhale...inhale. And I just say it. "I'm afraid of water."

"Water, like..."

"The ocean. I abhor the ocean. I'm...I'm land-bound."

I can feel his surprise in the stillness. In some subtle flicker of his mouth, a tiny movement of his brows over those discerning eyes. I can feel his questions, unsaid weights that make the air around us thicker.

"You're trapped here."

The truth of those words makes my eyes well. I nod at the

ceiling. Despite the care I've taken to keep steady, a tear escapes the corner of my eye and streaks down my cheek, running toward my left ear. I wipe it and sigh. "I don't get emotional unless I'm over-tired, Carnegie. I blame you and this rabbit burrow. We could be up there—" I point to the ceiling— "crushed by rocks under the open sky."

He chuckles softly, but it feels half-hearted. Somber. Afterward, he lets a long breath out and shifts onto his back beside me, propping one thick arm behind his head. I can feel his gaze on my face for a bit before his quiet question.

"Why are you scared of the sea, Siren?"

I'm not sure if I'm surprised he asked. Perhaps I'm not. He doesn't seem the sort to shy away from something he wants—and I suppose he wants to hear me speak of it.

I rub my lips together, aim my gaze toward his shadowed form.

"I'm thinking of speaking of something horrid. You should tell me not to."

"Horrid's my middle name, though."

"I believe that." I smile, and I think I can feel him smiling despite my refusal to look over at him.

"I like ume candy, Carnegie. Once a tourist from Japan sent seven pounds of it over prior to visiting. A sort of pre-greeting, I suppose. I ate most of it and had to have a tooth filled after."

"You're right, that is awful."

"You're awful. Be quiet and listen."

"Yes ma'am."

I sit up, because I can't lie down. Not for this. I peer down at him, and he looks up at me, and I continue in a quiet, steady voice. "I like colored telephones, the rotary sort, in orange or neon green or pink. If I had a need to, I would own more than one. Also, I'm incredible at knitting. I can knit a long, warm scarf in under a quarter hour. My hands just...understand. When I throw clay, that's also quite natural for me. I'm good at it. I'm bad at swing dancing, and truly I don't care for telly. It seems so distant and irrelevant. Why would I care what these people are doing? Books are different. Books feel real. I've got a few books in my pack because I can't go anywhere without a book, not ever. I have three dear friends, two of whom helped welcome you that day at the café. They're younger and naive, and I believe that day was magical for them."

He gives me a funny little smile, but offers no comment.

"The four of us came up together, learned alongside each other at the schoolhouse. I've never been in love," I whisper, "but I—I've been close to someone. I'm not so strange, I promise. When I tell you this, you're going to suspect I am, but I am not this story, okay? I'm a piece of ume candy or a constellation. Aquarius, in fact. January-born." I take a deep breath, and find I feel I need to sit up straighter to bestow these facts upon him.

"Are you ready for this melancholy, Carnegie?"

He sits, too, and in a way that feels magnetic, we're shifting to face each other. "Ready, Siren."

The pet name brings a deep sting to my eyes, but I blink past it. Best to spit it out, or else I never will.

"As you perhaps already know...when I was seven—on my seventh birthday—I went with my parents in a boat on an excursion." Saying that, just that, makes my throat feel so tight, I have to stop and swallow. His eyes hold mine, and I let myself be hypnotized by their dark shine. He doesn't blink or move, not while I put a hand over my mouth then move it down and draw a shallow breath.

"A storm came and...my father—he pitched overboard. Mummy went in after him." I don't mean to close my eyes. They slip shut because I'm not seeing his somber eyes; I see her halo. Flowers in the white caps. "Mummy and him drowned—" It doesn't feel real, even saying it. "And I remained on the boat...floating, unmoored, as you can likely recall. For seven days."

I open my eyes and am relieved to find his face impassive.

"On the seventh night, the boat ran aground on Gough Island. The one place, as it were, that I could run aground and be found by those searching." I suck back a breath and force myself to carry on. "I believe your father was on the boat that found me." I didn't realize that until much later, when I saw his face on the world wide web. "Gammy, Mummy's mother, took me in after. I grew up in your cottage. We flew kites in that field between the house and the cliffs there at the plateau behind it, and for a brief time Gammy let me use my bedroom's walls as a canvas before we painted over. Gammy was a good mum, to my mum and me. She made the greatest pies you've ever tasted, and she loved the scent of lemons."

It's there on the tip of my tongue, a terrible addendum to an unthinkable story. *I didn't speak for ten years after...*

I look at his face—his now-familiar face that I can sense is waiting before jumping to expression. I look at his painful-hand-some face that makes me feel like someone scooped my guts out. And I can't tell him I was broken.

I say, "I won't go near boats now." What I mean, of course, is that I barely *look* at boats and wouldn't get in one to save my mortal life. I don't even go down to the harbor. Cresting the hill just after he arrived was the closest I'd been to the ocean in years.

I don't remember anything about what happened after I lost sight of Mum. I never have been able to, not even during the two years a specialist made visits to the island to try to help me. But I know I can't get in a boat. I know it the same way I know I can't hold my breath indefinitely. It's a limit that I can't exceed, no matter how much I may need to. Any plans toward that are simply...silly.

The Carnegie blinks at me, and his mouth softens.

"I'm an all-star knitter, remember? I forgot to mention—I, too, make great pies. There are many things about my life that are quite wonderful, so don't go feeling badly for me. That's the story of my phobia. I'd like to know if you remember any of it—you were visiting here at the time—but I'd also like to stop speaking about it now. So it's your turn. What's your fear?"

I watch him from the corner of my eyes as he lies on his back again, so I can't see his face as clearly. I watch as his chest rises and falls. He waits a while to speak, so long I think he isn't going to.

Finally I feel him look at me. He props an arm behind his head, and his eyes close. After another small moment, he opens them and gives me a small smile. "Confining spaces."

I lie down beside him, feeling strangely light and also quite heavy.

"Like my knitting and pie-making," I say finally, "you seem quite good with a hammer. So that's fortunate."

He chuckles softly. "Yeah, I guess I am."

FIFTEEN
FINLEY

"So what do you think?" He holds out a copy of *The Paris Review*, topped by chunks of chocolate-chip granola. "This look like a breakfast you could choke down?"

"Jesus, Mary, and Joseph!" I leap from my bag and launch myself at him, knocking a small chunk of granola onto my sleeping bag as my arm goes around his shoulder. I give him a squeeze before shifting back into a crouch beside him, my hand hovering over the granola. "Where was it?"

He grins. "Bottom of your bag, in a zipper bag underneath a pair of pink socks."

I pop a piece into my mouth, closing my eyes. "Heaven." I gobble down a few more bites before frowning at him. "Did you have some?"

"I'm good."

"Speak now or forever I'll hold your piece."

His smile widens, and he hands the magazine/plate to me. "All yours, Siren."

I can feel the chocolate melting on my tongue—real chocolate, not the sad brown casing that coats the outside of the Atkins bars. "I was going mad with those horrid bars."

"Why do you have them?" He's got his knees folded up toward his chest, his thick arms propped atop them.

"There's a story there. Joshua McGillin's diabetic, and he spends much of his time out at the Patches. Elderly gentleman, quite set in his ways. We ordered some meal replacement bars for him—two dozen, early this past spring—but something happened and the crate contained twelve dozen."

I shake my head, laughing at the memory. "It turned out he didn't care for them at *all*, so they were divvied up among the ones of us whose duties keep us out of our homes at times. Normally if I'm about the slopes, I pack another snack. Often a number of other snacks. I don't know—I suppose the bars got pushed down in my pack and I forgot them."

"It's good you did."

I sigh. "I long for an apple or a Pop-Tart."

"There are Pop-Tarts here?" His brows shoot up, making me smile.

"Indeed. Brown sugar cinnamon."

He makes a soft sound, like a laugh that doesn't quite launch. "Nice."

"When we get out, I'll go to Gammy's place and put one in the toaster for you."

I tell him to turn around, and I go to the stream, where I change into another pair of shorts I found in my bag and a white tank top. I clean myself as quickly and discreetly as I can, using the inside of my dirty clothes to dry myself, and then wash those and hang them out to dry. The clothes I wore the night we fell into the burrow are near-dry, finally; I imagine they took such a while because it's slightly damp here.

When I return to the cave's mouth, I find Declan swinging the hammer, standing atop a pile of fragments that's impressive.

"Did you sleep at all last night, Carnegie?"

"Some."

"Liar."

His eyes are ringed with exhaustion. His bearded face looks leaner now, and a bit somber. My gaze dips to his lips, and I find they look in need of moisture. "You need lip balm, *buddy*." I flash him a silly grin, and he touches his mouth, looking a bit zombie-like.

Poor Carnegie. I decide I'll fetch some for him.

"There you are." I pass some cherry ChapStick to him, watching as he glides the tip over his lush lips then caps the stick. That's how I notice his fingers trembling. Really trembling, like he's terror-stricken...

I reach out and wrap my hand around his. Declan freezes, his expression carefully blank.

My stomach does a slow roll as I look up at him. "What's the matter?"

He frowns. "Nothing."

"Yes it is. You're shaking."

He pulls his hand away from mine and holds it out, long fingers spread. "Not shaking." But his voice is too steady, his tone a bit too ardent. I grab his hand again and thread my fingers through his, finding his hand damp and cool...and shaking.

His eyes close as his fingers relax. I wrap both of my hands around his larger one, and I can feel his whole arm trembling.

"Oh, Carnegie...are you quite sure you're okay?"

He nods once, but doesn't lift his eyes open. His hand between mine feels heavy. I give it a rub. "I don't believe you."

As I peer up at him, he opens his eyes to look at me. His face is utterly unreadable as he holds my gaze and squeezes my hand. "No one said you had to, Siren." He lets my hand go and turns away. "I'm going to keep digging now, okay?"

Is it okay? Surely it isn't. What would make him tremble like that? He's put his blood-stained shirt back on for reasons I can't fathom, and even with the cotton stretched over his back and arms, it's plain for me to see he's trembling all over.

Could it be anxiety? He told me he's afraid of being confined. I'd like to ask, but he won't look at me, is now striking the rim with what appears to be unbridled force.

I wait for him to turn back my way, to relent and explain, but he keeps bashing the wall, making me feel a bit abandoned, and then quite ashamed of myself for caring so much how he behaves in the first place. He is not my friend. Being trapped here with him—and only him—is addling my brain.

I get my stone and join him, bashing the cave's rim until my body aches and dust from flaking rock stings my eyes. Tears fill them as my throat tightens unexpectedly. *How can we be trapped here, with no one having come for us? How is that possible?*

As if he hears me, Declan looks over his shoulder. I set my rock down before my tears spill over and walk quickly to the stream, where I sit cross-legged with my hands over my shameful, hot face.

Crying is useless. Sure, it can be clarifying, but it's mostly wasted time, a spilling over of emotions best left in their own allotted cup. I take a few fortifying breaths and tell myself I've endured worse.

We'll keep chipping at the cave's mouth until we get a different angle on the stone that's blocked us in, and at that time, we will break free. I believe it. That's one thing I do believe in: believing. Outlook cannot be overrated.

More tears leak from my eyes, even as I tell myself how absurd I'm being. I hurry to wipe them as I hear him approach.

Not your friend, I tell myself.

I'm feeling frightened and out of sorts, but he is not my friend. He's an interloper who'll be gone soon. There's no point in making any headway with him. The fact that his presence makes me stupid is even more reason to put distance between us.

I wipe my eyes and straighten my spine, and then he's at my back, crouching beside me. I feel his attention settle on me, even as I'm looking down at my lap. I feel his hesitation, and I hate that I enjoy it. I enjoy his eyes on me. Like a forlorn child seeking acknowledgment...beyond pathetic.

"I think if we hit this hard—if we both do," he starts— "if we go harder than we have so far, I can shift that stone enough to get my hand in there beside it. It's been moving more now when I push a certain way. Trust me, we're just about out of here. Just gotta go a little harder for a little longer. What do you say, Siren?"

It's Finley, I want to scream. Instead I snip, "Of course."

I let him help me up, and we walk toward the cave's mouth, where we resume working with renewed vigor. We work the entire morning, Declan taking frequent breaks to splash himself with water from the stream and me swinging my stone so hard, my shoulders feel as if they're broken.

Every so often, he stops and shoves upward against the boulder, and I hold my breath, my head spinning with hope and dread and fear—but nothing happens. We press on. We work until sweat drips off his hair and soaks his shirt, and spots are dancing in my eyes. He pushes up against the stone again and again. He's correct: we can feel a wee, wee bit of breeze, so we can't be far from breaking free, but he can't lift the boulder.

I can tell it's driving him quite mad. When I stop for lunch, he keeps swinging his hammer. Then he drops it—more like tosses it across the way. From my spot atop the sleeping bag, I see his muscles flexing, hear him panting as he strains beneath the boulder.

Stubborn male. He should wait for me so we can try together.
"FUCK!"

I jump reflexively, but when I blink I find him bent at the

waist, his head in his hands, his broad back and shoulders pumping.

Oh, no.

Before I make it more than a few steps in his direction, he stalks past me with his head down, anger radiating from his form. I watch as he crouches by his sleeping bag, rubbing his hands roughly through his hair. Then he's on his feet again, his face stony as he walks back toward the cave's mouth, not sparing a blink for me.

There, instead of picking up the hammer, he scoops up one of the fallen stones and hurls it at the wall with so much force it crumples.

"FUCK!"

He grabs another stone and hurls it, then another and another. I watch with bated breath as he loses his composure, bashing the offending boulder in a sort of fury-frenzy, using the hammer to rip into the rock wall with freely flowing rage.

"FUCK! FUCK!" He hurls the hammer across the burrow. It lands with a thud, and he sinks to his knees.

I can scarcely swallow as I watch his back, crisscrossed with shadows that dance as he pants. He lets out another growl of rage, his fist tugging his hair, before he slowly stands and walks back to his sleeping bag. He lies on his side, still breathing hard, though silent now, and covers his face with both hands.

I hear something like a groan, and then a choking sound that makes my chest go hot with sorrow for him.

When I sink down beside him on my own bag, he rubs his forehead with such force, his knuckles whiten. "Sorry." His big hand sinks into his dark hair, fingers tugging harshly at the damp locks.

"Don't be sorry. Next, it will be me."

His hands drag down his face, one covering his throat as the other rubs at his temple. "Finley?" It's near-whimpered.

I lean closer. "Yes?"

His body shudders as his jaw clenches. His hand, covering his face, curls like a claw, and the hairs on my arms feel like they're lifting.

"What's the matter?" I whisper.

"Could you...put some stuff around my head?" His voice sounds tremulous and strange.

My mouth is open to ask what he means when his body starts seizing.

SIXTEEN
FINLEY

It seems to last eternity: his body jerking as his head lolls back against the blankets. Each time his muscles jolt, his arms twitch, fingers curling slightly in the air. His face is slack, so he looks like a stranger lying helpless on his back there.

When it's over, his mouth remains a bit open. A line of blood drips down his thick throat. I note the paleness of his skin, the stillness of his body—so still that I throw myself at him, pressing my shaking fingers to his jugular. I find his heart racing. Then my hands are on his face, they're in his hair; my fingers push at his brow.

"Open your eyes!"

I jostle him and slap his cheek, and then his eyes crack open. He looks pained.

"Declan?" I'm not aware I'm weeping until I hear his name in my thin, breathless voice.

He blinks. His lips tremble. "Where am I?" The words are thick and slow.

My hand rubs his chill-covered arm. "You're in the cave." His body starts to quiver again. "We've been confined here together —remember?"

His mouth twists, a bit of a wince. His eyes close. When he opens them again, they seek my face.

"What's...your name?" His voice is raspy.

"Finley!"

He flinches at the volume of my proclamation.

"Siren." His lips scarcely move around the word. His gaze is hung somewhere over my shoulder—so although he says the word, his face remains a frightful blank.

His hand comes to his chin. He frowns when he draws it away and sees the smear of red there.

"Why'm...I bleeding?" His eyes shut as a shudder racks him. He tightens his jaw, and I can't keep my hand from stroking his hair off his forehead.

"I think...you had a seizure."

His eyes open. "I did?"

I nod. I stroke his hair again, and he exhales. "I...like that."

Though his eyes remain open, they're glassy and unfocused. His hand moves over his mouth again, the fingers shaking.

"Siren...I don't feel good."

"I'm so sorry." I press my fingers gently to his jugular as his eyes cling to mine.

"Tell me how you feeling, darling."

His big hand clutches his face. Then he's shifting onto his side, flexing his legs, arching his back as if he's in discomfort. His chest pumps as he breathes.

"What can I do?" I whisper, moving so I'm right in front of him.

He holds his fists out, and I wrap my hands around them. He spreads his fingers, and I lace mine through his damp ones. "Slow breaths."

One of his hands breaks free of mine and covers his eyes. I lean in closer, cradling his hand in my lap, stroking his arm.

"I'm sorry." It's half groaned.

"Don't be sorry." I swallow as his entire body begins quaking. "Don't be frightened. I'm here with you." I feel chill-bumps on his skin, and I rack my brain for what could be the matter. "Have you ever had a seizure?"

I'm startled by the speed with which he's sitting up and crawling away. And then he's retching. He's managed to get off the blankets. He's there on the cold floor on his hands and knees. I come near and he swats at me, but he's trembling so forcefully, I'm frightened and I can't go.

I stick by him, trying to help brace his chill-swept torso. When at last he finishes, he grips my shoulder. "Fuck."

He crawls back to the blanket, curling on his side. I touch his shoulder. "Let's take off your shirt..."

My fingers brush his burning skin as I help him get out of it. After that, he simply lies there, pale and shaking, and my heart bleeds for him. I stroke his hair back, then lie on my side so that I'm level with him.

"If I can ease you—anything at all..."

His eyes open, reaching toward mine before closing. "Thanks."

I settle on my side, curling my body toward his even as he seems to fall into a solid sleep. He moves so little in the next few hours, I'm reminded of a hospice patient.

I repeatedly check his pulse, tuck my sleeping bag around him. When he twitches or shifts fitfully, I smooth my palm over his damp forehead. I'm so puzzled, so horrified and fearful for him, that I want to weep—but I know I don't have that luxury. I take my fear and frustration out on the cave's wall.

Perhaps it's the noise, but soon he's talking in his sleep. He jolts up, panting, looking terror-stricken. I rush over. When he doesn't look at me, I stroke his warm, hard-muscled arm and feel the chills that sweep his skin.

"There now. Let's lie down."

We lie together, and I wrap an arm around him. When I urge him closer, he leans in, his breaths near enough that I can feel their warmth on my chest.

I stroke his hair until he's quiet, and that's all I hear of him for hours. When I realize he should be drinking and attempt to wake him for some water, he shakes his head. Hours slip by as I lie with him, then wield the hammer, and then lie with him again, getting up when my fears mount and drastic notions flitter through my head. *What if he needs help urgently? What if it happens again?*

At long last, his blue eyes open slightly. They start to shut, but I'm there with a water bottle, guiding it to his lips, which look quite dry and cracked.

His whole upper body heaves, but he avoids retching. He's shaking again, like nothing that I've ever seen. I tuck the blanket around him. "I'm so sorry."

My fingers move through his hair, gently. His hand reaches up to capture mine. He brings my hand to his chest, folds his other arm around it, and sinks back into sleep.

* * *

Declan
2005

"Get her to take care of you, dude. Hot nurse."

Nate levels a glare at Farhad. His red hair sticks up everywhere behind the gauze around his head as he rolls his eyes. I can't help grinning as I think about the Texas word he always uses—"ornery." He looks ornery right now.

"No one's gonna be in here," he tells Farhad. "Except the real nurse."

Mrs. Beecham is a nice lady with pretty blue eyes that actually look a lot like Nate's. She's pushing centenarian status, though.

Alfonzo shrugs. "At least she always smells good."

"Ugh, that's just disgusting. *Ugh.*" Nate leans back against a pillow on a couch inside the ski lodge's great room.

Alf swats at Nate's pile of blankets. "Just tryin' to keep it real, brother."

"Real is taking pain meds when you bash your head open. Real's Alana's tits. It's New Year's Eve, and I'm stuck on the stupid couch."

This morning, Nate tried to kiss a fir tree—while skiing a black diamond. Mr. Laurent and Mr. Berns led a group up there, and since ole boy's been skiing since he was a kid, he thought he could hang. I tried to tell him he should wait, but brother's too competitive.

"Shut up." He sees me looking him over and gives me a glare.

"You look rough, dude."

"I've got thirty stitches in my fucking forehead."

"Language, boys." Makis strolls over, his eyes widening as he gets his first look at post-hospital Nathan.

"Man, you're fucked."

"See, he gets it."

While most of our seventh-grade dude posse fusses over Nate, I head back to the kitchen for a new ice pack and something else I think he'll like. They told him he can't have pain medicine for a few more hours, until he's out of the concussion zone, but I know something he could have—if just a little.

Ten minutes and a Benji to one of the nicer cook ladies, and I've got the ice pack and a pocket bottle of bourbon. The kitchen here at Pontresina stays stocked up because the staff likes to take those little bottles on the slopes.

I check my phone before I get back close to Nate and Co. It's been more than twelve hours, and he doesn't seem like he has a concussion. I don't think a little Maker's Mark would kill him. And it might keep the little bitch from being sad about not skiing at the fireworks with Alana.

I wait for Makis and Farhad to clear out—Farhad, especially, is a gossipy motherfucker—before I slip Nate the bottle. I could get busted for this, but his dumb face looking all happy makes it worthwhile.

"Cover it with cologne, man." I pull a bottle from my pocket, and Alfonzo laughs his ass off like a fucking hyena.

"You're just jealous because that chick you tried to hit on yesterday turned out to be the new Spanish instructor."

He shakes his head. "Boy be smelling like some Christian Dior."

"Shut up."

"Trying to impress that little—what's her name, Nathan, the little Finnish chick he likes?"

"Milla." Nate is smiling as he swallows the bourbon behind his hand.

I feel my neck get warm and want to strangle Alf. "It's not for Milla."

"Sure it's not."

"I brought it for Nate here."

Nate winks at me, and I roll my eyes. "Okay, gossip queens. I'm gonna peace out, catch some powder."

The slopes at night are probably my favorite part of our annual winter mini-mester at Pontresina. I like them almost as much as being home with Dad for Christmas. Even Christmases like this one, where I had to go to SoHo and see Mom and babysit her other kids on Christmas Eve while she went to a party with Rich.

Funny that I'm thinking of her as I ride the lift. My phone vibrates, and I dig it out to find a text from her.

happy new years declan

I frown down at it as snow kisses my forehead and catches in my lashes. Strange. No punctuation. As I squint down at the screen, another message comes up.

when I left when you were five, it wasn't because of you it was because of me. I wanted to be sure you know.

I stand up at the top of the slope, in the shadow of the lift shelter, and peer down at the little greenish screen for a few minutes.

Happy New Year, Mom. It's okay.

My breath clouds things up, so I have to hold the phone out as I decide what to add—if anything. I like the sound of what I have, though. It's short, but it gets the point across.

When I glide out from behind the shelter, there's Milla. Her blonde hair glows in the lantern light. Her snowsuit is Caribbean blue. She's standing with a friend in a pink suit, and when I wave, they both turn and smile.

Thank you, gods of New Year's.

We ski till almost 3 AM, and I refill Nate one more time just after midnight. By 1 o'clock, Alana is drinking hot cocoa underneath a blanket beside him. When I walk by, on my way to the john, I wink, and they both turn red.

Get it, Nate!

My night ends in the hall to the girls' rooms, with Milla hugged up to my chest and her friend, Hallie, wearing Alf's jacket.

Not a bad start to the new year. Not too bad at all.

I'm in bed with a pocket bottle of bourbon under my pillow and a popping fire in the fireplace beside me when someone knocks on my door. I roll over, not bothering to get up for some dumb shit in the hall.

The knock comes again. I look at the skylights, striped between the ceiling's rafters. It's still dark.

Again, the knock. It's more insistent now, so I sit up, thinking that it might be Nate. We share a bathroom back at main Carogue, but here we each have our own.

"Who is it?" I call as I jerk on boxers.

The knock comes harder this time. I forego pants and hurry over to it.

"Nate?"

I open the door, and there is...Mr. Laurent? He's holding a glass of what smells like liquor. He smiles when he sees me, but the smile is like the first clip of a film reel of an accident. I can almost see it slide off his face in the second right before it does.

"What's wrong?" The words are barely whispered.

"I apologize for the odd hour." He looks over my shoulder. "Let's have a seat."

I shake my head. I try to get a deep breath, but I can't.

"What's wrong?"

"Come." He takes my arm and leads me over to my room's couches. "Sit."

I do, because my legs feel strange and heavy.

"Declan. I'm afraid I've got some difficult news..." He leans slightly forward, and something in my chest catches.

* * *

"Declan! *Please*...wake up!" I hear her crying—Siren. Something's wrong. I can't remember...but I have to check on her.

I pry open my eyes to find her bending over me. I feel...really fucking shitty. Fuck, dude. I want to reach up for her, but everything hurts...like my joints. I don't know if I can.

She sees my face and bends down, kinda hugging me against her.

"You smell good." My voice sounds weird and raspy. I don't like how bad I'm shaking.

"Oh, Declan." Her hand feels good on my face. "What were you dreaming?"

"I don't know."

She asks me something else, but I can't track it. I can't even keep my eyes open.

SEVENTEEN
FINLEY

For the remainder of that awful day, he barely moves and rarely speaks. When he moves, he's stiff and shaky. When he speaks, his voice is groaned or tight with pain. His face is pale and slack, his blue eyes glazed and heavy-lidded. He shivers constantly and sweats so much, I fear he's contagious and we'll both die with it—underground, here in the darkness.

And yet...I can't keep away. When his fists are clenched, I stroke his hair and he relaxes. When he's rubbing at his forehead, I massage his pressure points—which makes him moan with what I pray is pleasure. Whatever feels good, that's my focus: fingers through his hair, my nails over his goosebumped skin. I swing the hammer in between, and when I need to sleep, I lie beside him, curling near his warm body as if we're not strangers.

I stroke his trembling, calloused hands and whisper to him. He mumbles in return. It's all nonsense. Once, he asks me for a napkin. Sometime a bit later, he's speaking to someone named Nate quite emotionally. His voice cracks, and I wrap my arms around him. He presses me to his chest.

"Siren," he moans softly. He inhales near my hair.

"I'm here with you."

When he seems more restful, I hammer the cave's wall like a madwoman, exposing perhaps another eight inches of our boulder.

I'm smiling at my progress when I glance at the pallet and find it empty. I turn a bit more and find him standing directly behind me, shaking like a blade of grass in a gale. He looks wild-eyed and exhausted, his hair sticking up comically.

My belly tightens. "Hi there," I murmur, stepping slowly toward him. "You got up quite stealthy."

"I'll be back." His voice is flat and hoarse as he looks past me, toward the scattered rubble pile. I watch as he disappears behind it. When he emerges, dazed about the eyes but still upright, I feel a crest of relief.

"Let me help you to the blankets."

I take his arm. He doesn't protest as I help him to the pallet, spread my sleeping bag back over him. I kneel there beside him, and he looks at me with tired eyes.

"How are you, Carnegie?"

His hand closes around my wrist, his fingers caressing my inner arm. "Soft," he murmurs.

Warmth spreads through me.

"I'll be better soon. Another day."

I feel a bite of horror at the notion—even one more day here is too much—but I don't show him that. "I'm making good progress without you—more and more rock falling."

"I'm sorry."

"You'll be better soon, as you said."

"I just...can't sleep." The words are whispered. Hoarse.

"What would help you?" I whisper in return.

He shakes his head, his mouth tight, and I feel near ill with sorrow for him. With my lower lip between my teeth, I lie beside him. Then, making a bit of a gamble, I wrap an arm gently across his chest. I feel his breath hitch, then a tremble.

"I'm not good...at getting off stuff," he says in a creaky voice.

I snuggle closer. "What do you mean, darling?"

"Subs aren't that bad. Makes me achy." He winces, one hand going to his forehead. "It's the benzos, I think."

"Is it?"

He nods.

"Two years is too long." His voice cracks on the words; then his mouth pulls taut, and I can see emotion quiver through his features.

"For what?"

"To be like this."

I've no clue what he's saying; it's all nonsense. I lean my head against his shoulder. "Why would you be...that way for two years?" I murmur.

"Because it's been so long."

"What's been long?" I ask, my voice soft and, I hope, hypnotic.

His eyes open, and he regards me strangely for a moment. "What did I just say?" His voice is rough and harder now, his body tensing beneath mine. His tired eyes look a bit delirious.

"You said it's been so long."

"What has?" He frowns.

"Benzos."

At that word, his face goes to stone. When he speaks, his voice is strong and steady, making him sound nearly like his old self. "What did I say about benzos?"

"You said benzos made you messed up for two years."

The look of shock he gives me is so startling, I look over my shoulder. He sits up. He holds his head and starts to breathe hard again.

Worry spikes through me. "Declan...what are benzos?"

He takes a few breaths—fast and heavy.

"It's okay." I rub the blanket. "Lie back down. I'm tired, too. I want to lie beside you."

"Did you say...I had a seizure?" His brows cinch slightly as his gaze finds mine. I'm startled to find he looks truly confused.

"Yes. But that was yesterday."

He looks around, and I can tell for sure he is.

"You've been poorly since then. How do you feel?"

He shakes his head, his eyes down on the blanket as his fingers tug at his hair. "You should keep on digging, Finley."

"Why?" My tone is slightly sharp, because there's something sharp and fearful lodged beneath my throat.

He shakes his head. I lean toward him, wanting just to get my arms around him as I've done so often in the last day. As I near him, he leans away. "What are you doing?"

"Nothing."

He looks skeptical, and I feel like a fool. "If you don't want me to, I won't," I whisper, drawing my knees to my chest.

"Won't what?" he asks.

"Won't touch you."

"Why would you touch me?"

I inhale slowly. Now I'm confused as well. "Because...we're here together."

"Did you fuck me?"

The breath leaves me like I've been hit in the stomach. "Why would you say such thing?"

He shakes his head and then he's up, stalking toward the stream. I find him standing by it, trembling wildly. I brush his arm with my fingers, wanting to take his hand but too afraid to.

"Sailor...please come lie beside me. I'm so tired, and tired of being here." My voice cracks at the sheer truth of it.

He looks at me bleakly. "I don't think you want me near you."

"You're contagious?" I swallow. "Is that it?"

He frowns down at me. I can feel dissatisfaction coming from him, but I don't know what I did to earn it. Finally, in a hard tone, he says, "Do you know why I'm here?"

My pulse quickens. "Would you like to tell me?"

His hand closes around my arm as his eyes shut. "I can't."

"You can and should. So I can take good care of you."

I step in closer, caress his face with my gaze before I dare to wrap my arms around his waist. I lay my cheek against his warm chest. His arms close around my shoulders. I can feel him take in two breaths—shallow, fast.

"Finley...you can't get what I have." All his muscles tighten as he exhales. "I'm an addict."

EIGHTEEN
FINLEY

"I don't understand." Perhaps I do, a bit, but my mouth runs away with me as I look up at his face. "An *addict*, meaning—"

"Addict. *Junkie*. Do you know what that is?"

"Yes, of course." I flinch at his hard tone, and I feel his body stiffen against mine. I lower my arms to my sides and look up at him.

"I'm afraid I—I can't imagine you...as that. You're so—" What I want to say is, he's so handsome. He looks strong and healthy. "Sensible" is what I stammer instead. "Smart," I add. "And you're...well, you're Homer Carnegie. How can that be true?"

I watch his jaw tighten, his nostrils flaring slightly as he inhales. His eyes close on the exhale.

"That's why you're here? To dry out? Or the equivalent?"

He nods once.

"Why didn't you tell me?"

He rubs his forehead, his face angled toward the ground. "Figured we'd be out in time."

In time...for what? "To avoid withdrawal?"

His hand covers his face, though I see his lips; I see them twist as he bites his cheek. "I was tapering. That night you came in...I was fucking stupid. I had everything in that one bottle." He sighs softly. "And I dropped it in the tub."

My mouth opens. "That's what you were doing with the water. You jumped up and..." I can see him in my memory, which makes my cheeks warm. "You were tapering your dosage, to decrease...to quit. Therefore you had brought some along. And...was it all ruined?"

He nods, his gaze meeting mine for one small moment before dipping back down to the ground.

"That's what you were at the clinic for, the time I saw you in the street?"

He exhales. "I was going to ask the doctor. But I saw you." His mouth tugs up a bit on one side, revealing his dimple.

"Oh, Declan. And I suppose that's why you offered to help with the herding? To butter me up?"

He rubs his head, and then gives me a guilty look.

"Well, that backfired quite spectacularly."

He angles himself slightly away from me, and I sense more than hear him take a long breath.

After that, he sits down. I can feel it—him turning away from me. He got the secret out, and now he's feeling...bare. Perhaps ashamed.

"You could feel the seizure coming." I'm thinking aloud. "That's why you went at the rocks that way. It wasn't out of temper."

"No—it was." He sighs.

I stand over him for a moment before sitting by him on the cave's floor.

"I didn't know," I whisper.

His hand is on his knee. I see it trembling and move to put

mine over it. That's when he turns himself away. And there's a choice for me to make. If I'm brave enough to touch him. But it's not a choice. From behind him, I wrap my arms around him.

* * *

Declan

If there was one thing I could change, it would be the shaking. I hate the unsteadiness. The Red Sox hate it worse. Since my last detox—Alaska in November 2016—I've never quite come off the Valium. When I cut below a certain point, my hands just...shake. And I can't throw. We tried some other stuff, but nothing stops the shaking. My fingers sweat and I can't focus. Even months after.

The rehab before that—Connecticut in spring 2015—I cut everything and got completely "clean"...and nearly lost my starting job to fucking twitchiness and paranoia. So the board covered for me. Not the whole board...mostly just the chair. We worked together with a few others from the club to game "random" screenings. They weren't frequent anyway, because the league had never really known. Before my draft, some people whispered, but it never was substantiated. Mostly due to school being in Switzerland. I never did rehab in college, stateside. Not a quitter.

I can't tell if Finley heard me when I whispered, "Please don't." She doesn't let go of me. I can't stand her touching me right now. I stand up, forcing her arms off me, and she stands, too, looking like I just killed her kitten.

"I'm so sorry," she murmurs.

"It's fine."

It's not. Even my voice shakes. As I walk back to the sleeping bag, I hear this static kind of thing, like several voices talking at once. Spooky shit like that has always been a problem for me when I try to get off benzos. Makes my heart beat triple-time, and my head throbs so badly that I'm pretty sure I'm going to get sick again.

Thank God, I hold that shit off.

She doesn't know how much I hate the blankets. Hate the softness of them. Hate the air without them. How I hate it on my side and on my back and on my chest. Everything...so uncomfortable and just...miserable. The way that feeling wraps around your soul. There's no way for anyone to understand who hasn't been here. I feel like I can't take it, but I can't will my heart to stop, so I just pull my hair. It's something I can do that won't scare her.

If I was at home...needles. Any needle does it. Rated PG, baby—no syringe required. I just need the bite to fake myself out. For a second after spiking something pretend, I can feel a little bit of relief.

I have a trail of sharp, white knife scars down the inside of my thighs. Before I started spiking shit, before it was about the needle, I'd come down from something snorted or swallowed and need something to...lift me. Lying here, I've thought of that; I could get a sharp stone.

But...Finley.

I don't want to scare her. I don't want her knowing...any of it. I have never wanted anyone to know. I got in trouble a few times at Carogue—shipped off once, my last year there—but all the other times, I detoxed in my room. Coke and pills and even Xanny back then—it was easy to come off it.

I stretch out on my back. Finley sits beside me. With my eyes shut, I can't see how close she is...but I can feel her.

"I don't want to crowd you." I can feel the tension around us;

tension that I've caused by being such a fucking freak. "Can I ask you a few things? If you don't want me to—"

I nod, because I'll do whatever she asks. It's not her fault she's stuck here with me.

She leans over—too close. Before I told her this shit, I kind of liked her soft hands on my face and in my hair. But now I don't think I can stand it.

"I just want to understand, so I can help you." She sounds nervous. "Does the word 'benzo' mean benzodiazepine? Like...the sort of tranquilizers?"

I nod, taking care to keep my face impassive. My eyes are still shut.

"What about subs. Could you tell me about that one?"

"Suboxone." I put my hand over my eyes and force myself to say it. "It helps you stay away from heroin."

I'm not looking, but I fucking *feel* her shock.

You can dissolve the strips and spike them, too, if you want.

"It's not the good stuff, but it can keep you from the bad withdrawal and...keep away temptation." I exhale slowly, turning my face away from her. "A lot of addicts end up on it."

"That's what you dropped into the tub, then? Suboxone and...what else?"

"Valium, GABA, 5-HTP, Sam-e, Clonidine..."

I see her face in my head: her doe eyes widening, even as she does that thing with her mouth where she bites her lip, trying to look chill when she isn't.

"You were taking those then?"

I almost want to laugh. Her tone is cautious—as if I'm made of fucking glass.

"It's the subs and Valium I was coming off. When you're quitting benzos, Valium's just the thing you taper off. And Clonidine and the other shit is just to make it better."

"I'm not sure I understand."

"The other shit was shit to help with withdrawal."

"It was all in the one bottle?"

"Smart, huh?" I had important shit in one giant ibuprofen bottle I could carry around when I was jonesing, and over-the-counter stuff in another one. When she walked in on me, I had been squeezing it, trying not to take a top-off dose of Valium.

Silence swims between us. Even though I'm distracted by my throbbing head, I can feel her biting her tongue. Not asking the thing she really wants to know. So I just spare her.

"Always been an addict, Siren." I want to add *since seventh grade*, but I know that I could never get that out. "Started early. I can quit. That's not the problem."

"What is? Do you relapse?"

I nod. I've detoxed—big detoxes—twelve times total, but I can't stay clean. It's my superpower. All-star pitcher. Carnegie. Closet addict. Puts the junk in junkie.

I rub my eyes. I'm tired of my own thoughts, the endless looping track of them.

"So now you know my secret." I force myself to look at her. "I'll be better on my feet soon and can help you more."

"But now?" It's murmured. Siren's looking at me through her lashes—one of her shy tells.

"Right now, you're on your own, chief."

"That's not what I meant," she says softly.

"Sleep will help me."

I wait for her to call bullshit. When she doesn't, I wonder if she's noticed I can't sleep...I just lie here. If she knows, she doesn't call me on it.

Pretty soon, that drifting thing is happening again—the one where I feel like half of me is somewhere else. Like all the blood in my body is blinking. Once, when I was herding on the Alps, I ran into someone's electric fence. That's what this is like: like that first half-second when your muscles jerk, before the sizzle.

Still, I feel her there beside me. Blood booms in my ears, obscuring all my other senses, but I feel her worry. I wish I could tell her not to. Someone who doesn't know benzos from subs shouldn't have to deal with this shit. She shouldn't be stuck in here with me.

I turn my back to her again and sink my hands into my hair.

NINETEEN
FINLEY

I can scarcely stand to swing the hammer at the rock, despite knowing it's the best thing. Everything in me yearns to go to him...to sit beside him, talk to him. To joke with him. Even, I realize with alarm, to touch him.

I do nothing of the sort, however. He's made his desires clear —from the moment I hugged him beside the stream and he murmured "please don't" to the end of our conversation, where he turned away from me. Declan doesn't want me nearby.

I've spent enough time in his presence now that I can read his face. I can see how poorly he is. He's still pale, with those poor, lost-looking eyes. He can't stop shaking, can't stop sweating or tossing about the covers. He must be so miserable. But he doesn't want my comfort.

Where before, he looked at me and spoke to me to fill the hours, now when he sits up and peels open a bar, he won't even lift his head in my direction. He chews a bit—not much, I think— and turns back on his side, away from me.

I see him writhing, hear him panting.

When I check on him a while later, offering some water, he won't move his arm from his face.

"Hi there, Sailor. I've just come to offer water."

"I had some." The words are half groaned.

"Is there anything you need...that I could—"

He shakes his head. He's quiet and still, and then he's trembling again. I curl my hand into a fist and press my lips together as I look down at him. "Tell me if there's something I can do to ease you. Do you promise?"

He nods.

I return to work, going hard until I feel delirious. As I'm swinging the hammer, I notice him get up. He walks to the stream and then back toward me, stopping a few meters away to steady himself with a palm against the wall. After a long moment, he walks to me without looking at my face. His eyes are lifted to the cave's mouth. Standing near me, he frowns at the boulder. When he doesn't remark on the truly massive amount of rock I've brought down around the rim, my stomach flips.

"Declan?"

His eyes move over me. The look is fleeting; flat. I watch as he walks behind the rubble pile to tend his business. I wait for him to emerge. When he does, he's staring straight ahead and walking slowly. He walks halfway to the stream before abruptly stopping. He sits against the wall across from his pallet, knees raised, his hand curving around one of them.

I watch as he rubs his hands back through his hair. He appears to stare out at the pallet. I can see his shoulders rising... falling. Another few times with his hands back through his wild, dark hair, and he gets to his feet. He walks toward the cave's rear, pacing with his shoulders heaving. Even from a distance, I can feel him working to contain himself.

Back and forth he paces.

I don't know him, I realize. I know nearly nothing of him.

Only that entrapment is his greatest fear, and he can't bear life fully conscious. I've had thoughts of that myself, looking at the bottles in the clinic. They say ignorance is bliss, and numbness surely is the chief respite of any feeling person.

I wonder what kind of pain he must be in, and, once again, I ache to go to him.

I turn my want into brute force and bring down showers of stone.

Finally, he returns to the sleeping bags, this time stretching out face-down. He wraps his arm around his head and shifts onto his side...then stretches back out on his belly, flexing his legs. He's breathing so deeply, his back pumps.

"Declan?" It's so soft, he doesn't hear it, so I set the hammer down and go to him. I kneel beside him, touch his back.

He moves like a viper, so fast I can't process. I see nothing but the cave's ceiling rocking in my field of vision; he's on top of me, his body warm and heavy as his forearm pins my throat. I try to scream, and when that doesn't work, I sink my nails into the arm that's propping him atop me.

Declan blinks down at me. He looks dazed, confused, and then his eyes pop open wide in horror. He scrambles away from me.

A sob escapes my sore throat as I sit up.

"Finley?" He looks anguished.

I put a hand out, warning him to stay away, and watch as his face crumples. "Oh Christ, did I say *Laurent*?"

"What?"

"Did I hurt you?"

"You were dreaming." Even as my voice cracks, I feel calmer. I see sweat roll down his temple, and I'm quite sure that I've never seen his face so drawn and weary.

His shoulders start to heave as he clutches his brow. "I'm sorry."

"I know you were dreaming." I swallow, rubbing my throat. "What was it about?"

"If I say that name again, just get away."

"What do you mean?"

"I can't wake up."

I wait for more words, but he doesn't offer any. He lies on his back, drawing his knees up before shifting onto his side, tugging at his hair so hard it surely hurts.

"Jesus..." He breathes like a woman in labor. His wide shoulders jerk, as if he might weep, but he doesn't. He just breathes, and rubs his shoulder.

"Come here."

I'm in front of him in an instant, close enough that I can feel him trembling.

His dazed eyes peek open, lifting to mine. His hand kneads his shoulder. "Press it back..."

"What?"

He rolls the shoulder. "Push on it." His voice is thick.

"Why?" I whisper. At that same moment, he rasps, "Please."

I put my hand there on his shoulder. It feels warm and damp under my palm, the muscle hard and thick and twitching with his tremors. "What now?" I whisper.

He shifts onto his back, his left hand cupping my hand. "Push on it. Hard as you can."

"I'm afraid of hurting you."

"You won't." When I don't reply, he grits, "Please." His eyes are squinted with pain, his sweat-slick face contorted.

So...I do what he asks. I lean over him and hold the place between his throat and shoulder with my left hand, while I cup his shoulder and push down hard with my right.

"Harder," he grunts.

I push harder, and he moans. The way his eyes and face flash open in alarm makes me let him go. "I hurt you!"

Something glimmers in the corner of his eye as his face twists. His left hand clutches his shoulder, and guilt racks me.

"I'm so sorry!"

"Wanted it." The words are almost slurred. "That's why...I had you do it."

"Why?"

"Because—" His eyes blink slowly. "I don't...feel *real*."

"What do you mean?"

He shakes his head, closing his eyes again. He rubs his forehead. When he looks up at me, his eyes are more unfocused than I've ever seen them. "Sorry...and thank you."

"How do you feel now?" My heart is racing.

"Okay." But his face is drawn in pain.

I lay my hand over his heart, feeling its fast thrum. Declan's sweaty, shaking hand comes over mine—and then, as if he realizes he's sweaty, he lifts it, cringing.

"Sorry for..." His lips are trembling ever so slightly. Behind his eyelids, I can see his eyes moving as if he's dreaming.

I lean in closer, stroking his hair off his forehead.

"Finley?"

"Yes?"

He looks up at me, and then his eyelids fall shut.

I smooth his hair back a few more times, hoping it'll rouse him, but he doesn't move. His forehead is cool and clammy. I check his pulse. There's no question that his heart is beating more quickly than logical considering he's scarcely moving.

As I'm leaning over him, his body twitches and his eyes snap open. When he sees me, he starts breathing hard, and then he scrambles back, wide-eyed.

"Declan?"

He holds his hands out, shaking hard. Then he looks down, murmurs something.

"Are you all right?"

He looks confused.

"It's just Finley...here to help you."

He looks up at me, but the terror on his face won't dissipate.

"Sailor...you know me, right?"

I watch him swallow.

"Siren," I say gently. "We met on the island."

Once again, he looks around. When his gaze lands on me again, his features twist into a grimace.

"Finley..." he rasps. "Something's wrong with me."

When I close the distance between us, he pulls me up against him, burying his face in my hair as his big body quakes against mine. I cling tightly to him, wanting to make him feel he's not alone.

Instead, he makes me feel that way. His hand smooths over my hair, his fingers spreading gently over my head, lightly massaging even as he shakes and pants.

"This is...just a phase of it," he manages.

"Of course. It will fall away, and you'll feel so much better."

His grip on me tightens. I feel him struggling to breathe.

"Let's lie down, darling. Is that all right?"

His eyes cling to my face as we lie on our sides. I cover him with my sleeping bag and reach beneath the blanket for his hand.

"You're so strong," I murmur, stroking his trembling fingers. "I'm so sorry we're still here. I tried to get us out. I think we're almost there."

"It's okay."

He seems tired now, half asleep. I move a bit closer to him and tuck his fist between my hand and chest to warm it.

"How long since you've slept, my darling? Really slept?"

He blinks at me, and I push back the hair that's fallen into his eyes.

"A while," he whispers.

"How long?"

"Like...back in November."

He's shivering again, and I feel tears burning my eyes. "I think you need to sleep. Do you think that's possible?"

"I don't know." His voice cracks.

I stroke his hair back, and his glazed eyes cling to mine. It's as if there's more he'd like to say and can't, so now it's bleeding out his eyes. My chest aches so sharply as we look at each other that I have to cast my gaze away.

"You're always doing that," he murmurs.

"Doing what?"

I look at his face and find his mouth tugged up at one side. "You don't like...to look at me."

"Untrue."

"I don't blame you."

"No, I only worry for you, Sailor."

"I'll be better." His eyes close as he exhales. His face tenses as he inhales.

"What's happening when you breathe that way?"

His eyes open. His lips tremble.

I hold my hands out, hoping he'll grab onto them. He flexes his fingers.

"Sweaty." It's more mouthed than spoken.

I wrap my hands around his wrists and draw both of his sweaty hands against my chest. His fingers are partially curled. I fold my hands around his. His eyes close.

"When we get out of here, you know, I'm making you soup."

His lips twitch, and one eye lifts open. "Soup?"

"Just to show off." I smile. "I make incredible turmeric soup... it's pure perfection. Homemade bread as well. I know you'd love it."

His eyes close again.

I stroke up and down his arms, running my nails along his damp, goosebumped skin. "Your arms are like carved marble," I murmur, running a fingertip over the muscle. "It's a bit ridiculous, you know."

I spot some dot-like scars there at the crease of his elbow and, on impulse, drag a finger over one. I realize how they must have gotten there when his eyes open. Even dazed, he looks alarmed. When he shuts his eyes again, I can feel his shame.

I press my hand over the spot. "I don't pity you, Carnegie. You're too pretty for that—and you're filthy rich."

His lips twitch. He's trying to smile, and that's all he can manage. My throat aches terribly.

"Tomorrow, you'll feel leaps and bounds better. I'll let you swing the hammer while I watch with my heels up."

I see him try to smile again. It looks painful. I watch as his face tenses and his breathing picks up. He breaths like the air is out of oxygen, like people do when they're in horrid pain.

With his hands still curled against the base of my throat, I draw closer to him, wrapping one arm over his warm shoulders.

"You can do this, darling. I know you're so poorly, but you're so strong. Every part of you is strong." I drag my nails down his nape, and Declan makes a low sound in his throat.

"Does that feel good?"

When he breathes harder, I do it again. He groans.

Relief streams through me. Finally—something I can do. I twist my wrist a bit and start to knead his neck in earnest. He gives a low groan, his body tensing against mine.

I follow my mental map of pressure points around his hairline, and he curls closer to me. Finally, his head is on my shoulder. His panted breaths tickle my chest, making me feel warm and oddly...needy. For what, though, I can't say.

I rub with a bit more force; his breaths come fast and heavy. My fingers find a tense spot on his neck there, rubbing hard, and he stiffens against me. I hear his breath catch. Then one of his hands squeezes my shoulder.

"Siren..." I rub harder, and his voice cracks.

"Just relax." I drag my fingers up through his hair. "Let me keep on till you fall asleep." I wrap myself around him, pressing his large body against mine in a tight hug.

My fingers play through his hair, then stroke gently down his nape.

He moans. "Siren..."

I feel his hips press up against me. Then his mouth catches my jaw.

For a moment, I'm suspended by his breath against my ear, his scruff against my cheek. Then it's me who shudders, my legs shifting against his as he rasps, "Stop."

The word leaps from my mouth before I can stop it. "Why?" My throat is tight, my eyelids heavy.

His forehead touches mine as he moans, "Feels...too good."

I'm not sure how I know. Perhaps the oldest, basest intuition. I look down our bodies. Declan draws his rigid frame away from me, and there I see it, jutting heavy from his hips, straining against his pants: a rod that's long and thick, outsizing what I believed possible. It's so large, it can't even tent the fabric of his shorts. The tip of it seems pushed against the shorts' waistband, the thick shaft bent in its confinement.

As I stare at it, he reaches down, melding his hand around it. As my gaze sweeps upward toward his face, I see the bare tip of it trapped between his pants and chiseled belly.

For the love of all things holy!

Desire courses through me, making my breaths quicken.

I was right, then, back at Gammy's. He's endowed quite like a bull. Something clenches in the region of my hips. I press my thighs together as I blink up at him.

Declan's hand spreads over his abs, partly hiding his sex from my eyes. But it's so long and thick, he can't completely shield it.

With his free hand, he kneads his forehead. "Sorry," he whispers, eyes shut. "When it's...like this—" His jaw tightens.

"Like what?"

He shifts his hips, his face twisting. "Getting clean." His voice is breathless, almost groaned. "Everything hurts...but this." He shifts his hips again, rubbing at the bulge of his sex.

"What does that feel like?" I swallow, my poor heart hammering as if it might give out. It's surreal, this moment, in this place. It doesn't feel like reality, and I'm not behaving like myself.

He wraps his hand around himself as best he can, squeezing. Hot saliva fills my mouth as I watch his jaw clench, his eyelids lift open slightly.

He's breathing hard and heavy as he lets go of his stiff sex. I watch as his hands fist.

"Fuck." He shifts his legs again in clear discomfort. "Get up, Siren. Go away and I'll..." He sucks a breath back, grips his temples.

I feel as if it's someone else's voice that whispers, "You'll do what?"

"Shit. What do you think? You rubbing on me—" He shakes his head. "It felt good." His voice is hoarse. "Just...go. I can make it fast."

As he says that, he cups himself, his raised knees spreading wider. I watch as his hand delves inside his shorts, and then he's pushing them down.

His thick sex springs up, stiff and rigid, lying like a hose against his abs. I note the darkness of his glans, the bulbous thickness of it. At that moment, he wraps his hand around it, squeezing as he tweaks the thick tip with his thumb. He tugs at it again, letting out a ragged groan. It seems to hurt...but perhaps not.

He wraps one hand around the length as the other delves

down to— *Holy virgin!* Still swathed in his underpants, but those must be his testes. They're...massive.

I have the thought *how does he move about with those*, and then he's pumping up and down the rod of his sex, squeezing the tip as his hand curves around it, gripping himself just below and then stroking up and down while with his other hand, he's stroking his awfully swollen testicles, tapping his fingertips against their sac.

I realize as I watch his face twist and his body writhe, his hands working frantically to find relief, that this was surely part of his discomfort. I know males swell and stiffen for the act, but this seems quite extreme. I've never heard of one so long and thick, not even during arousal.

Declan's breaths grow ragged as he works himself into a fervor. His knees lift a bit, his chest pumping with frenzied breaths. I can't tear my eyes away. How horrible that he's in so much pain, because it's quite majestic...and compelling.

As I watch, I feel my senses heighten, spurred by ancient magic; I grow warm and breathless, feel a needy clenching where my own sex would receive his...were we to copulate.

I'm about to turn away—all this is well beyond improper—but at that moment, he grunts and shifts onto his side, his hand releasing his sex as the other rises up to knead his shoulder...that right shoulder. He lets out a long, unsteady breath—it makes his thick sex jut toward his navel. When he inhales again, the hand on his shoulder moves to cover his face.

I hold stone still until he resumes stroking himself, one hand pumping his shaft as the other fists his hair. I tear my eyes away from his member and realize he's clenching his jaw.

At that moment, his eyes open. "Finley." His face still looks tired, but his voice is hard. "What are you doing?"

My cheeks burn so hot, I feel my eyes tear. "I'm sorry," I whisper.

"You were watching," he says darkly.

I look at my feet, and then I start to turn away.

"Why?"

I freeze. *Why? Because I love to watch you all the time...*

That forbidden thought sends shockwaves through me.

"Siren." His low voice is clear and quiet. "Have you ever seen a man without his clothes on?"

I shake my head, unable to turn fully around to face him. My eyes throb. I bring a hand to my forehead, clutching. "Please don't be...offended."

"Not offended." He sounds husky.

"I'd be mortified if someone looked upon me that way. I'm terribly sorry."

My gaze affixes to the pale glint of the stream. I start to move toward it when he laughs. "The more you look, the easier it is."

His words drop like weights inside me, as if I had swallowed them. I hear my own unsteady whisper. "I'm not sure I—I don't understand."

"Turn around, Finley."

I obey with bated breath—and find his maleness covered with a blanket.

"Have you ever touched yourself?"

His question pierces like an arrow, making my eyes well with tears of shame. I shake my head...then, to my horror, I feel myself nod. Looking at him, with his desperate face, one thick forearm still snaking down behind the blanket, I find myself incapable of deceit, even what's needed to salvage my wayward sense of shame.

His lips twitch. "You liked it, didn't you?" His voice sounds strange, a bit too low. I note his arm is moving; he's stroking his sex as he speaks. "It's supposed to feel good, Siren. There should be some pleasure, don't you think? Something to ease the pain."

His eyes close as he says that. His arm moves more quickly.

I sense myself in motion half a breath before I am, moving slightly closer to him. Declan's eyes open to meet mine. He looks dazed as he strokes himself behind the blanket—eyelids heavy, his face more relaxed now.

"So...it feels good?"

I watch his throat move as he swallows. "Yeah."

His eyes are closing, even as he strokes. I realize that I've crouched beside him.

Time freezes around us as his breaths grow faster, heavier. I can see his jaw tighten, his features tense as if he's deeply focused.

Then he shifts his hips. The blanket falls away, and I'm stricken to my core by what I see in front of me. His thick sex is fully revealed, his underpants tucked behind the mighty orbs below. His long sex looks painfully engorged, its dark tip pointed toward his navel. Around it, his thick hand curves, moving back and forth from tip to base, each long, solid stroke making his swollen testes bounce and wobble.

"*Ohh.*"

The noise slips from my lips, and Declan's gaze moves to mine. I should look away, but I find I'm not able. I look instead down at his sex, at his hand around it, pumping smoothly up and down. I watch the way his fingers twist over the tip, tugging upward as his knees spread wider and his slack face tautens. I see a mist of sweat along his hairline. Now there's color in his cheeks.

And I can't look away.

I have never seen a sight like Declan pleasuring himself. As I look down at him, my knees tremble. His hand slows its frenzied pacing, squeezing his glans. His molten gaze licks up and down me.

"Come here, Finley."

I kneel by his muscle-corded leg. My breath is caught in my throat. My pulse races as his eyes hold mine, and his hand squeezes the thick tip. I watch as he swallows, his eyes half closing. Then he lets himself go.

Jesus, Mary, and Joseph! The way it stands out, pointing proudly upward. It's so...thick. My gaze traces a vein from tip to base. It's a marvel—the perfection of it.

"Go on, Siren." His voice rumbles. "Touch it."

Heat zings through me—so much heat I'm sweating. For a moment, I can't find the words. They stutter out. "I...can't."

"No?" His hand strokes, lazy, down the shaft, then spreads below to cup his swollen sac. He squeezes slightly, and I nearly die from desire.

Jesus himself help me, but I want to touch it. Heat suffuses my face, and I'm realize I'm now panting. I scoot back, but I can't wrench my wanton gaze away. I watch his big hand play it like an instrument, his savvy fingers rolling his testes then tugging upward on the thick shaft.

"You don't have to." His eyes close. "Knowing you're watching is enough."

His fist grips beneath the flared tip, moving firm but gentle, up and down. His legs fall open wider. He does something with his hand—his thumb stroking over the tip in precisely such a way so I can see a tiny slit there at the top...and all around it, something wet and shiny.

I'm leashed by propriety, by twenty-seven years of Catholic learning. I am bridled by my past, by proper vows and chastity and even simple decency. He is not mine.

And yet...I know before I reach for him that I will. Not because I want to touch him but because I must.

Declan moans as my hand covers his. Then his hand moves over mine, urging my fingers around his sex. I gasp at the feel of it —so hot and soft. As he urges me to stroke, his silky skin glides over the core of steel beneath. He exhales, and I feel him swell in my grip.

Holy virgin...

I adjust my hand. My fingers can't reach all the way around him, but I think the grip should be firm, as his own appeared to be. I glide toward the base, and then back up, and he moans.

"Fuck."

I spread my fingers, rubbing over him with the skin between my thumb and forefinger until I reach the tip again. I trace the rim, and his hips jerk. *"Siren."*

"Does it hurt?"

He shakes his head, but still, I feel unsure until he juts himself against my hand. His hands stroke up and down my arm, and I explore the little slit, prompting a ragged groan.

I'm afraid of hurting him, so I return to what his hands suggested: stroking up and down the marble-stiff length. When I reach the base this time, I hold it with one hand and use the other one to test the swollen sac below. I feel it draw up at my light touch. Between my own legs is a yawning ache.

Declan shifts his hips again. His hand presses my palm against those tender globes, as his other starts to pump his sex again. Gripping him gently, I join in. Can he feel my fingers shaking? I watch his hand, turning slightly as it grips the thick shaft underneath its tip.

I tickle his sac, and he groans. *"Shit."*

I move with growing confidence up and down him, stroking the shaft as his thumb tweaks his tip. With his other hand, he grabs my arm.

"Finley."

I stroke him again, and his hips lift off the floor.

"Squeeze harder."

I do.

"Harder...*please.*"

I grip him harder.

"Faster."

I stroke so quickly, so firmly, I'm afraid I'll hurt him. His hand grips my shoulder. I can feel him shaking.

He moans. "If—" My hand stills, and his urges it to move again. He shudders. "If you don't stop soon...I'm gonna come."

I find his warning leaves me undeterred. I feel eager, almost frenzied, with the urge to see him come undone. I've only heard a bit about what techniques men like most, but I act on the knowledge.

I look into his eyes as I run my hand up and down his swollen sex. I can feel it throb as I do.

"Relax," I whisper as his breaths begin to come in tugs. "What do you like?"

I trace my hand from top to bottom—teasing, languid. Then I grip his tip, as I saw him do, and I rub my thumb over the tiny slit as I cup his balls.

"Finley..."

"I like this." I sway them a bit and his backside lifts off the floor. I stroke from mid-shaft to the tip and feel more moisture.

"What can I do?"

"Rub...your palm around." He's grunting.

I do as I'm told, rubbing over the wetness. With a gentle squeeze, I release his heavy sac and stroke his sex. His hand rubs over my arm, the fingers trembling as he drags air into his lungs and groans it out.

"I'm close."

I quicken my stroke, run my thumb over the wet spot where he's leaking, and then, when I'm positive he's just swelled further, when he starts to writhe and grab at me, I close one hand around his sac and pump my other up his length again.

When my closed fist brushes the notch there at the rim of his glistening tip, he gives a mighty jerk and grabs himself.

My head spins as I feel his sac harden against my palm, as I watch his thick cream spill between his fingers, dripping down the taut engorgement of his sex.

He's panting, but his face has slackened. I watch his pulse thrum at his throat and want to lick it. Bite it.

My gaze attaches to his heavy pecs, finding his perfect, brown nipples erect. I'm aware as my hand lifts away from his sex that it's time to step away. He's relieved—I've eased his discomfort—but between my own legs, I feel heavy. Heavy and...riotous.

He runs a hand over his length, and I throb. I can't say where. Perhaps it's all of me. I press my thighs together, feeling odd and slightly fearful.

His eyes open. "You okay?"

He looks near asleep.

I hear myself laugh. "Yes, are you?"

He inhales deeply. "Great."

I turn around and get a towel, setting it atop him.

"Thanks." He's still panting a bit, so I decide I'll clean him up. It's quite strange to run such ordinary terrycloth over his slackening sex. It's still enormous. As I wipe it tenderly, it seems to flinch.

He groans.

"I'm sorry."

"Fuck no." His eyes open again. "Hey, do you want..." His brows draw slightly together, and I can feel the question in the ether.

My pulse races as I shake my head. His gaze remains on mine, as if asking, *Are you sure?*

"No thank you," I murmur.

"That was so good, Finley."

And, at that, he's gone. Sunk into dreamland.

After I cover him, I go stand beside the stream, where I touch the inseam of my shorts with quaking fingers. I imagine my hand gliding up my thigh, beneath the fitted seam-line of my own white underthings...over my dark, coarse curls.

I can't stop myself. I glide my fingers over my sex, stunned to find it slick and swollen. When my fingertip nudges the slit between my lips, I have to bite my cheek to keep from moaning.

Oh, Declan...

I need my finger in that place. I need something to fill where I feel needy for his harsh engorgement.

I'm breathing so hard, it echoes. I close my eyes and I imagine his smart fingers parting my forbidden crevice. I'm so very, very wet...could he fit in?

I push a fingertip inside and cry out. I'm throbbing, my entire body aching with the need to feel...him. In my fantasy, he's lying flat as he was, his sex jutting up. I tug it toward me, push its thick tip to my swollen flesh.

I imagine spreading my legs open for him. He would push inside—so large and long—and I'd be filled completely...to the point of sinful madness.

I see his taut jaw, then his parted lips. I see his dazed eyes and that kind smile he gives me at odd moments. And I can feel his cheek beside mine.

My beloved.

The words chill me. How...ridiculous. And shameful. Sinful. I feel ill as I dip my hand into the stream and wash away the evidence of my wicked thoughts.

TWENTY
DECLAN

I feel...better. It's the first thing I notice as I blink up at the craggy ceiling. All the fucking dread, the racing heart shit—gone. Along with the surreal sensation I hate so much. I've still got the empty-chested feeling, but it's physical. That shit, I can handle. Pain and discomfort—that's the easy part.

I roll over, hoping to go back to sleep. That's when I feel it. *My shorts...*

The surreal feeling's back, making my stomach roll as I reach down and find...*oh, thank fuck*. My hand brushes the towel on my crotch, and then I know I didn't dream it.

Finley really jerked me off. I had a giant, detox hard-on and she...helped.

Again, with the fucking roller coaster. My heart bobs like a buoy up into my throat, so I can hardly breathe. I shut my eyes, and I can see her lower lip between her teeth, her long, red hair over her shoulder as her hands rub up and down my cock. Pale, tentative hands...that pumped my dick—and rubbed my back.

Warmth spreads through me like some kind of Harry Potter shit. Shame kicks up behind it. Shame and something heavy, like a metric fuck-ton of regret. That this is who I am. That she saw me this way and...I don't know. What did she think?

She grabbed my dick.

I tell myself that means she doesn't think I'm scum, and when I've got the nerve to look around, I spot her over by the cave's mouth, standing with her hands on her hips and her face tilted toward the boulder that's blocking us in.

I let my gaze run up and down her. *Siren.* She looks like a siren...or a mermaid. She's on the taller side, with curvy hips, a nice, round ass, and big breasts. Her face has that extra clean look some women have. I think it's something with her skin. It just looks soft. I can't see her very well across the cave, so I close my eyes and see her face. A few freckles across the nose...and those lips. Damn.

She gives me these looks sometimes where she's got her brows raised and her eyes wide and her lips pursed, and she looks like a sassy schoolmarm. I can see her sitting by me—leaning over me—her face framed by a few loose strands of hair...and I can hear her soft voice.

"Darling."

It feels weird to have a woman act like that with me. Even more so because I liked it. I glance at her again across the burrow and it's just...weird. I've known her less than a week, but it feels like a lot longer. When I look at her, I don't see a near-stranger. I see Finley.

I guess I could go back to sleep, but now I sort of feel like talking to her. We're stuck in here together, after all, and I'm not losing my damn mind for once. I probably will be later, when the benefits of sleeping wear off. But right now, I feel close to normal. And I want to see her. I want to see her blush when I walk over to her.

I pull my pants up, moving carefully, so I don't draw her eye yet, and then get to my feet. My body doesn't ache as much as it does sometimes. I feel so much better, I can't help a cheesy grin as she looks over at me.

The second our eyes meet, Finley's brows arch and her lips round into an "o." As I close the distance between us, she looks back up at the boulder again and then, reluctantly, at me. Nervous.

As soon as I'm beside her, I give her a *how ya doin'* look, and she drops her gaze down to her feet as her cheeks flush.

I knew it.

"Whatcha see down there?"

She laughs softly and tucks a strand of hair behind her ear. Woman is so shy, she can't even answer me. I swat her messy ponytail.

"I see something."

She turns to me with startled eyes, and I wiggle my brows. "Something in your hair."

"What was it?"

"Bug." I smirk.

She makes a face, and I tug her ponytail again. "Got it that time."

"Thank goodness."

When she still won't look at me, I close my hand around her ponytail and smooth it gently down. "How many times do I have to pull on this to see your face?"

Her eyes lift to mine, and I'm relieved to find a small smile on her lips. A shy smile. I let go of her hair, and she looks down again.

"Don't be shy, Siren."

Her blush deepens. "I'm not."

"Yeah you are."

She shakes her head, pursing her lips as she examines the floor. I crouch down in front of her, and she laughs. "You're so odd, Carnegie!"

"I've been told that."

"Get up now." Her fingers stroke my hair. "I want to show you something."

I stand, and she points up at the boulder, which looks bigger than it did last time I saw it.

"Damn. You got a lot of rock down." I hold my hand up, palm out, for a high-five before I remember she's not a Sox bro, but she high-fives me anyway.

"Push on it," she whispers.

I do, and it moves so much, my knees nearly give out with relief. "Well, hell. I think I might be able to move this fucker." I look over at her. "Can you spot me?"

She lets out a little squeal then bounces on the balls of her feet. "Wait! What does that mean?" She laughs.

"Just push up on it like I am. If it gets unstable or I'm pushing and I lose my grip on it, I'll give you some warning, and you can duck out of the way."

"Are you fine to do it? You don't want to wait till later?"

"I'm good."

I push up, grabbing the edge I now can reach since she cleared more rock from the cave's mouth. I get my hands around the edge of the cool stone, noting that it's not that thick: maybe eight inches. Using all the muscle of my arms and back, I push. When I feel it give and shift, I shove harder.

Wind caresses my hands and my wrists, and I hear Finley laughing. I don't dare look up. I push harder. No movement. I inhale, and then I push again. A bolt of hot, near-paralyzing pain shoots through my shoulder, but I keep on. I feel Finley pushing with me. When it doesn't budge, she whispers something that sounds like a swear word. We both shove.

There's a scraping sound, and when I look up, I see blue sky. *Oh, fuck.*

That's enough space for Finley to slip through. I push the

motherfucker one more time and the space widens. Finley's shrieking.

Her body smashes into mine, her arms wrapping around my waist as her face pushes against my chest. "Oh, sweet baby Jesus! We did it!"

She squeezes me. I spread my hand out on her small back, feel her shake beneath my palm. She laughs but then it sort of sounds like crying.

"I am not a crier."

"Sure you aren't..." I rub big circles on her back, and Finley sags against me.

"I can smell the ocean," she sighs.

I look at the swatch of sky. Then I scoop her up and lift her toward it.

"No!" She locks her arms around my head, her legs around my waist. "I won't go up without you, crazy man."

I set her down, and she gives me a look of disbelief.

I shrug.

"We're a team."

I nod. "Partners."

I hold her pack as she stuffs everything inside. When we're back at the cave's mouth, she laughs. "Thank you!"

"You did most of it. Chipping all that rock away is what did it."

Before I lift her up, I wrap my hands around the ledge of the cave's mouth and ease my torso partway out. My burning shoulder makes my forearms quake. The sunlight hits me like a brick. But I can see the difference in the landscape. The slope-side and the valley—all of it a sea of broken rock. I look to my left and find the peak we traversed missing its archway and the rock spires.

"You were right," I tell her, easing back down. "That arch fell, and most of it is right on top of us. I'm gonna lift you up into a field of rocks—but it looks stable."

Shock moves over her face. "Did you see anyone?"

I shake my head, and she blinks.

"C'mon, Siren." I shove her pack up through the gap and wrap my hands around her waist. A moment later, Finley's smiling down at me.

"There's so much wind! C'mon!"

My shoulder blazes as I lift myself, but coming out under the sky is worth it. Grass and wetness, stone and sea fill my nose. The sky has never seemed so big, so blue. I look up and down the valley.

"Rocks are everywhere," she murmurs.

I nod. If they came looking for us, there's no way they would have found us.

Finley touches my leg, laughing softly. "Your shorts." I look down. They don't look like khakis anymore. "They're filthy!"

Fuck, they're hanging off my hips. I fold my hand around the fly to hold them up.

"Showing your underpants," she chides.

"You like it."

We walk through the valley like we've just stepped off a spaceship. The scent of grass fills my head. Finley turns a circle, grabbing my hands as she comes to face me. She grins.

"You look horrid. Do I?"

"Oh yeah." I ignore the sudden dip of my stomach and smile back at her. "Like something the cat dragged in."

That makes her giggle. "We need baths."

We don't try to go over the peak where all the rock fell. Instead we move through the valley toward the ocean, toward the Patches. Toward the road where I'm hoping the SUV I drove here will be waiting. When we round the peak's grassy side, the ocean's surface flashes brightly, making my heart beat off-rhythm.

Finley's hand finds mine. Our fingers intertwine. "You need a rest...in bed."

"I'm cool."

Her sad smile says she sees through me. By the time we reach the Land Rover, my legs are shaking.

She reclines my seat, hands me some water. The cap's off, but I don't notice till it spills on my lap.

"Blimey..."

My head aches. My stomach feels somehow both sick and hollow.

"When we get to town, they'll likely crowd the Land Rover. I'll lock the doors and only open mine. I'll get out and explain. I believe I'll tell them you've got a concussion. Perhaps a cracked rib. If you'd like, we'll drive directly to the clinic."

I shake my head lightly, try to get my rubber mouth to form words. "Not there," I whisper.

I fall through silence as our tires bump over gravel.

"Okay," she says. "Gammy's house, and I can bring what you need."

I try to stay awake, so I can listen if she wants to share more thoughts as she drives toward the village. But I guess I fail. When I open my eyes next, I see a sea of faces through the windows. Finley's chair is empty. I can't find the energy to lift my head again.

Sometime later, I feel her move back inside the car.

"How are you?" she murmurs.

"Okay. You?"

Everything is shaking with the tires over the road, and I feel fucking sick. The car stops, and I crack my eyes open, finding she's parked right by the house's door. She has it held open when I get to the porch.

"There now...come on in."

She takes my arm. I let her. The house smells like lemons, and my head hurts really bad.

I can't follow her voice, but I know it's nice and soft.

The bed she urges me into is even softer.

"That's right...let me cover you up."

From somewhere that feels like a dream, I hear a phone ring. Not a cell phone.

"Someone's calling. I'll be right back, Sailor."

The next time I open my eyes, dawn glows through the pale curtains, and I'm alone.

TWENTY-ONE

FINLEY

I didn't realize until after Gammy passed, but she began work on Mummy's wedding gown the week after Charles Carnegie departed. I know only because I treasured the gown dearly and was therefore quite familiar with its look and stitching. I found Gammy's design sketches tucked into *The Grapes of Wrath* after we tucked her into her grassy resting place. The date was scrawled up top in her angular pen.

Henceforth, I was left to wonder if the dress was made in hope or in surrender.

Perhaps Mummy asked Gammy to make it, told her Charles would be returning to ask her hand. In the days just after he departed, I believe Mum surely felt emboldened by their dalliance. So it may be that Gammy set about sketching a gown fit for a Mrs. Charles Carnegie.

Or it may be entirely the opposite. Charles departed, and my wise Gammy knew that Mum would wind up married to my father. She figured if it wouldn't be a love match, at least Mummy could get married in a lovely dress.

I stand before the mirror at the doctor's quarters, pressing the dress to my naked body. I fold an arm across my chest and the dress, freeing up my other one to pull the tie from my hair. I spread my hair over my shoulder and I tilt my head a bit—so I look matronly. More like the Mummy in my memories.

I tried to don the gown anew a few moments back, but over the years I've fattened up and I can't fit into it.

Tears well in my eyes as I peer at my reflection. I'm still drying from my shower. Anna shoved me in before she and my dear ones left. After Holly and Dot asked ten million questions about Declan, and I fed them quite a large number of lies.

I look at myself, covered by the gown, and I open my jewelry box and remove Gammy's diamond. It fits my finger flawlessly—along with the band. I lay the gown over a chair and twirl through the quarters wearing nothing but the jewelry.

The phone rings off the hook, and not from anyone in need of doctoring. More people want to bring food. I told them back beside the Land Rover that no one should disturb Declan as he rests—so all the food's been brought to me.

One of the many times it rings, I answer, and it's Doctor again. He called at the cottage, having heard from his friend Father Russo I had gone there, but I feigned connection troubles. Now I feel like I've swallowed a fish as he says, "If it isn't dear, lost Finley..."

I try a weak laugh. "I've been found."

"Russo said you arrived in the village, both fairly unharmed."

I swallow. "No one was seriously hurt. It was just the fallen rock that trapped us in a...more burrow than cave."

"No way out?"

I nod, licking my lips. "It was horrid."

"I'd imagine. What's he like? What did you eat?"

"I had those Atkins bars that came for Joshua McGillin. Just a half dozen. We had those."

"You and the great Homer Carnegie."

"He's quite...regular. You'd get on nicely, I think."

"Is that right? Too bad we'll miss each other."

Doctor's ship returns after Declan's departs. "It is."

"So no injuries for you? My beloved nurse is well?"

I nod. "I was quite lucky." I lick my lips again. "How are you, Doctor? How is your father getting on?"

"Someone should hold a pillow over his face."

I laugh. "You must be joking."

"Insufferable bastard."

"That's really too bad."

"Without the bottle, he'd just as rather be gone."

"I'm sorry to hear that. It mustn't be easy on you."

"Counting down the days until I'm back there. Try to tend my caseload, will you? No more disappearing. Gave me quite a fright."

"I'm sorry."

The line crackles. "We'll talk later. This has been a long ordeal. I'd like some rest now."

My heart pitter-patters. "I do have a question for you."

"Yes?"

I feel the sharp blade of his temper even through the phone line. I inhale...then let the breath out. "I need the location of the safe's key. You know—"

"The only one. Yes, I know. What for?"

"For him—for Carnegie. He's got an injury, a shoulder that's giving him pain."

"Injured in the fall, then?"

"I'm not sure when."

"Weren't you there?"

"Well, yes. But—"

"Is it an old wound or a new one?"

I bristle, as I almost always do in the past year when we speak. "Likely old. Truth be told, I didn't ask."

"What do you need the safe for?"

"Well, for the controlled substances. For the pain. I'd hoped to give a bit of something."

"Did he ask?"

"He wouldn't ask. But I can see it pains him. I didn't want to broach the subject without having the safe's key."

"Broach the subject? Is it a tough one then? I'm quite sure I'm missing something, but I don't know where. Care to enlighten me?"

I shut my eyes. "Doctor...he's got a bit of history, I believe. That's how I know he'd never ask."

"A history? And you want to give him more? Are you out of your gourd?"

My stomach clenches. I feel foolish, as I always do around Doctor. "I don't like to see him hurting."

"You're too soft."

"Perhaps. Is there something I could give to help him rest or help with pain that isn't those things?"

"Nothing that you'd need a safe key for."

"What if the pain becomes unbearable?"

"You won't know then, will you? You just said he wouldn't ask. And if he does ask, how can you trust him? That's the trouble with you native Tristanians. Never having lived off the island, you're ridiculously naive."

My stomach twists as anger builds. "Don't be unkind, sir. I'm simply advocating for a patient. You know we can't gauge injuries like that here on the island. Something in the shoulder could be torn or broken."

"In ordinary society, this is why one has what's called a family doctor. Let him contact that person if he has a need, get a prescription. They can contact me. Until then, offer NSAIDs. And Finley?"

"Yes?"

"Be wary of him. Sort like that—he's damaged goods. Quite likely to do near anything."

My throat is tight as I whisper, "Okay."

There's no arguing with Doctor, but my eyes well as the line goes dead. I put the dress away and start on soup. I'm chopping onion when I slice my fingers. Blood pools all around the rings, so dark there in the shadows that it looks black.

I put the rings away, bandage my hand. I curl up in an armchair while the soup burbles. The house feels empty.

I can't bring myself to call him.

I don't sleep but remain curled there in the chair until the sun is up. When other voices echo down the lane, it feels safe enough to rise.

I open the door to find Dorothy standing on my small porch in a dreary fog. She's grinning wickedly as she leans against the door frame.

"Tell me all of it, trollop. You know I need to slurp back every detail."

"Slurp?" I lift my brows, and she lifts hers like a mirror.

I run my gaze up and down her, taking in her lovely yellow dress and red sweater, her vibrant lipstick. "What have you got on, then?"

She runs her hand down the fabric, which looks a bit like silk.

"You were there when I made it. Saturday night sewing..." She twirls her hand in the air as if miming someone with a duster, and I swallow back shocked laughter.

"You're dressed for him!"

She makes a duck face. "I'm dressed for me, but he could benefit."

My belly goes all topsy-turvy at her tone, but I make sure not to show it when I snort and say, "Saucy."

I turn back toward the kitchen, and Dot follows, her ludicrous heels clicking against the pale green linoleum. She spots some wedding cookies in a tin and pops one into her mouth.

"Careful there, Madonna. You might ruin your lipstick."

She holds up a tube of it, and I realize she got it from a small, brown purse. Dot never carries a purse.

"Ready for the ball then, are we?"

"Aunt Bea lent it to me."

"Oh, I'm sure." Dot's Aunt Bea is a mere six years older than her, three older than me. She married poor Oliver Green but sets her sights upon the tourists like she's hoping she'll be spirited away.

Dot makes a silly face—a pretty face.

"You've got white powder..." I wipe a cookie smudge off her chin, and she smiles. "What's he like, though? Really, Finley. Humor me. I'll help you carry everything."

I pile her arms with casseroles and cakes and send her to the red Bronco she drove to fetch me. For the next few minutes, I focus on loading the automobile. I unlock the door between the doctor's quarters and the clinic and fetch a bag of things I need for Declan.

I feel nearly ill with remorse for not returning to him last night. Absolutely wretched as I buckle myself into the passenger's seat.

Dot turns the Bronco toward Gammy's and smiles over at me. "Would it hurt so terribly to indulge me? You've never been one to go seeking out a sweetheart, but do think of the rest of us. Think of me! I'm not the scholarly sort, as you well know. I'll never go away to university. I'll have to settle for Mike Green, and isn't that a bit creepy?"

"Terribly so, Dorothy. He's still a child!"

"Homer Carnegie is so gorgeous. All I want to know is what

he talks of. How he smells. Could you smell his body there, inside the cave?"

I cover my face because it's unbearably hot, and Dot squeals with laughter. "Forgive me."

"Always with the pin-ups...and the bath tub faucet."

"Shut up, cow! That's secret!" Her hand slaps my shoulder, and I curl myself up more tightly. "I've the least options of anyone, being born at the worst time."

I can't argue that. Everyone within five years of Dot is female —just a stroke of poor fortune.

Fog rolls over the windshield. Through the haze, the amber lights adorning each stoop still shine brightly in the misty semi-darkness. As autumn marches on, the days grow even rainier. I get a deep, quiet breath and move my hands off my face. *Must behave like normal.*

"I don't know, Doro. He's...like a man. He's actually quite kind. He worked tirelessly to dig us out." It's not untrue. He was frantic to free us before the dawning of the werewolf hour, as I've come to think of it.

"After the first day, we assumed you likely were together, seeing neither of you surface."

"What sort of talk was there?"

"Only a few talked."

"The usuals, I suppose."

"But most felt he'd protect you. Baseball players, they're an honorable sort, after all. I think no one worried for your virtue."

I nod, staring at the glove box in front of me.

"Tell me, though—was it simply glorious to be so near to him? I'd never tell a soul, but even so, who wouldn't understand if you admit it was?"

I shut my eyes so I can't see the lovelorn look on her face. "It wasn't glorious, Dot. We were trapped there."

She sighs, and guilt moves through me. Guilt and a twisting sort of sensation, like my insides being tied into a knot.

"I'm glad you made it back in one piece," Dot says finally. "If you'd seen us when the two of you were missing..." She smiles faintly. "I'm not sure what was worse: the desolation over losing you or the horror at losing a *Carnegie*."

We both have a good cackle at that.

"Old Tom was going wild, raving about you ruining the island, were he to perish. Quite the fury he was in."

"Miserable old clod."

By the time Dot parks the Bronco at Gammy's, we're wiping laughter tears from our eyes. Dot hugs me, and I cling to her. I shut my eyes and tell myself nothing's amiss. No matter what's said to him, he'll be discreet about what went on between us. It wasn't purely lustful. It was comfort and...companionship. The sort of incident that occurs at times that are difficult and fear-filled.

I banish the topic from my mind because my belly feels as if it's dropped into my thighs. I can't breathe properly as Dot knocks on the door, bearing a covered pound cake in one hand and a basket of jams in the other. Her back is straight, her chin held high as misty wind tousles her updo. When he doesn't answer, she knocks twice more.

Then I realize— "The Land Rover isn't here."

She whirls around. "Where is it?"

We turn toward the village as horror falls through me. I've this primal fear he sailed away while I was resting last night—or somehow passed.

Dot steps off the porch, and I squint through the misting rain.

"I see! I can see that green of his Land Rover at the café," Dot says.

"The café?"

"Oh I'm sure Miss Alice has done breakfast. No surprise there really. Someone—likely many someones—came and dragged him out of bed."

"Contrary to the doctor's advice!"

She snickers. "Quite an awful lot, these scoundrel breakfast-makers."

"No one rang me," I say with mock indignation.

"You're not a Carnegie, are you?"

My throat aches as I force a smile. "I suppose not."

I steel myself as Dot parks the Bronco in front of the café, where everyone and their lamb has gathered.

Lamb! Baby! Jesus, Mary, and Joseph! I realize Mrs. White has Baby. When I got back to the clinic quarters yesterday, I didn't even think to call her. Oh, how awful of me. Perhaps she's here now. How is poor, wee Baby? Guilt drags at me. I blink to find Dot's hand waving in front of my face.

"What on earth?" she asks.

"I realized Mrs. White has Baby."

"Indeed she does. She's done a fine job, as you'd assume. Come now, you can worry over that later."

Dot and I leave the food there in the Bronco and make our way through the mud to the porch, where I get shoulder pats and one-armed hugs.

"So delighted to see that face," crows Mrs. Burns, my old piano instructor.

I smell cheese and eggs, perhaps cinnamon milk toast, as Dot escorts me through the café's doorway. We step inside and someone pats my shoulder—Mr. Braun, my dear diabetic patient.

"Glad to see you, lady."

We chat for a few moments. As we do, he shifts his weight, moving slightly rightward. The café's rear corner comes into view over his shoulder, and my eyes snap to him: *Declan.*

Oh, but he looks radiant. He's seated at round table, surrounded by adoring fans. His dark hair is neat—a wee bit wavy —and his handsome face clean-shaven. He's clad in a pale blue Polo shirt, one thick arm resting atop the table as he nods attentively at Dot's Mike Green.

As for me, I'm ensnared in greeting after greeting, but it's all a dull buzz.

Between answering questions—it's the same few on repeat—I catalog the motley crew seated around him: Holly, bottle Mac, Mike Green, Baby's Mrs. White, Horris Ballard, and Father Russo. Declan moves and speaks as if he's quite accustomed to the spotlight. I see his smile more in my periphery than perhaps I ever have. His low laughter makes my belly curl. My legs feel like a colt's.

Dot and I move through the room together. Her eyes press at me in sidelong glances that I don't return. She takes my hand and moves me toward the kitchen, where Miss Alice throws her arms around me like a mum.

"My dear girl..." My cheek presses against her mighty bosom as she squeezes me. "Rubbed the color off my beads."

"I'm sorry."

She steps back, her warm hands cupping my shoulders. "Don't be. Apologizing for what's not your fault is a disservice to yourself." A fond smile crinkles her face. "You look well enough. So does that young man. I'll suppose it's you who kept him safe and not the reverse." She winks, and heat suffuses my cheeks.

"Thank you for your faith, Miss Alice."

She moves in for another hug and whispers, "You know I worry for you. And I love you."

"I love you more."

My eyes are welling as I step away, and my mind races. Now I've got to go into the dining hall and speak to *him*. What has he heard in my absence? What will he think of me? The more he hears...

I'm distracted from my worry by Rachel and Maura, who step into the kitchen through the back door, bearing a large pot of stew. Rachel is a year younger than Dot, and Maura two. Dot is closer to them than I am, so when she sees them, she rushes over. I think of the questions Dot just asked me and cringe. If I stay, there'll be more of that, so I head off into the dining hall.

Mrs. Dillon appears out of nowhere, looking a bit like a fat bird in a mauve dress and feather-adorned pillbox hat. Her perfume is overwhelming. My head aches as she hugs me. "Oh you poor, unlucky dearie!"

Over her shoulder, I see Declan standing by his table. Old Mr. Button has him by the arm.

"We searched for days," Mrs. Dillon murmurs. "Days and days."

As she releases me, I hear my name called. I turn to find Rachel coming out the kitchen's swinging doorway. Her blonde hair's done up in dozens of tiny braids. As she throws herself at me, I smell something sweet—perhaps her lotion.

"So delighted," she cries.

Mrs. Dillon pats me on the shoulder, taking her leave, as Rachel smooths her hand over my hair. "You look a bit thinner but essentially the same! Not at all as if you've been trapped underground." She squeals, hugging me again. "How are you feeling?"

Rachel means well. This I know. So I oblige her, answering her questions while attempting to behave politely. I'm prattling on about our luck finding a stream in the cave when I feel something behind me.

Then his hand is on my shoulder. I know it's him without turning my head. I know because the blood drains from my cheeks and my poor heart throbs sickly.

I turn to him slowly, aware that Rachel's eyes are on us both.

Oh, but he's a sight up close; he looks so clean and strong and handsome. I tell myself I've got to behave casually, and so of course my eyes well. I stare at the stubble on his jaw before I feel mellowed enough to meet his gaze. So blue. In the dark, I couldn't tell how blue his eyes are.

His mouth twitches. "Finley."

I feel like I'm in a film as I say, "Hi there." I shift my gaze to Rachel. "Have you met Declan?"

She beams, buoyant as a schoolgirl. She holds her hand out. "Not exactly." Declan takes it, and I can see he's not sure what to do with it. He gives it a slight shake before Rachel tucks her arms around herself.

"We're all so elated that you made it back safely! How are you feeling?" she asks.

He looks tired about the eyes, but he says, "Good." His voice is low and warm. It sounds sincere.

Rachel smiles, glad as you please. "I'm delighted to hear it. Now that you're above ground, nothing but the very best. Would you like tea or coffee? Finley, you as well. What can I get the two of you?" Her cheeks blush, much as mine do.

"I'm satisfied as I am. Thank you."

"I'm good too. Just had some cinnamon..." He frowns, as if he's forgotten the name.

"Milk toast." Rachel laughs. "I can't believe they served him milk toast." She makes a face at me. Behind her hand, she tells him, "We've much better."

He smiles. "It was just fine."

"You're unfailingly polite."

"Nah. Just hard-up for anything that's not an Atkins bar."

I watch as Rachel's face transforms in understanding. "That's what you had in your pack?" she asks me. "Those horrid bars for

Mr. McGillin?" She laughs, looking beautiful as her lips curve. Youthful and unencumbered...

I watch Declan's eyes. That's how I find they're not on her.

"Get yourself some French toast," she's telling Declan. "Or Miss Alice's berry muffins. They're the absolute best." She waves as she turns to go.

I feel as if I'm caught inside a dream as she walks off and I look up at Declan. At least his gaze still feels familiar even as the rest of him looks like a polished stranger.

"You look...clean," I manage.

His eyes search my face. When he fails to find whatever he's seeking, his dark brows notch. "Let's step outside."

Even his soft voice sends sunlight rolling through me. It's soft and husky, and it's Declan. Odd and disorienting what a premium my poor heart seems to place on that alone: his mere Declanness. The blood in my veins glows as I follow him toward the door, barely aware of the room swirling around us.

Outside, we move past a group of school-aged kids kicking a bean sack on the porch. They whistle and clap as if we're celebrities—well, as if we *both* are. I can feel their eyes on my back as I follow Declan through a patch of grass into the muddy lane. He leads me around about the side of the café, away from eager eyes.

When we're there, his keen gaze sweeps me. I fixate on his lips, and then a bruise along his cheekbone.

"Are you okay?" He's frowning.

"Of course."

"Are you, though?"

"I am. Why do you ask?" My heart pounds so hard, I worry a bit for myself.

"You look like a ghost, Finley. When I touched your shoulder in there, your whole body tensed up. You won't look at me."

And I didn't return to him last night.

I look into his eyes and find them cool, his prince's face unreadable.

"I don't know. I suppose I'm trying to keep...proper."

"Where'd you go last night?"

I can see the hurt in his hard features. It's there in the tightness of his jaw. He looks down at his shoes, and my gaze follows. They're boots, made of brown leather, and they look quite fine. I watch as a breath moves through his thick shoulders.

Then those piercing eyes are holding mine. He blinks, biting his cheek on the inside. There's something like the shadow of a smile, as if he'd like to but he can't. And he says, "It's okay." I can tell he means it, which is sort of awful.

"No it's not. I'm sorry." I'm looking at my own shoes now—worn Mary Janes. "I went to the clinic, and the visitors were there late. Then I worried you were sleeping." I swallow hard and force myself to look up at him. "How are you feeling? Did you rest?"

He rubs a hand back through his hair, revealing scabbed gashes across his knuckles. "I'm okay."

I can hear the tightness in his voice. His face, though, is flawlessly impassive.

"I need to give you a check-over. Particularly your blood pressure, and I'd like a look at that shoulder. Could you come to the clinic in a bit, perhaps? Or I could come to you if you'd prefer."

It's there for a mere instant: the tiniest chink in his armor. His brows crease and his mouth tightens before he locks it all away. He nods once, jaw hard.

"Yeah, sure," he says in forced tones. "I'll come by."

"To the clinic? Will that be all right? I've got to make a house call. Afterward, I'll be there all day."

"Not a problem." His jaw remains hard as his gaze laps at me. "You feel okay, Siren? You sure?"

I nod, as I can't seem to speak.

"Good."

I can feel how much he wants to touch me as he starts to turn away. How much it hurts him as he walks around the café. His body moves with easy grace, but I just know. He rounds the café's front, and I hear voices rise in greeting.

Fog kisses my face. I take a few steps back, pressing my shoulder blades against the café's white-washed brick wall. For the longest time, I stand there alone.

Soon, he'll understand. But I can't tell him.

TWENTY-THREE
DECLAN

After I talk to Finley, I kind of lose my grip on things. It's like walking on a wire from one high-rise to the other. I can't look down. I don't have good balance.

If I'm not paying attention, my teeth chatter. My hands always shake, so I have to keep them fisted or shoved in a pocket. Someone wants to shake one, and I have to squeeze them hard enough so they can't tell. The space behind my forehead feels empty, and there's a heaviness behind my eyes that reminds me a little bit of being drunk. It's hard to keep them open sometimes, nearly impossible to act normal.

Following a conversation makes my chest go tight just from the effort of it. I try to smile and laugh at the right times, but time's not steady for me. Sometimes it rushes by, a breaking wave that kind of startles me with its fast passage. Other times, it feels as thick as honey. I know it's just detox—this shit's always like a bad trip—but that doesn't keep my mouth from going dry, my palms from sweating. Doesn't make it any easier to thank the cook and try to keep track of who to say bye to before I walk out on my plastic legs.

I've gotta drive back to the cottage. I make it past the village before pulling over to get sick. My palms are wet around the steering wheel. Inside the house, I walk past a box of fruits and veggies someone brought this morning and sit on the couch's edge to take my shoes off. When my fingers shake too much to do the laces, I lie back with them still on, stare at the ceiling.

Now's one of those moments where everything feels big and forceful. I feel kind of untethered. Need to sleep, but I don't think I can. I lie on my side. My mind races, all bad stuff and nonsense. My shoe connecting with Laurent's ribs, and his blood sinking into that rug. Walking into my shared bathroom. The haunted feeling stalks me across time.

I can't help but think of Finley. She looked like a painting come to life wearing that beige blouse with her hair down. I cover my face with both hands.

Don't.

I can't hang onto anything else, though. I get a pillow, hold it to my chest, and close my eyes.

"Try to relax, darling."

I think of her hands in mine, and it works like a pill.

I'm extra grateful for the little bit of sleep when I wake up mid-afternoon and can't stop shaking. My joints hurt so much, I can barely move. Somehow I make it to the tub and sink into the hot water. I stay there for hours, running more hot water when it cools.

When I awaken to a dark room and a quiet cottage, I pull some clothes on and step onto the back porch. A crescent moon hangs over the cliffs. A long way below, waves break against the rock. I pull my boots off and walk over the scrubby grass with my bare feet. I fold my arms and press my lips together till the tightness in my throat abates a little.

Then I go into the kitchen, open the cutlery drawer. They're there on the countertop, though—knives encased in a wood block.

I choose a chef's knife and an apple. Wash the apple. Wash my arm. I prop it on the counter, palm up. Shut my eyes as I run the tip over the soft hump of my veins. *Median cubital...cephalic.* Old friends.

I get a good, deep breath just feeling that slight sting. I can't put it where I want it, though—not if I want to wear short sleeves when I help dig trenches for the cable.

I roll up my shirt sleeve to the shoulder. My heart pounds. My lungs lock up.

With my fingers bent around the blade and the tip held at a slight angle, I press down, take a deep, slow breath, and draw a line around the inside of my bicep. The release is not unlike what Finley's hands did for me. In the rush I get right after, I laugh. Didn't even check for gauze...

But she's got some. I wrap it. Think of taking Advil for the joint pain, then decide I want to feel it.

I clean the knife off. Slide it back into the block. Then I use the paring knife to peel the apple.

I like apples.

I like cigarettes.

I put my boots back on and head into the dark.

Finley

"And then?"

"And then he kissed me!" Holly grins like a naughty child, and I stop breathing—and walking—on the right side of Upper Lane.

"Did he really?" I ask when I can breathe.

Baby presses against my legs, reminding me I still possess them.

Holly nods, still smiling smugly.

"He kissed you on the lips?" The gray clouds tilt.

"Well, no—not on the lips of course. How forward would that be? His mouth was here..." She points to her forehead, and I begin to burn.

"As you were dancing?"

She nods, red lips still upturned smugly. "As we were dancing."

Holly whirls and skips ahead of me, her yellow skirt bouncing around her lean legs. "Homer Carnegie kissed me," she sing-songs.

We're en route to the Brauns' cottage, so I've no choice but to follow along behind her. "And you were drinking liquor?"

"Just a bit." She grins over her shoulder. "Dot saw, too. You should have seen her green eyes."

Holly's smirk makes me feel as if I'm running out of air. I tug at my collar.

"Why...would he be doing that?" It's asked more to myself than her.

"Well, he is an athlete," she says, "but I've heard athletes can be quite unruly off the field. Maura told Blair and me that she looked him up just weeks ago back on the café computer and the world wide web still painted him as quite the bad boy."

Holly gives a little growl, complete with cat-scratch miming. "Blair danced with him near as much as I did. Little trollop. She's so twiggy, though, and all the acne..." Holly shrugs, and I gape at her back.

"I can't believe you said that."

"Well I'm only speaking truth! She's lovely on the inside, but that doesn't matter, does it? Not for dancing..."

I'd quite like to strangle Holly.

My new...*ignited* feeling doesn't leave me. Not as we wash the sore on Mr. Braun's foot nor as we pretend to savor Mrs. Braun's flavorless porridge. Nor when we walk back to the clinic, where we work our way through several more appointments. Holly stands as my assistant at times. Today she offered. I know why now.

When she leaves at four-thirty to "get a soak" in preparation for the night's festivities, I drop into a crouch and rub Baby around her soft ears.

"Everything is horrid. Simply horrid," I whisper against her fluff.

Declan never dropped by the clinic on that first day we were back. The next morning, I had planned to seek him out after I stopped at the warehouse to get a bit more washing soap. There I heard Tad Price and Weston Green discussing how they'd spent time at the bar with "Homer." Maura laughed behind the counter, revealing she was there as well.

"Some of us were there much later than you teenieboppers," she said, haughty. "Mr. Brenton didn't lock the door till half past two. He's quite enamored with our new friend, much as anyone. He had Homer signing cards."

I left the depot with a sinking feeling, but that didn't stop me seeking him out. I'm the fill-in for Doctor, therefore it's my duty to check up on Declan. I found his green Land Rover parked at Mrs. White's and later heard he'd taken an interest in her orchids. After that, he and Mayor Acton walked the village, charting a course for the new cable. I lost track of him during a house call, but someone said he'd been invited to supper with Rachel's older sister and her husband, Steven, the village electrician.

The next day, Monday, the crew began digging trenches right at dawn and worked quite late. That was the first night Holly saw him at the bar, although I suppose he might have gone before.

Yesterday, I walked over to the digging site—they're moving

slowly along Lower Lane—and delivered some of the goodies people baked for me. I'll never eat them all. Some of the men thanked me, but Declan scarcely looked up.

Now, having heard what Holly reported, I feel...horrid. There's no other word. My throat aches. I feel ill at ease in my own skin.

When the phone rings, I rush over to it. I don't feel the normal flare of dread accompanying calls that come when Doctor's gone, because there's dread inside my heart already.

I answer, and who is it but the man himself?

"Finley. How are you?"

"I'm quite well. How are you?"

"Head above water," he says. "Went on a short trip, so I've been away the last two days. I had my mobile phone of course."

"I didn't call."

"How are you faring? How is everything?" He means the patients.

"Everyone is well enough. Mr. Braun has got another foot sore. Holly helped me irrigate it."

"Is there pus?"

"Not much at all. We caught it early, and I applied the Bacitracin."

"Very well then." There's a pause in which my senses prickle. Then he says, in low tones, "What of our Homer?"

I swallow at his use of the word *our*. "Honestly...I don't quite know. I asked him to the clinic for a check-up and he never dropped in."

Static cracks between us. I imagine a line stretching over the ocean. "Wonder if he's got something from somewhere else."

"Something?" I ask.

"A sort of painkiller. Tell me there was nothing at your Gammy's house."

"Of course not. Why would there be? I'd have moved it here if there had been."

"At least you've some sense."

I swallow my retort. It's always better not to anger Doctor.

"Is he draining the bar dry?"

"I'm not sure. I don't go there, you know."

"Yes, but have you ears?"

I grit my teeth. "I've not heard that. That he's draining it dry."

"But is he going?"

"That I *have* heard."

"Well, it makes a bit of sense, then. If he doesn't want a check-up, you can't force him. Let him be."

"I will."

We talk a bit more before someone knocks on the door. It's a fine excuse to end the call. I find Anna on the porch, holding a foil-covered plate, wearing a tired smile.

"Give me refuge. Kayti won't stop wailing. I had to get out or I'd have gone mad." She holds the plate out. "I made friendship bread. And iced it."

She gives me a wry smile, and I tug her inside. "It's cold and wet out. Take off your coat and sit a bit. We'll walk over—" I gesture to the adjoining house— "and I'll make you some chamomile with sugar," I say, teasing her in return for her icing jab.

"We need our sugar," she agrees. "It's all that keeps me going some days."

She leans down to stroke Baby. When she stands back up, she tilts her head, giving me a curious look. "You look like you need the icing, love. Why aren't you eating?"

"Oh, sod off, I'm eating plenty."

"You're a wretched liar."

"You're just wretched."

We step through the door into the house. Baby's hooves click on the hardwood floor behind us. Of all the homes here on the island, only Doctor's has hardwood. The rest have mostly cement flooring. I suppose the wood is meant to lure physicians. I find the clicking sound of it a bit unpleasant.

I fill the teapot and Anna slumps down at the kitchen table. She runs her hand over a braided placemat. "I like these. Where did they come from?"

"Gammy's. I thought they added a bit of something."

"Certainly. Makes the place more homey." She sighs. "Tell me, Finley. Tell me what's the matter. I can see it plainly."

I set the teapot on the stove, glad for an excuse to put my back to her. "Nothing is."

"You've had quite a week. Are you terribly tired?" When I turn around, her lovely Anna face is soft. "Are you lonely? Was it very frightening to be below the ground? You never really told me."

My eyes fill with tears, and Anna rushes up to hug me. "Oh, I'm sorry, dearie."

I weep only for a moment. When she pulls away, her freckled face is filled with understanding. "It makes perfect sense that it... reminded you."

I nod and swallow, staring at the floor.

"It's good at least you weren't alone. Freddy helped with the digging today and said Declan is a humble, kind man. Not at all like what you might imagine."

I nod.

"Have you spoken much with him? Are you two dear friends now?"

I press my lips together and shrug. I have to summon all my courage to lie compellingly to Anna. "We are friends, I would say. It was good to have him with me. He was always kind and understanding, just as Freddy said."

"I'm so glad of that. I suppose you heard about the dinner tomorrow?"

"Come again?"

"They're doing a dinner for you—for the two of you. Celebratory. It's at the Burger Joint." Anna laughs, and I realize I'm scowling.

"Don't you want to tell the story one more time?" She grins. "About the Atkins bars and how you dug fair Declan out?"

"I didn't dig him out."

She shrugs. "That's what he told Freddy. We all know you can be overmodest. At times," she teases.

"Do you think I ought to go?"

Anna chortles as she uncovers the plate she brought. "You'll have to at least stop in, you goose. You can sit with Freddy and me. Holly's working on the setup, and you can guess where she's seating herself."

I groan, and Anna makes a sympathetic face. "I know that's got to gnaw at you a bit. It's understandable."

I nod once. I've confided in Anna about my feelings regarding Declan's father and my mother. The strangeness of knowing Mum was telling me Prince Declan stories just before he and his father arrived. And she'd been writing letters to Charles Carnegie. It's quite difficult to name the feeling it brings me. I suppose it's one of...fate. Making me think of the oddness of it. If they'd survived the outing on the boat, would I have grown up in America?

I can't put my thoughts into words, so I nod again. "I can't imagine losing Holly or Dot," I say softly.

"I can't imagine being swept away." She smiles, a bit dreamy, and I think of the seething ocean—not of Declan—as I say, "I wouldn't want to be."

I make Anna's tea, and we eat too much friendship bread. She heads home a bit after nine, and I tuck in early, falling right away into a dream in which I'm locked inside the clinic, pacing the wide room alone as my hair grows down past my backside and turns gray. Doctor grabs my backside, his hand squeezing.

Sometime after midnight, noise breaks through the dreaming. I open my eyes to find Baby curled up on the rug beside the bed. As I sink back into dreamland, I hear it once more: the sound of someone knocking. A peek out the door reveals an empty stoop.

TWENTY-FOUR
DECLAN

"So how was she?"

I stop with my foot on the shovel and look across the trench at Mark. He's got his cap off, re-tying the red bandana he wears as a sweatband underneath.

"How was who?" I get another scoop of dirt and toss it over my shoulder.

"Oh, you know...the doctor's lady."

I frown. "Finley?"

He nods, fitting his cap back over the bandana. He goes back to digging on his side. I look up and down the trench. With the island's only mechanical digger broken, we've spread out, one person digging every four or five feet on opposite sides of the trench.

"What're you getting at?" I ask quietly, because I don't want to draw more eyes and ears.

He gives a chuckle, as if he knows my uncouth implication. "I'm asking how *is* she. Did she give an ordinary sort of appearance? I only ask because the missus and I are seldom ill, and so I've never heard her speak."

I hold my breath a second, trying not to let frustration cross my face. Sometimes it's hard to understand the thick Tristanian accent, and I've got a searing headache. "I'm not sure I get it, man."

"Finley—she's the mute."

"What?"

He smiles. "Ahh, so then you hadn't heard. I suppose I've answered my own question." He looks satisfied and resumes digging.

I dig for another minute while my head throbs and my body does that shit where it feels like it's flickering. Then I can't help myself. "Mark—what did you say?"

He looks up. "What part then? Ms. White Coat being mute?"

"You said *mute*?"

"Not anymore of course. That's been a few years past. Before her time in the schoolhouse ended, Doctor arrived, she got helping at the clinic, and she resumed speaking. When she was a younger girl, she didn't speak. I don't suppose she told you."

My throat tightens. "No." I keep digging, harder now. I wrap my hand around the shovel's handle till my knuckles ache. "She didn't speak at all?" I ask him tightly.

"It was the queerest thing. Her parents—they both passed on in sort of tragic fashion. Drowned with her there in the boat when she was just a wee one. Though I suppose your father and you were here visiting when that went on. I remember that. Do you?"

I nod. "I was six, so I remember some of it."

"When we got her back, she wasn't right up there." He points to his head, and my stomach does a slow roll.

"What do you mean?"

He throws some dirt over his shoulder. "Didn't speak a word for I don't know how long, suppose near ten years."

Ten years.

My hands shake so hard I can barely hold the shovel.

"So what, then one day she just...started talking?"

"Something like that. Her grandmother was a lovely woman. Helped her quite a bit. I've heard she passes as quite ordinary now, but I've never spoken to her. Wondered if she had a voice at all."

"She has a voice." His bushy brows lift, and I realize my tone was too sharp. I force a laugh to cover for it. "Trust me on that."

That gets me a chuckle. "All the woe-men do."

I feign another laugh and dig as fast and hard as I can. By lunchtime, I've run through all the dirt in my path. I pull my jeans off, revealing running shorts, and swap my boots for Nike sneakers.

"Be back," I tell the group's de facto leader as I pass him.

He gives me a thumbs up, and I'm gone. We're at the Patches side of Lower Lane, and this time, I take off out that way. Other days, I've run up to the cottage, beyond a small plateau on top of the cliffs that rise up just behind it, past the hardened black lava field—a relic from the 1961 eruption—and toward the ponds. I've done that run a few times, and I know I can make it back to the trench spot inside an hour.

Today, though, I don't want to pass the clinic on the other side of Lower Lane, so I run along the lonely road that points toward the Patches. On my right, the ocean swirls and simmers like a vat of acid. Overhead, the thin clouds shift. Everything is cast in pale green light.

I run until my toes feel numb and the air seems to tremble. My heart hammers like it might explode behind my ribs. On the way back toward the village, I get sick beside some rocks. Small price to pay for a clear mind.

* * *

Using the shovel makes my shoulder hurt, which keeps my detox dick down. But the drive home gets me every fucking time. The car bounces over the rocky road, getting me half hard. The walk from the car to the cottage's front door drags my boxer briefs over my head and shaft. Then I'm standing in the living room, sweaty and shaking from the long day, feeling weird and empty and not real, my dick ripping a hole in the briefs.

I've got a routine going. Kick off boots, get some water, limp back to the bathroom. By then I feel like I'm rolling with some blue diamond on board. Once, I almost blew before I got my pants off. Run the bathtub water, sink into the tub, and finally, I get a chance to squeeze it.

I run the water hot so it'll burn and I'll last longer. Never works. I squeeze my head and stroke my shaft. My fingers wander over my big, puffed-out balls, and that's all I'm good for.

It's intense. So much so, I don't think much. There's no time to work up fantasies. I imagine shoving inside a hot, slick pussy, but it's just a pussy. Ghost pussy. Belongs to no one.

If I'm lucky, I'll pass out for a few minutes. Slip into the water...slip into a fifteen minute dream state. When it's over, I feel rested. That's where I am now. Fifteen minutes of good shut-eye is a game changer.

I climb out of the tub feeling more alert than I have all day. I dry off with one of the good-smelling towels and lie on her sweet-smelling bed and cover myself with the blankets she tucked around me that afternoon when we first got back. I just have to hold on for an hour, until it's late enough to not stick out for being at the bar.

I feel worse the longer I'm at the house alone. Fucking pathetic.

I walk down to the village at six-thirty and walk back around midnight or one. Don't want to be the first in, don't ever want to be the last one out. The bar guy's got my back. I think he gets it that I only ever want the one drink: Macallan 18 in a snifter, always at the tail end of the night.

I'm halfway down the hill that leads from the cottage to the bar when I see Holly coming toward me in the dark. That's when I remember what night it is. The dinner thing started at six. The thing to celebrate our "escape."

I'm sweating as I talk and try to laugh with Holly on the walk down to the little place the locals call the Burger Joint.

Bikes and a few cars line Middle Lane before we reach the yellow building. People spill through the front doors, over the porch, into the dirt-patched grass. They're playing country music. Holly takes my hand, and I see her friend Dorothy smiling on the porch. When she presents me with a mini bottle of Rumple Minze, I toss it back.

* * *

Finley

"Well, your partner in crime has finally arrived, and he's downed the mini bottle of liquor the Australian tourist gave Dot at Christmas."

Anna slides back into our booth and takes Kayti from Freddy. I watch Kayti lift her fuzzy head from Anna's shoulder.

"Dot gave Declan her liquor?"

Anna makes an odd smirk.

Freddy shakes his head. "She's shameless."

"Perhaps more so than Holly, which is quite a feat," Anna says.

Half-hour ago, Holly went in search of Declan, claiming

they're dear friends and she felt she should be the one to fetch him from Gammy's.

I clench my teeth, then bring my Coke's straw to my lips and have a nice, long sip. "Well," I say when finished, "I suppose it's good he arrived."

"How long since you've seen him, Finley?" Anna pats Kay's back.

"Mm, not quite sure. Perhaps five days...or six."

"I'm a bit surprised you haven't spent more time together," Freddy says. He takes a large bite of his burger, and I want to slap him with the mustard-covered bun.

"Perhaps we had our fill of one another." The words escape my mouth before my brain can screen them. I feel the blood drain from my cheeks. *Perfect.*

"Look at her." Anna points, and Freddy's gaze lands on my face. "I think she should be checked over. You're not yourself since getting back, and who could blame you?"

"I'm exhausted," I say. There's no need to fake the edge in my voice. "Everyone falling, stabbing themselves, getting impregnated." I roll my eyes and tuck a strand of hair behind my ear.

"It has been a busy few days," Anna says. "Is Audrey excited?"

I keep up as best I can while watching Holly, Dot, Declan, that horrid Bea, and Mike Green file through the doorway. They settle somewhere out of my range of vision.

I feel tethered to the booth. My brain's a fog.

Mayor Acton comes to the table, giving me a basket of bread made by Mrs. Acton and a round of fresh congratulations.

While I swallow leaden bites of burger, someone starts the music. Rachel and Mike push booths out of the way, and although I try not to look, I glimpse Dot drag Declan out onto the mock dance floor.

He's wearing a white shirt, which only enhances his dark beauty.

As time creeps by, people stop to hug and greet me. My head pounds. My chest feels funny, like there's something wedged behind my sternum. A short time later, I frown down at the pager I keep on hand. Then I hold it up toward Anna.

She gives me an "oh no" look. I make a sad face, as if I'm disappointed, and just liket hat, my freedom has been earned.

I head into the kitchen, past the phone table, and out the kitchen's back door, which leads into a short hall that smells perpetually of grease. I stop in front of the battered wood doors marked with smears of pink and blue paint. Laughter bleeds from below the pink one. I feel my cheeks burn with emotion, and I know I've got to get away before I boil over.

With no time to make it onto the back porch, I duck into the supply closet, where I press my back against the door and sink slowly to my haunches. With my forehead against my knees, I cross myself and let the tears flow.

Stone the cows!

I push my hands into my hair the way he does and curl over, letting out a muffled sob. *I messed it all up! Every shred of...everything.*

I think of Declan coming through the door with Dot and Holly, and I want to rage. For what my life is. For the mockery I only now can see. I think of Mum and Hudson, Mum and my father. I think of the village's elderly—often a widow or a widower, though sometimes a couple. I think of how they squabble. How they smile together. I think of the ones alone—widowed or never wed—and how we bury them alone and they have small, square, solitary grave stones. I think of my grave stone.

"*Finley.*"

My body freezes and I start to tremble, shaken as if I'd heard a phantom speak. I lift my head slowly, half expecting that. But there he is, so tall and strong and handsome, leaned against the closet's back wall with his arms folded in front of his chest.

His face is grave. His face is flawless. His eyes hold to mine until I lose my self-control, and my gaze rushes up and down him. *Declan!* He looks taller, broader than I recall from in the burrow. Clad in a long-sleeved gray tee shirt that clings to his chest, chino-style pants that hang from his hips, and black boots, he looks like the worldly man he really is. He blinks, and my heart gallops with such force I feel it behind my eyes.

How is he here? Something like panic grips me as I rise to my feet. One look at him and I feel blown wide open. So much so, I can't bear it.

As I turn toward the door, I feel him step to my side.

"What's the matter, Finny?"

My heart pounds fast and hard, and I can scarcely keep my voice steady as I whisper, "Nothing of significance."

What a liar I've become. I can't look at him, have even shut my eyes. "You never showed up at the clinic," I whisper.

In the ensuing silence, my blood crashes between my ears.

"You didn't come and find me either." The rumble of his low voice makes me shiver, and I think dimly, *this is what they speak of.* He's standing so close now, I feel the heat of him.

"I never said I would." I wrap my hand around the doorknob.

Declan's hand touches my elbow. "Hey...why won't you look at me?"

I do, then. I look at his face, and I'm arrested. It's illogical. Insensible. It shouldn't be this way. I shouldn't feel he's air and water.

His gaze is searing, as if he hears my thoughts. I tear my greedy eyes away from the vortex of his. I'd like to not look at him, but I can't stop myself from taking in his dark brows and his predatory eyes, the feline-high cheekbones and sultry mouth. He's got no business with a mouth like that—a woman's lush lips.

I note the prickle of his shadow...the dark smudges beneath his eyes. And then my belly clenches as I realize *he looks ill*.

My hand goes to his cheek, the pad of my thumb brushing the sharp stubble there at his jaw. His eyes shut, as if it pains him. As I lower my hand, he seals his long fingers around my wrist. His grip loosens, feather-light. His jaw clenches.

When he speaks, the words are whisper-soft, nearly inaudible. "You should go."

I've never touched a man so tenderly, never felt the urge except with him. So I'm holding my breath as I lift my hand, letting my fingers brush his dark hair. His fevered eyes meet mine again, and I feel the closet tilt around us as my fingers stroke his forehead.

His eyes shut. I watch his jaw flicker with tension. And then he wraps an arm around me, pulls me to him. With my body pressed to his, he steps toward the door, bracing one big palm against the doorframe as his hips push against mine. I feel a prodding thickness at the curve of my hip for a mere instant before he shifts himself away.

"Finley—go." The words are ragged. He looks tired and strained, his blue eyes barely open as he stands there with his fists at his sides, his erection jutting at the fabric of his pants.

I turn to go, but I can't open the door. I feel my legs tremble the merest bit, weakness vibrating from the knees. And then he steps behind me. His chest brushes my shoulder blades, and I feel the stiffness of his sex against my backside.

"Tell me to stop."

When I don't, his arm slides around my waist. His hand spreads over my ribs as his mouth moves in my hair, his warm breath making something pulse between my legs. His cheek presses atop my head as his hand delves under my blouse, his rough palm moving over my bare belly.

"Tell me no," he rasps, rocking his forehead against my hair.

When I don't—I *can't*—he presses my backside against his sex.

"Finley..."

His hand on my belly trembles. My head spins. I understand it now—the power other women speak of. Declan's breaths are ragged pants at my ear. I don't know why he didn't come to me; he sought me out not once since we spoke outside the café the day after arriving back. And suddenly it doesn't matter. Doesn't matter that it's sinful and beyond forbidden, doesn't matter that I mustn't.

Declan.

Behind me, he's big and thick and sturdy. With each of his breaths, I feel his long erection nudged against the curve of my buttocks. He lifts the hair off my neck and begins to kiss me there.

His mouth is soft and hot, his fingers gentle as they stroke above the button of my pants. He sucks at my neck. I'm not sure I like it. Then I'm moaning. *Saints be praised!* It feels like he's...biting me.

His fingers delve into my pants. They're stroking lightly as his lips brush my ear. I'm aware I'm panting, but I can't stop. His big hand strokes lower, low enough that he's there at the top of my underpants.

"I've been wanting this." His low words vibrate by my ear. He nips gently at the lobe, and his deft fingers pet me. His breaths come heavy as he strokes my soft curls. His large body quakes behind mine. He trails one finger lower, pressing his thickness against my backside as he very, very gently strokes my most forbidden place.

"Siren..." He sounds desperate as he rocks against me.

I push my rear against him. He groans roughly, and his fingers part me. His mouth stills on my throat, and with his gusted breaths there near my ear, he dips a fingertip into my crevice and paints gently up and down.

Exquisite pleasure rolls through my legs. They give way. His arm is tight about my waist, holding me against him as his lips drift over my shoulder. His hand makes me quiver and gasp. He rolls his finger around something that lights up the world, causing me to lose myself for an electric moment. Then he drags his finger gently downward, resting right there, where I—

"Fuck, Siren."

He prods right where I'm slick and needy. The sounds coming from my throat are foreign to me. Wanton. When he pushes his sex against my backside, I rock against him, eager for unnamed relief. And then his finger curls, pushing inside me.

He hugs me against him as bliss unfurls within me. I feel so full and...good. I hear a ragged gasp—my own—as his thick finger pushes deeper. He's doing something...else. Up at the other place —*my clitoris*. It makes me cry out.

"Quiet." His breath shakes. "Gotta...stay quiet, okay?"

I whimper, feeling almost fearful at the pressure building beneath his hand. He does something to my clit that makes me rock against him. As I do, his finger in me strokes, and I can't help a ragged groan.

"Someone's going to hear," I whimper.

"Nah. Just stay quiet."

I bite my cheek as his thumb grazes my clit, and his finger delves still deeper. My legs quake. My body sweats and tenses.

"Ohh!"

"You're okay, Siren. I've got you." I feel his arm secure around me, his thickness behind me. And then his thumb performs some witchery. He drags his finger partway out and pushes in again, and at the same time, his thumb circles me. Pure, ecstatic bliss streaks through me as my hot flesh pulses, followed by a wave of throbbing pleasure so intense I lose track of my mind and body.

When I come into myself again, I'm trembling and breathless, feeling like I might weep. He's easing his hand out of my panties, still hugging me against him.

I whimper his name. He kisses my hair, and then my shoulder. One hand cups my hip. His lips are pressed against the top of my head. I can feel his breath there.

"Jesus, Siren..."

I turn around—too bashful to look at his face—and then I do, and he gives me a small, heartrending smile. He folds me against his chest, and there I feel the rhythm of his breaths: a bit unsteady. I can hear the thunder of his heart. His chin is tucked atop my head. His shirt is warm and damp under my cheek.

I laugh—a small, soft sound—and hug him.

That was...bliss. It was the greatest thing I've ever felt.

His arms around me tighten. As he strokes his hands down my back, I can feel the shaking in his fingers.

"How're you feeling?" It's a whisper.

He runs a hand over my hair, smoothing the tresses down against my nape the way he often does. I can sense the answer in the way his fingers hesitate before he says, "I'm okay."

I want to tell him I can't get the medicine he needs. That I tried and failed. But I decide against the mention of it. I've only ever craved sweets...and Mum, but when I'm wanting something badly, mention of it hurts.

I stroke a hand down his back. I've closed my eyes, and I'm working on discerning whether I can feel his thickness pressed against my hip when he murmurs, "You should go first."

I swallow as my eyes well. My heart aches with too much want for a body to manage. I feel so satiated in his arms. Once I step away from the anchor of him, I'll be lost again.

I feel as if I'm stepping out of myself as I step back. Our gazes hold. His face is leaner. Sharper. I can see it plainly, and it makes my heart bleed.

My throat stings as I rasp, "Thank you."

"Of course."

There's a certain sweetness on his face, a gentle boyishness about his small smile. *Imagine if I'd met him in the schoolhouse.* The thought hurts, so I wipe it away, giving him a tremulous smile before I push back through the door.

TWENTY-FIVE
FINLEY

There's only five of us at morning mass: old Mr. Button, Mrs. Adams with the poodle hair, Mrs. Dillon on the organ, Father Barnard, and myself. Father Barnard wears his purple Lenten vestment with the small stain on the left sleeve and blows his nose four times on a kerchief.

I wear a mint-green dress that snags a few times on a rough spot on the pew. The dress is one of those we received last year in a mass order. The green was my size; I look fair in green, so I bid for it. Many of the dresses were for smaller girls...like Holly. I won't think of her now. Not in church.

I clutch my favorite rosary—the one with ocean blue glass beads that belonged to Gammy's mum—and steer my inner monologue so it flows from the blessing to dismissal to my silent prayers after I've bid everyone goodbye.

O my Jesus, forgive us of our sins. Save us from the fires of hell. Lead all souls into heaven, especially those most in need of thy mercy.

I can whip through the rosary more quickly than an auctioneer, but I work through the prayers slowly as I trek from Upper

Lane to Lower in the soft, blue morning. The words are like an incantation, warding off all thought, obstructing sorrow. I don't notice until I reach the clinic that the morning's oddly quiet and cold enough to numb my ears and mouth and nose.

I slip the key into the lock on the door of the residence, and I hear Baby's hooves click. When I step inside, her warm, wee body presses to my stockings.

"Hi there, fluffins."

She peers up at me with her sheepy eyes, and I crouch down beside her.

"There's my wee ewe." I stroke her soft head, and she presses against my dress. "Did you miss your Mummy?"

She peers up at me, and I think she looks happy.

If nothing else, I still have Baby. I've made her a leash and collar out of a bit of red canvas I fashioned for her at the sewing machine. I attached a pink and red hair bow to the collar last night after my crying jag was over. It was mine when Mummy was still here. I laugh every time I look at Baby in her collar.

I spent the remainder of the night baking. Now I pack it all into a woven wood basket. I spend some time poking through the bathroom cabinet as Baby rubs her fluffy self against the coolness of the tub.

"You silly ewe, you."

We emerge with several of my favorite oils and tinctures. In the kitchen, with Baby pressed snugly against my legs, I write out instructions for my favorite vodka-based sleeping tincture, which includes a bit of skull cap, ashwagandha, chamomile, hops, and rhodiola root. I label a bottle of capsules filled with valerian, and two others containing B-vitamin and magnesium supplements (both being good for the mind). Then I've got a bit of passion-flower. I toss in some melatonin and Unisom for good measure, along with a note explaining he ought not use all the remedies at once.

After that, I walk into the bedroom, where at the bottom of the quilt-clad bed there is a purple velvet blanket folded into a large square. I scoop it up and hug it to me as Baby looks on.

"This is Mummy's special blanket. Gammy made it for me with the weight inside it long ago, and recently I re-covered it with this fabric." It smells of lavender and feels like home.

Biting my lip, I roll the blanket tightly, bind it with a strand of white ribbon I braid into my hair for weddings and receptions, and wedge it into the picnic basket alongside soup, breads, and cookies. I pack in a jug of my honeyed green tea and load it into Doctor's white Land Rover. It had been with Gregory Green, who was patching an oil leak, but I got it back late yesterday evening.

With the passenger's seat scooted back and Baby standing like a fluffin princess in the floorboard, I drive up to Gammy's cottage. His Land Rover is there—of course it would be—but I don't let that deter me. I walk to the small porch, set the basket down, and ring the doorbell once. Then I drive off.

He'll take us from here. If he doesn't reach out—and I doubt he will, based on history—it's quite possible I might never speak to him again.

* * *

I start making bargains with myself. I didn't see him yesterday after I dropped the basket off. If I don't see him today—Thursday —and I likely won't, as I'm working through appointments at the clinic—I'll build on that; I won't seek him out tomorrow. I won't even walk near where they're digging.

If I don't see him either day, I'll tell myself it's well and truly over—for the best.

What happened in the closet was a moment of shameful weakness. For us both. He's still poorly. I'm the only one who knows about his suffering. I've soothed him before. And I'm that sort, besides.

There's a reason I became Doctor's assistant and de facto nurse. There's a reason I'm here cooing at a lamb clad in a diaper and a bow-bedazzled collar. I'm a nurturer. I remember pasting a Band-Aid onto Mummy's finger once, and she said, "You'll be like Gammy."

"How so?" I asked.

She smiled. "A healer."

Shortly after Mum and my father were lost, the island hired a licensed physician to live here fulltime, working on a two-year contract. As we cycled through doctors Ahuja, King, and Greer—who stayed for two "terms"—Gammy used her healing powers less and less, except to teach me tincture-making. But a healer she was. Mrs. White told me that way back when, she would take the mental cases and see to the infants. Gammy doctored wounds and sprains, crushed fingers and concussions and the like.

I feel warm, remembering my Gammy as I wait for Mrs. Glass to arrive at the clinic. She rings the bell, and I pull the door open to her radiant smile. Fluffy, fading red hair falls around her face. I look down and see that in the hand that's not propped on her cane, she's holding a Tupperware box.

"You didn't!"

"Well, you know I certainly did."

"Mrs. Glass." I tsk, then take the box of berry muffins as she coos at Baby, whom I pick up to ensure Mrs. Glass' safe passage through the waiting area and over to the first of the clinic beds. She's got something neurological that flares at times—something that resembles multiple sclerosis—but she won't leave the island for treatment. Not at her advanced age, she says, though she's only sixty-three.

She asks all about Baby as I conduct her monthly neurological exam, checking boxes off a photo-copied list on my clip-board for each question I should ask, each small test I should do. Doctor wrote it out for me before he left.

"I'd say you're as good as last time, at least your reflexes appear to be. Your eyes are holding strong, I believe. Tell me how you've been feeling?"

I listen as she discusses toileting and her numb toes.

"Mr. Glass has been massaging them as you suggested," she reports. "I believe that does help."

"Lovely of him."

She smiles proudly. "I did well."

"Mr. Glass is quite a fellow, that's true. What's he writing now?"

"A story for the younger boys, Asher and Josh." It's Jacob, but I don't correct her. "It's about a rogue penguin."

"That sounds delightful."

We work through the rest of her vitals, and she talks of winning a bag of freeze-dried strawberries at bingo and "that poor dear" Sarah, who styled her hair a bit wrong last week at the salon.

"I quite hope my cousin can instruct her a bit more before retiring."

"How has she been—Cindy? I last talked to her a few days back."

"You know how she is. Not a thing wrong with her," Mrs. Glass huffs.

"That's not true, though," I say gently. Cindy Glass has always suffered with depression.

"Mind over matter, as I see it."

"For Cindy it's more difficult, I believe."

She pats her hair, sighing. "Evidently."

And that's all that's spoken about that.

"How are you feeling?" she asks. "I can scarcely believe what happened with you and that Homer Carnegie. I heard he moved the boulders one by one until he cleared a path for those wide shoulders." She winks, and I feel a flush creep up my neck.

"We dug out at last. We were thrilled to see the sky."

"Oh, I'd imagine. He's not hard on the eyes, though, so I suppose the alternate view was near as good. A bit sinful perhaps, but quite memorable."

"Mrs. Glass." I tsk again as I pull the blood pressure cuff off her arm. "You're too naughty for me."

"How is Dr. Daniels? How's he faring?"

I update her on Doctor, who's away visiting his ill father.

"You must be exhausted. Ready for his return."

"Certainly so. But I'm faring quite nicely for the moment."

"It's a bit of pressure, I suppose. Bearing the responsibility for so many poorlys."

I laugh, and she smiles quite charmingly, and that's a person for you, I think—any person. Bits of good and bits of not-so-lovely. I've learned to take the bad with the good. It's all that one can ever really do. I find other people quite foreign—especially after years of silence—but there's almost always something to love.

I send Mrs. Glass away with a freeze-dried pack of strawberries Mayor Acton's sister gave me when she came by for assistance with an ingrown toenail.

As she starts toward her home, across the lane and two doors down, I hold Baby's hoof up in a wave. Mrs. Glass chortles.

A few moments after I step back into the clinic, I hear a soft thump outside. With a vision of dear Mrs. Glass tripping on the ramp, I yank the door open and nearly suffer heart arrhythmia.

Declan.

He's leaning over, his long arms bracing against the wooden rail beside the stairs. As I watch, wide-eyed, he turns his head toward me and straightens.

"Hi." A soft smile curves the corners of his mouth. His hair is messy, dimple showing. I realize he's wearing sport clothing and breathing like he's just been jogging.

"Hi." I can't help smiling, even as I realize with some horror it's the first time I've seen him since the closet.

He brings his hands together in front of him, and for a moment, I feel he looks perhaps a bit bashful. "Thank you for the basket."

My cheeks burn. I nod. "You're welcome. I'm glad you found it."

Something warm pushes at my calves.

"Baby." I scoop her up, holding her against my frantic heart. "She's a wee rascallian."

He grins. "She's what?"

"A wee rascallian." Now I'm blushing.

"What's a rascallian?" He look so smug, I'd like to pop him.

"I don't know. It's like a rascal I suppose." I pet Baby's head, then stroke her soft nose. "Your people created duck face." I smile up at him. "So don't you say a word."

His easy smile widens. "What's duck face?"

"You know...duck face."

"Show me." He smirks.

I give him my best ridiculous pout, and both his dimples show. "I scarcely noticed them inside the burrow." I nod at him.

His hand runs over his wild hair. "What?"

"The dimples. That one's deeper." I point to his left cheek.

He flattens his mouth and smooths his face out, giving me an exaggerated, "o"-lipped face. "I don't know what you're talking about," he says without moving his mouth.

I roll my eyes. "As if there's not a fan club for your dimples."

"What?" He looks a bit puzzled.

"Women adore dimples. It's a known fact."

"Is it?"

"Don't be a duck, Declan."

"I'm Declan again now?" He leans against the railing with a faint smile.

"Only because your surname is so tedious."

"Tedious?" I love the way his face lights up when I've surprised him. "You think so?" He's grinning now.

"That's what I said, I believe."

Baby squirms in my arms, and I set her down. She blinks up at Declan.

"Hey there." He kneels down beside her. I watch as he holds his palm to her face. "God, they have the softest noses." His eyes close a moment. Then he runs his hand over her head. "She glad to have you back?" He's looking up at me now.

"Over the moon. You, she's not so sure of."

He remains crouching there on the stoop. My eyes sweep his shoulders and my body warms uncomfortably.

"To what do we owe this honor?"

He stands, pulling something from his pocket. It's a small black packet. He holds it out, and I squint.

"Pop Rocks..." I take it from him. "What are Pop Rocks?"

He lifts his dark brows. "Guess you'll have to open them and see."

"Something edible?"

His dimple deepens. "Open them."

I tear along the top of the packet and peer inside at a pile of tiny, pink-red rocks.

"Here." He takes the packet, holds my gaze with his blue-gray one. "Hold your palm out, Siren." I do, and he shakes some of the candy pebbles into it.

"Now put those in your mouth."

I laugh. "I don't want to."

"Do it." He grins brilliantly.

"Is it going to hurt?"

"You think I would hurt you, Siren?" The seriousness on his

face makes my neck flush. When I stare skeptically down at the Pop Rocks, he pours some into his palm. "Here."

He puts them in his mouth and opens it wide—and I hear popping.

I laugh. "What?"

"C'mon..."

"Witchcraft!"

He closes his mouth, making a funny, smirky face, and I hear the pop-hiss of the candy.

I squeeze my eyes shut, pop my small handful into my mouth, and gape as they sizzle and fizz. "Stone the cows!" I say around them.

He laughs. "What?"

We stand there laughing in the damp air. When I swallow, I say, "Stone the cows. It's a perfectly valid expression."

"Is it?" He makes a skeptical face, and I notice he looks a bit strange. A bit pale, perhaps, and there's something about his eyes...

"What?" His lips twist in a not-quite-smile and I realize something. "You look poorly. Tired," I add gently.

"Nah."

But he does. He's paler than he was mere moments ago.

"You're a hopeless liar, Carnegie. And anyway, don't lie to me."

His eyebrows notch as he shakes his head, raising his hand to his hair as he does when he feels uneasy. "I'm okay."

"Did you use my remedies?"

"Not yet."

"Are you afraid to try my funny tinctures?"

He gives me a strained smile. "I'll use them. Did you make them?"

"Of course."

"Thanks for sending them."

I want to scream at him to just act normal—how we did inside the burrow. But that wasn't normal, was it? And I'm not acting that way myself, besides.

What you really need is for him to leave.

I hear myself say, "Come inside."

His eyes widen a bit, and I open the clinic door. "I never got a chance to check you over. Step inside and I'll do something speedy."

I hold my hand out for his. He doesn't take it, but he follows me into the entry area, where there are two small love seats angled 'round a wooden table stacked with old magazines.

"Wait here for a moment." I point to the mauve love seat and go fetch a few things from the cabinets and counters. I return to find him sitting with his head in his hands. Baby stands at his feet like a guard dog.

I sit beside him, speaking softly: "Take your shirt off, Sailor."

That makes his lips twitch. He removes his shirt, and I feel tingly at the sight of so much heavy muscle. I try to take a deep breath, but my face feels hot, and my heart starts to race.

I press the stethoscope to his chest. Chills cover his warm, smooth skin. I check a few spots on his chest and move to his broad back. His muscles flex as he shifts under the bell of the stethoscope.

"A bit fast," I murmur.

He rubs his face. As if he's avoiding my eyes?

"Let me get your blood pressure."

He holds his arm out, staring ahead as I work the cuff up his forearm. It scarcely fits over his bicep. When I get it there, I realize I'll need to change it. His muscle is simply too thick for the usual size. While I do that, he avoids looking at me, and I wonder why. Is he embarrassed? Irritated? Perhaps I erred in urging him inside.

I get the reading and remove the cuff from his arm.

"Do you always tend a bit high?"

He shakes his head, so slight I nearly miss it.

It's likely a side-effect, then—of his withdrawal process. That or he intensely dislikes sitting near me.

I look at his handsome profile, gone from jovial to serious.

"May I ask...what was your last dose? Of medication," I manage.

He blinks, his gaze still pointed straight ahead, and I realize my hunch was correct. He doesn't want to look at me. "Tapered down to eighty," he says.

"Eighty..."

"Milligrams."

I lick my lips. "Of..."

"Valium." His eyes find mine.

Eighty? Eighty milligrams a day of Valium was his *low* dose? My brain stumbles. I realize my mouth is open. I should say something. Something affirming. I just can't process.

"Into the bath," I manage.

Something harsh crosses his features. "Right." He exhales and starts to stand.

"Wait."

"I'm fine, Finley. I can't be in here." He tugs his shirt over his head and strides toward the door.

"What do you mean?" I call after him.

"What do you think?" His tone is hard, but as I reach his side, he pauses with his arm stretched toward the door.

"Because of all the medication?"

"Never let a junkie in the drug store, Finley. Didn't someone tell you that?"

I see his hand shake as it wraps around the door handle. I don't know why—perhaps because I can't stand to see him trembling as he does—but I wrap my arms around his waist from behind.

I can feel the pumping of his torso with his too-fast breaths. I press my cheek against his back and hear his heartbeat thunder. "I'm so sorry."

"Why are you sorry?" His muscles clench as a shudder jerks through him. He turns around, escaping my grip with the movement, and I find his eyes are hard. His face is pale.

"For asking you inside. And—" I swallow against my aching throat before I whisper, "I'm sorry I can't help. I asked for the location of the key to the controlled substances safe. I couldn't get it from him. From Doctor."

His eyes shut. "I don't want it," he whispers.

I'm not sure if I should touch him when he's clearly upset, but I find I can't help myself. I grab his hand, linking our fingers as his eyes open to find mine.

For the longest moment, we stand there staring at each other —and I feel his pain. I feel how lost and tired he is, how difficult it must be for him to endure. Then he tugs me closer, strokes his hand back through my hair, and lowers his mouth to mine.

His lips are firm and soft and warm. I feel like I'm falling through space and time as his tongue nudges into my mouth in a velvet surge that makes my limbs quiver. My fingers—still laced with his—curl.

Then it's in and out; it's sinuous and slow...tender and firm... and I can feel my body throb and clench as I try to return his kisses. His mouth is hard and forceful. Mine feels soft and stupid. I can't breathe as he devours me.

Then his arm laces around my waist, bringing my hips flush with his erection.

He steps back.

I'm panting as he says, "Goodbye, Finley."

And he's gone.

TWENTY-SIX
FINLEY

Every time he throws the ball, a cold sweat prickles my skin.

"Did you see that?" Anna laughs. I curve my hand around my forehead.

"I'm not looking! Someone's going to lose an eye."

Anna chuckles, and I peek around my fingertips to make a face at wee Kayti. She gives me a gummy smile, and I peek at the field. Declan's pulling his arm back to throw. My belly flips so hard, I fear I might be sick, so I look at my feet again.

A moment later, Anna says, "You can look back up, you ninny! Mayor Acton struck out."

I lower my hand, forcing my gaze to sweep the mayor first. The tactic is a bit of a fail, though, as he's exchanging words with Declan. I school my face before I dare examine his, finding he looks sheepish underneath the bill of his Sox cap. Sheepish and utterly delectable.

The afternoon is gray and misty. He's wearing a baseball shirt —white at the torso, dark blue on the arms—that stretches over his chest and shoulders. Paired with it, cargo-style khaki shorts and sneakers. Every time he throws, his strong calves bulge and his forearm muscles tauten.

I can't watch without a flipping feeling deep down in my belly. It's like an illness. I can't shake my automatic response. It's not just my body, either. My mind is like a train that's confined to a circular track, running as fast as its engine will allow but never getting anywhere new. I feel dazed. Hyper-focused on him. I'm lost in the shape of him, the way he moves. The way his mouth curves at the corners a bit shyly. The way he laughs.

Near the game's end, Declan hits the ball off Daniel Smith's comparably snail-paced pitch, and it sails high into the milky white sky. For a moment, he hesitates before he runs the bases. Then he's moving like a golden god, and I have no good excuse not to watch.

"Quite amazing," Holly says, echoing my thoughts.

"Might be more amazing if he wasn't any good."

The minimizing comment is designed to deceive. The truth is, I feel shaken by the force of my ardor. I've never felt this way before. I fear my voice could tremble at the mention of him. So I try desperately to appear nonchalant.

I pick at a cuticle as Holly and Dot cook up a plan to offer him some homespun cotton candy after the game wraps.

"You two are horrid," I murmur, and turn around to patty-cake with Kayti.

Anna whines about the casserole she promised Freddy she would cook, and then she's tucking Kayti back into her wrap so she can greet him by the field.

"I've got a check-in call coming from Doctor," I say, by way of an excuse for myself. I can't bear—indeed don't *dare*—to walk down to the field with Dot and Holly.

And yet, I can't quite tear myself away. I chat with Molly Green, a school girl, aged fourteen, who wants to learn to throw clay. I explain my wheel is still at Gammy's house and Declan's staying there.

"When it's time for him to go—that's in near two months—we can get started. How does that sound?"

She beams. Over her right shoulder, my traitorous gaze hones in on Dot, Holly, and *him*.

Someone taps me on the shoulder. Anna. She's gotten caught up gabbing before going down to Freddy. Since I'm still about, she wants me to walk down to the field with her to congratulate him. He got a poor hit—but still a hit—off one of Declan's supersonic balls.

I feel robotic as we file down the wooden bleachers to the makeshift fence, where I stand beside Anna feeling like a flashing light. I try to fill my lungs with air, but I can't seem to. I focus on Freddy and then on Mark Glass as he stops over to chat. Declan's not in sight. For that I'm grateful.

Finally, with a glance at my watch, I break away. I walk behind the bleachers, clutching my unused umbrella's handle, chewing harder than is strictly necessary on a bit of gum, and start toward the Away dugout. Everyone is congregating at the Home side, so it's good I need to head away from it to amble toward the clinic.

Much as I crave an encounter with him, I don't need one. Certainly not with so many others about. Who knows what might be said?

Thinking of that weighs on my heart. It's only a matter of time really. All of this—this infatuation—has an expiration date. I feel a horrid swell of empathy—of sorrow—for Mum; surely, she felt similarly. My eyes blur and I wipe them.

The sky has darkened with encroaching evening, and no one's walking near me. I take a few measured breaths and start around the rear of the Away dugout.

And there he is.

He's leaned against it, holding his injured shoulder with one hand and a red-tipped cigarette in the other.

His eyes are closed. They open for me, and the world curves in around us.

"Hey there, Siren."

My heart turns over at the soft twitch of his lips. My body flashes like a light bulb.

"Hi there."

It takes me a moment to realize the particular look on his face is perhaps a bit of bashfulness.

"I couldn't watch you throwing." A grin splits my face. "It worried me for Sean—the catcher."

That makes him grin in return.

Spurred by a bit of madness, I pluck the cigarette from his fingers and take a choking drag. I blow it out in circles, like that caterpillar in *Alice in Wonderland*.

Then I hand it back and squint against the smoke. "They're bad for you, you know."

He chuckles. "All the good things are."

I wink, and he says, "Come with me tomorrow."

"Where to?" I fix my face in an impassive look, as if I wouldn't follow him to hell and back.

"I thought I'd hike up to the peak."

Behind us, I hear someone's laughter. In that sliver of time before whoever rounds the corner, I give him a coy smile. "Perhaps I will."

Then, before we're seen alone, I trot away.

* * *

Declan

Knowing how she feels about propriety, I get to her door before the sun is up. It's cold out. Cold enough to turn my breaths into white puffs and make me wish I'd worn more than a fleece. Overhead, the moon shines, casting a pearly sheen over her porch and gleaming on the door's six small glass windows.

I should knock. I shake my head at myself, grinning. I feel like a kid at Christmas. Finally, I give a few hard-but-not-too-forceful knocks, then wrap my hands around the straps of my daypack and wait to hear footfall. If she doesn't answer, I figure I'll go at it again.

A couple seconds later, the door opens, revealing Finley and her wide-but-sleepy eyes. She's got on a soft-looking brown robe, and she's wearing a funny little smile.

"The sleepy Siren."

"Declan!" She laughs. "What are you doing here?"

"Came to take you on that hike."

She laughs again, her pretty face incredulous. "Right now?"

"It can be the other way around if you want—you can take me."

"Of course it will be. Silly interloper." She looks down at her robe, then up at me again. Her eyes are dancing, her cheeks round with a suppressed smile. "I can't believe you're here! I suppose I've got to get dressed."

A small, white head peeks around her robe-clad legs, and I crouch. "I've got something for you..."

Finley laughs and whirls away. "Wait there, kindly. No coming inside."

"I'll be here."

I reach into my pocket and get a little piece of apple, holding it out while Baby sniffs it. She takes it from me, and I smile like an idiot as I listen to her chomp.

"That's the good stuff, right?"

A second later, her eyes rise to mine in a request for more.

I've got a bunch of little bits of apple, so I keep her busy while we wait for Finley. When the door opens again, she's got her hair in braided pig-tails and she's wearing dark leggings, a light green jacket, and boots, with a hiking pack flung over one shoulder.

"Is that apple?" she asks.

"Hope that's okay."

"What do you think, Baby?" She reaches down and scoops the ewe up. "Her first apple." She peers over Baby's head, her lips quirked up and pressed together, making her look a little like an angry duck. "Very crafty, Carnegie. Win over the ewe."

I laugh like I have no idea what she's talking about. Like I didn't spend a bunch of time dicing up an apple, mostly to impress Finley.

While she disappears inside with Baby, I step off the small porch, pacing over to some brush near the cliffs behind the doctor's quarters. I hear the thunder of waves breaking below. I think of Finley, only ever looking down the cliffs—no thought of leaving. I wonder if she even looks down at all. Maybe she can't.

A moment later, she reappears, closing the door behind her and pressing a small sticky note to it. She doesn't speak, just smiles, a little bit mysterious as she steps off the porch and joins me in the grass. She covers the distance between us with one long stride and stops right by me. Near enough that my dick perks up and I want to touch her.

"Careful, Sailor. Just beyond the vegetation here is a steep drop-off."

I look into her eyes and feel myself smile. Watch as my fingers brush one of her braids. "I like this." My voice sounds low and husky, like I'm talking with my hard-on. Because I am. *Fuck.* I grit my teeth and shift my weight as she looks away shyly. "Thank you."

"Let's get moving while we've got a little darkness left. You good to go now?"

Her thin brows notch as if she doesn't understand.

"Can you be away from work this morning?"

"Oh...mm, yes, I believe. For a bit. I left a note." Her gaze moves to the door, and I adjust my pants. Goddamn, I love her voice. Love her accent, love the way she can't look at my face. I feel a bolt of pure lust. Not just lust but *life*—that wasn't there before I got here this morning.

"Did you tell them who you're going with?" I smile as we start toward the dirt road.

She shakes her head, laughing. "Wouldn't want to cause alarm. Who would trust the two of us together on the slopes?"

"I had that thought."

"Don't worry," she says softly. "I'll be a better guide this time 'round. I know all the trails, of course, and all the lookouts. It's a bit of elevation, but you can choose how high we climb. I have perhaps six hours before I'll be missed."

Her elbow brushes my arm as we walk along the lane's edge. Suddenly, I can't think of a single thing to say. I think she just questioned my physical fitness with that shit about how we can stop whenever I want to. But I can't even get my brain to work enough to toss that back her way.

"So, Carnegie." She blinks up at me. "Tell me how you like it here."

"Demoted to Carnegie again."

She smiles, but it's a little tight...or maybe coy. "I'd like to hear your impressions," she says crisply. "What you've enjoyed and not about our island."

Just a little hesitation over how to answer, and a cold sweat hits me. That's how this shit is. Stuff that doesn't ever make a normal person nervous makes my hands shake. It's like this every day, though. I know how to hide it.

"I like it," I say. "Good people, good food. Hey, that reminds me. I didn't realize you moved out of your place for me. Thanks for doing that."

She gives me a smile, and now I'm sure it looks a little strained. "Of course."

I bump her arm with my elbow and smirk down at her, hoping to get her loosened up. "The tub's my favorite."

"Using all my bath salts, are you?"

"Nah. I used them a couple times, but not too much. I know you can't get more."

She waves her hand, not really looking at me. "I'll get more eventually. I could put an order in and they'd come on the next ship. Not the next," she amends, frowning, "but the one after. You'll be gone then, I suppose."

I swallow. "So what is that? How many weeks?"

"The next ship with supplies will arrive July." Her face tilts up to mine. "Does that seem quite absurd to you?"

I lift a brow. "You ever heard of Amazon?"

"The river? Oh." She snaps her fingers. "No—the mega-store."

I grin down at her, and she elbows me. "I've heard of Amazon."

"Welcome to 2018, Siren."

She giggles. "You're an arse."

I catch her by the wrist. "Finley Evans. Did you just use a dirty word?"

I lace my fingers through hers, lightly swinging her arm as I aim a mock disapproving look down at her. With our joined hands, she punches at me. "Only for you. I never use perverse language except when influenced unduly."

"Unduly influenced? Is that right?"

She lands a light blow to my chest.

"Finley, Finley..." I squeeze her hand. "What am I gonna do with you? Lashing out at me, using the devil's language?"

She's grinning, but I see her lips bend downward at the corners, like she's trying to fight it off.

I stroke her wrist with my thumb. "Siren. I've been missing you."

Color spreads across her cheeks. She bites the inside of her cheek before she presses her lips flat.

"Odd. You didn't seek me out for company for near a week before I walked into a closet with you."

Our path curves as we crest a small hill, and I see my borrowed cottage over on the left. Its underground window shines in the soft grass.

I squeeze Finley's fingers. "Maybe I wasn't sure you wanted me to."

"I tried to track you down for your check-up. You were never there."

"Did you?"

"I did."

My pulse kicks up a little as I think about that first night back, when I woke up without her. All the other days... I exhale. "I'm sorry."

What can I tell her? I'm too fucked up to be alone in a house so I kept going to the bar, but I hugged my pillow and I thought about her lots? I rub my thumb over her knuckles, hoping she won't pull her hand away from mine. I touch a Band-Aid taped atop her hand and trace its rough edge. "What'd you do here?"

"Slicing something in the kitchen." Her pretty eyes are still on her feet. I can feel her brooding, and it makes me want to wrap my arms around her.

Instead of that, I draw our clasped hands to me. I don't know what I'm thinking. That I'll kiss the back of her hand? Some kind of Casanova shit? Another wave of cold sweat sweeps me, and I wonder if my hand feels sweaty.

I take a slow breath as we pass the cottage.

Finley glances at its front door. "I'll be by to pull the weeds soon."

I swing her hand. "I can do it."

"You're not grooming my stoop, interloper. You're the guest. You're meant to relax." She gives me a smile plus side-eye. It's so fucking cute, it helps me get my bearings.

"Is that right?"

"Of course. Listen to the ocean and endeavor nature walks. Get lots of rest and use up all the bath salts."

I nod at the trail ahead, which disappears around the cliffs that lead up to the plateau. "I guess I'm doing this all wrong, then."

She looks up at me, and there's this sweetness on her face; it reminds me of the looks she gave me in the burrow. Like she's happy she's here with me.

"Tell me more of your impressions, city boy. I've heard a bit about your comings and goings. What are you drinking at the bar? What Tristanian dishes have you tried, at whose home? Have you seen things you consider odd here? I'd like to hear it all."

I squeeze her hand. "Hmm, well, I saw Mrs. White's orchids."

"All nine hundred ninety-seven of them?"

I laugh. "They were nice."

"Oh, sure."

"I like flowers."

"Sure you do."

"Mrs. White is a nice lady."

"Sure she is."

I can't stop laughing. "Spitting fire today, Siren."

"What does that mean?"

"I had an Alabama nanny when I was a little kid who would have said, 'She's in a mood.'" The memory makes me chuckle.

"My mood is perfectly fine."

"Sure it is."

She sticks her tongue out at me.

"I'll tell you what I've seen—I've seen some homemade tinctures. Not something you see every day." She smiles shyly. "I found out the other day there's only two more bottles of Macallan 18 on the damn whole island. Kinda stopped that nightly routine."

She laughs. "For the best, perhaps."

Our dirt path takes us past the plateau that overlooks the village—and her cottage. I point toward it. "I've been up there some. Does that count as relaxing?"

"Vloeiende Trane," she murmurs.

"What?"

"Cascading tears," she says dramatically.

"What language is that?"

"Afrikaans." She wiggles her brows. "Is it one you don't know, Sailor?"

Sailor again now. I shake my head. "How dare you name your cliffs in a language I don't know?"

She laughs, her eyes on her feet again, as if she's too shy to look me in the face. When she looks at me again, she flashes me a pretty smile. "How many do you speak? How many languages?"

"A couple."

"A couple is two. You've already admitted to Italian, German, and French. And English."

"So that's four."

"Do you speak more?"

"Would you be impressed if I did?"

She laughs softly. "Perhaps."

Our trail forks, the left side veering toward the little lakes I ran to a few times, the right tilting up into the fog. The sun is rising, but we can't see it through the heavy cloud cover. It's turned the darkness gray-blue, but it doesn't offer any warmth yet. The air feels thick and cool around us.

"What about you?" I ask. "What ones do you know?"

"Only French and Spanish."

"I like Spanish," I say as we skirt a patch of muddy ground. She looks down at her boots, and I admire her profile. In the burrow, she looked beautiful—and more so because she was so fucking nice—but I couldn't see her clearly due to how dark things were. Now that I've got a good view, I can't pull my eyes away from her smooth, freckled skin, her wide, expressive eyes.

"You ever read Pablo Neruda?"

I watch as her mouth falls open in what looks like happy surprise. "Pablo Neruda? He's my *favorite!*" She swings my hand. "You like him?"

"No," I deadpan. "I just said the name to mess with you."

"You're smirking." She laughs. "Why are you smirking?"

I swing her arm again. "I don't know. Just had a feeling you might like that stuff."

"And why is that, pray tell?"

I smirk down at her. "Because you say pray tell."

She ducks her lips up like she's pissed, even as she's fighting a smile. I tug one of her braids. She swats me.

"How do you know of him?" she presses.

I shrug. "Poetry class."

She wiggles her eyebrows and waves her arm dramatically. *"No estés lejos de mí un solo día, porque cómo, porque, no sé decirlo, es largo el día, y te estaré esperando como en las estaciones cuando en alguna parte se durmieron los trenes."*

"Don't leave me," I continue, "even for an hour, because then the little drops of anguish will all run together. The smoke that roams looking for a home will drift into me, choking my lost heart." I wink. "I learned this one in English."

Despite my recitation in the wrong language, her mouth is open.

"Oh, may your silhouette never dissolve on the beach," I recite, suppressing a grin. "May your eyelids never flutter into the empty distance. Don't leave me for a second, my dearest, because in that moment you'll have gone so far, I'll wander over all the earth, asking will you come back. Will you leave me here...dying."

She gives a little squeal and drops my hand so she can clap hers. "Bravo, you! I couldn't be more surprised."

I laugh. "Should I be insulted?"

"Absolutely you should not. I'm impressed. What woman doesn't love a man who quotes romantic poetry?"

I watch her face twist up in horror as she realizes her faux pas. She blushes tomato red as she covers her eyes with her hands.

"Pardon me." She stops walking. "I can't walk with my face covered."

I step in front of her, laughing as I try to pull her hands down. She fights me, so I let her leave them...but I pull her up against me. "I can't see your face now," I murmur, wrapping an arm around her soft back.

"Don't be embarrassed," I whisper against her hair. It smells like flowers. "The verdict is in, and apparently I'm pretty loveable."

She shoves me. "You're a clod." Her face is still tipped down, but I can see she's smiling.

I laugh. "What's a clod?"

"A stupid person."

That makes me laugh...which makes her laugh.

"Your cheeks are red," I tease.

"Because I'm the clod." She strides ahead of me, but I lunge forward and catch her hand. "Finley." I lace my fingers through hers. "You're not a clod."

"I'm inexperienced and awkward." Her words are whisper-hisses. She's glancing down at just the right angle so I can see a teardrop in the corner of one of her eyes.

Shock moves through me, making my hands shake a little. Then my chest goes warm and heavy. I squeeze her hand. "Hey now. Let me tell you something. Experience is overrated."

"Is it?" She peeks up at me, and it takes some effort not to pull her up against my chest again. To keep my tone light, like I don't want to fucking hug her.

"Oh yeah. If I could get a redo, I'd go somewhere just like this. Appreciate the everyday shit. One type of gum. Mail runs every third month. You know everybody. Everybody looking out for each other."

"Is that what you think it would be like?" I can hear the censure in her soft tone.

"I don't know." I rub my forehead. I know there wouldn't be any covert trips to Mass Avenue. I know I'd never swerve around some fucker sprawled out in the middle of the road and foaming from the mouth—because even though I've got Narcan in my glove box and I'm certified at CPR, I can't stop for him. Homer Carnegie isn't supposed to be there with a bundle of smack at 4 a.m. on a fucking Tuesday.

I feel the heavy shaking start in my shoulders and vibrate down my arms. Her fingers squeeze mine as we walk toward a rocky ridge.

"You didn't tell me you were mute."

It's the next thought that crosses my mind, and it falls out of my mouth with no forethought, surprising me and stopping Finley in her tracks. I feel her hand slacken in mine as her gaze snaps to my face.

"Who told you?"

I rub my forehead. Shit—my heart is fucking pounding. I can feel it right behind my eyes. I try to keep my voice steady as I say,

"One of the guys digging. Asked what you were like, said he'd never heard you talk."

"Who was it?" Finley's tone is impassive, but she's gone ghost pale.

"Mark Glass."

Fuck. I feel like shit for blurting that out like I did—and even more so when one corner of her mouth quivers and she presses her lips together.

"He heard me at your ball game," she says tightly.

"This was before."

She blinks at the sloping field beside us, her chin raised, her face statuesque.

"Shit. I'm sorry, Finley. I wish I hadn't said that."

Her eyes shift to my face. She gives me a stoic look that makes my queasy stomach knot up.

"Quite all right." She blinks down at her boots before locking her focus on me. "Not untrue," she says softly. "I didn't speak for ten years...after. I'm aware that I omitted this fact from my tale of woe back in the burrow. But who's to say you wanted to know? Even if you had," she murmurs, "I suppose I didn't want to tell you."

"Why?"

She tugs her eyes away from mine and starts to walk again, her arms rigid at her sides and her gaze set on the trail. I follow her for a long minute, hating myself for how bad my hands are shaking, for how hard it is to breathe. My heart pounds like a fucking drum, and I feel like my chest is empty. Like I'm only half here.

"To this day I'm—on occasion—" She shakes her head. Her eyes dart my way as she picks up her pace. "I'm referred to as 'the mute.' I suppose there are those like Mark who've never heard me speak. Even though it's been years since that time." She steps around a stone in the path, not looking back as I hang half a pace behind her.

"No one here before me ever stopped speaking." Her words are forceful, almost harsh. "Some assumed the stint at sea had ruined my mind, but those who cared to realized that I wasn't daft. I would write a note at odd times...although mostly I got on through nods and other methods. And still..."

She folds her arms across her chest as we walk through a blanket of fog. "Some treated me as if I couldn't hear either. I've been privy to more secrets than you can imagine. Like a priest a bit in that way."

Our path slants down into a grassy valley at the base of the peak, which looks large and dark, mostly in shadow. Her strides lengthen. So do mine.

"There are others who assume I'm simple," she continues. "Some don't speak to me, because for years they felt there was no point in doing so. They've checked the box beside my name that says *non-entity.*"

She looks over her shoulder at me. "Do you want to know the truth, Declan? The truth is no one ever courted me. I was never kissed under the arches. Others got sent off to university, but never me. I'm a fixture on this island but I'm never truly seen. I haven't been since Mummy was alive and never will be again. It doesn't matter how much pottery I sell and ship out or how often I bandage a mashed finger. When I'm buried I'll be most known for lacking my voice—because someone like Mark Glass has failed to notice when I use it."

TWENTY-SEVEN
FINLEY

I tell myself to slow down, but my legs rebel. Perhaps because of my confinement to the boat for those days, I've become a runner of the worst sort. When I'm emotional, I flee. This is worse than usual, because I'm fleeing *him*.

The more my own words echo through my mind—the more I picture him on my heels, his handsome face contorted in shock and dismay—the more I feel I simply must keep moving.

I dart up the packed-dirt path as it tilts at the foot of the peak. My harsh steps startle a bird. I can feel mud spitting off my shoes.

The trail's not marked because we locals know it, and we don't allow the visitors to summit alone. So it's possible that I might lose him if I'm speedy enough.

I duck under some vines that hang over the trail and dash around a wide rock. When I hear footfall, I move faster.

Now he'll know how mad I really am. Not merely some unknown girl, but the island's wretched outcast. I'm assuaged by a feeling of loss—the loss of something I can't name. A sort of twisted hope, I suppose. Hope that sprung forth anew when I realized a bit earlier he doesn't know my darkest secret yet. He hasn't heard.

Still, I flee him like I should have fled the moment we escaped the burrow. Like someone who's got everything to lose, whose life is altered each time she gets near him. My pack bumps atop my back, and my heart hammers.

If he turns back, that will be the end of things, and I can move forward on my life's track...however desolate that may be. I could even go to him a bit before he's due to leave and spill my own secret...and ask for help. A voice inside me screams "no" at that prospect.

My chest feels tighter than a rubber band, my throat a vice clamp as my poor, unfeeling body rushes up the cool slope. When I'm above the wind-bent grass and scattered stones, when the path before me has gone stark with elevation, I hear him. I *feel* him.

And then his footfall is too close, and his thick arm captures my shoulders, locking my back against his chest. My eyes close, and I feel the heat of him, the bulk of his thick body. I can smell him—the slightly spicy, uniquely Declan scent that stirs some sleeping dragon in me.

"Siren." It's an exhalation.

He turns me around to face him, and I do so like a good doll. I look at his face, his indecipherable face. His handsome features are impassive, but he always fails to lock away the feeling in his eyes. I hate his eyes the most—the kindness I see there, the concern.

"I don't need your pity, you know. I'm pretty like you, and though I'm not absurdly wealthy, I am talented and clever."

I watch as his face transforms, its hard lines bending as he grins, then gives a low chuckle. It's a rich and husky sound that warms my bones.

I close my eyes and bow my head and pray perhaps he'll just jog off and leave me be. But I have no such luck.

His hand captures my chin, his long fingers curving around my jaw. "C'mon, Finley. Look at me."

"I can't," I whisper.

"Why not?"

Against my will, my lips quiver. I press them together.

"I'm looking pretty strung out for someone clean. You scared to look at me, Siren?"

I peek up at him, my gaze drawn to the dark circles beneath his eyes. "Don't be moronic."

His jaw hardens. "Finley, do you think I give a fuck about your past? That I would judge you for it? Me?" His eyes are so angry, my heart lurches a bit.

I freeze as he scoops me up and sets me on a nearby boulder, at the edge so that my legs hang off the side. He wraps his hands around my elbows and stands so close, my knees are forced to part around his waist.

He blows a breath out, strokes his warm hands down my shoulders. "Jesus, Finley." He leans closer, wraps an arm around me. "Think of who you're talking to." He holds me fast against him as his hand crawls up my back, stroking over my nape into my hair. I feel him inhale as he tucks my head against his shoulder.

"I know who," I whisper. "Homer Carnegie."

It's a catty thing to say, I know, but I can't seem to help myself.

I feel his diaphragm expand on a deep breath. He steps slightly away, so that a cool breeze twists between us. When I look up at him, I find his face hard. "Have I ever said that's my name? Homer?"

I look down, and his hand cups the side of my face. "C'mon, Finley," he groans. "You don't know the half of it with me." I feel a tremor move through him. "I've been trying to outrun myself since I was fucking thirteen years old."

I blink down at the space between us: a swatch of dirt where an ant hauls a bit of leaf atop its back. My eyes well with relief at his desperate tone. I'm not the only damaged one for once.

Tell me more. Please, Sailor. I send a prayer up to that effect, but as I watch his shoes and feel him breathing, he says nothing. Finally he leans in closer, smoothing his hand down the back of my hair, caressing the nape of my neck.

"Don't ever worry, Finley. Not with me."

Something moves through me, a sort of dark force. I'd like to lash out at him, shove him away. What I'd really like to say is "you'll soon be gone." But I do none of that. I feel like a statue in a snow globe as I hear myself say, "All right, then."

He lifts me off the rock and sets me back on the ground. Even now, when I'm so agitated, standing near him makes me feel like a lamb near its shepherd. I steal a glance at his face. *I'm tired of resisting him.* But when our eyes catch, his blue orbs are remote, as if he's locked himself away a bit.

Something throbs below my throat—a sort of tightening sensation. Because I want to know—I feel I even need to know— about him. I feel like sand at low tide as I walk beside him: *thirsty.*

For his part, his strides are long and slightly brisk. His hand-some face is perfectly impassive. He seems focused on the path ahead, which tilts more vertically as misty rain drifts over us. For not the first time in his presence, I don't feel quite real as I trod near him. I need his eyes, his hands on me to be corporeal.

Finally, as the path cuts leftward in a zigzag toward the summit, he looks over his shoulder. Now his face is clearer...perhaps calmer. He reaches for my hand, his fingers catching mine and lacing with them as if nothing heated passed between us. We walk on, and I think oddly of the animals in Noah's Ark. Two of each kind...

"Tell me something," he says, low.

"What sort of something?"

His mouth is solemn, but it curves a bit as his warm eyes reach for mine. "What's your favorite color?"

I can't help a small laugh. "What?"

"Tell me all your favorites, Siren. Tell me everything."

My body warms from scalp to soles as I smile at him. "Everything? I'm not sure there's so much to me." I feel my cheeks burn, and I hate that I can blush at my age.

"Everybody has a favorite color." His brows waggle. "Mine is gray."

"Gray?" I snort. "It can't be gray. That's not a color!"

He grins. "Tell that to the good folks at Crayola."

"It's a color, but it's..."

"Gray." He tilts his head.

"It's flat and sad."

He smiles with dimples. "Not to me."

"It can't be your favorite. Choose another."

"Gray."

"A runner up of sorts."

"Dark blue."

"The color of a dark sea? I'll accept that."

He smirks. "What about you, Siren? I gave you two, now I want two."

"That's easy, and you'll see that mine are valid. Green and purple."

"Favorite food?"

Our path veers rightward, running flat as we traverse the peak's significant width. Frost gleams on the vegetation. Out to our right, sprawling past the fog-dappled valley, we can see the ocean stretching on for eons.

"That's a bit of a tough call. Perhaps a York Peppermint

Patty. That's my favorite thing I eat consistently. As well as apples, I suppose. And yourself?"

I feel a tremor in his hand and squeeze it slightly. "I guess maybe tacos."

"We don't eat that here really."

He blinks down at me. "Someday."

"What does that mean...someday?"

"Someday I'll come get you in a plane and take you to get tacos."

I laugh. "You can't land a plane here. There's no air strip."

"Not all planes need landing strips."

"That's not what I've heard."

He smiles. "Trust me on this, Siren. Planes are my hobby."

I file that bit away, meaning to ask more later. For now, I stick to topic. "Where would you take me to get a taco? Mexico?"

"New York."

I laugh, and he looks abashed. "I know it doesn't sound authentic, but New York City's got the best taco place. It's not in Mexico, but the owners are from down there. Now I want some," he says, husky.

"What have you been eating here?"

I feel his shoulder lift on a shrug. "Different stuff."

"What's been your favorite?"

"I don't know. It was all pretty good."

I rub my finger up along the side of his wrist, where I can always see a bone protruding. His body is so different than my own, even his wrists and hands. "I worry you should eat more."

He laughs at that, and lifts one dark brow at me. "Wasting away, huh?"

"Well, of course not. But I worry for you. I'm a worrier, I suppose."

"I'm good."

Our arms bump lightly as the path curves in its zigzag, headed back the other way now.

"Are you really, though?" I stroke his knuckles with my fingertips and feel his fingers tremble.

"Yeah." He gives me a tight smile, and my heart aches a bit.

"Tell me more about Declan-not-Homer," I say. "What's your favorite book? Do you re-read the ones you really like, or is that just for those of us without a reliable connection to the world wide web? What were your favorite parts of your life back home?"

He chuckles. "That's a lot of questions."

"You answer first, then I will."

* * *

Declan

I smile down at her. I'm always smiling at her—all the fucking time, until my face hurts. With my free hand, I rub at my aching cheek, trying not to let my smile turn into laughing. Trying to breathe deeper so my hands will stop shaking.

I'm kind of surprised I can handle her holding my hand when shit's like this, but the truth is...I like it. I don't know why it's different with Finley. I guess because of how we met—that time inside the burrow.

Despite what she said back there, she doesn't know me as "Homer." She can't imagine what my life is like back home. She doesn't know who I'm supposed to be. And she doesn't treat me differently—not like an addict and definitely not like a celebrity.

"I'm gonna have to go with something that's kind of embarrassing."

She grins up at me. "Yes?"

"It's not a board book," I warn.

She giggles. "But it *is* a kids' book. I can sense it."

"Bullshit. How can you sense it?"

"You're blushing." She waves at my face.

I roll my eyes. "Guys don't blush." I jab her ribs. "But I know someone who does."

"Sod off."

I chuckle.

"Out with it."

I shake my head and swallow my pride. "I'd really like to say something like *The Odyssey*. Or Marcel Proust."

"But..." She's grinning. Little witch.

I sigh for effect. "But...it's Harry Fucking Potter." I watch her face as a gorgeous smile spreads over it.

"Of course it is. They are the best books of our time. It should be on the list with Shakespeare. What house? That's what I really need to know."

"What house do you think?" I crook a brow at her, and she crooks hers back as our path narrows and steepens.

"Somewhat difficult to say. I don't think Slytherin. You're too kind for that."

I scoff. "Kind? Me?"

She rolls her eyes. "I'm voting against Ravenclaw, although perhaps I shouldn't, since you can recite poetry."

"You calling me a Hufflepuff?" I give her a skeptical look, and she laughs. "Actually...perhaps." She taps her chin. "I've narrowed down to Hufflepuff and Gryffindor, but I can't quite sort you. You're likely too ambitious to be Hufflepuff. And perhaps a bit competitive. You do play games professionally. And I believe you like to win."

She laughs, and I realize I'm smirking at her.

"The sorting hat says...Gryffindor!"

I nod, smiling at the geekiness of this shit. "Hufflepuff for you?"

"How did you know?" She narrows her eyes at me.

"I had you sorted from the second day in the cave."

"Not the first?"

"I was getting Slytherin vibes before that." I laugh at my lame joke, and she hits me with our joined hands.

"Likewise." She makes a snake sound for that house's mascot.

"So you're a Hufflepuff. Who likes the colors green and purple, and likes reading. Favorite book?"

"*Wuthering Heights*. Followed closely by—" she cringes— "*The Great Gatsby*."

"What's wrong with those two? What would you rather have said?"

"*Little Women. Harry Potter*."

"But you didn't, because?"

She shrugs. "I enjoy a bit of drama." A small smile tilts her lips. "A bit of melancholy, I suppose."

We walk in easy silence for a while, trekking horizontally across what's getting to be the middle part of the volcano's wide base. We follow the trail up a set of stone stairs before starting back the other way, the ocean to our right now.

I watch Finley out of the corner of my eye. I catch her gaze on me a few times, too.

I think about the last question she asked: What was my favorite part of life in Boston? I've realized since she asked that I don't know. Every month leading up to November, things got worse and worse without me realizing...and at the end there, I'd stopped doing everything I liked.

She tugs my arm, and I glance up to find a boulder over to our right, jutting out over the zigzag path below.

"Look out there." She points out at the ocean. "Do you see that?"

She hurries over to the boulder and tosses her bag down, digging in it frantically. "Hurry!"

I climb up behind her, taking the binoculars she hands me and focusing them on the water. "Are these...dolphins?" I squint.

"Whale dolphins. They're two-toned, correct?"

I nod as I watch them jumping. "Black with a white belly, looks like."

"That's right."

I watch them for a while before handing the binoculars to her. Then I watch her watch. She's so damn pretty. She could be a model if she wanted to. Finally, she sets the binoculars in her lap and digs into her bag, smiling as she brings out a package of Pop-Tarts.

"Step up from an Atkins bar."

She opens them and passes me one. I'm not hungry, but I never am. I bite into it.

"I'm right, aren't I? You're still feeling poorly. You like Pop-Tarts—you said so—but you look queasy at this moment."

"Do not."

She peers at the ocean out in front of us, and her mouth bends into a frown. "It was dolphins that took us to sea. That day," she adds softly. "It was my birthday...and I wanted to see dolphins."

It takes me a full second to realize what she's talking about. Then I'm not sure what to say, what's adequate. "Fuck. I'm sorry, Finley."

She shrugs, nibbling at the un-iced edges of her Pop-Tart. I wait for her to say more, but she just blinks at the ocean.

"I want to tell you something," she rasps. "Ask you something. But I'm nervous to," she whispers.

"Ask away." I sit up a little, propping my elbow on my knee as I lean closer to her.

"You may not say that if you knew the question."

I turn more fully toward her, sitting cross-legged. "You can ask me anything. I'll try to give an honest answer."

I watch as she swallows. She looks down at her legs, stretched out in front of her. Then she crosses them. She looks into my eyes again. "When I was a small girl, my mother used to tell me stories."

I nod slowly.

"They were of a princess—me. And her dear friend...a prince. Prince Declan. Do you know why?" she whispers.

I shake my head, feeling my pulse pick up.

Her brown eyes hold mine. "It's because she loved your father."

I feel suspended mid-air, that sort of paused sensation that comes with a shock. At the same time, everything I've ever heard my old man say in recent times about the island floods my mind.

"You can't go wrong there. Especially where you are, son— with your temptations. If there is temptation there," he laughed, "it won't be a pill."

I'm thrown back into my room at Pontresina. Answering the door that night, and Laurent leading me to the couch. What he said, and how he handed me that Xanax after.

"Declan?"

Her hand on my arm makes me blink. I realize she's leaned in close. "Sorry."

"Are you all right?"

"Yeah."

I can see concern on her face—the rumpled brow and taut mouth.

"I'm sorry. I wasn't sure if I should tell you," she says.

"Tell me what?" It comes out hoarse.

She looks down, biting her lip. She looks up at me. "That they were lovers," she says. "Here. Before they married others.

They were lovers and...you know—" She clenches her jaw, looking like she thinks it's time to shut up.

"What?" I ask quietly.

She licks her lips. Inhales and blows the breath out. "Do you remember visiting here?"

"Some. A little bit."

I tell her first that my parents split when I was five. So she won't feel bad for asking about my trip here with my dad the next year. If he was coming here to see her mom or something, that's not going to upset me. Mom left him.

"I remember he pitched it as an adventure to me. We flew to Cape Town, and I had this little green travel pillow that looked like a dinosaur." I shake my head, smiling at the randomness of that memory. "I remember seeing the boat we came on. It was pretty big, and it was headed to Antarctica for something."

I look at my lap, because I'm not sure how to say the rest of what sticks out to me.

She whispers, "What else?"

My throat kind of knots up. I'm surprised by that. I suck my cheeks in, swallow. "Ahh, I think I met your grandmother."

She asks about that, and I tell her about kneading bread, and Finley smiles. "That was likely Gammy. She did love to bake and make bread. She could eat bread at every meal."

Her eyes go to the ocean again, and with them fixed there, she murmurs, "Did you remember me? I heard you were here when..."

When they found her. She can't say it.

I swallow again, and take her hand.

"You sure you want to talk about that, Siren?"

"I asked."

My thumb strokes her smooth hand.

"Yeah, I do." When she says nothing, I go on, trying to tread lightly. "That's a lot of what stuck with me. I guess just like...the mood of people. How focused they were. How everybody tried to sort of stay busy. There was like...this weight hanging behind things. Things like making bread. Nobody told me exactly what had happened, so I didn't really know."

Dad told me someone had gotten lost, someone important. And I could tell he was upset. He was upset the whole time. I remember feeling kind of nervous about that. Because I didn't know what was wrong. Just that something was.

"I saw you," I finally say. "When you came back. Dad was on that boat."

Chills cover my skin as I remember how everybody looked when the boat pulled up to the dock, and someone stood up, holding her. I don't know how many people were there standing on the dock with me, but I'd imagine probably at least a handful, despite it being nighttime. And I guess at that first glance, when they first saw her, they all must have known that it was only her.

I remember everybody crying, but trying not to. And someone was holding her. My dad was right there by her, too, and he looked really weird. Really upset.

I look at Finley's face and find her eyes a little wide. That's all, though; besides that, she looks impassive as she stares out at the ocean. "Didn't know that. I didn't know you two were here at all. Not for several years. I suppose it didn't seem quite relevant— or perhaps a shade too relevant. Your father's presence here then."

I want to tell her how the glimpse I got of her eyes was my first time ever seeing agony: that bright blaze roaring like a fire in her dead, sallow face. I couldn't place it, so I rolled that memory over like a pebble in my hand for years. Till after my own shit, when one day I caught the same soundless blaze in my eyes in a mirror.

"When I thought of coming back here, I thought about you." I manage to keep my voice steady.

She looks at me—for just a second, her eyes touch mine, asking, *What?* Then it's back out at the ocean. I squeeze her hand.

"I heard you were still here. And I wondered how you turned out. How did you keep going? I wanted to know."

She's so still, so frozen, my hand on hers shakes from being worried I upset her.

Her lips tuck up, a barely-there motion. She still won't look at me, but her hand in mine tightens. "There is no how." The words are thin. Fragile.

"I think of my mum, and for her, too...I believe there was no how about it. Your father left. She wouldn't go with him. Too frightened, I think. And so she married my father. And that's the part that strikes me most, I believe." Her tongue moves over her lower lip, her mouth pressing flat for a second, and her eyes grab at mine again. "There's endurance, I believe. And within that, there can be no how."

TWENTY-EIGHT
DECLAN

Her voice trembles a little on those words, and I fold both my hands around hers.

"Ask me," she says thinly. "What you're thinking. Don't just sit there silently. I'm not so fragile."

Her fingers thread through mine, as if she wants to reassure me that she's not upset. I look out at the ocean, too, like she is. "What was your dad like?"

Her tongue darts over her lips; I see her in my periphery. "Truth be told?" She looks down before seeking my eyes with her watery ones. "He was horrid."

My heart feels like it's lunging out of my chest. I know Finley's okay—she's right by me—but I'm so fucking jittery and shit, I start to sweat.

She moves her hand off mine and draws a finger underneath her eyes. "I'm sorry. I've never spoken of this before, to anyone." She sniffles softly. "No one asks about them."

"Hey...there's nothing to be sorry for."

I wrap my hands more tightly around hers. With her chin up

and her brown eyes spilling tears down her cheeks, she looks almost holy—like some sort of warrior saint.

"I hate to think of her life with him." She inhales, wiping at her eyes again. "My mum was...lovely." She sounds breathless as she shields her eyes with one hand. "My father was the last of the unmarried males near her age." She looks at her lap as she whispers, "He wasn't good."

"What do you mean?"

She looks at me, but it's more like she's looking through me. She draws her legs up to her chest and wraps her arms around them.

"I hate to think of her that way." Her throat sounds tight. Her head is kind of down there on her arms. That's how I notice when her shoulders tremble.

For a second, I'm not sure what to do. Despite what she said, she seems fragile. Like if I fuck up, I might break her. But I can't watch her cry without touching her. So I scoot closer. I sit right beside her, and I wrap my arm around her back. When she doesn't tense or push me away, I wrap my other arm around her in the front and scoot still closer.

Finley's body slackens against mine. "I killed them." Her voice quavers. "I killed my mum." I feel her shaking ramp up, and I squeeze her tighter. *Fuck.*

"No." I shift her weight a little, so she's in my lap—she's in my arms—and wrap my hand around the back of her head. "I know that's not true."

"I did." Her voice is tight and thick.

I rub her back as she shivers. I can feel her chest pump, as if she can't get enough air.

"Hey..." I rub some circles on her back. "Just take some slow breaths. Do it with me, sweetheart."

I inhale, pushing my chest out so she feels it. I feel her ribcage expand on a breath. Then she exhales with her cheek pressed to my shirt.

"That's right." I stroke her soft hair, drawing my fingertip along her pig-tail part. "You're okay." I hold her tighter.

"I pushed him." It's hissed against my chest. "It was supposed to be...the two of us...but he came along at the last moment." She starts to really shake, and I wrap her tighter against me. "They were fighting, and he held her head into the water. So I shoved him. I didn't know he'd go in. Mum went after him, trying to save him." Her body is shaking so hard now that it almost scares me. I hold onto her, and she inhales, a little gasp. "She was wearing... this halo. Flower halo, from my party. I can see it...floating away." Her shoulders shake as she weeps. "I did that."

She wrenches out of my arms and dashes off the rock, her boots smacking the dirt of the trail as she lands on it. I'm on her heels, ready to run after her...except she doesn't run. She leans over with her hands braced on her knees as I touch her back.

"Siren..." I run my hands over her shoulder blades, then think what I'd want if I was losing my shit and scoop her up. I carry her to another rock, a smaller one on the other side of the path, and sit down with Finley curled in my lap. I lock an arm around her, and she turns her face into my shoulder and sobs.

Fuck. Oh fuck.

I close my eyes, squeezing her as tightly as I can without hurting. Her whole body quakes as high-pitched, broken sounds come out of her.

"You're okay, Siren. I've got you."

I focus on my arms and then my hands, rubbing big circles on her back the way I liked when I was little. When her crying doesn't let up and my chest is tight with feeling helpless, I shift our position on the stone a little bit and kind of rock her.

"I've got you, baby." I trace down her spine and then back up, holding her by the shoulders, pressing my cheek against her head.

I keep on whispering and holding her real close like that. And slowly, her sobs turn to little gasps. Her body quivers with those little crying aftershocks, and I realize this one spot on my chest feels kind of damp.

I hear her sniff and feel her forehead press against my fleece's collar. She exhales, this little whimpering sound that makes my throat knot up. I run my hand along her spine again, slow up and down, until I feel her body stiffen, and she leans away, looking up at me with swollen eyes and a soft mouth.

Little strands of hair have come free from her braids and become pasted to her damp cheeks. I stroke the hair back off her face, and she blinks at me.

I don't know why—I kiss her forehead, then her cheeks...and then her lips. She tastes like salt and feels just like the whole damn universe right here where I can nibble at her throat and wipe her eyes and breathe her breath until I'm dizzy.

She returns the onslaught with her hot mouth and her grasping hands, until we have to break away to breathe.

Her molten eyes are wide and slightly dazed. In a voice that cracks, she says, "I shouldn't do this."

"Why not?"

Anything she says, I'll honor. I don't want to hurt her. But she doesn't speak. Tears pool in her eyes and spill down her cheeks, and I kiss them off because I just...can't not. I've never felt this way before. Like all my moves are played out for me. I can only follow.

"Let me tell you something." I frame her face with my hands, looking into her eyes for a second before pressing my cheek next to hers. "Before I left...back in November...we had this field trip group at headquarters." I run my hand over one of her braids and feel her chest move as she leans against me.

"Bunch of first graders that came to tour the place where we train. So we do all this stuff with them, right? Show them the locker rooms, give them all T-shirts and shit. And then it's time for them to eat. And corporate's got these little cracker bags and juice boxes. Like one in ten of them could open up the bag and get the straw into the juice box." I lean back a little bit, so I can look down at her. "Right when it was time for them to go, I heard one of the little fuckers got lost in a stairwell. Pissed himself. One of my buddies had to donate boxer shorts to this kid. Seven years old.

"You see where I'm going with this? These little dudes—they were from a Catholic school, all boys—they weren't real 'with it.' Didn't strike me as a bunch of masterminds. And I thought —*seven*. I was at Carogue at seven. Doing my own laundry. But that's little. Seven's just a little kid, Siren. Seven-year-olds never hurt anybody."

She nods as more tears fall. I kiss her eyes, her cheeks and chin, and she kisses my mouth. Her tongue is warm and soft, her hand cool on my hot cheek. When I push my tongue into her mouth, I think of her pussy and wish I could be there. Pretty soon, my dick is hard, and I'm gritting my teeth.

She laughs, a soft, unsteady sound, and, to my surprise, pets it. "Quite opportunistic."

"Sorry."

"Don't be sorry." She looks up and down the trail and then back at me. Her face is splotchy, but her mouth is bent into this dirty little smile.

Finley

I look up and down the path once more, and then down at the bit of it below us that's within my range of vision. When I feel reasonably confident we're in the clear, I lay my hand over his bulge and squeeze a bit.

"You came here uninvited, didn't you?"

He laughs, but it comes out a groan. "Finley..." His hand circles my wrist, but still I pet him, smoothing fingertips over the outline of his long, stiff sex until it's straining at his pants.

"You came here of your own accord, and I tried to dislike you, remember?" I catch his head in my fingers and rub my palm against it. "I didn't want to be your friend. I didn't want to be your lover, either, but we were trapped, and you were very, very easy on the eyes and quite a bit too kind for me to freeze out, weren't you?"

I can see him try to focus on me as I speak, but I'm making it difficult for him with my hand.

"Then we arrived back at the village, and the choices were impossible for me."

His chest pumps as I work his sex with my hands. His head is leaned a bit back, so I can see him swallow. Even his neck is a thing of beauty.

"I felt that I should tend to you. I wanted to be near you quite against my will, you see. I tried to stay away, but that's not how it went, and now I'm telling you my secrets—all the things I sought to lock away and just...forget. And you're touching my hair as if we're lovers. Making me *feel* as if we're lovers."

I look around again before unfastening the button of his pants. I delve inside until I find him, hard and hot and ready, and I begin stroking.

"I don't know how you know that women adore having their hair touched, but I've got a fair idea, Carnegie. I don't think you realize it's pure torture being near you." I clasp my hand about the base of him and tug my way back up his thick sex, loving how he looks in this moment, with his eyes narrowed in confusion and his head tilted back.

He looks like a fallen demigod upon the rock, and that thought fuels my raging heart.

"I'd like you better if you were a bit less handsome or a bit more mean, but you're neither, and it's too much for me. It's too much for someone like me. Because you're leaving, see?" I work the head of him until he groans. "And I'll be here without you. And I know how that works out, you see. It doesn't work out pretty."

Suddenly, I want to slap his face—for teasing me this way. For dangling himself in front of me like a carrot I can't help but bite, except the carrot is his warmth and kindness. It's his hands and that hot mouth that makes me shiver, makes my lose my sanity.

I stimulate him as best as I know how—which likely isn't very well, in fact—but I give it my all, and I assault him with my words and hands until he seems quite lost, until he's at my behest.

I can tell he wants to speak—he puts his hand over mine to halt me so he can—but I won't let up. As my fury builds, my hands feel smarter and more skilled. I'm a bit rough, perhaps, but he's so hard he could cut marble, and he's wet there at the tip, as if he's very close to losing control. So I suppose I'm doing something correctly.

I ease up a bit, and when he opens his eyes, I look into them. I try to tell him the things I cannot say. I try to say them with my eyes, because now that we're here, and I've said that, and he's kissed my tears, I realize I can't speak to him—ever again.

As he moans, I work him faster. I drink up his moans, his lovely grunts...the way he stiffens further, groaning. Then the moment comes when his hips jerk and his warmth overspills my hand.

I cried in his arms...but he spent in my hands.

I want to wipe it up and laugh and lay my cheek against his chest. I want to feel his fingers pushed where I feel soft and wet. But I can't.

"I can't do this with you."

I jump up and grab my bag and race off down the path toward the village. Where I live. And suddenly I understand my mother more.

PART II

"If you want a happy ending, that depends on where you stop the story."

—*Orson Welles*

ONE
DECLAN
JUNE 20, 2008

"Happy seventeenth, mofo." We're in the junior common room, a big square at the center of the Carogue campus high school boys' apartments, shoving New York-style pizza into our pie holes, when I reach into my bag and lift out a handle of Saloon Moonshine.

"Well, dammit. I don't think it's big enough." Alf's dark brows jut into his mop of hair as Farhad swipes the bottle from me.

Nate reaches across the table, grabbing hi`s birthday gift. He turns the bottle around, checking out the label before giving me a funny grin. "What the fuck is this?"

"Came from Texas, cowboy."

"How the fuck did you get moonshine here from Texas?"

"I've got my ways."

And my dad has a jet he and my cousin Bryant flew here on back in December. Avoided customs and all that. I can see the wheels turn in Nate's fat head.

"Bryant?" he asks, catching on.

I laugh.

"You were planning birthday shit for Cowboy in December?" Makis gives me bug-eyes, and I roll my own.

Nate turns the bottle around again. "A hundred and eighty percent." He gives a low whistle, shaking his head. "You must wanna kill me."

Alf snorts.

"I think you've got the monopoly there," Farhad mutters.

Nate doesn't even blink at Farhad's jab as he shoves his chair back. "Hands off, ladies." He pushes the bottle to the center of the table and stands, nodding toward the hall behind the table as Alf makes some wise-ass crack about the two of us and "swordplay."

I get up and follow Nate, because I'm not worried about that dumb shit. Last night, I fucked Ms. Keller, the new ninth-grade history instructor—but if I wanted swords, I wouldn't let a bunch of fools like Alf and Farhad make me feel bad for it.

Nate strolls down the hall and steps into the laundry room.

"Check this out." He grins darkly as he reaches into his shorts pocket, pulling out a bag of...oh fuck, that's a lot of pills.

"Knock-off Xannies?" My throat damn near closes off.

"Oxy."

"Fuck, dude. Where'd you get it?" That Ziploc must be stuffed with a hundred of the little oval-shaped pills.

He laughs. "I don't wanna tell you that now, brother."

I've got half a second—maybe more like a quarter-second—to decide how to play this. I'm afraid I know exactly where he got them, but I don't want to spook Nate. He's been skittish as fuck since last summer, starting on his birthday, actually, when he got too coked up and Makis found him razor-blading his wrist in the shower. Had to call a goddamn ambulance.

"If it's who I think it is—" I'll play it low key— "you should be careful."

He snorts. "Says the kettle to the pot, man." Something crosses his face—some kind of look that wants to be aloof but falls short. His thick eyebrows narrow. "You think you've got the monopoly on Laurent?"

Hearing his name makes my stomach knot up. "What does that mean?"

He laughs, shaking his red hair like a mane. He shakes the bag in front of me. "It means your days of having to share Xanny with your boy are over."

"How'd you get him to do it?"

It's there on his face. The way he smirks, and how his freckled cheeks round on a smile that's unmistakably smug.

"How did *you?*" he asks.

My body goes cold as the air leaves my lungs. "What do you mean?" The words echo through me, hollow and surreal.

"Laurent told me."

"Told you what?"

Nate laughs, a low rasp, and the floor tilts under my feet.

"What did he tell you?" I don't realize that I've grabbed his shirt till Nate steps back. He holds both hands out.

"Calm down, bro. Laurent is...like a mentor to a lot of us." He can barely get the words out without snickering.

"He's not your mentor."

"No." His face cements into a serious expression as he stuffs the baggie back in his pocket.

"For how long?" I rasp.

"Long time, brother."

"Did he—"

He holds his hand up, shakes his head. *Don't ask.*

I'm so stunned, I don't feel anger.

Nate. Holy fucking shit, how did I not see?

"So you're saying—"

He chuckles. "Since Caitlin."

Jesus Christ. I can't draw a breath as Nate claps my shoulder and leaves the room. It's my fault. Holy fuck, it's my fault that this happened. Holy fuck.

Somehow, I say bye to my buddies, still eating their pizza. Nate is opening the moonshine. In years to come, I'll remember how he looked as he took off the top. How his eyes held mine for just a second too long, asking if I was upset. Asking, maybe, how I felt about him being gay.

I rip my gaze away from his and mutter, "Happy birthday, fucker."

Then I'm down the stairs and out into the breezy night. I find the old man in his place across campus, watching 30 *Rock* with subtitles and wearing a black bathrobe. When he opens the door, I break his fucking face—for the second time in five years. I unleash the threat I've never had to make; instead, I blackmailed him, promising to keep quiet about what he did to me if he kept me stocked with the pills I needed.

"I don't give a fuck about that now, you fucking piece of shit!" His blood splatters the rug. My knuckle splits as I knock one of his teeth out. I kick him so hard he can't walk for days, I later find out. Then I kick him again.

"You fucking pedophile. You fucking freak!"

When he tries to tell me Nate came onto *him*, I kick him harder. Caitlin was three years ago. This piece of fucking shit has fucked my friend up for three fucking years. I think about the razorblade stuff, and I want to kill him. Then I think of Nate. I think of me and what I'd have to fucking say if someone calls the cops, and I get out of there.

I've got his blood all over me, so I can't go to my room; Nate and I share a bathroom. I spend that night at Ms. Keller's place, letting her suck my dick and patch up my knuckles.

She's young—just a few years older than me, and likely years younger in experience. She never notices something is off with me. When I fuck her from behind, wrapping my arm around her neck, she giggles and she gasps and sighs like it's a game. I'm glad it's a game for her. She isn't scared like I was. I get off pretending she is.

I fuck her three times that way, each a little rougher than the one before. After the last time, I lie down facing away from her, and she touches my back. I lose my shit and fucking yell at her, then say I'm sorry and let her pick out the movie. Some royal shit about King Henry.

Nate won't answer any of my texts. I figure he's fucked up or maybe mad at me for Laurent—that is, *if* he's heard already.

I stay up all night, paranoid as shit that I'll get found out for Laurent and sent to fucking jail or something. I can't sleep. I can't breathe, and I dropped the Xanax that was in my pocket, maybe at Laurent's place.

That's why I walk back to my room at five-fifteen in the morning. I leave Ms. Keller a note, calling her Rachel and saying I'm sorry for the yelling.

Walking across campus to my place, I realize what they told me last year at that two-week program Dad forced me into was right. There's something wrong with me. I can't use Xanax or, fuck it, *anything*, without becoming like this. No way Laurent keeps getting me stuff after last night, and maybe that's a good thing.

I feel just a little better as I open up my dorm-room door. My hands are shaking, but it's no big deal. Now that I know there's a problem with the Xanax, I can stop it—easy.

Something's off about my room, but I can't figure out what. Maybe it's just me. I get the baggie from inside one of my boots and take a Xanax, laughing. What a fucking addict. Then I strip my bloody clothes off, open up the bathroom door to bury them at the bottom of my hamper.

That's how I find Nate. He's slumped over on the padded

bench that lines the bathroom's back wall with a belt around his arm and all those pills swimming around his cold, bare feet.

TWO
FINLEY

Doctor has a wardrobe full of yellows, greens, and reds. I stand in the closet adjoining the master bedroom in the clinic residence, and I thumb through his shirts. I suppose he'd never be caught wearing gray or black or dark blue.

I bring the hem of a bright green shirt to my face and inhale the slight, soft scent of washing soap.

Here is a man who is within my grasp. I could have his babies, serve the people here, and help make Tristan stronger. Yes, he's puritanical and patriarchal, but I can't live with that? Mummy endured worse without losing her brains or running off, as I've dreamed of so often recently. (Not that I *could*, given my fear of boats). Mummy endured everything and always did her best for me.

I wander out of the closet and curl up in bed, and I don't leave until it's time to make two house calls. After that, I scurry back to Doctor's and soak in the bath. I'd like to cry, but I feel nothing.

I remember the morning and try to sear his touch, his lips, his voice into my memory.

I doubt he'll come back 'round this time. Why would he? I know what my assets are; I realize I'm not utterly without them, but I'm not exceptional. I'm just a girl locked on an island, and he's him.

Yes, he holds my hand and gives kisses that reach down to my soul. But he's a natural-born romantic. He knows Neruda; how could he not be? He loves tugging at my hair and giving me his dimpled smiles. He's got a big heart; I suppose it just spills over onto who's nearest. Here, he's had no one but me. No one else who knows his demons. No one whom he trusts with his deft, shaking hands. That doesn't mean he needs me, I tell myself.

Still, I dream of getting on a boat with him, sailing away. I think of what it might be like, but then my chest feels like it might collapse on my heart. I'm locked inside a cage, and I feel it. I've got to get out, even merely for an hour.

I crave the wind on my face and the moonlight in my eyes. I know where I want to go, but I clean house instead, arranging all the knitted pillows neatly on the couch and picking lint off the rugs as if the queen herself might drop in for tea. Finally, when even Baby is tired out, and I feel numb enough for comfort, I put on my coat and boots and slip into the darkness.

Night has always been my favorite time. When I was young, I'd sneak into the grass beside the house and lie there looking at the constellations. When Mummy would catch me, she'd chastise me for going out so late, but then she'd pinch my cheeks and say, "I see you in a space helmet one day, my wee dearie."

Before I spoke again, before I learned to throw clay, I spent my time painting nighttime landscapes with the watercolors Gammy ordered from our old suppliers' magazine.

For years, it's been my habit to walk up to Vloeiende Trane at night and sit there on the moonlit plateau talking to Mum. The nights are often cold and windy, but that matters little to me. I button my jacket to the neck and wear the hood if needed.

As I walk up the ribbon of a road that leads to Gammy's cottage, I think of my mother. What would she think of me now? I'm not an astronaut, nor am I brave or strong or happy. I've failed her.

I hear Gammy's voice, though, and I think about her favorite quote, which says that if you want a happy ending, it depends on where you stop the story. My story's not over—that's true. But I know down in my soul that it will never be a fairy tale. I've made choices that have locked me in, and that's my burden to bear.

As I near the cottage, my heart sits like a lump of steel in my chest. The house is dark except a light that shines on the back porch, where there's an awning that wraps partway around the house, covering my potter's wheel.

I assume he's sleeping. I'm a horrid person for the way I left him there, for using pleasure as a weapon. Perhaps I'm twisted from my perverse past. The idea makes me ache.

I take the trail that winds toward the volcano, following it up the hill that leads to the top of the plateau. It's mostly barren here, but there's a single cluster of these massive shrubs that grew up in a circle. I think I might lie there at the center, watch the stars move till I don't feel so horrid.

I do just that, lying on my back with my knees drawn up, watching my breaths drift in puffs of fog to be tossed by the sea breeze. I hear a whale's song, which my mother used to tell me was the merpeople. That's all it takes to fill my eyes with tears, smearing the stars.

The ground is cool. It chills me through my jacket. Even though I thought it would be good up here...it isn't. It's just the barren earth and the projector image of the starlight. A bit of wind to chill my nose and numb my hands. The reality of things is quite different than daydreams.

"I've nothing to say," I whisper to her.

More and more it seems a cruel trick—all of this. I see no

meaning in my own existence. Nothing sweet or special, nothing even offering a bit of comfort. There are only obligations and the feeling that I'm no different than the cows. I'm just a thing to step about the grass and color up the matrix of our island. I am nearly nothing, really.

I wonder how the others do it. But I know the answer. It's as meaningless for them as me, but they're not alone as I am. Anna lives for Kayti and for Freddy. I suppose Kayti's wee, round belly and Freddy's arms around her in their bed at night must ease the pain, lessen the numbness. That's what makes her warm, what gives her universe its starlight.

I wipe a tear from my cheek.

Holly has her dreams. Nothing's happened to her yet to make her doubt their power. Holly's got both parents, and they worship her. I've been in her house at night when her mum makes that lovely bisque and her father does his crossword by the wood stove. Holly lives next door to Dorothy, and they'll look at magazines and file each other's nails for hours. I adore them both, but all of that is foreign to me. It seems...silly.

I look at my own plain nails, curl my freezing hand into a fist. I use my fist to blot the moon. My hand looks like it's glowing. I've still got it stretched up when I hear footfall—heavy steps, and moving quickly. I sit partway up, then lie back down and tilt my head in the direction of the path that runs up toward the volcano.

When I hear movement on my other side, my stomach drops. Someone's on the plateau with me. I roll over slowly, careful not to make a sound. When I see him silhouetted in the moonlight, all the breath leaves my lungs.

He looks taller, wider, from my vantage point here on the ground: a shadow figure stopped perhaps a meter from the cliffs' edge. I watch as he folds his arms in front of his chest. He stands with his feet a bit apart, as if he's bracing for the wind...which I suppose he is.

Watching him, I feel a clawing sense of want, a sort of breathless desperation for him. It doesn't do for me to be so near him. I shut my eyes and pray he'll pass by quickly. Will this be the last time we're in such proximity? I count down the weeks till his departure as I sit frozen with my eyes closed. Nine weeks—plus or minus. Do I hope for the former or the latter?

I breathe deeply, losing a bit of my balance so I have to open my eyes. When they latch onto him again, I'm alarmed to find he's nearer to the edge. His head is down, as if perhaps he's looking over.

Don't be foolish, Declan.

What's he thinking? Is he tired? Cold? Sad? I want to know it all, and yet it isn't mine to know. I grit my teeth as tears fill my eyes. I wish I could steal away without him hearing, but I don't believe I can.

My throat tightens so fiercely, I can scarcely draw a breath. It's the latter, I decide. I'd like him to leave sooner. I can't even look at him without aching.

As if he hears my thoughts, he steps much closer to the cliffs' unstable edge.

Careful, Sailor.

As if in defiance, he takes a small step. Terror swells in my chest. I feel like I'm in a dream where I should run, but my body is frozen.

When he moves again—to sink down to the ground—I nearly expire from fear. I tell myself he's only sitting, and he's perhaps half a meter from the edge, not there at it. I watch as he brings his knees up to his chest and drapes an arm over them. His hand strokes back through his hair. Then his head bows and one arm comes over it. His hand rifles through his hair, tugs at the tresses. I watch as his shoulders rise and fall.

Lord, give him strength. Give him peace. You alone can ease his pain.

Despite my prayer and my deep belief that God can ease him, I'm swamped with a desperate feeling. One of panic, same as in my drowning dreams. I feel ill with the need to go to him, to hold him as he held me. It's the only thing I want, and yet...I can't.

I wipe my eyes. I lower my hand in time to see him scoot still closer to the drop-off. He drapes his legs over.

My heart stops—and then I'm moving, gliding toward him with the iron will of an angel. There's no question. I *will* reach him.

The frigid breeze slaps my cheeks as he shifts there the ledge. Overhead, the stars pulse. Then I'm dropping to my knees beside him. I can't even breathe his name, can only latch onto his shoulder with a low moan.

As he turns toward me, I see his face has got that lost look I remember from the burrow.

"Declan?" I can't tell who's trembling—he or I? Panting fills my ears as I cling to his arm.

"Shimmy back..." I gasp, "before you frighten me." A cracked laugh squeezes from my throat. "Please."

I look up and find his face looks frozen, his eyes fixed on the sea.

"I loathe this ledge. So dangerous." I press my face against his shoulder as I breathe in deep pulls. "I hate heights." My voice quakes as I imagine the rock below us breaking away.

Declan's hand squeezes my shoulder, and I open my eyes. Then he reaches back with both arms, palms against the ground as if he might push off the ledge. I throw my arms around his neck and lock on.

The next second is a riot of sensation. I dig my nails into his nape as the fall flickers through me like the old films they projected at school. The sharp air and the dizzy plummet twist my senses as my mind plays out a reel of our demise. I'm so certain I'll fall with him that when instead he shifts *away* from the ledge, my mind can't quite comprehend.

"Finley?"

I'm gasping as he stands.

He frowns down at me. "Why are you here?" he rasps.

I look up at him between strands of my wind-blown hair. I swallow hard. "I saw you." My still-racing heart stammers. I can barely rise up on my quaking legs. I'm pulsing with adrenaline. But stand I do.

Bright moonlight hides his features from me as I step closer. My hands curl into fists. "You must be mad! Or have a death wish!"

I pace around him. From a different angle, I find his shadowed face a mask of apathy. "What was going through your mind? I'd bloody like to know!"

When he doesn't move, I shove him. "You could have fallen, easily! That rock sloughs off daily!" I can see the muscle at his jaw tic. *Good.* "What were you thinking? Fancying a midnight swim? It takes eight minutes to drown in the ocean. Have you ever put an egg timer for eight minutes and thought of that? Because I have!" A sob catches in my throat, and he strides to me.

"Fuck." It's so soft, I'm not sure he actually said it. His strong arms encircle me. They're damp and shaking, as is his chest.

I breathe deeply through my nose, too furious to cry.

"Why are you here, Finley?" His big hand rubs circles on my back. "Are you okay?"

I feel him inhale deeply, and I want to strike him—so I step away.

"You nearly died! A stiff wind would have blown us over." Thoughts race through my mind, but I can't seem to fold them into language. Even these few minutes after, panic grips my heart. I realize my eyes have sprung a leak and wipe my face. "I don't think I've ever been so frightened!"

His face is a mask. "I'm sorry." Such a flat voice.

"Were you going to jump?" I laugh, the sound a bit unhinged. "You think you have wings, Declan Carnegie?"

His mouth tightens.

"Is that a yes or no?"

"No."

"Are you quite sure?"

"Yeah, Finley." He shuts his eyes. "I'm fucking sure."

"Then you're the biggest fool that's ever traveled here! Dangling your legs off that way..."

He rubs his eyes with one hand. I can see his taut jaw. "I'm sorry I scared you." One sharp breath, and then release, and his eyes open, peering at me. "Should you be at home?" He tilts his head behind him, toward Gammy's. "You need a ride?"

His voice is low and soft. It makes me want him. When he breathes, it makes me want him. Wanting him sends fury beating through my veins.

"Have you got a car up here then?" I wave around the moon-drenched plateau, and his lips quirk. *Unbelievable.*

"I could drive you from my place." As he says it, he looks down. It takes a moment for his gaze to rise to mine again. When it does, his mouth is soft; his eyes are cautious.

"I'm quite fine. Are you, though?" Tears well in my eyes as I replay what happened.

"Yeah. I...uh...went running." He glances down at himself, and I realize he's in dark sweats and a pale tee, wearing runners. "Figured I'd stop here and...you know. Watch the water."

I nod. My throat stings as I try to keep my tears in.

"I'm sorry I scared you." I watch him shift his weight. In the darkness, I think he bites the inside of his cheek—one of his tells. "And I'm sorry—" He blows his breath out. "I'm sorry for what you said. Before." He breathes deeply again, his big shoulders sinking. "You were right."

He's looking down again, the fingers of his right hand touching his left elbow. For the barest instant, his eyes touch mine.

He's quick to turn away. "Just knock if you want a ride, okay?"

And he's off.

THREE
DECLAN

I'm just rounding that big field behind the house when I hear her behind me.

"Declan?"

I turn to Finley with my eyes throbbing, finding her maybe fifteen feet behind me, one hand drawn up to her throat as if she thinks she needs a shield. "Right about what?"

It's windy. She pushes her hair out of her face.

I jam my hands into my pockets. Rub my lips together till I'm sure that I can keep my voice steady. Then I say, "I was selfish. Just thinking about me—what I want." My heart pounds as she steps closer. I shift so my left arm stays behind me.

"What do you want?" she whispers.

I shake my head. "Don't do this, Finley. I'm fine, and you'll be okay, too." In the moonlight, she looks like she's shivering. I think maybe I see tears on her face. She steps closer, and I'm sure.

"Hey..." I take a half-step toward her before remembering *I can't touch her*. "You should let me drive you back."

Her mouth trembles as she shakes her head.

"Want to come inside...just for a second?"

She shakes her head.

"What's the matter, Siren?"

Tears spill down her cheeks. I step closer to her, but I don't know what to do. Can I hug her? Would that make things worse?

"C'mon, S...I wasn't gonna jump off. That's just crazy."

She shakes her head. "I'm haunted." It's a ragged whisper.

Shit. "I'm really sorry. Keep in mind that I'm a lot heavier than you are. I couldn't get blown off. And the rock was steady. I'm a climber. I could tell. Maybe it was a bad idea, but I wasn't going to fall."

"Weren't you, though?" She steps closer, peering at me with her leaking eyes, and I feel like she can see right through me. "I miss you." Her face crumples, and her shoulders jerk a little as she covers her face, speaking from behind her hand. "Since this morning...I miss you."

She puts both hands over her face, and I start shaking like the freak I am. More than anything, I want to put my arms around her, but what she said today still stands. I know her well enough to know it's her statement of record.

Please don't break my heart.

I swore to myself that I wouldn't.

I put a hand over her shoulder, because that's all that seems appropriate between friends. And I can do that. I can't *not* be her friend. "You'll feel better after some sleep. Everything looks better in the morning."

Her head lifts, her brown eyes flashing. "What bollocks is that? I won't feel better in the morning! If anything, I'll feel worse as time elapses...without you." The word cracks.

She holds her forehead, and I give in. I put an arm around her back and draw her carefully against my side. "C'mon, Finny. Let me take you home. I didn't mean to fuck your night up. I'm sorry."

I glance at my left arm, but I think the bleeding's stopped. I got most of what was dripping blotted off at the plateau. She won't see it if I'm careful when I steer.

I shut my eyes for just a second as we walk toward the car, trying to memorize the feeling of her body against mine. After this, I've gotta stay the fuck away from her.

She stops when we get to the car and stares up at me. "You can't take me home," she whispers. "All the chatter."

After a second, I realize she means people would talk.

"Oh—what happened?" She reaches across me, pointing toward my left arm, and my stomach nosedives. "Did you hurt yourself? Are you all right?"

"Yeah." I run my right hand back through my damp hair so she can't see my left side as well. "Going hard. Ran into something." I square my shoulders, keeping my face impassive. "You want some company on your walk?"

She looks at the ground, then up at me again. "Why don't I walk you in and peek at your arm? That way I won't worry for you."

She looks weird, like she might cry, and I feel like the biggest dick alive. What was I thinking when I touched her in the closet at the burger place that night? If I'd kept my damn hands to myself, we wouldn't be here right now.

I suck a breath back, knowing damn well I can't refuse her. I say, "Sure. If you want."

As she walks into the house in front of me and I step in behind her, I imagine kissing Finley. I could take her by surprise, make her forget why she came in, and keep my arm behind her. *Hide.* It's every addict's first instinct.

We wind up in the living room, and I'm shaking because I can't do that. I can't kiss her. She told me to keep my goddamn distance. It's not her fault I crashed her party, losing my shit on the fucking cliffs. That shit is my fault. Now I've got to make this right, then get her home.

"Sit down." I wave at the couch. "Take your coat off. Someone brought some good stuff by—Miss Laura?"

"Miss Alice's twin," she murmurs with a nod.

"Yeah." I don't remember who Miss Alice is, but I walk toward the kitchen as I say, "Sit down. I'll get you some."

It's darker in the living room than here in the kitchen. I hope she'll wait there. When I don't see her in the doorway, I run the sink's faucet and stick my arm under the cold water.

Fuck. It still looks like shit. Like one big bruise, but you can see the needle marks along the hump of my vein. Would she know what that means? *Yeah, dickhead. She's not an idiot.*

My gaze flies to the knives. The worst of the damage is right there in the crease of my elbow. That bad bruise is probably what she saw in the moonlight. If I could make a little cut there, she might notice that and not the other shit.

With another glance over my shoulder, I grab the knife and set it in the sink. I look back again before pulling the plate of bread closer, like I'm fucking with that. Then I lower my arm into the sink and, with shaking fingers, drag the knife tip over my skin.

As I set the knife back into the sink's trough, she says, "Declan?"

Shit.

I nearly jump out of my skin as she strolls over.

"Oh, it's friendship bread. We do a lot of that here lately." I fold my arm up as she looks from the plate to me. "Have you tried it?"

Sweat prickles my hairline as I feel blood drip off my arm. Right on target, Finley's eyebrows scrunch up. Then her eyes pop open wider, and she looks me up and down. "Are you all right?"

Her gaze dips to the floor and then snaps to my arm.

"Oh no. Sit down there." She points at the kitchen table. I pull a chair out as she leaves the room. Then I double back and stash the knife back in its slot. *You fucking idiot.* I sit down and dig my fingertips into my bicep, raise the arm over my head.

Just take some deep breaths.

I do that, so I'm not shaking quite as bad when she comes back with a first-aid kit. Her brows are drawn together in concern, and her red, puffy eyes are kind enough to make me feel another wave of hatred for myself as she sits in the chair beside mine.

"There now. Let me have a look..."

I don't want to show her, but I'm out of options. I stretch my arm out, shut my eyes. I feel weird and sweaty, kind of tingly. Her hand on my forearm makes me feel like I'm about to get sick.

I pull in some deep breaths, waiting for the gasp or murmur. Instead, she tears a packet open.

"All right. I'll get cleaning it. All I have is alcohol on hand, so it will burn more than a bit. I'm terribly sorry."

It does burn. I feel it in my head and throat—a deep, deep sting that makes my eyes and mouth water. I must have gotten veins with that knife cut and not just flesh. After she's done cleaning the gash with alcohol, I start to shake again because... endorphins. Pain—and then the absence of it—feels like pleasure to me.

I feel calm for just a minute. Calm enough to get a few deep breaths with my face hidden behind my right hand. Then her fingers drift along my vein.

She's quiet as she cleans the puncture marks, but I've got my eyes shut, and everything feels like it's spinning. She said she didn't want to see me anymore, which means she doesn't want to see this shit. I dig my fingers into my temples. She rubs something over the marks.

I can hear the beeps and robot voice of the defibrillator. For the thousandnth time, I wish I'd never been brought back. I think about the lines of light crisscrossing—light on water; of the sinking and the thick, pervasive cold that was my death dream... and I feel so much worse.

Finley rubs my forearm. "I'm going to do a gauze wrap so the Band-Aids don't tug at your hairs here."

She wraps my whole forearm, starting at the top, where she takes for-fucking-ever wrapping the cut. Before she ties it off, she whispers, "Does it feel all right?"

I nod, and she does the rest. I know it's stupid, but I can't look at her. Not even when her hands are off my arm, and it's becoming weird not to. I run my hand into my hair and hold my forehead. Force myself to swallow. Speak. "Hey—could you go now?"

I fucking pray she'll take the out. When she doesn't reply, I exhale slowly. "Just a sewing needle." I train my eyes on the table-cloth. "Kind of like a fake-out...for cravings."

I can see the moonlight on the water up above me. That's how I know it's a hell nightmare and not some peaceful heaven vision. The way it squiggles? That part's how I know that it's the ocean: waves. As I drift underneath the surface, I feel pain in every part of me. Not just my chest, where it makes sense because they were doing chest compressions as I dreamed.

I feel fury. Agony. A helplessness that's so profound, I feel it ripping at my fucking soul. I remember trying to kick my way up. It felt so urgent, like I'd be okay if I could just get to the surface. Up to...someone.

I was dead, but I remember someone waiting for me up there. Ever since then...

I squeeze my eyes shut as I hear her push her chair back.

* * *

Finley

He can't look at me. That's what hurts the most, I think: to see him with his eyes averted, asking me to please just go—so that he doesn't have to speak about it.

I imagine that he must have struggled quite a lot and jabbed himself to simulate a pleasure feeling, and then run to fire up his endorphins. When that didn't work, he wound up at the cliffs, racked with so much pain he thought of jumping.

I think of how he seemed outside, the odd look on his face as we stood near the automobile. Just a look of pain, really. I saw it mostly in his eyes, the sort of squint about them. Now I understand. He was poorly the entire while, even as he offered to drive me home, telling me I would feel better tomorrow. My poor Sailor.

His hand remains over his eyes. I see the tension in his frame, his shoulders. How long has he struggled this way? Since the burrow? Thinking of the burrow brings to mind the time when we stood by the cave's mouth—just before he moved the stone—and he crouched down in front of me so I'd be forced to look at him.

I take a deep breath, and then I sink down to my knees beside him. I crawl partway beneath the table cloth and tap his knee. When he shifts a bit, I laugh.

"Peek down at me. Please," I whisper.

"What are you doing?"

"If you won't look up..." I scoot my entire body beneath the table, and he gives a rough laugh.

For a second, he won't move. I'm just sitting by his knees. I lean my cheek against one of his thighs and wrap my arm around his calf. I cross myself. Then, with whispered words, I gamble.

"If you knew how wonderful I find you...simply lovely—really in all ways. And I know you're wildly wealthy and quite sought after." I smile. "But that part doesn't matter to me." I press my cheek against his thigh, against the softness of his running pants, and hug his calf. I feel him trembling. "I could never pity you because I have so much affection for you, Carnegie, that I can tell you only from beneath a table. Because you're right. I am shy." I stroke his hard calf, feeling a bit surreal.

"I know you must be in such a horrid state, but that's not what I see most clearly. I simply adore you...and it's *you* I see. I think I cannot stay away." I gulp a breath back, my heart racing even as my words are soft and measured. "Before tonight, I was afraid of being hurt. Then I saw you on the ledge, and the fear I felt..." I shake my head. "Not only was I terror-stricken, but... I wanted you. My heart ached the moment I saw you." I blink against my tears, and his leg shifts slightly.

"I've decided I don't want to stay away. If it hurts—if feeling this way for you simply *hurts*—I'll bear it. I want to be near you. I want you to hurt near me. I feel certain that together we'd be...better."

I feel him shift a bit. I peek up, but I don't see his face. I duck out from beneath the tablecloth and find him with his head down, his forehead resting on his right forearm. For once, his body seems completely motionless.

"I'm frightened now." I try to laugh, but the sound catches. "If you feel I'm mad... If all of that seems quite apart from how you feel—"

He lifts his head, and I see that his eyes are red. His face is stoic.

I wipe at my tears. "I suppose I simply wanted to jump for you, and to hell with the consequences."

His chair scrapes the floor, and then he's wrapping me against his chest, holding me in a near-crushing hug. I feel his ribs flare, and I cling to him with returning force.

Then he's scooping me up, carrying me through the living

room as a groom carries a bride, his strong arms beneath my back, behind my knees, my cheek against his warm chest. Never, as he carries me to the bed, does he look at my face. Neither does he as he stretches out atop the covers beside me, drawing me against himself, his hands trembling.

He presses his cheek atop my head. I wrap my arms around his neck.

"Since the burrow," he says hoarsely.

He breathes deeply, and I kiss his throat as my heart hammers wildly.

"The first night back, I was afraid," I whisper. "I'm so sorry I left you."

A tremor moves through his shoulders. "Don't be sorry." He kisses my hair, hugs me closer. "You're so fucking perfect, Siren. Sometimes it's the only thing that gets me through."

"I'm so sorry that you're suffering." I run my hands into his hair. I kiss his throat, and then his chin. I stroke his forehead with my fingertips. "My poor darling... Is it this way every day?"

He gives a little lift of his shoulders, shuts his eyes.

"You're so strong. A lion," I whisper. "You're so good and kind. Relief will come."

His fingers strum my back like a guitar, even as I feel him trembling.

"You're so brave." I lean back a bit to look into his eyes and find them closed. I kiss his cheek. "I won't leave you alone again. I'll stay here with you."

His mouth covers mine, and together we groan.

FOUR
FINLEY

He kisses deep and hot and hard, as if he means to claim me. One hand fists my hair. The other cups my cheek as his tongue cravenly explores my mouth, its probing rhythm making my thighs press together as a warm weight drops low into my belly.

I'm spun 'round in the frenzy of his onslaught: his rough cheeks scratching mine, his mint-tinged breath in my nostrils, the way his lips are bruising mine and my mouth is opening for more, my jaw aching till we wrench apart to breathe in frenzied tugs.

Then he's moving, shifting so he's crouched above me. All I see are his eyes, asking questions that I try to answer with my own. He lowers his hips atop mine, and I can feel his thick erection.

"Siren—are you sure?"

I can't answer for my tight throat, but I grab his shoulder, pulling him down on me. His head nuzzles my throat, and then he's kissing me there. His hips rock against mine, his sex dragged over my softness until I cannot take it anymore.

I'm pulling his hair, groaning. "Please..."

"Please what?"

I wrap my arm around his hips, pressing my palm against his back, and lift my backside so my sex rubs his.

He groans, and then his mouth is moving over my throat. His kisses are so hard, I feel heady with a sort of fright which fuzzes into to velvet bliss and then near pain as his long, stiff sex rubs against me and my insides tremble in primal response.

I can't stop myself from stroking every inch of his warm skin. I drag my nails along his sides, caress his shoulder blades. His muscles quiver and his breathing quickens. We reach a point where every time his sex catches on mine, we moan and thrust our hips. I hold his face between my palms. His eyes reach into mine.

You know what I want, Carnegie. Now give it to me...

His mouth finds mine—tender, slow, an answer. I can't discern if it's "yes" or "no," and so I simply kiss him back and tell him that way: *Yes, I want this. I want you.*

I want you.

I want you.

We pant with our foreheads pressed together. Then we're back in motion, nothing but our hungry mouths and grasping hands. He can't hold out much longer—I can feel it in the tremor at his hips, can hear it in the way his breaths come from the throat.

He takes my pants down...then my panties. He's there where I'm slick and ready, rubbing his round tip through my folds.

"Ohhhhh."

My back arches, and suddenly he's off the bed. "Hang on a second." And it is merely a second—just a breath—before he's returned, sitting on his haunches with his large sex jutting from his hips. I hear the rip before I see him roll the condom over his sex.

He looks back up, his dark eyes wide and glassy. "Tell me no if you don't want it." He crawls over me, tracing his fingertip over my puffy slit. "I can lick this pussy, make you come like that."

"I want you," I whisper.

When he presses his tip into my slit again, I moan and thrust against him. My heart races, and my head feels light and hollow.

"It's gonna hurt." His words are groaned, as if he'll feel the pain as well.

He rubs his thick tip where I'm slick, the latex-covered head of him brushing deliciously against my clitoris before he drags himself back through my folds, making me lift my hips. Then he's there—he's where I'm pooled wet with desire and swollen with need. I can feel the pressure of him as he fits himself against me.

But instead of pressing in, he leans back over me, his lips and tongue teasing my nipple, his sheathed sex pressed into the crevice between my hip and thigh as our taut bodies quiver.

I run my fingers through his soft hair, tugging. "Let it hurt, then."

He gives me his eyes—careful as ever; even beneath the glaze of lust, I feel his kind concern for me—and then he's bowed again between my thighs, lapping at me with his silken tongue when what I need is his thick sex. He's stoking my fire, and I can scarcely bear it.

"Please...oh please!" His tongue skates around my clit, making me gasp, then groan low. Finally, he fills me with his fingers. He pushes in and then drags out, and my knees clench around his shoulders.

"Oh!"

He probes deeper, and his mouth—

I try to fight what's overtaking me, but I can feel it rolling in—the sort of tide that stretches smooth before it gathers in a round fury and crashes hard against the rock. I come apart like white caps spraying, making rainbows.

Then I'm fuzzed about the edges, so much so, I nearly fail to notice him; he's risen up onto his knees, and his large hand is wrapped around his sex. He's pushed it down toward his thigh, out of the limelight. But I can see it, long and condom-white and thick, still begging for attention.

Tears are drying on my cheeks. I laugh though them, and when he smiles at me, his handsome face is warm and kind —indulgent.

He shifts, as if he's moving to stretch out beside me. I shove at him.

His eyes round in inquiry.

"Sit up—please. I want to see it."

He does—and I do. It's standing tall and thick and proud, its thick tip pressed against his navel. The weighty globes below look taut, distinctly darker than the pearly latex.

"May I...touch it?"

Just the barest hesitation, then he's stretching out beside me, lying on his side with his hips near my shoulders, putting himself within my reach. I grab hold and rub gently from tip to base. Then I cup his balls, my fingers trembling as I stroke there.

His eyes close. The rough sound from his throat is both grunt and groan. Something in me coils more tightly.

"Does it feel good?" I trace a fingertip around the flanged rim of his tip, and his whole lower body jerks.

"Ahh...*Jesus*."

There's a notch there on the underside of his head. I can see it plainly through the latex. I press there, and he barks out a groan so loud, I jerk my hand back.

"Fuck." His arm covers his face, and his hips rock toward me. I feel so wet and ready, somehow both heavy and empty, buzzing...as I rise up on my knees and urge him onto his back. His sex juts over his flat belly, inviting me to wrap my hand around it. I lean down, curious if I can lick it...and I do. I lick at the tip, grinning as I find it tastes like candy.

He fingers thread through my hair as I tease him with my tongue, then suck the tip of him into my mouth. Anna told me what to do, the way you need to stroke the shaft and do as much as you can to the tip; men like to be teased there. If you take it into your mouth, swallow back deeply and don't let your teeth touch.

I do everything I know to. It works like magic. Throaty moans and raspy whimpers come from his throat, and his hands cinch in my hair. I can feel it building in him, feel his hips shift as he tries to keep himself from shoving down my throat. I suck his thick tip, tracing the rim with my tongue.

My hands tremble as I realize *I'm doing this.*

This man is my lover—this beautiful man. I want nothing more than his pleasure. I draw more of him into my mouth, and his backside comes off the mattress. He starts breathing hard and heavy, groaning as if he can't help himself. I can sense his burgeoning discomfort. It's in every line of his big, smooth-skinned body with its thick, round muscles and its hard, male angles.

"What do you need?" I'm quite evil, and what's worse is I delight in it. He cannot even answer for a time, just smooths my hair out of my face as his intoxicated gaze clings to mine.

"Wrap your hand around the bottom." His eyes squeeze shut as his jaw clenches. "Just...go up and down."

Instead I rise on my knees, scooting closer before rubbing him where I need him.

"I want you here."

His eyes peel open. They seem pained, and when he speaks, his lovely, warm voice vibrates. "No."

"Why not?"

"I can't—" His eyes squeeze shut, then open. "Finley."

It sounds like a plea...or prayer.

"You can't tell me you don't ache for it. You're desperate to press into me...and I want you there." My voice catches. "I crave it."

I lie on my back beside him, handing him the reins. My heart hammers as we lie there, side by side, both panting. Then he's up. He's on his knees between my legs. His eyes are molten as his hand works his stiff sex, stroking from tip to base, making his balls bounce with each firm stroke.

"Finley..."

I reach for him, stroking the twin globes as he tugs his sex. He groans raggedly.

"I need you," I whisper.

"Oh fuck...*Finley*."

I wrap a hand around his shaft, and with the other trace the seam between his testes. Something like shock flickers through his features. Then he rubs himself against me. I can feel the pressure of him, feel the tremble in his arm, the one that's holding him up. His eyes focus on mine as he rubs me harder with his firm tip.

"You're so fucking perfect."

"You are."

I laugh, and his eyes squeeze shut. I stroke his arm and lift my hips.

"Are you sure?" It's raspy, an apology in a question.

"Yes."

His eyes open to hold mine. His hand grasps my hip. I can feel him rubbing at me, pressing there.

"I'm sorry," he rasps.

The next moment, he thrusts. I'm torn open, soul and body. He's in me. He's in me. Oh—I feel him deep inside. The stark invasion has me panting, my legs quaking as I try to make sense of the massive presence, of the stinging soreness of my flesh, and at the same time, such a heady, stuffed sensation. I shift a slight bit, and he presses at my insides, making me groan.

I'm shaking, my eyes leaking. Over me, he's panting as his hand smooths my hair off my forehead.

"You okay?"

"Yes."

"Fuck. Ahh, *Finley*..."

He sounds desperate. I can feel him trembling, too. I grip his arm as sweat rolls down my temple. Then he pushes deeper.

"*Ohhhhh.*"

It's exquisite. I feel filled—too full—and somehow in need of precisely that. I shift my hips again, and he moves his—so carefully at first, withdrawing slightly, stinging. Then his wide eyes burn mine, and he presses fully in again, his eyes closing. He makes a grunt-like sound...and I'm impaled. I'm simply stuffed full, all my nerve endings flashing like lightning and rolling like thick thunderclouds.

Light rolls through me—blazing, golden.

"Oh fuck. Fuck..." His body quakes above mine. His face twists. I feel his legs quake. He's in so deep, I cry out at the pleasure of it. And then he draws out nearly all the way, his hand gripping my shoulder as he pushes back in.

"Oh!"

"Finley." He's out and then he's plunging back in, tightening my belly, trembling my knees.

I can't help a grunt as he draws out and repeats, filling me with so much pleasure, I fell near to bursting with it.

He groans, repeating the thrust two more times, until he's buried fully in me. I feel heavy, something tugging at me. At the same time, I'm swelling. I'm starting to spark.

Then his hips begin to thrust more rhythmically. His eyes are shut tightly, his dark brows furrowed, full lips parted. Every time he fills me, I can feel it building. Pleasure rolls through me, lifting me up.

I feel when he's near release—the frenzied pace, the way he

fills me tighter. I'm groaning, grunting, grasping at my own tendrils of bliss.

I slam against him, crying, "Harder!"

He gives what I ask, and two more thrusts—

I scream as his chest comes low over mine. I can feel him trembling, then we're panting; we're both panting, and he's dripping sweat. I'm weeping and he's whispering, his voice rough and concerned. I'm kissing his salty shoulder.

"Did I hurt you?"

"Yes," I laugh.

He lifts himself up, and I clench around him. My hand squeezes his hip.

"I like it," I whisper drunkenly. "I like it."

My awareness ebbs as he withdraws and moves off me. A rush of cold air sweeps my damp, prickling skin. Then his arms are coming beneath me. I'm being lifted. I'm held against his chest, and his eyes are on my face.

I can't read his face as he strides into the bathroom, where he sets me on my feet in the cold tub and leans over to start the faucet. He uses his hands to direct the water away from me before it's warmed up.

I smile at that.

His gaze swings to mine, and I find his blue eyes wide and cautious.

"What's the matter?"

He gives me a funny little smile, but I can feel the tension underneath it. "Are you okay?"

"I'm lovely."

I watch as he swallows. "Are you sure?" His voice is low.

"*Yes.*" I reach for him, my fingers gripping his forearm. "Get in with me."

His eyes scan the tub.

"Get in. I don't care how. I'll sit on your lap."

When he doesn't move, I rise gingerly on my knees and wrap my arms around his neck. "Carnegie..." I kiss his cheek as he reaches down to put the stopper in the tub.

When he looks at me again, his face is gravely serious. I stroke his cheek and lean in close. "What's the matter, darling?"

He won't look at me.

"Did it hurt you?"

"No. Fuck no." He stands up, and I scoot toward the faucet. "Sit behind me."

After a moment's hesitation, he climbs in behind me, stretching his strong legs out around me. As I wonder if I've ruined this somehow, he wraps his arms around my waist. He folds my back against his chest, one arm below my breasts, and I can feel him breathing.

I cling to his forearm. When he kisses my shoulder, I rub his leg with my foot. Then I need the reassurance of his eyes. I turn to face him. Instead of kissing me, as at first I think he will, he pulls me to him, hugging me so hard it nearly hurts.

I hug him back. I stroke his shoulder, kiss his pec.

"I'm sorry." His voice vibrates.

"Why are you sorry?"

He shakes his head. He shakes his head again, and I can feel him inhale. "It's been a while." It's whispered.

"Was it..."

"It was good. I'm glad I had the condom."

I press my hand to his chest. I can feel his heartbeat, hard and fast. "Tell me what's wrong."

His eyes shut, and he shakes his head once more. When he speaks, the words are soft—so very soft, near murmured. "I don't want to hurt you."

"I'm not hurt. It felt amazing."

I frame his face with my hands, gently forcing his eyes to mine. Troubled eyes.

I stroke his cheeks and neck, and then his shoulders. His eyes close. Then his hand comes to his face, his fingers tunneling into his hair.

I hug him.

"I don't do that...with virgins." It's a raspy whisper.

"Why not? Does it...hurt you?"

He shakes his head. "Doesn't feel fair." His eyes open. He looks dazed.

"Why not?"

He shakes his head again.

"You're far from a virgin. Is that why?"

He nods once.

"I knew. I figured," I amend. "You're gorgeous and wealthy...a sports star." I'm trying for a bit of levity, resurrecting the sentiment I expressed in the burrow—that I won't pity him because he's so superlative. I want to prompt a smile.

Instead, he holds his head with one hand; with the other, he grips the bath's side. "I can't fuck you up, Finley."

"You won't. You didn't. Come here..." I try to kiss his mouth and end up kissing his chin. "You would never hurt me. I know that, and I'm not worried at all."

His eyes lift open, and his mouth takes mine. He kisses me deeply...with a sort of hunger. Then he wrenches away. I feel as if he'll lean away. Instead, he pulls me to him, holding me against his chest, where I can feel his heartbeat. "When we got back, I was fucking haunted by you."

When we got back—from the burrow. "Likewise," I whisper.

He inhales. Blows the breath out. "I don't do this." It's half groaned. He's got his head bowed near my shoulder.

"Do what?"

"Nothing more than sex. Ever." The words are rough and soft. Confessional.

"So...no dinners. No dates. No snuggling or kisses...or baths."

I brush my lips along his jaw. "You don't want those things?" I whisper over his skin.

I feel him shiver before he shakes his head. "Not good at it."

"I'd argue that on baths." I smile a bit as I feather a kiss over his collarbone. "You're sitting up. Staying afloat. In fact, you're keeping me afloat. Without support, I simply sink. Quite like a stone."

His mouth curves up on one side. He's still got his eyes closed, so he doesn't see me coming as I kiss one dimple, then the other.

"Let me tell you something, Carnegie." I wait a beat until his eyelids lift. His mouth is still quirked up a bit as I say, "I'm not like your other girls."

"How so?" He's smirking, despite the heaviness that's clinging to the rest of his face.

"I don't know. I don't know what they're like. But I'm not like them. I can sense all your malarkey."

He grins—just a flash, but it's radiant. I run my hand down his arm till my hand meets his, and then I squeeze. "I think you're romantic. It's your secret, I believe. I can't imagine you dismissing me after what we just did. But you're saying that's what you do normally?"

He casts his eyes away from mine, looking at the flowing faucet. After a time, he says, "It's different there. Sometimes they want that, too."

I regard him with my eyes narrowed, my head tilted. "You need women in your bed and bath. You hate to be alone."

He makes a skeptical face—a bit exaggerated, silly—as a cover for the weight of things. "What makes you say that?" Now he's looking at me again.

"You're a barfly. And the whole world knows you throw massive parties. Besides that, I feel it."

His lips press together, seeming tremulous despite the way he widens his eyes and arches his brows; he's trying for a silly a face, a much more casual impression.

I lean in, sighing as I rest my cheek on his shoulder. "In any event, I'm not leaving your bath or bed. Tell me you don't want me to," I whisper.

His cheek rests on my hair. I hold my breath as he inhales slowly, perhaps deciding if he'll give me honesty. After a long second, he says, "I don't want you to."

He takes my face in his hands, peering into my eyes before kissing me. His mouth is hard and firm, his tongue forceful and smooth. We kiss until my hands are squeezing his shoulders. I need air, but I don't have the self-control to pull away.

When finally we part, I gobble down a breath or two, and then I'm laughing.

"What's so funny?" His eyes burn into mine.

"I'd rather kiss you than breathe."

I run my hand down his side, and he cups my breast. A moment later, he gathers me in his arms, slowly stands, and, holding me to his chest, grabs a towel, which he folds around me.

He grins down at me as he carries me to the bed, where he tucks me in and delves under the covers. He rests his cheek on my thigh, and I stroke his shoulder then his bicep with my foot. He kisses the back of my knee. I'm panting as his mouth crawls upward.

Then his lips and tongue are where I'm warm and needy. And for all my talk—all my bluster in the tub—I'm reduced to whimpering. I come so fiercely, I'm near-instantly tugged under afterward.

I feel him situate beside me, pulling me against his chest. With no ado, he folds himself around me, and we sleep.

FIVE

DECLAN

I told her I wasn't going to jump, but that's not completely true. I didn't *want* to jump. I fall asleep with that thought in my head and sleep a few hours before waking. I lie still for a while longer, my body curved behind her smaller, softer one, my lips wanting to kiss her hair—although I don't.

At five, when I don't think I can keep from rubbing my erection against her ass, I climb out of bed and start on pancakes. While I stand there flipping them, I think that it feels like I *did* jump. Not in the way of the relief I think that would be—I feel like I'm in a free fall.

Should I be fucking her? Obviously not. It's been high school since I fucked a virgin. There's a certain type of woman I go for back home, and it isn't never-been-kissed. I prefer the older ones, the one-night-standers who tell me from square one all they want is a night full of Homer. Or the married ones whose husbands fuck around my circle, so I know it's okay to take them for a quick spin out of wedlock; there are no expectations.

The best ones are the so-called "bat bunnies"—the ones who

fuck the whole damn team—the unattached ones, anyway—then tag us all on Instagram or post a pic in someone's boxer briefs.

If a girl in Boston, or New York, or LA looks younger than me, I give her a second thought. I try to say "no" if she's fucked up on something, if she mentions anything about the future, or gets breathless when I kiss her. If she even hesitates unbuttoning my pants, sometimes I'll get cold feet and throw the brakes on.

I feel like a stranger to myself when I think of Finley curled up back there in the bed, probably just a little while away from waking up sore. Sore because I let myself take what I wanted.

But—*fuck me*—I can't seem to do things differently. I can't stay away from her. Even if I wanted to, I can't. The worst thing is, I *don't* want to. I've got no sense of restraint when I'm around her. No self-control. I don't like that. If nothing else, I want to be someone who's...not predatory.

She seemed like she knew what she wanted, but does she really? How will she feel when it's time for me to go home? How the fuck do I respect her right to decide what to do with her own pussy and also protect her?

By not fucking her, dipshit.

Just say "no."

I move some pancakes from the skillet to the plate and think hard on that option. Thinking of ending things with her makes my stomach lurch. Gives me that bad free-fall feeling.

I'm still thinking when I spot her in the doorway. She's got on the same clothes as last night—dark jeans and a plain gray, long-sleeved shirt—but her hair's flowing down her shoulders, and her face is soft, her eyes sleepy. When she sees me, she grins like she's won the lottery. She bounces over, throwing her arm around me as she laughs softly.

"Look at you." Her hand comes to my neck, and I frown before remembering I put an apron on. I shake my head, and she hugs me.

"That was Gammy's. It looks better on you, though. What are you doing in here?" She looks at the skillet, and her green eyes widen. "Incredible."

"You think I can't cook?"

She laughs. "Of course. I'd imagine you'd have a harem of lady chefs who feed you grapes in bed."

I snort. Then I wrap my arm around her, pull her up against my side so I can hold her up against me while my free hand flips the pancakes. "I can cook a few things, Siren. Mac and cheese. Bacon. Cheese toast." I chuckle. "Pancakes...waffles."

"These smell lovely."

She breaks away from me, setting up the table for us. I can feel her eyes on my back as I finish cooking. While we eat, my heart starts kind of racing and my hands start shaking, but I keep on talking—we're debating whether aliens will visit Earth (she thinks yes, I think maybe)—and keep eating, even though I've got that never-ending seasick feeling.

When we've almost finished off the pancake pile, she drops a piece into her lap, and my hand dives under the table cloth. Our eyes meet, and instead of moving back to the table, my hand curves around her knee.

She looks at me with wide eyes and an "o" mouth and those pink cheeks, and I can't help smiling.

"It's the shy Siren." I stroke her denim-covered thigh.

Her hand covers mine, and she smiles shyly. She looks giddy. Like a kid. We lace our hands together, and that's how we sit while we both finish eating.

We end up fucking again after. I don't want to push her, but in the end, it's Finley who pushes me. We're on the couch, and I'm about to push in when I realize I don't have a condom. I have to run go grab one. Finley laughs her ass off as I try to get it on.

"It's far too tight!" She chortles.

I shake my head, tugging and pulling at the damn thing.

"Are you too oversize for ordinary condoms?"

"Oversize. Now that sounds like a bad thing."

"Oh, it's not a bad thing."

My gaze catches on her bare breasts and her legs, spread slightly, giving me a peek at that plump pussy. I can't formulate a reply. My dick is desperate to be in that tight cunt. I dirty talk her some and tease her, rolling my head around her dripping slit while she squirms, looking gorgeous with her hair everywhere and a little smile on her lips.

I make sure she's nice and wet before I push in. Then I hold her hips, gritting my teeth as I restrain from the hard fuck I want to give her. It's her second time; I've gotta take it slow. That's okay, because it feels so goddamn good...the way she squeezes me. I try to remember anything before her—the last time I fucked a woman and felt good after.

Shit, when was it? Last summer? I don't like to think of that, so I focus on my breathing and her little murmurs and her sharp cries. I bring Finley pleasure, and I have myself one hell of a hard come. Afterward, she crawls into my lap and teases my cock in its condom. She runs her warm palm down my happy trail, and I get hard again. Then she cradles my balls and gets me panting like a teenager.

I growl. She giggles.

"I wouldn't do that if I was you..."

I laugh, and I feel like I should get up. Toss the condom, find some way to get my dick down. Siren follows me back to the bedroom. When I step out of the bathroom, still hard, sans condom, she's there in the bedroom doorway with her nipples peeking out from under her long hair.

"Dammit, woman." My hand wraps around my cock, and Finley saunters closer. "What're you trying to do to me?" My words sound hoarse...like it's me who was the virgin.

She runs her hand up my chest slowly, tickling with her fingernails, but her brown eyes are wide. She's watching my face.

I run a hand into her hair and kiss her cheek, and then her lips. I'm going to kiss her and then tell her she doesn't have to fuck me all day, but I can't seem to stop once I get started. We kiss until we're both panting. When I pull away, her face looks startled.

"You okay?"

She nods, still wide-eyed...but they're glazed now. Like she wants it.

I rock my dick against her leg. "That's because you're fucking beautiful, and you feel so good. When I'm with you, I want to be in you. Every time." She reaches between us, running her hand up and down me. *Fuck.* I take a deep breath as she strokes me. Force myself to go on. "You don't have to, though. Okay?" My hand cups her shoulder, squeezing lightly as her hands send pleasure rolling through my belly, down my legs. "Anything we do...is enough."

She gives me a solid tug and whispers, "Is it, though? What's wrong with more?"

I don't want to hurt you. I'm going to say it, but it feels so damn good, what she's doing. I end up leaning on the bed, and then I'm on my back, with my legs hanging off the side. And Finley's got her lips around me.

She's giving my head these tentative licks, teasing that little slit with the tip of her tongue. It's making me moan. I pull her hair...then stroke her hair. She keeps kissing up and down my shaft. I'm about to shove my dick down her throat if she doesn't take it herself. That's a lie, though. I just groan and flex my legs... and she eases my head out of her mouth and looks up at me, grinning like a fucking minx.

"I adore those noises you make."

That's the last thing I process before she reads my mind and deep-throats my dick. I can tell she's new to it from how she gags —I rub her hair and rasp out some instructions—but she's damn good. I try to pull out when I feel it building, but she won't let me. I come so hard I see stars.

Afterward, I can't move off the bed. I feel wrung out, like I might even fall asleep.

"I've got an idea," she murmurs. I can sense her walking off. She comes back back a minute later. She tosses a blanket over me, and I move my legs fully onto the bed as I squint up at her.

"Do you trust me?" she murmurs.

"I don't know how much I like that question."

She kisses my forehead. "Yes, of course you trust me."

She holds something up, and I realize it's one of those little potion bottles. "Let me give you a bit of this. Stay here and rest. I've got two patients today and one errand. I'll bring Baby with me when I return, we'll wake you in three hours. Then I'll cook you lunch and dinner."

I can't swallow as I peer up at her.

She runs her hand over my arm. "I'll report you ill, and there's my excuse for returning to see you, should someone spot me en route. Perfect."

I inhale slowly, and she leans down, rubbing her cheek against mine. Her lips tickle my jaw, making my dick twitch. "I know every herb by heart, all the ones that could potentially help you." She strokes my hair, making my eyelids heavy. "This will be a good thing. Say yes."

I do—because she's smiling so angelically. Also, I don't figure it'll really knock me out. I open my mouth like a little kid, and Finley gives me something from a dropper. Then she kisses me, stroking her tongue into my mouth, which tastes like liquor and strange sweetness.

"I'll let myself in when I return since I know you like that. I'll wake you."

I drop into sleep like parachuting off a plane and drifting down into a field. I dream of her hair, her sweet smell. I can feel her kisses on my throat, her hand around my dick. And then my eyes are open, and she's really here. She's straddling me. Her long hair is tickling my chest, and she's biting my nipple.

Fuck.

I feel her hand on my cock, and I realize she's been jacking me off. Holy fuck, I'm hard.

"Ready to go again," she giggles.

"I don't—" My eyes shut as she rolls my balls in her hand. I can't think, can only pant and grit my molars as she works me. Then I'm groaning. "I don't think I have another condom."

I'm surprised to see her hold up a black package. "Got the large size from the clinic bins." She laughs, and strokes me faster.

Christ—I must have died and gone to heaven. Finley rolls the condom onto me—"I read the brochure," she whispers smugly—and then lifts my cock away from my abs, pointing the head at herself.

"I'd like to try on top...if that's all right. Only for a moment, just to feel it."

I laugh—a sound of shock—and then she's crouching over me. With her eyes on mine and her mouth a little unsteady with nervousness, she presses me against herself and slowly sinks down.

Holy fuckshit...

I'm engulfed in heat. Her pussy squeezes me. She's so damn tight, I nearly blow right then. She rocks slowly forward, kissing my chin before I can't take it another second; I lift her by the hips and thrust up into her as I lower her back down.

I'm breathing hard and heavy as she finds her rhythm. Then I'm getting fucking. I'm grunting and groaning, still fuzzy from her potion, and so damn stiff and hot and hard...even my balls are hard.

"Finley. *God. Fuck.*" I feel it coming, and it's like a dream, this whole damn thing. She's bouncing on me, her mouth open and her eyes closed tight as I come. I hear a guttural sound from my throat and I sort of laugh at that, but then my eyes are rolling back into my head. I hear her panting over me.

"Did you come?" My head feels heavy, and my voice sounds rough.

Her fingers stroke my chest. Her soft laugh sends light spinning through me. "Yes, of course."

I feel her moving off me, and I drag my eyelids open. I reach for her, and she takes my hand. Kisses the palm.

"You're...so good." My throat is tight. The word cracks.

"You're better, Sailor."

* * *

Finley

I know how to pleasure him. I'm heady with it. If he feels the way I do...*during*, and just after... I would like to do that for him every day. And I plan to. It's as if a switch flipped last night. I'm "all in" now. This is what I'm doing, and I want to do it well. I want to well and truly be with him before he goes. Today, as I pondered all of this between patients, I concluded it can be quite freeing, letting go. Falling with no though of safety nets.

What do I have to lose? I laugh quietly. One might say I'm desperate. I'm willing to gamble with my soul—if that's the price of following my heart. I realized after our moment at Vloeiende Trane: life is never going to be perfect. So I choose the next best thing. I'm choosing perfect for a time. I'm choosing bliss for all the moments we can find it. When the game is over, no regrets. Even though I know I'm going to lose.

I clean myself up, sifting through my drawers and then his bag before deciding to tuck in beside him sans clothing. I climb carefully over his legs and curl up beside him, covering myself up to the shoulders. Then, gently, I rest my cheek on his bicep. In his sleep, he stretches his arm out. It feels like an invitation. I stare for a moment. Then I fit myself against his side, melding my curves against his angles. His hand curls around my shoulder before slackening as sleep reclaims him.

I snuggle up against him, shut my eyes, and let myself disperse into the rhythm of our breathing. I follow his pulse, inhale his scent, and meditate a bit.

I am here, and I am fine.

I am here, and I am fine.

I am here, and I am fine.

I'm better than fine.

What will happen? I push that errant thought aside and go on drifting.

I mean to enjoy him. Nothing more and nothing less.

About the time the light that's seeping through the curtains darkens to a dusky indigo, his eyes flip open. They're wide on the ceiling. Then they move to my face, and he startles.

"It's all right." I stroke his forearm. "We were napping. You're just waking up. It's dusk."

He draws a deep breath. I can see the grief in his eyes.

I whisper, "Are you feeling poorly?"

His eyes close. "It's...just like this sometimes." His words are so quiet and low, I scarcely hear them.

I lie back beside him, wrap an arm over his chest. He muscles tremble as he inhales deeply. Does he want me near him? I'm relieved when his arm wraps around my back. Pulled up against his chest, I hear his racing pulse.

"It's a bit like fight or flight, is it?"

His cheek presses against my hair. I believe he nods, but can't be certain.

"Do you feel frightened?"

He's still for a long moment. Then he lifts his shoulders.

"It makes sense," I murmur. "Given what those drugs do—" the ones he's withdrawn from— "it's completely sensible." I shift so I can hug him more tightly. "Does this help a bit?" I whisper.

"Yeah."

But his breaths are fast and shallow. I shift more, so we're on our sides, facing one another. His face is somber; his blue eyes are closed. His nostrils flare with every inhalation. I cup my hands around his full lips, trying for a paper bag effect.

Instead, he kisses me between his gulping breaths. His arm loops around me. His hand delves into my hair, pressing our mouths gently together as his tongue strokes mine. Then we're devouring each other.

When we break away for air and he's breathing more slowly, I stroke his face, look into his eyes for some clue how he's feeling.

"Better now." The words are raspy.

"Good." I brush my lips over his temple. "Are you hungry?" I lean back so I can see his face. "Perhaps a bit of toast?"

He nods once.

When I return with cinnamon toast, I find he's shifted onto his side, facing the door. He's clutching his phone, and I can see his large hands trembling. When his gaze finds mine, his tired eyes look lost again.

"Hi there, Sailor."

He tries to smile for me, but it's a twitch of his lips. I stroke his hair, and he pushes up on one arm...then sits fully up, taking his plate. He won't meet my eyes as I sit on the bed's edge, eating my own piece.

"Thank you," he says after a moment.

"I hope it's decent."

"Yeah, it's good." Now his eyes are on me—watching me with care and all the usual perception. "You okay?"

"Of course."

"Not too sore?" Now his voice is low and husky.

"I'm deliciously sore." I can't help grinning. I expect him to return it. Instead he rubs a hand over his face, back through his hair, and does another sad not-smile that makes my stomach knot up.

"If you need to go, I'm good," he tells me.

"Oh...I know. I don't want to, in fact. Is that all right?"

"Yeah."

I stretch out beside him, pressing my face to his thigh and hugging his legs.

"My Declan." I squeeze. "I forgot! I meant to make you tea. It's tea time."

He gives a hollow laugh—a bit surprised, I think—as I flounce from the room, feeling a bit giddy. Everything will be well. All he needs is someone to be with him. That won't solve all of his problems, but it should go quite far.

When I return with the valerian/peppermint tea I made the lazy way, using the microwave, I find him crouching beside Baby on the bedroom rug. He's rubbing her head as his eyes find mine. Such somber eyes. Yet when he stands, I feel him trying to play normal.

"What's this?" He smirks at the metal tea straw jutting from a mug I made.

"Valerian tea with a bit of mint. I prefer it loose leaf."

His lips curve a little as he reaches for the mug, despite his shaking fingers. "What will it do for me?" He quirks one brow.

"It will make you grow a horn—of the unicorn variety." He draws the mug to his chest, and I smile. "It should sort you out a bit," I tell him softly. "Valerian, if you note the name, works a wee bit like the other."

I don't want to say Valium, lest it trigger something for him.

Understanding passes over his face, and his blue eyes flare a bit in reaction. "Thank you."

"Have you ever used a tea straw?"

He shakes his head, and I lean up to kiss his dimple. "Want to come into the den with me?"

While I was steeping the tea, he pulled on a pair of soft-looking plaid pants and a long-sleeved gray T-shirt. He looks a bit better just now, I think. A bit tired-eyed and still a bit pale, but less pained, I believe.

He follows me into the den, where I sift through the drawer in a small table by the front door, fishing out a faded *Little Mermaid* valentine. I think of his shaking hands and unfold it for him, holding it open so he can read.

To Prince Declan

from Finley. the princess

The corners of his lips twitch as he reads it. His eyes move to my face.

"I wrote it the year after. When I was eight. Don't know why it survived these years, but I found it somewhat recently near the back of a cabinet."

He takes it from me, peering down at it. When he looks back up, his eyes are clearer. "I thought about you, too. Used to ask my dad about you."

"What would you ask?"

He shakes his head, as if to say he's not quite sure. "If you were okay."

"You remembered me."

He nods. His eyes dip to his feet then rise to meet mine. "Saw you as they brought you in. Down at the docks."

He told me that before, up on the peak as we looked at the dolphins. But I didn't ask about it then.

"What was it like?"

He takes a sip of his tea, his eyes closing for a brief moment. "This is good."

"You can tell me," I murmur.

His lips press flat, revealing dimples. "I remember mostly... this is weird," he murmurs, "but I remember your eyes. They were dazed...but kind of lit up. There was this...just something there. Kind of like an energy in them. Almost this magic. Everybody else was at the dock, but you were somewhere else." He swallows. "I had never seen a person look like that. So I remembered." His lips press flat again, and his hand goes into his hair as he shifts his weight.

"Later...years later, I realized that's how people look when they're going crazy with pain. But you were stoic, Siren." His lips press together again. He looks back down at his feet and then back at my eyes, and I can see it bothers him to talk to me about it. "You seemed dignified...even though you were so tiny. I remembered that a long time."

My eyes well. I blink quickly. "Come outside with me? I want to show you something else."

DECLAN

She teaches me to throw clay. I'm too tall to sit with my knees under her wheel, so I kneel beside it, my knees on the cold stone of the patio, with Finley leaning over and around me. Her hands shadow mine, teaching me to flare the vase's bottom, run my thumbs along the rim.

For the longest time, my fingers shake. When it's really bad, I use the base of my palms, and that works. Other times, the focus I'm exerting seems to keep my hands steady.

Finley's soft breasts press against my back, her soft arm tickling mine. When she's in front of me, just watching, she smiles like she's happy. She likes teaching me. And at the end, we have a vase. An actual vase.

She holds it up like Simba from *The Lion King*. "We'll put it away in this Tupperware for a bit—" she gestures to a tub that's pushed against the house's wall— "so it will dry evenly despite the wind. Afterward, you can paint it and we'll set it in the kiln."

I'm squinting as she talks, and I picture the bowls and plates in the kitchen. "Wait...those plates inside?"

Her cheeks redden as her mouth curves—a little bit mysterious, just like a siren.

"Damn." I arch my brows. "You're really good."

She shrugs and does a girly spin thing, sort of like a pirouette. She looks happy and...I think that's maybe bashful?

I step over to the rubber trash can where she keeps her clay. There's a foot or so gone off the top of the pile, cleaved away with something circular.

"You used up all that so far?"

She nods, and I run a fingertip over a ridge in the clay. "Those lines are your fingers." I smile.

"Yes," she murmurs. "Their imprint."

"Did you do the mugs, too?" I get mine up off a table by the wheel, running my finger over its teal-with-gold-flecks sheen.

She smiles shyly, and I cup her chin in my hand.

"What?" she whispers. She's smiling, but she looks embarrassed.

"You're an artist, Siren."

"I'm not sure about that."

"Come here." I catch her hand in mine and lead her back into the house. As I'm walking toward the kitchen, I notice how good my body feels. Like...this sort of calm. I can breathe easier. I squeeze her hand. "That tea."

"Yes? Did it make you feel nice?"

"It did."

In the kitchen, I take out the plates and set them on the table. Some have mermaids, some have fish, one has a whale, another dolphins, one a boat. The style reminds me of an oil painting, with chunky brushstrokes and bold colors she blends so they look a little magical. It's a testament to how terrible I've felt since I got here that I didn't wonder before about who made these.

"You know you could sell these, easy."

"I do...sell some of my work. But no one orders much from

the island's web site. Perhaps twice a month, though less often recently because I haven't posted new work for a bit."

I run a finger over one of the mermaids' tails. It's so realistic, I expect the plate to be grooved atop the fin. Instead it's nice and smooth, her painting just tricking my eye. "I can help you get a site up. Your own website. I bet you could bring in some good money."

She smiles softly, and I realize what I'm saying. I shake my head, then step close enough to grab her hands. I swing her arms a little, just because I like to touch her. "What do you buy if you have some extra money, Siren?"

She smirks. "Money's nearly always extra. But...I buy paints. Clothing on occasion. Sometimes pens. The lovely sort of pens."

I pull her close and kiss her. "You like pens?"

She shivers, and that makes me chuckle. I run a fingertip over her earlobe, and she does it again.

"Fuck..." I walk her slowly back against the counter.

"What a horrid, dirty mouth," she murmurs.

When she kisses my neck, I rub my dick against her hip and kiss her lips until she's panting. I nip at her throat, and she does the little shiver thing a third time. My cock throbs. "Love when you do that."

Pretty soon, I've got my fingers in her pussy, and her legs are quaking as she tries to fuck my hand. I'm damn near ripping through my pants, so I carry her to the couch, strip her from the waist down, and lean down for a feast.

Midway through, I trail a fingertip along her slit, and Siren moans.

"How's this pussy feeling?" I murmur.

"So needy..."

I stroke my thumb over her clit, and Finley arches off the couch.

"What do you want?" My words are rumbled.

"You."

I roll a condom over myself, rub my tip between her lips.

"Oh heavens…"

I grin as I press against her slick heat.

"Oh yes…"

"You want it?"

"Please!"

I smile down at her closed eyes and her open mouth. "You gotta tell me what you want before I give it to you."

"Your sex." Her eyes peek open as she lifts her hips, so she's rubbing against me. "Fill me with your sex, please, Sailor."

"So…what you're really saying is you want to be fucked." I'm just messing with her, kind of hoping she might blush the way she does, but Finley shuts her eyes and whispers, "Yes—that."

Holy hell.

I fuck her till we lose our minds, and afterward, I put her clothes back on, perversely pleased to know she's wet and likely sore in her lacy, pink panties.

There's a little table over by the front door—the one that held my valentine. Atop it, there's a chess case. I lead her over to it, waggling my eyebrows as I hold the case up.

"Do you play?" she asks.

"Do you?"

"I'm a star."

That first time, I can't help letting her win. Then she's smug as fuck, tossing her hair around and all but finger-snapping in my face. I bring it on game two. When I've got her in checkmate, she shakes her head slowly, folds her arms under her breasts.

"You're like a card shark but with chess. Carnegie! I've been had."

I'm grinning like a fool. Mostly because her tits look great pushed up that way. She takes it as arrogance and tosses her queen at my chest. It bounces onto the floor.

She's laughing as she kneels to scoop it up. I let her set it on the table before scooping her up...setting her down by the door.

"Put your shoes on, Siren. And your jacket."

* * *

Finley

"I should ask where we're going."

"Are you going to?" He smiles over his shoulder as we follow the moonlit trail.

"I don't suppose so. There's only so many places to go."

Declan laughs, a husky sound that I feel echoed through me. The white cloud of his breath stains the dark. His assessing gaze slides to me. "You're not cold, are you?"

I stuff my fists into the pockets of his jacket, a smooth, suede number which he said is insulated with wool. "Actually, a bit warm."

He links his arm through mine then fishes my hand out of my pocket, lacing our fingers together. I give his a squeeze. "Your large hand makes mine feel child-like."

He snorts, and I feign outrage when I understand the innuendo. I elbow him. "Scoundrel."

He gives a low laugh.

I believe we're going to the ponds, but I'm not certain. Also this way, north of the cottage, is Hidden Cove. He could have come upon that some time earlier, and now he's taking me there with no thought to high tide. Silly interloper.

In the end, we crest the hill before the valley that contains the ponds—three crater lakes off to the right—and Hidden Cove

—part of the craggy cliffside on the left—and he looks toward the ponds.

"You come out this way much at nighttime?"

"I rarely go out anywhere at night." There are rules for such endeavors, though I don't say that. It doesn't matter for now.

"I found this little spot between the middle and the lower lake." He's whispering, like it's a secret. That makes me smile.

The clouds move, spilling sheets of moonlight over us, and in that bright light, I notice his eyes—how they sparkle. His mouth is curved into an easy smile. The relief of seeing him this way is a warm rush.

"I adore this valley," I say. "It's so far from everything, and it's lovely how the ponds reflect the starlight."

We start down the slanting trail. On each side of it, tall grass bends in the breeze. I see the three ponds out before us and the ocean to the left, and I think of another trail, another time, a murmured story that my mum told me under the dark clouds as the grass bowed around us.

"Tell me again about the prince and princess..."

From some corner of my mind, one of St. Thomas Aquinas's philosophies burbles up. Predestination. God knew and has always known all. He knew some of us would damn ourselves with our choices. It's an idea I've known of for years, but I feel jolted by the idea now. Could it be I'm one of those? Have always been, and simply didn't know it?

I reach for Declan's hand and feel his eyes assess me as his palm meets mine. I want to tell him I don't mind the conse-quences. More and more so, I suspect that I was born for this. I *am* one of the transgressors. How odd that after many years of pious living—or attempts at that—I would prefer to lean in to my wicked destiny. I feel a rush at the notion. At what it could mean for me, and the choice I later make.

"You okay?"

I nod, offering him a small smile, and we stop there on the trail, descended halfway into the valley. We kiss gently, cling to one another. I feel him inhale. Then his chin is propped atop my head.

"You feel so good." It's half groaned.

"You do." My throat feels so choked, I can scarcely whisper.

We hurry the rest of the way to the ponds. They're each about the length of a ship. The top one flows into the middle; that one flows into the lower; and the lowermost lake spills down the rock-strewn hillside to the sea.

Declan leads me around the lowermost pond to a place beside the middle where water spills downhill in veins that glint moon-white in the dark grass. The spot he found is somehow dry and slightly concave. He makes a nest of blankets there, and we lie down together. Then he pulls more from his pack and covers us.

The stars look clearer than ever I can recall. I lie against his chest, and his arm wraps around my back, and I watch him as he watches the sky.

"I summited Mount Kilimanjaro and a couple others," he says quietly. "After high school."

"Did you?"

He nods, staring at the sky. "One of the only other times I've ever seen the sky look like this. Brings back memories."

"I had no idea."

He smiles, tight. Of course I didn't.

"You didn't die," I offer.

"Nope."

"Was it awfully dangerous?"

He smiles a bit. "A little."

"How old were you?"

"I was nineteen...almost twenty. Took a gap year after high school."

"That's a year off?"

He nods. "It had been a dream of mine since I was a kid."

I think of kid Declan dreaming of scaling a mountain. I remind myself to ask later about photos of wee Sailor. Perhaps there are some on his phone. "Who went with you?"

"This guy from my class, Farhad. We didn't really like each other that much, but we both wanted to do it."

"At the end, did you care more for one another?"

He smiles. "Oh yeah. We still keep in touch. He climbs for a living now."

"That's possible?"

"If you're fucking crazy." He smiles fondly, and I hug his chest.

"Do you have photos? Of the summit?"

"You know...I might. I uploaded some old stuff before I left."

He reaches under the covers and pulls out his phone.

"Ever-present." I give a teasing laugh.

"Damn Americans. So obsessed with their world-class technology."

"Touché."

I peer at the phone's screen as he scrolls through what appear to be thousands of teeny images. His thumb slows its movement on the screen, and I catch views of what I think must be his journey here. Snapshots of men in baseball garb...a snapshot of a sleek car. The images are so clear; they seem unreal to me.

"The quality is incredible."

"Yeah, these things are like computers. Let me see..." He slows a bit more in his scrolling, and I see an image that stops my heart: Declan, with his eyes taped shut and stickers on his face and a thick tube in his mouth. It's gone the moment my eyes focus on it.

I grab at his wrist. "Wait!"

"What?"

"Back there..."

He chuckles. "I just flipped through like five years of pictures."

"May I see it?"

"Which one?"

I shake my head. I mean the phone. When our eyes meet, he frowns. Then he pulls his gaze away; he tilts the phone's screen away.

"Carnegie," I rasp. "Are you ill? Or were you?"

His eyes close, and my heart pounds sickly. I move off his chest, where I'd been lying, and he sits up, staring blankly at the pond in front of him.

I watch him swallow. Then, so quietly, he says, "Yeah."

I feel faint with alarm.

What's the matter?

He breathes for a moment, still as a stone. His jaw hardens as his eyes move to mine. "Back in November," he says evenly, "I overdosed."

He offers nothing more, and I can't seem to find my voice. My chest feels like it's frozen solid.

"I was in the ICU." I see his hand flex, making a fist in his lap. "On a ventilator for a little while."

I drag air into my lungs. "All the tubing?"

"Yeah, that's what that was." His eyes find mine again for a brief moment. Then he's stretching back out on his back, one arm behind his head. His blank gaze points at the sky. Conversation over, then?

I lie on my side, my cheek propped in my palm.

Is that really it? I've no clue what to say back. *I didn't know.* Of course not. *I'm so sorry.* Is there anything more trite? *What was it like?* Quite prying.

I've no clue what to say, so I scoot closer. After a moment feeling like I've just swallowed a fly, I rest my cheek against his pec. I wrap my arm over his chest. When he doesn't stiffen, I relax against him.

It's okay. My fingers rub the softness of his jacket. *It's okay, Carnegie. You're okay now.*

I try not to think of it. I don't want to think of him there, with his face red and his eyes taped shut, his lips around a tube because he can't breathe for himself. I saw the image briefly, but his chest and face were covered with so many wires and tubes. I've seen nothing like it—ever.

I drape my leg over his, shut my eyes.

You're where you should be now—with me.

I feel a breath move through his torso. "My uh...cousin had a flight to catch, a redeye...headed here. To Cape Town. He remembered that he had this box of balls. Baseballs. So he came by." A cool breeze makes me shiver, and his hand rests on my shoulder. "He's the one that found me."

My throat knots up. I swallow hard and feel him inhale.

"It was pretty fucked up...but they got me back." A tremor moves through him. Again, he inhales deeply.

"Got you back." I dare a peek at his face, finding his eyes closed.

"They gave me Narcan. There was a defibrillator."

Narcan. That's the medicine that helps if someone's given— or takes—too much opiate-based medication. We have some here, for dire emergencies.

"When I woke up—" I feel him shake his head.

"What?" I whisper.

"After I got out, I decided no more rehab."

"No?" I'm stroking his jacket, smoothing the fleece fibers as if he can feel it.

He shakes his head, and I can feel his breaths quicken. He inhales, long and slow, and seems to steel himself.

"That shit doesn't work." Another big breath. "It's not rocket science to get clean. Afterward—" He shakes his head. Locks his jaw. I feel him inhale deeply, and he says, "Sorry you saw that. I should have been more careful."

"Please don't be—sorry." I shift my weight a bit and ease my hand into his jacket's collar, stroke his warm neck. "I can handle anything. It's what I do, that—caring for the ill. And there's no pity," I add softly.

"Yeah." He's not looking at my face, though.

I push up on my arm and peer down at him. On a whim, I paste myself atop him. I wrap my arms around his neck, and kiss his jaw and chin and lips.

"You're so strong. So wise, choosing to come here. I know there's a path for you. A better path." I whisper it between kisses. Then I feel him move beneath me, and his mouth joins mine. We're kissing slow at first, then harder as his tongue delves into my mouth.

I run my fingers into his thick hair, tugging gently at the dark locks. When we break for breathing, I say, "You're so strong. And you're here. You made it to me."

He kisses me so hard, I moan into his mouth. His arms lock around my back, and then he flips us. I'm on my back on the blankets now, and he's above me. His gaze glows as it holds mine. Then he's rocking back a bit.

He's jerking my pants down...my panties down. He pulls a blanket over his shoulders and kisses softly down my belly. He stuffs a finger into me, and then another. I moan, and he licks me, clit to core. I feel his body tremble.

I grab at his neck, wanting his mouth on me. His fingers shove in deeper.

"Oh, is it like that?" he goads." You think you're in charge?"

I thrust my sex against his hand, tipping my head back. "Perhaps I am." I grab at his hair. "I loathe...that I wasn't there. Didn't know you." I gasp as his fingers pump. "Now I know you."

The tip of his tongue circles my clit. He drags it wetly down between my lips as his thick fingers surge inside me.

"You think you know me?" He laps at my slit as his fingers thrust.

I tug his hair, and then I'm too lost to find words. I moan as his fingers push in and drag out; his hot mouth licks me to a frenzy. When I lose myself, I shout into the night. I open my eyes to find him on his knees. His face is hard, near angry. I can see his sex straining at his pants.

"Do you have a condom?" I murmur.

He stares at me. "You can't fix me, Finley. If you met me anywhere but here, I would have never touched you."

My heart quickens. "That's malarkey. You'd touch me because you wanted me. Because we're meant to touch each other." I lean up, rubbing at him where I know he's aching for me. "And besides, I met you here."

His jaw clenches. I rub up the hose of his shaft, drawing my thumb along his rim. "As it happens, I don't think you're broken or need fixing." With my left hand, I explore the soft bulge down below his shaft, causing his thighs to tremble slightly. "If I knew you someplace else and couldn't get you to see reason, I would chain you up out in the wilderness and keep you there."

He barks a laugh—his surprised laugh. His hand grips my shoulder. "Think you're strong enough for that?"

"I think your money can buy someone who is."

He gives another rough laugh, but his hand moves from my shoulder to his forehead. He rubs at his temples even as he presses his stiff sex against my hand.

"You can't do shit like that," he rasps.

Like locking him up, I suppose he means. "Why not?"

"It's illegal."

"I don't care what's legal."

I unbutton his fly. He grips my shoulder as I tug his pants and boxer briefs down to his knees. He groans as I stroke his bare sex.

"I would never let you hurt yourself." I work his shaft the way I've learned he likes, and he breathes fast and heavy.

"You don't have a choice," he groans. "That's why it's fucking toxic." I tease the notch there on the underside of his thick tip, and he makes a hoarse sound.

"You should lie back now." Our eyes hold like magnets for a long moment. Then he eases down onto his back. He's thick and hard and heavy, masculine perfection. I roll his heavy sac in one palm, work his long sex with the other.

"I'd figure you out. I know it."

"Too much on you," he breathes. "It's too fucking much on anyone."

I stroke him harder. "Perhaps you've been spending time with the wrong people." I squeeze him and he moans, thrusting at me a bit. "If you were...from somewhere else...you'd get it," he breathes.

"Perhaps I would hold your tourniquet."

A harsh groan rips from his throat. His hand captures my wrist. "No." With gentle pressure, he stops my hand moving. His dazed eyes hold mine. "I would never, *ever* let you near that shit. Not in a billion years."

"I'm not so fragile."

"No...not fragile. *Precious.*"

I can feel a flare low in my belly at the word, and suddenly, my throat aches awfully. He releases my wrist, and I start on him again, working steadily until his chest is heaving and his eyes are squeezed shut.

"I meant what I said," I murmur. "I'd never give up."

He shakes his head.

"I know myself. I'm loyal." I laugh, given what we're doing, but it's true. I'm far too loyal. That's the core of my problem.

"If you...ever do leave...it can't be with me." His voice is hoarse and low. His hand fists in the air atop his bare abs. "I would fuck it up. And you would hate me."

I run my thumb over the slit where he's slick, and Declan moans. I feel his shaft thicken, and it energizes me; I work him more quickly.

"You'd hate me," he says, "and I couldn't stand to hurt you." His voice cracks on the last word as I lean down and suck his tip into my mouth.

I draw my cheeks in, teasing him like a moment before swallowing him more deeply. I inhale slowly through my nose, working to settle him, until it's difficult to breathe around his hard girth, and he's moaning desperately.

I take him as deep as I dare, and then I suck hard as I ease him out. I wrap my hand around his balls and stroke their seam until his eyes peek open.

"I don't think you'd hurt me."

His eyes widen slightly, but he's too lust-filled to speak. I lap at his tip, tasting the saltiness. Then I lick the sides of his sex.

"Oh fuck." I suck his head into my mouth again, and his hands cinch my hair. "You don't know me. Not...that...version."

I suck him until my mouth is aching, till I taste a bit of his seed; then I ease him out again. "There's no version that would hurt me. That I know."

He's shaking his head.

I suck him in again, swallowing with care to get him lodged in my throat. I feel his hips tremble, and I can feel he wants to press in deeper.

"Do it," I say—but of course, it comes out humming.

He barks a groan and rocks his hips. I choke on him.

"Oh fuck." His hand trembles as he pets my hair now. I suck in my cheeks around his base, and he moans loudly. "Ohhh fuck."

I hum more, and he tugs my hair, groaning gutturally. And

then it's in and out. I ease him out and take him in until I want to cry from the ache in my jaw. Sweat rolls down my temples. Tears roll down my cheeks. I give it my best, and I suppose I'm getting better all the time.

This time, when he reaches his climax, he makes a sound like a harsh sob.

SEVEN
DECLAN

She lifts her head, and cold air hits my dick. I reach down for it—shit, that's cold—but she's already on the job; she's pulling up my underwear. I lift my hips to make it easy on her, and her eyes move to my face. She gives me a small smile and then tucks my dick into my boxer briefs. She pats it lightly with her palm and smiles softly at me again.

I try to smile back, but my face feels kind of weird and shaky. Finley doesn't notice. She's working my pants back up my legs now. It's the dark gray North Face pair I've had forever. They're pretty loose; I remember as she gets up to the fly. I can tell she notices. Her fingers feel around the button, like she's checking to be sure there's not another one or something.

Then she's stretching out beside me, her eyes on my face as her soft fingers stroke my hair back off my forehead.

Fuck. My eyes go hot, and I can't blink without them spilling over.

Finley snuggles up beside me, and she hugs me hard. Like she can tell I've grown a pussy and I need some TLC. I drag in a few deep breaths. A shiver hits me.

Fucking worthless addict.

I cover my face with my hand, and her grip on my chest tightens.

"Did it feel good every time?" It's such a quiet whisper, it takes me a second to process her words.

"You mean what you did? Hell yeah."

"No...not that."

I blink at her hair. Does she mean using? Would she ask something like that? I get a slow breath. Cold sweat flashes through me.

"I was curious. Perhaps it's too prying. If so, hum your favorite song, and I'll attempt to guess it. I have quite a few records for reference—"

"No," I rasp out.

She goes quiet and still, but I can feel her interest. Why the fuck she wants to know...

I don't get it. But Finley's stubborn, and that picture got her thinking. That was my fault. I made her upset. I owe her something more now, don't I? I shut my eyes.

"No," I offer quietly. When she says nothing, I look down at her hair, dark in the moonlight. "Toward the end...it never felt good. Rarely."

"I want to ask," she murmurs, stroking my arm. "But I'm afraid to."

Good. You should be. I keep my voice light and steady. "What do you want to know?"

She lifts her head off my chest, and her small smile is so sweet, so fucking gentle, it makes my throat tighten.

"If I ask," she murmurs, "will it make you...want it?"

I squeeze my eyes shut. "No." I don't know how best to explain it. Not to someone like her. "It wouldn't change things that much." I fix my eyes on a bright star and focus on that. "For me, the cravings are...more physical. Usually. They happen at certain times of the day."

"Early evening?" she whispers.

I nod. And all night, almost every night. I don't want to tell her that, though. I don't want her pity. Even though she says she doesn't feel it, I'm pretty sure she would if she knew how much worse I feel than I let on.

"To me, you're so near perfect. Not perfect as in a silly facade. Just...I value you so very much the way you are. And I think I would value you if you were still...actively ill. I would move heaven to keep you safe. But I would view you the same."

I squeeze my eyes shut. *Shit.* Where is she going with this?

Her hand strokes my hair, and what's in my chest—this little ball of tension—melts away. My fucking eyes ache.

"It's not like that," I manage. In the real world, this shit is nothing like she thinks. She's trying to get it, but she's romanticizing. Simplifying. I can't blame her. "You might value me." I laugh, a cold sound. "Siren, that's exactly what would ruin you in the end."

"Because I'd value you and your safety but...you wouldn't?"

I laugh dryly. "Not that. I'm still human. Everybody values their life." Until they don't. Until it's too hard for too long. But I would never, ever say that out loud. Not to anyone—but definitely not Finley.

"How did you carry on, then? Weren't those two desires at war?" There's a tremor in her voice, as if she's nervous. I strum my hand down her back.

"These are good questions. I'm not upset you asked. You're all good, Siren." She hugs me harder. "When I don't feel like this—" I exhale. I inhale again and swallow hard to keep my voice smooth. "I value my life like you do." *Liar.* "But...I'm not normal without it." My voice dips down on that. I press my lips together. Lock my jaw.

"Why is that?" She asks so clinically, so smoothly, I find that it's easier to answer.

"Mm...because I used for so long. Different stuff." A tremor rolls through me as the next thought scrolls across my mind's screen. "It's like my brain's just...broken now." It's whispered. "Doesn't work right."

I shut my eyes, try to pretend that she's not lying on me.

"That's the part that everybody bullshits you about. They'll say one year, two years." My voice sounds hard. "And then you go on forums and it's five, ten. *Never.*"

I suck back a breath, and she lifts her head, frowning. "What do you mean?" Her brows and mouth are pinched.

"People don't get better. Sometimes. You got hooked for a few years—yeah. Five years, six years, seven. Fine." I shake my head. "If you've used a really long time, like me, people don't come off the subs. They don't stop taking Valium."

I can see the wheels in her head turning. I'm kind of impressed at how she keeps her face so clinical. "Why does it matter, that bit? Is it a poor quality of life? If you don't...stop it all entirely, that is?"

I swallow back a dry laugh. "It depends on who you ask. And how they do on that."

"On what?"

"A maintenance dose." I air-quote that shit.

She gives me a little frown, then tilts her head as her lips press together. "What's the difficulty? Sticking at that dose?"

I nod. Someone like me—I can't stick to it. I always want more. I drape an arm over my eyes and chuckle hoarsely as I feel her tuck the blankets back over my chest. I peek at her from underneath my elbow, watching her moonlit features as they shift between troubled and concerned.

"If I didn't know better, I'd think you're a fucking angel," I whisper, smiling at her. "Not a siren."

I watch as her face lights up. She sits up straighter, then adjusts what I think is an invisible crown. She moves her shoulders so they're more squared, and I swear, I think she's miming wings. It's so fucking funny that I forget myself and sit up.

She blinks her eyes a few times fast, and lifts her chin. I wrap my arms around her, then lay back again, pulling her down atop me. I kiss her cheeks...her lips. She's pushed up on her arm now. She pulls gently away, smiling down on me.

"I won every schoolhouse game of mime for many years." She gives me a huge grin, then laughs. I urge her head into the corner of my shoulder and wrap my big leg over both of hers.

"Am I imprisoned?" She giggles.

"You bet your ass you are." I squeeze her ass for emphasis.

About that time, I see a shooting star. It's like...a shooting star, I guess. It's big, dark gold, and unmistakable. And right above us.

I laugh at the sight. She frowns at me, but I don't explain. I inhale. It's easy. I can breathe. Like, really fucking breathe. I feel...*good.*

It's like Cinderella's carriage. Doesn't last more than those few hours. But I know how to get the magic back. She comes over every day when I get home from laying line. And usually, she stays the night.

Finley

Every afternoon or early evening when I knock at the cottage, he pulls the door right open—no delay. It takes me nearly two weeks to realize that the only way this is explained is if he's waiting by the door. One night, he's awake in the wee hours, feeling poorly for the first time in a few days, and I ask about this.

"Yeah." It brings a smile to his tired face. "After I shower, and I change Baby's—you know—the thing..."

"Lappy." I laugh. "A lamb nappy, that's what it is." Ever since she's been staying as a pet at Gammy's, this is what we do for her.

He shakes his head. "Yeah. Anyway, Baby and I wait for you." His arms squeeze around me. "Is that too much?" he asks softly.

"I adore it."

When I began my nightly visiting, the Carnegie couldn't cook—he'd burn toast—but as time passes, we begin to cook each evening after we make love. By perhaps the third week of this, he's learning. One night, I arrive later than usual on account of Mrs. Dillon slicing her thumb open, and I find dumplings in the boiler pot.

We twirl around the kitchen, with me giggling because I'm so tired and he's so lovely, and my Carnegie trying not to grin with pride about his dumplings.

"You're adorable." I pinch his cheek, and his face reddens.

"Dudes can't be adorable."

I giggle. "Yes, they can."

Three nights and three lovely dishes later, I realize he can likely do near anything. "You're quite multi-talented."

He snorts a bit and sticks his hand out. "Hey there pot."

"I suppose that makes me kettle, though I'm not."

He scoops me up and carries me to bed, and from between my legs, he murmurs, "You're the kettle. Don't deny it, Miss Nurse-Potter-Lamb Mom."

"You're a better shepherd than I."

His tongue skates velveteenly over my most secret crevice, and I tug at his hair. He grins rakishly and does it again, and I come up off the bed. He chuckles darkly.

It's a waking fantasy, this thing we're doing. He's quite better than expected, really. Frequently, he runs the bath for me. He learns to cook what I can, and on nights I arrive late, I return to a lovely meal. We paint pottery together, go on moonlit romps with Baby. I take him to the Hidden Cove—a partial cave with black sand and its mouth half full of ocean, and on its roof, pearly white stalactites—and he grins and says a cove sounds like a place we ought to make love...so we do there, on a blanket on the cool, black sand.

There's a village gathering at the Burger Joint mid-May for that month's birthdays. We arrive and depart separately but step into our old closet for kisses.

"Last time here," he murmurs, "I was going crazy missing you."

I laugh softly. "You were why I wept."

He kisses my cheeks, my eyes, my forehead as we grind against each other. "Never let me be the reason that you cry. You got that?" He kisses my mouth, and it's a breathless kiss, a bruising kiss. "That's our only rule."

"No sorries—we have two," I manage between gasps of air.

"No sorries."

As we walk to the cottage in the dimness of a dark night, he twirls me as if we're dancing, and the night breeze tosses my hair.

"It feels like a fantasy," I murmur.

"Good," he says. "I want it to."

The weeks fly by. I cannot catch them. Three weeks turns to four, then five, then six. The world is a new place. Even waking in the night at times when he's sweating or trembling with after-shocks from his body's ordeal—it's perfect. Our dim autumn sun shines more brightly. Love is all the books proclaim and every-thing the singers sing of. All is well...except my lover cheats at chess.

"Blazing blue bananas!" I wag a finger at him as we play one June evening. "You're a cheater! Cheating Carnegie."

He's holding his hand over his mouth, so I can't see the smug grin behind it. His eyes are wide. He blinks them quickly, as if to emphasize his innocence.

"How do you *always* win? I'm bloody good at chess!"

He moves his hand, revealing a suppressed grin and dimples.

"How did you learn, scoundrel?"

The grin falls off his face so fast, my heart drops. *Oops.* I bite the inside of my cheek as he begins to line his pieces back up. *Never mind.* I want to say so, but my throat is too tight. Looking apathetically down at the board, he says, "My mom's husband. Stepdad, Rich. He was a Wall Street guy. Machine at chess."

"He taught you?"

His eyes come to mine as he scoffs. "Fuck no." His mouth tugs up on one side, as if he's smirking, but his face is hard. "I learned how so I could kick his ass."

"So did you, then?"

"Did I kick his ass?"

I nod, feeling quite hesitant about this topic now.

"One time, yeah. Could have done it more, but didn't see him after that."

My belly does a slow roll as I try to stitch this information into what I know of his mum, which is merely that she passed.

"Christmas before my mom died," he says evenly.

I inhale slowly. "I'm glad you won. Who schooled you on your techniques?"

He lifts his brows, making his forehead crease. "I played with some friends from school."

I run a hand through my hair, then pull out the hair band and re-gather it. "Who was your dearest friend there? What was he like? Or she, I suppose." I feel that it's safer to shift topic.

As I'm speaking, though, his face is losing color.

"Never mind..."

His eyes fix on mine, unblinking for a long moment. He looks near robotic.

"No. It's fine." The words are odd, though—slow and soft. He looks at me for a moment—this look of concentration. After that, his face softens a bit.

"His name was Nate." The words come slightly slow, but sound near normal. "He was the one I talked about, from Texas."

I can feel my cheeks burn, as they do when I feel anything—in this case, regret for asking. "I'm sorry," I murmur.

He inhales, a quiet but fortifying breath. I can tell he's working hard to appear unemotional.

"Nothing to be sorry for." He stands stiffly. "I'll be right back, Siren."

He returns from what I suppose is the bathroom a few minutes later. We carry on about our night as if it's ordinary times. I teach him knitting, and he seems to enjoy it. Before bed, we don't make love, but then sometimes we don't. When we go to sleep, he's wrapped around me, just as usual.

I sleep soundly, I suppose, for I don't hear him leave the bed. When I awaken, it's pre-dawn. I hear the shower running. *That's odd*. I wait up for when he's out. I want to touch him...feel his arms around me.

Instead, when he returns to bed, his skin damp and warm, his hair dripping, he looks into my eyes for one long moment, then turns me around so I'm facing the headboard. His fingers slide into me from behind. His free hand grips my backside. I wait for his low voice, for his filthy, whispered words—he likes to goad me, and I like to clap back—but there's none of that this time. Merely the ripping of a condom wrapper.

Moments later, he's pressed at my entrance—prodding so deliciously, I can't help moaning. He shifts his hips, and then he's pushing inside. I gasp as he enters. It feels different in this position, much more visceral.

I feel a tremor in him as he buries his thick sex deeply in me. He's so large. I feel so tight around him.

"You feel so good." I wait for those words—for any words.

His hand squeezes my hip. His fingers rub my clit. And then he starts to thrust. It's slow at first, then faster as I bear back toward him. His hand strokes along my back, and then his fist cinches my hair.

I gasp at that. His hand slackens. He stops thrusting.

I groan, "More!"

He fills me so deeply, I cry out. Then his hand grips my hair again.

EIGHT
DECLAN

"People are stupid and naive. Do you think this is about love?"

The voice is so crisp and clear, so goddamn loud, it rips me from sleep. I bolt upright, panting as the motion tosses Finley off me.

OH, FUCK.

Just a nightmare.

Just a nightmare.

Off the bed, into the bathroom. What day is it? Fuck. I'm shaking. Phone is on the bed. Getting close to that day, though.

Deep breaths, man.

It's all good.

Finley's in the room right there. You can get in bed with her.

I fold my arms tightly across my chest and lean against the door. My heart is racing. Jesus. *Deep breaths.*

It's so weird when this happens. Now my teeth are chattering.

Nothing's wrong, dude. Just the same dream.

I drag air in through my nostrils...hold it. Blow it out my mouth.

Again.

Again.

I feel like a balloon that's floating off—my head hollow; my body fuzzy, cold. My heart's still racing. I shut my eyes. Take some deep breaths.

I don't want to pass out. Please.

I breathe through my nose, half close my eyes as I lean into the tub, wrapping my hand around the shower faucet. When the shower's warm, I sit in the tub and put my head against my knees. Inhale the steam and tell myself it's different than air. I can breathe steam, no problem. When having my eyes shut gives me that weird floating feeling, I thread my fingers into my hair and pull hard enough to make my eyes sting.

How ironic that it levels me out—the thing he did.

I try to guide my racing mind to Finley. *She's in the bed. She's naked. I can never leave her. What day is it? It'll be June 21 soon... and then I leave the next week.* I inhale and try to let my thoughts roll past without latching on. Like they taught me to at rehab. Mindfulness.

Hey, at least you're clean.

It's such an innocent thought—and it's true. I don't know why it makes my stomach heave. I lunge from tub to sink, trying to stay quiet as I dry heave. When I'm done, I wipe my face and brush my teeth and clean the faucet off with hands that shake.

You'll never be better.

Finley doesn't care. She said she'd never leave me.

You're okay. My sweet Carnegie...

I just want to get in bed with her. I still feel kind of weird and half-real. If she's not too hard asleep, she'll probably scoot up against me. That'll be good.

I look at the razor on the sink for a long, dazed moment before I step back into the bedroom. Back into bed, and it does feel good. The sheets are cold, the mattress soft. Finley is sort of awake. She lifts the blankets for me, and I wrap her soft, warm body up against my chest.

I do that little tremor thing—my body's last hiccup. Then her hands are touching my bare shoulders. I can feel her waking up more.

"Did you shower?" It's a whisper.

I nod.

"Are you all right?" Her hand runs down my tricep.

I nod. "Yeah."

But she can see through me. Even in the dark and half asleep, she knows I'm not. She hugs me with one arm around my neck, kisses my cheek. She's so soft.

That's all I need: to be inside her. It's the only place on earth I always feel good. She prods at my dick, then jerks me off. I eat her pussy. After she comes, she presses my cheek against the softness of her belly, and she whispers it like nothing: "I love you."

My throat twists. All the air in my lungs dissipates.

"Don't say it back," she murmurs. "Not right now. This is my moment to tell you." Her hand comes to my face. "I love you, Declan Carnegie. No strings attached, as they say."

But she's wrong. Every string I have is tied up in her. I don't know how I'll ever untie them. I blink. My eyes sting so fucking bad.

I want to say *I love you, too. I love you.*

I can't breathe because the words are stuck in my throat.

She reaches for my dick again. I put a hand over hers. Better if I do that tonight. Better when I feel her long, soft hair against my chest and throat.

"I want to say *I love you* with my sex." She grins as she murmurs the word. I give her the best smile I can manage.

Then I guide her onto her back. I love to whisper to her while I fuck her. I love to touch her face and kiss her lips.

I love you.

I grab her by the hips. She squeals as I turn her over onto her front.

"Ohhhh, it's this again...the deep dive." She giggles.

Cold sweat blooms on my skin. "Stick your ass up in the air for me, Siren. And put your fingers in your pussy."

* * *

Finley

I ponder it at the mid-June Monthly Market as I wait in line for all the usuals: enough eggs, meat, chicken, and grains to last, oddly, not four weeks, as the name might suggest, but six. Our customs need not make sense.

"For one or two?" I ask Maura, who oversees the market with her mother and two sisters.

"When will Doctor be back?"

"I believe the ship's arriving 'round about the first of August."

Maura scratches her freckled face with a pencil. "Well...the beef keeps. And chicken. Go on. Get a bit for the household."

I'll share a bit with Declan as well. My thoughts return to him as I move through the homegoods market. Would he need some shaving cream? New razors? I fill my basket for us both and grin behind my hand at how lovely it feels.

I return to the clinic residence, unload a bit of stuff, and get a hat I knitted for Kayti so I can drop by Anna's. If I don't go by often enough, she'll *know*—and that won't do. Not yet. Perhaps not ever.

When I arrive, Anna grins and tells me Freddy took Kayti to market. "I'm alone! Can you imagine?" She laughs, a bit mad with the freedom. "Do come in, my dear!"

To my surprise, she opens the bottle of wine the oldest Mrs. Glass gave her just after Kayti's birth.

"Shall we have a bit?"

"And what of your udders?"

"Oh, I'll have only a swallow."

"And I'll get sloshed?"

I laugh at that, but it's near what happens. By the time I leave a few hours later, I can scarcely walk straight. I remember there was something—something I should do or think of?—but it's quite a ways past midday now; I left before sunup, and now I need to see my darling.

I love him. I grin at that. Then I frown...because he didn't say he loved me, did he? I *did* ask him not to, though. And besides, I can feel he does.

But what of the odd intercourse? *That's* what was nagging at me. I was going to ponder why he's switched his preference. Every night and day this week when we've made love, it's been that way, where I can't see him. Is it odd? Does it perhaps signify he's putting distance between us? Or does he rightly think that I enjoy the angle?

I giggle as I weave a bit along the road toward Gammy's. I'm a bit sloshed. A wee bit, that's all. Will he think it funny? What will Baby do? I'm a git; the lamb won't notice. I laugh at my own madness.

I'm there on the porch before I realize my colossal error. I fix what's wrong and stash the evidence inside the tiny pocket on the front of my pans. Then I knock. I'm transfixed by my own fist moving.

I giggle when he opens the door. I watch as his lips bend into a frown and his blue eyes widen. "Finley. Are you...drinking?"

I'm howling. It's right hilarious how startled he looks. "Anna's fault," I wheeze between cackles as I clutch his shirt. His arm goes around me. "What did she give you?"

"Wine."

He laughs. "What kind of wine was it?"

"The whining kind." I dissolve into giggles again, and he scoops me up and carries me into the kitchen, where he sets me at the table. I giggle further as I wobble in my chair.

"Hold onto the table." He laughs, shaking his head. "Siren. This is a surprise."

"I'm such a git!"

I hear him chuckle behind me.

"Am I annoying?"

"You?"

I nearly fall again as I look over my shoulder at him.

"C'mon, Siren." He steps to me, and I feel his arm hand on my shoulder. "Hold onto that table for me, okay? I don't want my Finny getting hurt."

I giggle.

He looks into my eyes, and I watch as his lips curve slowly upward. "I think you need some water."

I belch softly. My hand slaps over my mouth. I hear his low laugh, followed by the sound of water running. "Don't worry, I've got ya covered."

He sits beside me with a tall glass of water and two small, round M&Ms.

"Advil." His strong-looking fingers push it toward me.

"Advil." I pout. "So...I swallow them?" I rub one with my fingertip.

"Siren, Siren..." He picks up the pills. "Are you pill first or water first?"

I tilt my head. "I don't quite follow."

"When you're taking something."

I laugh, airy. "I don't know. I take nothing."

"Let's do the pill first. Then you drink a little water, wash it down."

I love his face as he helps me. "You're so good-looking. It should be a sin." My eyelids feel so weighted suddenly. "I suppose it is." My words sound slurred.

"How much of the bottle did Anna have?" I hear him ask it distantly.

"Not much. Because her breasts are VIPs."

He chuckles. "Are they?"

"Not like mine." I poke my lower lip out, peer down at my chest. "Mine are talentless twits. Anna's make milk."

Something touches my leg, and I startle.

"Baby." Declan smiles. I rub her with my foot.

"Do you still like me, Carnegie?"

He makes a frowny face, but also a bit soft, a little smiling. "Why would you ask that?"

I look down at the table. He stands up and pulls me up against his hard abs. "Why'd you ask me that, Siren? Tell me."

"Because...of things," I whisper. I shake my head, picturing our odd lovemaking. "Can't remember now," I murmur. I try to stand.

He helps me up. "Let's go back to the bedroom. You can see a thing I knitted."

That sends me all giggly. "I adore a man who has smart fingers."

His hand grips mine as we walk toward our lovely lair. I note the yarn out on the bed. There's two mugs on the bedside table.

"Having tea?" I frown down at them.

"Yeah."

"You quite like it."

He nods. I frown as I sniff in his direction. "Do you smell that smoke smell? Oh," I laugh, "I bet it's you. You've been a chimney lately!"

He tugs at his shirt, takes it off. I whistle at his lovely, hard torso—or try to. He laughs at my failed attempt.

We're on the bed then. I'm collapsed on my back, and he's leaned over me. I reach up and pinch his pebbled nipples. "These are darling."

That gives him a good laugh.

"So much good here." I run my hand down his chest and realize I can feel the outline of his ribs. "What's this?" I run my fingertips over the hardness of him there.

"My body?"

He's grown leaner, I realize. But...it's rude to say so. I don't want to make him feel odd. I'll just feed him lots so he'll be healthy when he goes. *When we go.*

I look into his eyes. "I want to go with you. Did I say that yet?" His eyes widen, making me laugh. "I think not." I claw at his side—warm skin, hard muscle, the surprise ribs.

I can see him try to blink away the shock on his face. He tries to mask it as he peers down at me.

"I've decided I'd like to go to America." I wrap my arms around his, struggling to pull him down atop me. "I'm the princess, you're the prince. It's too soon...you leaving. We've only just begun."

I reach for his face, cupping his cheek with my hand. "I've known it's time for me to go," I whisper. "Believe me...I need to get away from here. You'll feed me liquor for the boat part...or we'll break the safe. Not break the safe," I muse. "That could be painful for you. No pain for you..."

His eyes are wide, and my mind's foggy. I fear I've said something untoward. "Don't be having wide eyes. And don't let me be afraid," I hiss. "If you tell me you love me, I can brave the boat." The words grow raspier as I whisper. "I'm frightened of the boat."

His eyes are wide and somber.

"Not now," I whisper. His face blurs. "Say it when you

want...I'm just talking nonsense. Kiss me." I grab his shoulder. "And let's be together."

He kisses me. Harsh kisses. He should tell me he loves me. I bite his lip in retribution. "You're a git." I yank his hair. "Tell me you love me."

"I love you."

The words spin round till they're evaporated. Did he really say them? I think so.

I fumble with his pants then push at his hands. "Take them down," I order.

I must be no good at drunken blow jobs. He's not even fully thickened up and firm.

"I'm sorry," I manage. I wipe at my eyes.

"Why?"

"I'm not good."

His hands on my shoulders, down my arms. Gentle. "You so good, Finley." His eyes seem to reach for mine. "You're so good. Never doubt that I think so."

My eyes shut. Our dizzy kisses. I adore the weight of him above me, making things feel better. Safer.

And then I've lost him. We're moving, and he's behind me. His hands build a fervor in me, make me want his sex inside.

"Your fingers," I hiss. "Not enough..."

His hand is gentle on my back. "Hmm, I don't know. I don't think I mess around with drunk girls."

"I'm not a drunken girl," I try. "I'm your girl."

He answers with a snap of latex. With his sex shoved into me. I'm numb on the surface, but deep there, I feel him. The sensation makes me grunt. It draws loud cries from me.

"You okay?" he keeps asking.

"Oh yes. Never better..."

I'm near climax when his hand catches a handful of my hair and tugs.

I gasp.

"Is this okay?"

"It hurts a bit," I squeak.

And then it doesn't hurt. He lets go. He reaches around and rubs me till I'm screaming his name. As I come, he slaps my backside harshly, and I feel the condom swell.

NINE
FINLEY

The weight of my drunken words grows nearly crushing as my mind clears and the headache comes on.

What must he think? I don't know, because Mark Glass has called him off. It seems Mark's washroom pipes have sprung a leak, and he's ripping up the tile floor. He came knocking as I soaked in the bath Declan drew for me, asking if Sailor wanted to help. Because why wouldn't he want to help? Cue eyeroll.

Before he left, I begged him not to mention me—in any manner. While they're working, though, what topics might arise? If my name surfaces, what more might Mark Glass say of me?

I pace around the house, talking to Baby before deciding to walk back down to the clinic residence and give Doctor a call. It's been a few days since I've heard from him, and it won't do to have him calling frequently, failing to reach me because I'm spending nights elsewhere. I'm checking the voice mail daily, but the notion of him catching on still frightens me.

He answers on the second ring and tells me that his father passed last night.

"Oh, I'm so sorry."

"It was peaceful." He says nothing more.

I open my mouth to solicit details. Doctor and I have seen two Tristanians through their final moments. We understand the workings of death in a way few do. But it's his father, and he didn't offer me the information.

"I'm sure it must have been quite difficult regardless," I add softly. "I'm so sorry." In the silence that follows, I feel breathless with growing disquiet.

"Perhaps you should return to us ahead of schedule." I blurt it, but as soon as the words leave my mouth, I recognize the wisdom of my subconscious. Were I really to steal away on Sailor's ship—the Lord forbid it—who would handle the ill in the month until Doctor's return? Mrs. White could manage some of it, but she's more elderly than she once was. She can't prop up a heavy man, for example.

I hear him clear his throat. "Perhaps that's not a bad idea."

"I don't know when the next ship departs. Could you return onboard the *Celia*? I know she doesn't always pass our way...but perhaps she could be persuaded to."

The *Celia* one of only three vessels that pass our way with anything approaching regularity. I know from long experience that she departs Cape Town the tenth of each month. Today is the fifteenth of June. That means he can't depart South Africa for some three more weeks, which gives me time to make a plan and carry it out—should I decide to—but puts him back here two weeks earlier. Perhaps it's more like sixteen days. The *Celia* is a smaller, quicker ship than the two others.

"Are you in need of me?"

I smile, stiffly, although he can't see that. "Always. Your guiding hand cannot be over-valued."

There's a silence where I feel his ego swelling.

"In that case," he says with pomp, "prepare for my return."

* * *

My Carnegie returns from the Glass house hungry. In the bed, he's quite himself—all deft hands, rough murmurs, hard kisses, and his stiff sex. Before we move into our new position with him at the rear, he holds me close and runs his hands over my hair. I'm greatly relieved to find it seems he still craves me. I told him that I'd like to run away with him, and he's not frightened off. I feel a thrill at that.

If he's perhaps a bit more quiet than even our new normal, I chalk it up to his sore shoulder. He so seldom mentions it, I sometimes forget it bothers him, but after we make love, we lie panting together, and I see him rubbing at it.

"Stay here." I press a kiss against his cheek.

Then I hurry to the kitchen, fetching a large Ziploc bag of frozen applesauce, two dish towels, a thin, silk tablecloth, some Advil, and a glass of tea with a straw.

His eyes are keen on my face as I drape the dish towels over his shoulder, meld the Ziploc over them, and use the table cloth to wrap the cold compress in place. He swallows water, downs the Advil, shuts his eyes.

"You're water first, eh?"

His lips twitch at the corners. "Yeah." His eyes lift open to give me a small smile, and that smile gives me courage to nestle in against his left shoulder.

Truth be told, I remain humiliated by my drunken proclamation. By his silence in response. Had he not said he loved me right after, I'd be drowning in the depthless sea of my own shame. As it is, I'd simply like to move beyond it—until it's closer to time.

"How was Mark and Maura's house?" I whisper.

"Wet."

"Sounds like quite a headache."

"Yeah. It kind of was. I was glad I could help, though."

We lie in silence for a long while, and I feel compelled to address my gaffe. It's important to me that he knows I'd never want him to feel obligated to me. I squeeze my eyes shut, exhale slowly. "I'm sorry if I worried you with what I said...when I was out of sorts. I've no expectation of you. In any way. Never feel I do, please."

I wait a breathless moment for his reply. Then I realize...he's dropped off to sleep.

I try to sync my breaths with his long, steady ones for quite some time. No matter how I alter my breathing, it seems I always come up a bit short.

* * *

I awaken the next morning to an empty bed. I find Declan in the living room, wearing only boxer briefs as he knits on the couch. My eyes move over what he's making: something teal and muted lime green.

"Is it a scarf?" I inquire.

He lifts his brows.

"You thumbed through my pattern book." I smile as I take a seat beside him. "What a fast learner you are."

I run my gaze over his face and find his eyes are sporting tired smudges below. A glance about him reveals an empty mug at his feet. That's my recent gauge of his anxiety.

"You didn't sleep well?"

He shakes his head.

"I'm sorry."

I pull a blanket over myself and curl up against his side. I'm relieved when he sets the knitting aside and hooks one of his long, strong legs around me. He pulls me so I'm lying with my cheek against his chest and wraps his arms around me.

"You're so warm," I murmur.

"You are." Now his legs are locked around me. I giggle. We do love a leg hug. Then he shifts a bit, and I feel his sex pressed against my thigh. It's so long. So thick and hard. I feel a clenching sensation between my legs as I reach down and wrap my hand around him.

His hips shift. I giggle wickedly.

In times past, we would make love here on the couch. He would cup my backside, keeping me from sinking into the cushions. This time, when we've worked each other to a fervor, he carries me back to the bedroom, where he positions me the way he likes me.

This time, he crawls between my legs, licking me until I sag over his face. I find my release screaming his name. Then when I think my legs can hold my weight, I get on all fours and wiggle my rear for him.

It does feel good this way. I don't mind the oddness of it. I don't want to ask him why the change. If this is what he likes, and I enjoy it, too, what does it matter? Perhaps the bit I don't know is this is the best position once you're stretched and flexible enough to try it.

This time, when he grabs my hair, it's pulled into a ponytail. When he yanks, it doesn't hurt quite as acutely. After a moment, I find I'm not throbbing at my scalp, but in between my legs.

Afterward, as he presses a towel over me, I whisper, "That was excellent."

He grins. "Good."

He showers shortly after that, not telling me until he emerges with a towel tucked about his waist that there's a men's baseball social this morning.

"I didn't know."

"I should have mentioned it," he says. "I just figured you'd heard."

"It's true it often works that way." I grab a shirt and pull it over my head. "That sounds reasonably bearable."

He laughs, shaking his head. "What an introvert."

I wrinkle my nose. "I'll be glad to frolic about in the field with Baby. I've got an old kite I'd like to try."

He laughs at that. "Are you serious?"

"Do I look like I'm joking?"

He steps closer after pulling on his boxer briefs. He runs his finger over my breast, tweaking my nipple. "You look like I want to get back in bed."

I wave my hand. "Go pursue your sport." I scoff teasingly at the last word, prompting his dimpled smile. "And don't speak of me. Remember we're the Catholic sort, despite some of the men's foul mouths. And although you're a gorgeous, charming sports star, you're an outsider. What we're doing would be beyond frowned upon. I could suffer for it."

His face tenses, and he runs a hand back through his hair.

"It's not hand-worthy."

"What?" He smiles a little, bringing out a dimple again.

"Don't go grabbing at your hair, Carnegie. Just don't speak of me. And hurry back."

As it happens, he's gone until near four o'clock. He returns with a nice, sloppy grin and heavy eyelids, reeking of liquor and cigarettes, craving my body. He throws two blankets on the living room floor and urges me onto my hands and knees. Then he lies on his back below me, suckling my breasts until I'm so wet between my legs, I've started trembling with the need for release.

"I can't take it..." I laugh, a soft quaver.

Declan shifts his lower body so he's lying directly beneath me. Then he unfastens his pants and lowers me atop him, rubbing his sex against mine through my panties till he's groaning and I'm clawing at him.

I feel him palm his sex. "Ah, hell. I need a condom."

I reach down and smile to find his steel-hard sex is weeping. "I adore this." I paint the illicit slickness down his vein-striped shaft, making him rumble low in his throat. Then I drag a fingertip over his taut balls.

"Ohh, *fuck...*"

I smirk as I reach atop the coffee table, where I stashed a condom in a bowl. Declan's jaw is taut, his eyes aglow with desire as I roll it over him.

"Someone's randy when he drinks."

I squeeze his thick tip, and he groans as if my touch is torture. I do it again. This time, he whimpers.

"Sit on my dick." His eyelids slit open as I cup his balls. "*Please...*ride me."

He's so stiff, his condom-covered sex is lying near-flat on his chiseled belly. I pull it away, wrapping a hand partway around the base, and he groans loudly.

"Oh fuck. Finley, please. I wanna be inside you."

I climb over him, my own sex piqued and dripping. I take just his tip inside. My legs tremble with need to stuff myself until I'm stretching.

"Oh God. Fucking hell, Finny."

I sink slowly down atop him till I'm so full, for a moment I can't get my legs to hold me.

He thrusts. "Oh fuck. I love you."

Then he flips me over, thrusting with such force, he has to hold onto my arms to keep me locked in place beneath him.

TEN

FINLEY

For the first time in a week or two, we climb into the tub together after. I rub his feet, marveling at his flawless arches as he reclines with bubbles kissing his pecs and his head against the tub's rim.

"This is how I found you—loafing, you'll recall."

I see a flash of dimples before he's panting as I tour the pressure points on his foot.

Afterward, he gives me back as good as he got, rubbing my feet as I perch on the bed's edge, wrapped in a towel and a blanket. He's kneeling on the rug, and Baby's looking at us both. I can't help laughing.

"Do you want to throw something? Er, pottery..." I laugh.

He stands, looking tired. "How about I watch you?"

"Of course. If you'd like to."

A while later, I cast a glance from my hands to his face and find he's nodded off, standing with his broad back against the home's external wall. His cheek is on his shoulder.

"Declan," I whisper. His eyes peel open.

"Dearest. Go inside and rest."

When I finish, though, I find him knitting on the couch.

"Who is it for?" I inquire coyly.

"Who do you think?" I can't see his eyes. They're focused on his hands and my bamboo needles.

"For Baby?"

He snorts. "She's got a built-in wool scarf."

"Could it be...me?"

He glances up for a moment, his lovely lips pursed in mock mysteriousness. I kiss his forehead and go wash my hands.

He's quiet for the next few hours. Markedly so. I read a bit as he knits. The scarf is completed as I dress for Saturday sewing. He puts it on with gentle hands, running his fingers through my hair as he looks down at me.

"Does it suit me?" I murmur.

"I think it does."

We share a simple kiss, and he helps me into my coat. I toss a spare pair of needles into my yarn-stuffed shoulder bag, and then I'm off, walking quickly to outpace the melancholy that's begun to bear down on me at odd moments.

His ship departs in near two weeks...

I remember, as I take an odd, out-of-the-way trail into the village, that Saturday night means I can't return to him. My chest aches at the prospect, but there's nothing I can do. On Sunday mornings, everyone is going to and from church. Were I to walk down from Gammy's, I'd be noticed in an instant.

My heart is heavy as I enter the post office through the unlocked front door. On Saturday evenings, the packaging room doubles as our sewing spot. I find Holly, Anna, Dot, Rachel, and Blair sitting in a row of rocking chairs that make us all feel geriatric.

"Fancy you should join us." Holly looks up from her cross-stitch.

I glance at them, each one looking down at their hands. "Meaning?"

Dot sighs. "We all knocked all afternoon, trying to tell you we'd be starting early."

My gut clenches.

"It's Aunt Bea's birthday," Anna offers.

"So it is." My words are soft and slow. My heart is pounding.

"Where were you?" Holly's voice is snippy.

I take my seat in the smallest, creakiest rocker. I can scarcely breathe as I say, "On the slopes."

"Did you have business with the sheep?" Blair asks as I bring my yarn out.

"Rain may be coming. Someone had to redirect a problematic gulch. Who better than me?" I roll my eyes as if it's quite the headache.

"I hadn't heard that," Dot says.

"Checked the forecast." I say a silent—*automatic*—prayer of thanksgiving when no one contradicts me.

Soon we're comfortably lost in our gossip. Blair's much younger brother, Randy, bit her calf when she stepped on his favorite Hotwheels car. She shows the bruise, and I fuss over it. Anna confides that Freddy's mother Sheila encouraged her to poke a hole in Freddy's condoms.

"It's Lord God's way," Anna quotes. "Can you imagine? The Lord favors lying?"

We all shake our heads. *Those liars, headed right to hell.*

"Wee Kayti's still so young, and...it's a risk each time," Blair says quietly.

Here on Tristan, pregnancy is never underrated for its risk.

Before too long, Holly starts fishing for Declan information. When no one offers any, she bemoans his disappearance from the bar. It's a bit of work for me to keep from smirking like a twit.

Then Dot reveals she got a kiss from Rob Glass, and there's the evening. Rob is nearly old enough to be her father.

"Thirty-eight," she whispers, her high cheekbones staining

red, and Anna nearly falls from her chair. Holly shrieks, which startles Blair, who drops her penguin cross-stitch. Rachel slaps a palm over her mouth.

"He *is* perhaps a bit handsome," Blair whispers. But her eyes are bulging; I can see she thinks it's mad.

Dot is quite demure at first, but then she brings us up to speed. They've been spending time together for three weeks. By evening's end, Holly's naming Dot's unborns, and Anna's doling out cupid advice. ("If he kisses your lips and slips his tongue in, don't attempt to duel him. You'll both choke!")

As we slip out into the foggy night, I see Dot hug Holly. They walk off that way—and I suspect I know why. Holly's feeling left out...as she does.

Anna walks me partway to the clinic residence, our breath staining the night in puffs of white. Before she turns toward her house, she stops mid-step.

"Wait—I had an odd thought. Where is Baby?" She tilts her head, as if perhaps Baby will materialize. "Did you put her back out with the others?"

"No." I give what I instantly realize sounds like an uneasy laugh.

"Well where's she gone to?" Anna laughs, too.

"Funny story, actually. The Carnegie has her."

"Does he then?"

I nod. "Quite the fluffin lover. Perhaps a bit lonely as well."

Anna gives an odd laugh as she turns to go. "Fancy that."

As soon as I get into the residence, I call Declan and stand by the counter for an hour with the phone's cord twirled about my finger. He doesn't say much but that he's feeling a bit poorly. I regale him with tales of my night, and then I offer to come to him. I could sneak back to the village for tomorrow morning's mass if I departed quite a lot before sunup.

"Nah. It's okay." But he's quiet, and my heart tugs a bit when we hang up the phone.

I call back after a hot shower. His voice is gruff when he answers.

"Were you sleeping?"

He snorts, and I shake my head. "Take your tincture and drink your tea, Carnegie."

He chuckles—and I note he doesn't promise he will. Silence spins across the line.

"You okay?" he asks.

I give a small sigh. "I miss you." It's the fourth Saturday since I realized I need to stay away if I want to attend mass on Sunday morning. It's important that I engineer perception, but it feels so horrid—being separated. It makes me think of July. When I do, I feel near frantic with fear and confusion.

He interrupts my musings with a husky whisper: "What part of you misses me?"

I close my eyes and lean against the counter and confess my craving. He whispers a wicked incantation. Till I'm on the floor. Till I'm shameless, with my hand between my legs. He says he's touching his sex as well. My flesh throbs with envy.

Declan

I lie in bed until I can't keep lying there. Then I put on boots and a jacket, fill a thermos with some of that tea. As I'm going out the front door, Baby darts up out of nowhere.

I crouch down to rub her head. "You wanna go?"

She presses her warm, fuzzy self against my legs. I swallow hard. "Okay."

I know she's an ewe, and sheep are great on rocks, but I feel weird about taking her up somewhere with such an epic drop-off. I tie a rope around the collar Finley made her and use that as a leash. I'm pretty sure Baby thinks I'm nuts, because as we follow the trail up to the plateau, she keeps looking back at me.

"I'm sorry." My throat's so tight, it sounds raspy.

I'm glad Finley isn't here tonight. I'm grateful for church, just this once. I'm fucked up today. Just woke up feeling...dark. Then at baseball, some guy slapped me on the back, right near my neck. I spun on him. Went to grab his collar, but I stopped myself in time. I think the mayor saw it go down, though.

Afterward, Freddy invited me to get some beers down at the bar. People kept buying me bottles to say thanks for coaching them, and I kept putting them away.

I said sorry to back-slap guy as I took off, and we shook hands, so I think it's all good now.

I can feel how drinking the beer wasn't good, though. Since I've sobered up, I feel like I've sunk a little lower than before the bar. It's that real bad, heavy, anxious, apathetic feeling. Fucking mess.

I stop at the back edge of the plateau. Hold my breath and then release it. It's darker tonight. Darker than the last time I was up here. I sit down beside some bushes, draw my legs up to my chest. Baby—fuck, she's such a good girl. She sits right beside me...like she knows. I want to hug her, but I'm sort of scared I'll hurt her. I wrap an arm around my knees and try to smooth my breathing out.

"I'm the princess, you're the prince."

I'm not. I'm not the prince. That's why I called my agent earlier...before I got in bed. Told him what happened with the taper meds and asked if he could get me out of here early.

There's a ship coming—right now. The *Celia*. Left from Cape Town yesterday, will be here the night of the twentieth. She's a research vessel. Not too many people on board. I've got a ride back on her, departing the twenty-first.

"It's too much for someone like me. Because you're leaving, see? And I'll be here without you. And I know how that works out, you see. It doesn't work out pretty."

With steady hands, I untie Baby's leash and stand up. Walk slowly across the plateau. I hear myself swallow, louder than the tide. It's pretty calm tonight, and quiet. No sunlight to turn the squiggle of the waves above me golden. But it's nice and dark. And peaceful.

She would never get over it.

You'd drown, like her parents.

Those thoughts make me feel like I should really do it.

Take yourself out. Piece of shit. If you can't do this right, you can't do anything. You already failed at living real life every time you tried.

I crouch down by the ledge, squeezing my head between my palms. My heart is racing so damn fast. I'm worried I might pass out. Fall before I'm ready.

Oh fuck. *Fuck.* I rub my eyes till I see golden shapes. I pull my hair. *Why does nothing help me? Maybe I'm not meant to be alive.*

I see the lines of light above me, feel the cold weight of the water. That's why I came here. Not for her. I came here to sink myself.

"I can't go back. I can't. I can't...I can't."

I cover my mouth with my hand. Sit back with my legs in front of me. I cover my mouth with both hands. I don't want to leave her. I don't want to sink like that. I hold my head as tears roll down my cheeks.

I'm so fucked up. She doesn't know. She doesn't know what it would be like with me.

I scoot closer to the ledge. I can't feel anything. I just want to be done with this. I don't want to feel this way. I can't be fixed. I claw at the ground. I punch the ground, ripping up my knuckles.

Something warm nudges me. Baby presses up against my back and...she won't move. I look out at the stars, so bright and unreal. My ribcage expands as I breathe. Baby doesn't move a hoof.

It's all I need. The crest smooths out. I breathe until my body feels less frenzied. Till my thoughts are coming in a straight line.

Finley. I just need to see her. Just another couple days...so I should take advantage of them.

Baby follows me home. When we get there, I feed her and whisper "thank you" in her velvety ear. Then I climb into the bed that smells like Finley, take some of her potion, and sleep.

ELEVEN

FINLEY

Perhaps I've got a sinner's black, blasphemous heart, for I feel no guilt as I step inside the church for Sunday morning mass. I still pray as if I'm one of the lambs. When it's time to ponder gratitude, I say a silent thank you for *him*. If the Lord truly knows my soul, he'll understand.

Will I be cast into the fiery pits? Will I truly? I wonder most of the service. I think perhaps it depends on whether I stay and live the life I committed myself to, the one I always presumed the Lord wanted for me.

But does He, though? What does the Lord want for me? And what of me? What can my heart bear? At this point, that's the question. Never before—*never before Declan*—had I given thought to what I needed...much less what I wanted. It simply didn't dawn on me. I never had a suitor. Never in the schoolhouse. Not for so long.

We don't want for happiness here. We take what we have and find happiness in it. This applies to all facets of life, and also love.

Am I sinful that I couldn't do that? That I can't be happy with my lot? I thought of *him* before he arrived. Before I even knew his face, I wrote him letters, sealed them up in bottles, tossed them to the sea. It was all quite pitiful. I knew that. Silly.

I suppose I wanted to escape. That was the narrative I knew. Prince Declan. I smile down at my lap as I think of how he behaved that first night I saw him. I was furious—less so with him, more so with my foolish self. And then...

And then.

After mass, I chat with Uncle Ollie for a bit, and then with Mrs. Petunia White. I find, by chance, I wasn't wrong about the weather. We're due two days of driving rain, starting this evening.

Father Russo comes to stand by Mrs. White as she asks after Baby. "How is that sweet love?"

"She's doing wonderfully. I haven't put her with the others yet, but it's in her future. Unless she says she doesn't want to leave me."

Mrs. White chortles. Father Russo's gray-black eyebrows scrunch, as if he's never heard a conversation like ours. Then he smooths his face out, unassuming—comically so. He puts his hand on Mrs. White's shoulder, but his eyes meet and hold mine.

"Finley. How are you feeling?" Father Russo's voice is like a bird's: nasally and so high-pitched it sounds like chirping when he speaks.

"No complaints, sir. How are you?"

"I would be better if I understood why you ceased attending weekday masses."

My face blazes. I can scarcely form words. "I suppose I have," I manage.

"Did I do something to offend?"

"Oh, heavens no. I'm sorry to cause...questions, sir. Father," I correct. "It's just that without Doctor, I'm more occupied with clinic duties. All of that...it takes up quite a bit of time."

"Is that so?" His eyes and mouth are round, as if he's

genuinely curious. He's such an odd duck, I can't tell if he's just being odd, or if he's actually unhappy with me.

"It is so, Father. But I'm sorry to have disappointed you. I'll do my best to attend mornings again quite soon."

"I heard your Doctor is returning early."

My stomach does a slow roll. "Did you then?"

He nods. "I'm ready to see my dear friend again."

"Oh yes. I'm so eager for that, too."

As quickly as he stuck his neck into our conversation, he's gone.

"Dear Father. A bit odd. What a true man of the Lord, though," Mrs. White murmurs.

"Absolutely."

I can't escape the church quickly enough. As I step out, I nearly bump right into Holly, who looks lovely in an apple red dress.

"Finley. You're just the one I wanted to see."

I imagine crossing myself, as I would like to. Holly walks me to the clinic residence, yammering the entire while about Dot and Rob Glass.

"I'd quite like to be...enthusiastic, but he's...simply so...well, *old*." Her brows draw sharply together. "He's like...the apple when the peel part, the outside of it, has gone a bit squishy. It's still edible—" I'm cringing along with Holly, though for different reasons— "but who would want to eat it? If we've enough apples, and the crop has been well, I toss those out whole at times when Mum's not looking."

Well, you're not the lady of the house. You can afford to behave like a school child.

I nod.

"I feel she'd be better off alone."

I clamp my molars on the inside of my cheek to avoid rolling my eyes. *I'm quite sure you would. Though not for Dot's sake.*

Holly needs a sympathetic ear, and never much more. She's a gabber. Needs to hear her own thoughts to decipher them. By the time we've reached my porch, she gives me a small smile.

"Thank you for listening. You're the best at listening." She hugs me, and I go collapse on the couch.

Moments after—truly *moments*—I hear knocking on the clinic door. It's old Mr. Button with a sliced his finger. Chopping potatoes. It takes me half an hour and three bandages to stop the bleeding. Then I have to explain to him that he ought not to be using large, sharp knives due to his severe tremor. I try never to presume that I'm a strict voice of authority, but Mr. Button cut his thumb severely this past summer, and it's only a matter of time before it happens again.

He leaves hunched over, looking like a just-kicked puppy. I feel villainous. I hang about another half hour—these Sunday things come in threes—and sure enough, there's another knock. It's poor Cindy, looking ill-kempt and quite desolate. I lead her into the residence and spend the next forty minutes talking with her, drinking tea and sharing slightly stale friendship bread.

Having suffered quite intensely in my own life, I can understand her pain—at least a bit. She feels ill like this a bit more often in the fall and winter. Unlike me, she needn't suffer anything particularly unusual to set her off. It's simply her body's weakness. When she leaves, she seems a bit brighter.

"Page me anytime," I insist. "Day or night. You know how I enjoy talking with you."

Thankfully, there's no third patient. Twenty minutes later, I'm out the door. I walk toward the Patches, then cut up into the hillside and back toward Gammy's cottage. It adds nearly half an hour to my trek, but lately I've been feeling more frightened of being found.

Which brings to mind Father Russo. What was that about? He's one of Doctor's closest friends and confidants...but I don't understand. Eventually, I'm feeling so overwrought that I shut down all my thoughts and focus on the landscape. The way the mist drifts about the volcano's peak, hiding it from view. The way the grass bends in the breeze.

How could I leave this place?

Focus on the dirt...the grass...your footsteps. No thinking.

And soon I'm at the cottage.

* * *

That night as the rain begins to fall, and thunder claps, and lightning flashes out the window, we lie curled together on our sides beneath the blankets. We're quiet, kissing at odd moments. His eyes simmer with some unnamed thing. Perhaps I'm simmering as well.

"What do you want for yourself?" I whisper to him. "In the future."

He shakes his head. His lips press gently together.

"Do you adore baseball?"

He traces a strand of my hair. His lips tilt at the corners. "Yeah."

"Could you picture yourself playing for a long time?"

"I don't know."

"But if it worked out? Injuries...the shoulder. Your team and you seeing eye-to-eye."

"I could see myself playing." His eyes move away from mine, then back. "Maybe not in Boston."

I don't need to ask why. Why *wouldn't* he want to get away—after what happened there?

"Where, then?"

His finger traces my jaw as his eyes hold mine. He shakes his head once. "Seattle? I don't know."

"The great Northwest Coast."

We're speaking in whispers, even despite the loud rain.

His palm cradles my cheek.

"Is it lush and rainy there? I think I remember talk of rain."

"It's rainy there, yeah. Sort of like here."

His eyes fall away again. *I can't make promises.*

I want to say, *I know.*

"What would your house be like there?"

Now our gazes latch again, and my heart feels warmer.

"Smaller." His chest sighs, although I don't hear evidence of it. "Nothing like the one in Boston."

"What is your home there like?"

"Too big. On a busy street."

"You want seclusion. Something warm and cozy."

He swallows.

"Something to remind you of this cottage."

When he looks back up at me, his face is apathetic, but his eyes—they're filled with fury. "You said no strings."

"There are no strings." And yet my pulse begins to race.

He shakes his head once, his jaw tight.

"You don't want to take me with you. You think I don't know it?" I sit up, blinking at the dresser, where Mum's photo faces down now. "I was drinking, but I still remember. You said nothing."

He sits up beside me. I refuse to look his way.

"I said I loved you."

I blink quickly. "Yes. I know."

"I love you, Finley." He wraps his arms around me, dragging me close. "Maybe I shouldn't have ever said it, but how can I keep that to myself?"

Tears spill down my cheeks. "Thank you for saying it."

"Don't thank me. I hurt you. And now I have to leave."

"That's how it goes. I knew it would be."

At the start, I didn't think I would feel this way. Couldn't fathom I might want to really go with him over the ocean. Now I can't imagine staying.

"I trust you," I whisper. "I trust you more than anything. More than I fear those awful waters."

"I can't take you with me."

Fury rises in me. "Why not? Tell me the official reason."

"You know why."

"You don't trust yourself to steer clear of temptation. You think it will hurt me if you don't."

"Finley, you'd be way out of your element. You'd need me there."

"I'd have you," I whisper.

He shakes his head, and I cover my face. I won't explain, won't share my secret with him, even though it's logical to do so at this moment. I find I simply can't.

He holds me all that night, folding me against his chest, his strong arms keeping me warm.

"I love you," I murmur near his ear. "Forever, okay?"

"I love you. I'm sorry. I'm so sorry."

"Don't be sorry. We said never sorry." I won't make demands or tug at his heartstrings. "One day, perhaps I'll find you. And you won't feel you have to be my watcher."

I stroke his face. His beloved face. We kiss until I taste my tears. But I don't think they're only mine.

When I look out the window and see how much rain is on the ground, it's nearly a relief. I've got to get up to the Patches. We hug at the door, and kiss deeply, and turn back for the bed.

Afterward, I dress for cold and rain. And I bid him goodbye.

TWELVE
FINLEY

Monday morning, there's a mud slide trapping two sheep and killing three others. I call for help via my repaired radio, and Mayor Acton sends Mike Green. He is, as ever, quiet and helpful. We spend Monday night sleeping in shifts in one of the huts down by the fields. Whoever isn't sleeping is keeping the sheep away from the thick gulches.

Tuesday, June 20, brings more rain, as well as Benny Smith to help in early afternoon. It's frigid, and the rain is mixed with sleet. The three of us are miserable as we use sand bags to redirect an overflowing gulch.

As the rain turns to mist, and then a thick fog, I allow myself to think of him. Ten more days. That's all I have left with him. I feel nothing at the prospect. I suppose I can't believe it.

We pile into Doctor's car at half past five. I'm headed toward Mike's family's home when Benny says, "I need my bones warmed."

Mike, in the front passenger's seat, looks over his shoulder toward Benny, in the back, and then turns to me. "Would you take us to the bar, Finley?"

"I don't see why not." Younger lads aren't meant to indulge, but when it's quite cold, or on a special day, they sometimes have a toddy.

"You should come in with us," Benny says. "You never do get out much."

"Finley doesn't hit the bottle," Mike says. "Everyone knows."

"I do on the rare occasion."

"It's a rare one when we lose so many sheep."

It's a rare one when I feel as poorly as I do. I can scarcely bear the thought of seeing Declan. My heart is so full—so battered, stretched, and sore—I fear seeing him will only make me ache. And yet, it's all I want. Perhaps one glass of something wouldn't hurt so. Only the one. Truth be told, I've lost that fear of becoming my father. I've become Mum instead.

As we walk to the bar's front door, where banjo music spills into the cold air, I notice the blinking Christmas lights draped around it and realize it's solstice—the longest night. How fitting.

There's a bit of a crowd just inside the doorway, so I'm stopped for a brief moment on the porch. I touch one of the lights and look up—and that's when I see between Benny and Mike. I see what's drawn the crowd.

It's Declan. Wearing dark pants and a pale shirt, he's whirling Holly to a fast-paced song. He's been on the bottle. I can see it in his loose movements. In the way he laughs, unencumbered, as his hand grabs her hip and she throws her head back at the song's end. Just behind them, I spot Dot, her Rob Glass, and Rachel, all smiling and clapping.

Dull weight settles in the hollow of my belly. As Declan and Holly head toward the bar together, the crowd shifts. Mike steps inside. Benny smiles back at me.

"It's a bit loud, but it's—"

I shake my head. That's all I can manage. Hot pain blazes just beneath my throat—an ache so fierce, I run the entire way back to the clinic, desperate to outpace it. Instead it seems to cleave me deeper. When I round the clinic's front corner, gasping for breath in the frigid air, my poor heart beating wildly, I nearly run right over Anna, clutching Kayti, who's wrapped in a blanket.

Anna's eyes rove up and down me, skeptical and then relieved. "I'm glad you're back. Kayti's got a horrid cough."

Inside, I find this to be true. Kayti's quite congested, and a peek into her ear canal reveals what seems to be an infection.

"Poor wee dearie. We'll sort you out..."

I feel Anna's eyes on my back as I poke about the cabinets, working out the proper medicine for Kayti and the proper dose.

"When did it come on?" I ask.

"Sunday evening."

"I wish you'd have paged me."

When I return to the chair Anna's sat in, bearing the bag with the medication and syringes, I notice the strange look on her face.

"What's the matter, Anna?"

She purses her lips and sweeps a strand of hair from her face, refusing to meet my eyes.

"I'm afraid I'm a bit confused."

Her eyes flash to mine. "Sunday night."

I ignore the tightness in my throat as I say, "I was at the Patches."

"No you weren't! Your car was here."

"I walked—"

"You walked to see *him!*" Her eyes glitter. "Maura saw you leave there in the early hours! She went for a hill-walk to the ponds."

Tears spill down Anna's cheeks. I feel so faint, I grab onto the chair by hers.

"No," I whisper.

She's shaking her head. Just shaking it in silence. I can see her lips quiver despite the way they're pressed together.

"I'm ashamed I didn't know. The way you spoke of him that day—when we had the wine. Just the barest mention, but it was there in your eyes." She dashes tears away. "It makes complete sense now. Ever since you returned from that cave, you've been someone different entirely. You think I haven't noticed?"

"I was trapped below ground!"

"You're a liar!"

Kayti starts to cry.

My throat feels as if it's turned inside out. I try to appear casual but end up whisper-hissing, "I was there to get measuring spoons."

Anna jumps to her feet. Kayti's eyes pop open. "Have you lost your marbles? What's possessed you, Finley?"

I think of Declan whirling Holly. Hot tears sting my eyes. "Nothing! He's gone in ten days! Nothing possessed me! I needed *spoons!*"

Kayti's rooting about Anna's coat. With one hand, Anna opens several buttons. She sits back in the chair stiffly, pushing her shirt up, and Kayti lifts her head, mouth open. I'm stricken by that sight: Anna shaking her head, her jaw tight with fury, as wee Kayti latches to her breast.

"I know it wasn't a love match, but are you purely mad? You should be chaste! Waiting! You'll be judged for this, God save you. I can't say I know you. Where is that girl? I don't know!"

Tears spill down my cheeks, and Anna shuts her gaping mouth. Her eyes soften despite her shaking her head. "How did it—"

I shake my head, pressing my trembling lips flat as I inhale deeply through my nose.

Her lips purse tightly, and her narrow shoulders tauten.

"Anna, *please!* Don't tell a living soul, especially Holly! I could...you know what could happen. Please tell Maura it was spoons!"

Anna juts her chin up. I can see her pulse in her throat. "If they find out, Finley, it won't be from me!"

She whirls from me, grabbing Kayti's blanket off a chair before she snatches the bag of medication from my hand and flies out the door. Good thing Kayti's dose is unchanged from her last infection; I never did tell Anna how much. I stand at the door for a few moments, breathing in great tugs, wiping my face.

Then I turn the lock, flip the lights out, and walk numbly into the living quarters. I should eat, perhaps. It's been near twelve hours. I pull out a round, white plate that was my Mum's, a loaf of bread, some jam and peanut butter. I stare at the plate's edge.

"Why use that plate for a simple sandwich? It's quite larger than the sandwich will be. Bit of wasted space."

I flinch at the voice in my head. It's been so long...I suppose I don't expect to hear him narrating my actions—no more. Once my brain is compromised, though, he won't hush up. Memories play like a record as my shaking hands assemble the sandwich.

"Why are you making that damnable soup again? Who asked for tumeric soup?"

"I've had a long day. Shouldn't my food be waiting? Or do you cook simply when you feel the urge?"

I stare down at the sandwich as it blurs about the edges. It looks perfectly nice despite the extra space on the plate. There's nothing wrong with how I make a sandwich. Just as there was nothing wrong with Mummy.

I set the plate down and walk woodenly into the bedroom, where I slip my shoes off, lie down in the bed, and pull the covers over myself. I haven't slept here regularly in so long, the sheets smell stale and odd. Beneath my pillow, I find my old, brown rosary—the one I got in girlhood.

I don't pray the rosary, but simply clutch it as I lie on my back, rigid as a corpse.

Please help me. Oh, please. Please help me. Please help me.

Tears roll into my ears, and I whisper the word aloud, half chant-
ing. "Please. Please. Please." Each time I say it, my eyelids feel
heavier.

Knocking wakes me. I'm aware of knocking, and my racing heart.
The quiet house. I wonder if I dreamed the knock, and then I
hear it again: two more raps, delivered with a heavy hand. A
male hand.

Terror rolls through me. I never checked the ship schedule...

I sit up. Take a thorough breath. The knocking comes again,
less rhythmic this time. I slip on my shoes and drift into the clinic.
It's all dark inside. Through the closed blinds, slits of white
moonlight. I can't see the clock on the far wall, so I've no idea
what time it is. Trepidation trills through me with every step
toward the door.

I don't know why I'm so sure it's going to be *him*. Sometimes I
get pulled into another place. Something happens, I'm flashed
back to the past...delivered to the clutches of my old, familiar
fears.

Were you as damaged as me, Mummy?

You deserved more.

If we are nothing but the flesh and motion summation of our
DNA, then I am her—extended. In my bones I know I'm certainly no
more. I'm like a bird I once saw flapping its wings just atop the rocks
near Hidden Cove. On first glimpse, I couldn't understand how it
could flap its wings so fiercely and remain motionless, not taking
flight. Then I moved nearer and saw its foot caught in some moss.

I have no hope, no expectation as I open the door. So I can
feel the warm life force that pulses through me when I see *him*.

His hair looks like a choppy sea. His face is swarthy with a
two-day pirate's beard. My hungry gaze falls to his mouth—that

lush, archangel's mouth, so out of place among the harsher land-scape of his nose, cheekbones, thick brows. Finally, I dare his eyes, and I think I now understand the phrases from novels. I could fall into those eyes, never emerging.

"Finley?"

I drag my gaze away from his. On his jaw there is a bit of reddish pink. I can smell Holly's perfume and the sharp stench of liquor. Cold air billows in around his broad form. My gaze darts to his.

"You're home," he murmurs. There's emotion in his voice—perhaps surprise, although naively I fancy that it sounds like wonder.

I want to rail that this is not my home. I'm homeless. Does it matter if I have a home besides? My life is over, even as he's fighting to determine if he wants to go on living his when he returns home.

"Yes," I whisper.

"Can I come in?"

Something flashes in his eyes—a sort of flame. I can't be sure because I look away again. Self-preservation. Love is reckless, and the heart gets out ahead of the soul. Mine feels like an anchor dragging me down through the floor.

I look at his face. This time, I won't cast my eyes down. "Did her mouth feel like mine?"

His lips twist as his brows gather. "What?"

"Did Holly's lips feel like my lips on your jaw?"

He frowns.

"There's lipstick on your jaw." I touch my own, and his hand lifts to mirror mine. His face is emotionless, although his brow remains a slight bit furrowed.

"I saw you dancing at the bar, and now you smell like Holly." I shut my eyes. Why did I have to love him? When I look at him again, I'm gripped by fury. "Why are you here, Declan? What do you want from me?"

"You were gone." It's whispered. He leans on the door frame, and then grips its top beam with his palm. I can see the liquor in his eyes, the way they're wide and over-focused on my face.

"Is that how it works where you're from, then? It's just whoever is about will do?" Despite my anger, or perhaps because of it, my eyes ache. "Oh, I know—" my fingers snap— "you're leaving anyway. That's right! You're leaving soon, aren't you? And there'll be other women. Ones who don't hold court in your bed or force you into bubble baths. They won't really know or care for you, or risk their *lives* to love you for mere weeks, as I have!"

His face twists again, and his brows notch in anger. *Oh please, try that!* I give a hollow laugh. "Go back to Holly, won't you?" I wave at him, shooing. "Holly wants you, no doubt Rachel as well! Go be merry at the bar, and we'll end this here! So much *simpler*. And that's what you like, isn't it? Keep it all risk-free and simple. Float through life without thinking too much beyond your animal-position *fucking*!"

He steps inside, his dark eyes flashing. "You don't like to fuck me, Finley?"

My heart beats so quickly, I fear I might pass out. "No, I don't in fact. I don't like *fucking* you. I like making love, and you stopped doing that. You won't look me in the eye now!"

He closes the distance between us. How he reeks of alcohol. His potent breath sends me back to my childhood, makes me tremble.

"You're a liar." The words are like velvet, and his face is set like stone.

"No, I'm not! Now go away from me!" I shove his chest without forethought and then recoil as fear pounds through me.

"Tell me you don't want me. C'mon, fucking tell me, Finley. Make it easy."

"I want you, and I hate it. *I hate you!*"

"Tell me you don't want my hands on you. My mouth right there." His finger points to my throat. I can't swallow. His hands run down my arms, the warm palms feather-light. His face is grave as all the universe.

I can say nothing. I've made unforgivable mistakes, so many errors in judgment. My foot is caught in moss I'll never break free of...and still I crave him.

"I don't want to want you," I say, the words barely there.

To my surprise, he laughs, his prince's mouth twisting before he tosses me over his shoulder and makes off toward the curtain, striking it aside to stride toward the beds.

"I don't want to either, so I guess that makes it even."

He takes his time lying me on my back, spreading my legs. For a moment, he stands over me, and our eyes lock. His are dazed and depthless. Were it not for his tight jaw, I'd have no clue he felt anything as he looks down at me.

"You thought you should stay away from me?" He shakes his head, the motion taut. He leans down, running his hand along my thigh. "You have no idea what I want to do to this body. God—so fucking thick. Nobody has an ass like this," he murmurs.

He squeezes mine, and then leans lower over me, unfastening my pants and taking them down. As he does, he looks into my eyes; he's giving me an out—but I don't take it. I can't.

He rips my pale blue panties cleanly at one side and then the other, snatching them away before he climbs atop me like a predator, lowering his face between my legs, rolling his tongue around my clit then dragging slowly in between my slit. It feels so glorious, I cry out, thrusting toward his mouth and grabbing at his hair.

"Heavens...oh...*mercy!*" He laps at me until I'm weak and

trembling, unable to properly breathe. All I want is that crest of elation. I lift my hips, urging his warm tongue over me, hoping that he'll fill me with his fingers.

I hear the rumble of his dark laugh. "Tell me what you want, Siren."

He licks upward from my core, his tongue hot and slick, tracing a circle 'round my clit until I'm moaning. Then he lifts his tongue away. I grab his hair.

"Relief...please!"

He leans down, refusing me his mouth as his breath warms my inner thigh. "Tell me how you want relief, Siren."

My belly coils, and then his fingers dip into my heat. It's just the tips at first, but he pushes them slowly inside then drags them back out as his thumb circles my clit.

"I want to come," I whisper, feeling my cheeks redden.

"That's right. And I've been wanting to do this..." His gaze flicks up to mine, unreadable, before he rolls his tongue over my aching flesh. His fingers probe me sweetly as his tongue makes me feel slick and breathless. I lift my hips, urging his fingers deeper, even as my legs tremble.

He wraps one arm around my backside, lifting me so he can pump with more force. His mouth contrasts with those firm thrusts, teasing my clit with gentle licks until I grab his head and push down in a desperate bid for satiation. Then I'm overcome by ecstasy, my body quaking as my hand on his hair gentles. I hear myself whisper, "I love you."

When I open my eyes, I find him stroking his stiff sex. His gaze grips mine. It's unapologetic. He looks as if he feels nothing for me. No emotion—only lust. Still, I need him. I'll take scraps.

I rise on my knees and kiss his mouth. I kiss him even though he tastes like nightmares and he smells like Holly. I feel ill but also rapt as I hug an arm around his neck, stroking his warm nape as our kisses deepen.

Then he's lying me down, spreading my knees as if he plans to take me in the way we used to. He's looking down, away, as he presses his sex into me. When he lifts his head, his blue eyes are closed. He thrusts deeper.

As he starts to pump his hips, I stroke his arms...but I'm afraid to touch him, frightened I'll drive him away. Instead I lock my hand around his thick forearm and focus on returning what he's doing thrust for thrust, on tightening myself around him so my sex hugs his huge erection.

In return, he plunges deeper, filling me more fully than perhaps he ever has, as if on this, our longest, darkest night, gentleness simply won't do. He grunts and groans, but he says nothing. Not once does he lean down over me and kiss my throat or stroke my hair.

I can feel it when he nears release; he thickens inside me, and then I feel a hot, soft, full sensation. That's when I realize—there's no condom. Worry cinches my chest, but it's there then gone, lost in the rush of ecstasy as I topple over my own ledge.

I open my eyes as he lifts his head and his eyes hold mine. Where before, when we made love in this position, I could see his feelings in his face, tonight there's nothing. He's no warmer toward me than a stranger might be.

Wordlessly, he separates our bodies. With a final glance at me, he moves down off the bed and bends to pluck his clothing off the floor.

THIRTEEN
DECLAN

"Is that it, then?"

I glance over at her. Then my shirt's over my head. The floor feels like it's moving. I almost fall over as I get my arms through the holes.

"Um, what?" I can't see her. It's dark in here, and kind of blurry. What did she say?

"So...you're leaving, I suppose?"

A crest of panic hits the back of my throat. Sweat rolls down my temple. "Yeah."

Where are my underwear? Fuck. I see them by a table and float over that way. I'm fucking drunk. She felt so good. Too good.

"Would you like company?"

I step into my boxer briefs and look back at her. I can feel my heartbeat in my eyes. They're kind of pulsing, which makes it look like her long hair is blowing in the wind.

"Uh—" I clear my tight throat, try to make my voice a little louder. "Yeah."

My shoulders start to shake...and then my chest and arms.

If she comes with me—

But I want her to.

I need her with me. Even though it's *that* night. I'm leaving tomorrow. I can't stay away from her on my last night here.

I nod—I can't get my mouth to move—and then she's getting off the bed.

"Wait here, if you don't mind? I need my toothbrush." My ears hear her words, but my mind's not processing, so I just nod. When she disappears, I feel a slosh of horror. She went next door, my real voice tells Drunk Me.

I put on my pants...and then my shoes. I can't get them tied, and when I try, my fingers tremble.

It's cold outside. Cold...like the refrigerator. I had that thought in a dream, but now it's here...and I'm awake. I feel my legs move like machines, and I'm there at the cabinets. It's dark, but I can see the pale refrigerator at the room's back corner. Every pharmacy has to have a refrigerator. She said she couldn't get what I wanted, but why would she tell me if she could?

Just a little, and I'll get through tonight better. I don't want our last night to be like this. I don't want June 20 to haunt me twice.

I walk to the refrigerator. My pulse is racing. If it's here, I'll get it. I could even tell her. But no. Why make her worry? Why let her know? If she sees me as a fucked-up addict, she won't love me—and I need for her to love me till I leave.

The door cracks open. I realize belatedly my hand's around the handle. The light is bluish. Cold. And then I've got it open all the way. I can't sort through bags and boxes fast enough. I spot it in the right-hand corner on the top shelf: just this little syringe, marked with a handwritten label. When I see it, I go so hot, and my head spins so hard.

I've got Fentanyl.

Holy shit.

I curl my hand around the syringe. All the room's dark, hazy edges sharpen. I can't get my breath. My heart's pounding too hard.

I could run. Bolt the door at my place, get it all set up just right. Really take my time with it.

Oh shit. I'm getting juiced up just thinking about it. But...I don't head for the door. My whole body breaks out in a cold sweat, and the shaking gets so bad, my legs almost give way. I start to gulp back air because I don't know what to do.

It's Finley's writing on the label.

I can't take it if it's hers. It's not hers...but she mixed it. If I use here, I'll never get clean. I can't steal from Finley. I need it so fucking bad. If I fuck up, it doesn't matter. I'm already a fuck-up. Put it back, it's Finley's. What would she do if she saw me? If I use, she can't come over. I could do it when she's sleeping. Would this be enough to get me fixed up? What's the milligrams per milliliter? What if I get fixed and can't remember our last night together?

I hear footsteps. My whole body flashes icy cold, then swelters. I can't breathe. My pulse throbs in my eyes as a wave of shame envelops me. It's so thick and dark, I can't feel anything but decimated as it rises through me, filling me up while weighing me down, like lead.

And then she's here. She's right in front of me, and she's the same, but I'm not. I am dead before her. I'm black matter and she's pure light. I can't move or speak or even think as she stops near me.

"Declan?"

How long till she sees it? I can't put it back now. She'll see it. She's gonna know.

Something large and heavy moves atop me, pushing me down. I feel like that nightmare dream I used to have after hearing that Houdini story: I'm buried alive and I will never, ever get out.

"Declan?" She steps closer to me. I watch as her face morphs in concern. She reaches out. Her hand brushes my arm.

"Darling?" I realize I'm breathing loudly. "Are you all right?" *Reassure her, fuckface.*

I feel like I'm going to throw up.

"Declan?" Her hand's gentle around my arm, but I can't stand the feel of it. I stagger back, and I can see her eyes pop open wider.

"Sailor...are you all right?"

I hold up a hand—the one that's not holding her syringe. *Fuck-up with the shaking hands, that's who I'll always be.* I'm trying really hard to breathe right, but I can't, and Finley won't leave me alone.

Her hand is on my arm again. She needs to let go. *She thinks she knows me, but she doesn't; she knows who I want to be, and I'm not him. I can't do this.*

"What's the matter?"

"Nothing."

"Here..." She tries to wrap her arm around my waist, but I step away.

"What's that? In your hand?"

I hear her let her breath out. I shut my eyes. But with them shut, I lose my balance. I can feel my shaking legs about to give out, so I crouch down. Then my knees are shaking, so I end up sitting on them—kneeling. I've got my hand cupped around the syringe. I don't want to see her. I don't want to be here like this. I don't want to be here. I see the gold lines, those waves. Why did I see those waves? What's the point of getting brought back if I can't do it? I can't do it. I'm scared. I've never felt this scared before; I didn't know before. I don't think I can do this.

I'm shaking so bad. My teeth are chattering. Every time I go to inhale, I can't, and I have to gasp to fill my lungs. I cover my face, or try to. My hand's shaking, too.

"My darling Sailor. Is it empty?"

I lock my fingers around it.

"It's all right. Just tell me what's happened, and I can help you."

"No...you can't."

No one can help me. I pull the top off the needle, jab it into my fingertip. Anything to get me steady, get my head back straight. Doesn't help, though.

I can't breathe, and now I really think I'm gonna pass out. Why is this happening, I wonder dimly. I open my eyes and find her face twisted. Tears shine in her eyes.

"I'm sorry."

It's the only thing I'm good at saying. I try to swallow...but I can't. Her face is fuzzing black around the edges. I hold out the syringe, or I try to, but my hand can't do it. It falls to the floor. In the breath of time when she looks down at it, I manage to fill my lungs with air.

She picks it up, I think, and then her hands are on my shoulders. "Breathe."

One of her hands goes to my throat. I think she's trying to get me to inhale, but I'm so cold and tired. I think of Laurent's arm around my neck from behind.

"People are stupid and naive. Do you think this is about love? I'll show you. It's about comfort. For the body. You're in shock right now from the news of what happened. You won't remember this discomfort. And next time, when I come to bring us both comfort, you'll be more ready."

I can feel his chest against my back. I can feel his arm. I feel it. I don't like it. Something's wrong with me. Finley is climbing on me. She's wrapping herself around me. Her mouth covers mine. I can't breathe. My ears ring. I hear her voice, the firm words. Her hands on my shoulders, squeezing.

"You're okay. Listen to me, Declan—you are fine. Look at me."

Why's she saying that?

I look up at her, or try to, but her mouth is over mine again. Am I supposed to kiss her? She blows air into my mouth, and I feel like I'm floating. Did she shoot me up, and I missed it? I'm slowing down now.

"Just breathe."

Again, her hot breath in my mouth. She's blowing air into my lungs. That's weird. Her arms are around me. She's warm and soft. I love her.

"Here we go again." Her hands around my mouth. Her hot air that I breathe into my nose. I don't like this shaking. Finley's hand is rubbing my arm.

She kisses the corner of my mouth, and then, again, she's blowing into it.

I must be hallucinating. Am I dead? I'm really tired now.

I manage to hold onto her so she doesn't get knocked over as I shift so I can lie down on my side. I feel my heart pounding, my cold skin, the colder floor. I'm really fucked up. But there's Finley. She's beside me.

"There now." Tears are dripping down her face as she strokes my hair. "It's all right." Her mouth on my cheek—just beside my nose. Her lips kissing my eyes. I'm confused. I inhale deeply, and she cups her hands around my mouth. I manage to kiss her. Just a little kiss.

I'm sleepy. Maybe this is just a dream.

"You're okay. Take your time...we can just lie here."

I look up into her eyes. I love her. I can't get my mouth to say it.

"I love you," she murmurs back.

I laugh—inside my head, at least. She read my mind.

Finley holds me, and it's me and her. It's slow and dark, and all that bad stuff feels a little bit better.

"This is my worst day." It's barely a murmur.

She hugs me closer to her. "Close your eyes, Sailor. I'll play with your hair... You'll tell me later."

My friend died. Because I was stupid and a coward, and I didn't tell. I imagine saying it. I see his face. I always see his face, especially when I dream: it's blue, with purple lips. I killed him. I kind of want to tell her that. So she can tell me it's okay.

"What's wrong with me?" My eyelids feel so heavy. "Did you give me something?" It's a whisper.

"Carbon dioxide." Her lips press against my cheek. "Just my breath. You were having an anxiety attack. But now you're okay."

I was?

"I messed up," she whispers. "The refrigerator... I'm so sorry."

I stare at the ceiling. "Would you go with me?" The question burbles up from nowhere. "Finley...will you marry me? If I get better?"

Her arms tighten around me. I feel her ribs expand. Her lungs expand. I love her lungs. More than I hate myself, I love her. Does it work like that? Does getting better work like loving something more than wanting to be dead?

A triangle moves across the ceiling. Something long and pale. I focus on it without knowing what it means.

"I would love to marry you, Carnegie. But—" Her voice catches. "Declan—"

Finley jumps up. I sit up in time to hear her loud gasp. "Doctor!"

Two figures congeal before someone flips the light switch.

I blink at the priest and someone else—a short guy with gray-brown hair. I'm getting to my feet when Finley runs into his arms.

He chuckles: a deep, Santa sort of laugh that doesn't match his small frame. "It's my wee wifey!"

FOURTEEN
FINLEY

When my world implodes, there's silence. Silence as I'm crushed against my husband's chest. Silence as Father Russo spots Declan on the floor. I hear a smack, but I can't turn around because I'm locked in Doctor's arms.

When I do, I find Declan lying pushed up on one elbow with a dazed look on his face, and Father Russo standing over him.

"What's this then?" Doctor frowns from me to Declan and then back to me, with drawn brows. "What's he doing here?"

"He's sick," I manage.

Father Russo crouches down beside him. When my gaze moves to Declan's face, I find his eyes are locked on me. His face is white as bone, but his eyes—they're blazing. I feel myself whither.

When I look to Doctor again, his hard eyes are on me, too.

He frowns at me, then strides to Declan. "Hello there. I'm the physician over this clinic." He kneels beside Declan, and I feel my legs shake. "Dr. Daniels. Or, as they call me, simply the good Doctor." He casts a glance over his shoulder at me. "Intoxication?"

From my angle standing over them, I see Declan's jaw lock. He shakes his head. "Tree nut allergy. Got near something with cashews."

I watch, wordless, as he somehow stands, putting a hand into his pocket for a moment before looking dead at me.

"Thanks for the Benadryl, Finley." He quirks a brow at Doctor. "Nice to finally meet you, Dr. Daniels." He nods, just the barest motion of his chin, and walks out of the clinic.

The sensation in my chest is one of tugging. It's as if my heart is trying to leave with him.

When the door clicks shut, Father Russo and Doctor speak at once.

"That is the strangest—" Father Russo begins, as Doctor exclaims, "Who the devil managed to get cashews?"

Father Russo shakes his head, purses his lips. I can feel his eyes move over my face as I glance down at the floor.

Doctor steps back over to me. He snakes an arm around my waist, then drapes his hand over my backside. "Who has cashews?" he asks lightly, as his fingers pinch.

His hand roves up and down as the priest shrugs. "I've not seen them offered in the catalog since '17." He gives me a pointed look, then steps toward Doctor, hand extended. "Welcome back, Daniels." They clasp hands, and he meets my gaze. "You'll do better with him here now."

"Yes."

I feel like I'm drowning as he moves toward the door. The air I'm dragging through my nostrils doesn't seem to make it to my lungs.

This time, when the door shuts, I'm alone with Doctor. The room seems to buzz around me as he grabs my upper arm. "Perhaps you'd like to explain where your undergarments are. And why I walked into *my* clinic to find my *wife* down on the floor embracing Homer Carnegie!"

His gray eyes widen slightly, and I note he's grown a bushy mustache.

I shake my head. "He came here...craving." My voice quakes, and he loosens his grip on me.

"That's why his hands were shaking?"

I meet his eyes, nodding slightly.

"That's why you were with him?"

I nod. "He arrived quite unexpectedly, leaving me no time to dress. He'd been drinking, as you noticed. He was out of sorts. I tried to help."

Doctor nods, pressing his lips together. He gives me a small smile, and for a moment, I glimpse in him what I did when we met four years ago: a conviviality that, if not actually kind, could at least be companionable. "It's been quite some time," he says softly.

"You've arrived early."

He reaches into his pocket and brings out something he holds pinched between his fingers. My pulse quickens when I see that it's a ring with a large diamond.

"Oh—I—" I swallow. "Thank you."

I take it from him, and he takes it back. "Hold out your hand, Fin."

My fingers tremble wildly as he slides it on my finger. I hold my breath, praying he'll mistake fear for excitement. When I glance up at his face, I find his thin mouth curled upward at the corners. "To replace that dingy one."

Gammy's. I nod. "Thank you, Doctor."

I wrap my arms around his neck, stretching up a bit too high at first. As I hug him, my head begins to feel hollow.

I pull away, and his eyes search me up and down before they move across the floor—to the spot where Declan was.

"It's been quite a journey. Lock up, Fin."

He strolls toward the residence, and I walk to the clinic door on legs that feel like rubber. I pause for only a moment to listen. I hear nothing, but even if I did, there's nothing I can do. I cross myself and walk toward the short hallway before I realize—*the bed!* My heart dips down into the hollow of my belly. I feel like I'm moving underwater as I rush over, straighten the covers. That's when I realize—where is the syringe? Is it still on the floor?

My heart thuds dully in my temples. I turn around, thinking I'll check the floor quickly. And there's Doctor. He stands just behind me, staring without blinking.

"Did you have a patient?"

"Well, yes. Homer."

"He was in the bed...then on the floor?" He arches one brow.

"I rushed to the door thinking it could be emergent. I was in my robe. I directed him here to the bed and went to dress." I wave down at my pants and sweater. "When I returned, he was near the medication cabinets. Perhaps wishing for...well, who can know? Then he went down to the floor. I believe he's quite poorly. Withdrawing, since he's been here," I say softly.

Doctor nods. He holds his hand out for mine, and we walk toward the residence together. Never has he held my hand. Not ever. As he closes the door linking the residence to the clinic, I can't breathe for crushing fear.

I flinch a bit away, a habit borne of only three occasions—but they were...*impacting.*

Tonight, though, he gives me his tight-lipped smile. "It's good to be home, dearie."

* * *

"How is it?"

"Adequate, I suppose. Perhaps a bit stale." Doctor sets the muffin down and shifts his gaze back to the newspaper.

"I'll try for more moisture next time."

He chuckles. "Oh, I trust you will. You're baking for me again now."

"What shall I make for you today?" When there's an ebb in our patient flow, and I've nothing to do out on the slopes, Doctor likes it when I bake sweet things.

"Do you have dough for friendship bread? Something that you can't foul up, and besides, I've missed the taste of it."

"I don't believe I do, I'm sorry to say."

He frowns, tugging at the chain attached to the arms of his bifocals. "Plum cake, then."

"Plum cake it is."

I'm not sure he'd mind if I left the adjoining den and kitchen area, so I start to spray the counters with some cleaner. When I'm finished, I stand near the table where he's sitting. "I'll start on your laundry now, I believe."

He says nothing. Likely too absorbed in what he's reading. As I step into the bedroom, I note that the clock on the bedside table says it's 4:49 a.m. Normally, Doctor is up at 5:30, but he's been in Cape Town—west—so his biological clock is a bit "off."

I sprinkle lavender oil atop the sheets to mask the musty, unused scent before making the bed. I had no time to do so last night, but it's better late than never till I get a chance to wash them.

I hold still a moment, listening. Then I walk to the room's doorway, holding my breath as I point my ear in the direction of the kitchen. When I hear nothing, I slip into the hallway and walk silently but briskly toward the door adjoining residence to clinic.

I find my torn panties beneath one of the pillows on the bed I shared with *him*. Scooping them up, my heart seems to skip a few beats, and my eyes throb awfully. It's the first bit of emotion I've felt in a number of hours—a stinging needle-prick of deepest longing for him. It's there then gone. I stuff the panties into my bra and walk quickly down the clinic's short hall. When I make it back to our room, I pull my contraband from my bra and nearly fall to my knees with relief.

A moment later, he clears his throat. "What's that you've got there?"

I whirl around, my body vibrating with terror, my blood roaring in my head. "What do you mean?" My voice is hopeless—weak and cracked.

He strides closer. "What's this then? Something you fetched from the clinic."

I hold the panties up, my fingers bending desperately to mask their torn appearance. "If you mean these—"

He snatches them from my hand. Holds them to his nose, inhaling.

"From the drawer," I whisper.

The back of his hand connects with my mouth, and I taste the stinging tang of blood.

FIFTEEN

DECLAN

I leave Baby in the house with a fresh lamb nappy and a full belly and walk down to the village.

It's really cold out. I think colder than it's been so far.

When I get to Upper Lane, I notice all these lanterns on the porches, and I remember that it's solstice. The twenty-first of June's the longest night here.

Every time I take a breath, I feel it in my chest. My chest is sore. It's kind of weird how bad it hurts. My whole body hurts. I kind of like it. It gives my mind an anchor.

When I get to the clinic, I don't know what to do. I just stand there in the dirt-patched grass beside the door and watch my breath fog. I forgot to wear a coat. I guess that's why it's so damn cold.

The sky is orange and pink this morning. Usually, then sun's nowhere in sight, so dawn is always blue or sort of purple. I rub my arms and sort of pace around for a minute. I spend a second being careful with my breaths, doing the breathing from my nose and letting it out my mouth.

It's okay. It's weird how when I think shit like that now—

when I tell myself something to calm me down—I hear *her* voice saying the words. Thinking of that makes my throat ache.

I need to get going. Earlier, I used my radio, which has spent this whole trip at the bottom of my bag, to talk to someone on the *Celia*, and I don't think they want to wait around too long. I need to get going.

I reach into my pocket and pull out a square of paper. The paper's folded around the stolen syringe, which is still full of Fentanyl. I step closer to the porch. I don't know where to leave it. The note doesn't say much.

I'm sorry I took this. I kept it cold, so it should still be good.
Thank You.

I underlined the "Thank You" twice with slash-looking lines, like maybe I'm just someone who likes underlining things.

I thought hard about leaving the syringe at her Gammy's place, but I thought of a few ways that could go wrong. Someone might think Finley gave it to me, for one.

I go around for a few minutes about where to leave the note and syringe. I rub my sore chest. It feels weird to hold the note, knowing that the Fent's inside it. I've had it on me for so many hours now, it doesn't tempt me quite as much.

There's no flower pot or anything on the clinic's stoop. And it's a little windy. I decide to walk back to the other porch. The one by their door.

I gulp down some cold air. Walk around the building's back corner. I think she'll find it here. There's an empty pot with just dirt. I set it in there. If he finds it—the doctor—it's not like it tells him anything. It shouldn't put her at risk.

I suck in some more cold air. Stuff my hands deep into my jeans pockets.

My eyes sting. I squeeze them shut. *Christ.*

Is he good to her? He looked older—maybe fifties—and I couldn't tell if he was a dick. As far as dicks go, I guess maybe he's not into using his, because...she was a virgin. I know that for sure.

I think of all those times she said things like "no strings attached," and tell myself she knew this all along. She knew he was coming back and I was going. She's okay with it.

I can't think much on how I was a fling for her. Because that was basically it. Finley's got the biggest heart on earth, so a fling for her is worth more than a lot of people's marriages. Thinking that makes me think of how she ran to him. My throat closes off.

I pant in white puffs.

Fuck.

I gotta go now.

I've got my eyes half shut, and I'm striding toward the clinic part of the building when I hear yelling.

That's a man's voice.

What the fuck?

I move closer to the clinic's white-washed, cinderblock wall. The voice is low and hard—not yelling now, but kind of clipped and...yeah, that's definitely angry. I listen, but I can't tell what he's saying. Then he's quiet. I can't move as adrenaline floods my system.

What the fuck was that?

Say more.

Give me a sign if I should stay.

The ever-present Tristan wind whips over the roof. I pace back to the house door. Nothing. Fucking hell.

I sit on the stoop and run my hand back through my hair. I need some kind of fucking sign. That she's all good with this guy.

Even thinking of that—of her with that old fucker—gives my chest this burning feeling.

I get the letter and the syringe out of the pot. Walk toward the clinic door. Maybe I'll knock. It's probably a bad idea, but I don't know...I've got a weird feeling. I clear the stairs with one big step and stand there with my eyes shut. *Please.*

Maybe I'm going crazy: I just want it to be bad for her, so I can swoop in.

I try the knob. It works. The fuck? The door is open at 5:35 a.m.? That's sort of weird, right?

I can step inside and...if they're in there—if *he's* in there —I'll...what?

If it's him, not her, I'll ask for Benadryl. If it's both of them...I don't know. Why would it be both of them, though? Mother-fucker was just yelling at her in the house part of the building. I don't dare to think of what I'll do if I walk in and it's just Finley. But if no one's in there, I'll walk over to the door that divides house from clinic, and I'll listen just a little more.

I rub my eyes and try the door again. I don't know what I'm thinking. That I'm in some kind of Bond movie? I push it open slowly, though. Real quiet, like 007. Inside the main room, it's dark and silent. *They're not here.*

I blow a quiet breath out. Step inside. And stand there. To my left is the little waiting area where she took my blood pressure just after we got back from the burrow. To the right, a long, pale blue curtain that divides the area with the beds from the big space in front of me, which has the cabinets and a receptionist desk.

If I go around the curtain to my right and pass the area with beds, I can walk into that little hall and listen at the door of the residence.

I keep my footsteps quiet on the pale linoleum as I make my way around the curtain. That's when I hear it—a grunting sound.

It stops me in my tracks and makes my body start to tremble. I know from the first sound...but I keep quiet, listening. I hear the grunt again, and the sound of a zipper. *Oh, fuck—NO.* The curtain to my right feels like it's tilting.

I hear Finley's whimper. No. No, no, no. But she's whimpering—this sort of groaned whimper that turns into a high-pitched whimper as I hear springs creak. He makes a low sound in his throat, and my head starts to float on top of my shoulders.

She whimpers. He grunts. She whimpers, and that's when, slowly, through the haze, I realize *Finley doesn't whimper like that.*

Does she?

No, she doesn't.

Finley is a screamer. If she's not screaming, she's gasping, groaning...whispering. She whimpers more, and something thick and hot and prickling starts to crawl up my neck. I can't move... and then I have to. I can't keep myself from stepping to the curtain's end and walking quietly around it.

Each bed has its own curtain, and the one around the bed where we were last night is pulled shut. She whimpers again, and her voice cracks. I pulse white hot as the whimper turns to a small cry. Finley starts to cry, and he says, "Oh, I think you shouldn't worry. You'll enjoy this."

I'm so hot, so frozen, so filled up with horror. I don't know how I get my legs to move me across the space of the floor to that curtain, but I reach out and snatch it back, and there they are.

She's on her back without a shirt on, and he's over her. For a terrifying, black hole second, I can only see the back of him, his asscrack and his legs, and I think *he's inside her.* Then I step closer, and I see Finley's underwear. Oh Jesus. Fucking Christ. My pulse gallops. My knees tremble with relief—and then he's up and coming at me.

"What do you think you're doing here?"

My eyes magnet to Finley, and I realize that her arms are down in front of her, cinched in a belt. Her pretty face is red and tear-streaked. On her left cheek, there's an awful bruise.

I don't know what happens, how it starts or anything, except we're on the floor, and I'm on top of him. I'm whaling on his face, and I can feel his bone, the sticky thickness of his blood as I try to rip his head off his body. He keeps trying to talk, and I'm laughing, and I'm busting through his face because he hurt her and *you don't hurt Finley!* It might be okay to hurt me but you never hurt her—

"NEVER. HURT. HER. Do you fucking hear me? Never—" *smash him*— "ever—" *fuck you*— "EVER hurt her or I'LL FUCKING KILL YOU."

Every time his head snaps back, I feel another shot of satisfaction. Someone's screaming, but it's dim and far away. Then someone grabs me from behind. Someone's arm is locked around my throat. Someone's on my back. I fight them like an animal until the fucker's on the floor. It's Freddy.

"Fuck."

He's bleeding from his forehead, and one of his eyes is swollen shut. I look at the doctor. There's a pool of blood around him. Finley's huddled by the bed, sobbing. I rush toward her, wanting to get that belt off. Someone shrieks, and her friend Anna steps in front of me. She waves her arms as pain blooms in my head.

SIXTEEN
FINLEY

The sea at dusk. I squint my leaking eyes, and that's what Anna's blue tin roof looks like. I can't wrench my gaze away from it. I'm lying on my back on Anna's marriage bed, but if I stare up at the roof for long enough, I can pretend we're in a boat out on these deep blue waters. It's twilight, and we're holding each other. "I'm so sorry. I'm so sorry, Declan. I'm so sorry."

I don't know I'm speaking till she whispers, "It's not your fault. He went mad, Finley."

I blink at the ceiling.

Where is he? I'll find out when Freddy's back. As Mrs. White and Holly worked on Doctor, Freddy and Father Russo dragged Declan off. I saw him upright outside, but Anna and Mrs. Acton didn't let me near him. Mayor Acton stayed behind while Anna and Mrs. Acton brought Kayti and I here.

Mrs. Acton took me into the bathroom and asked me what happened. I wanted to tell her, but I could only weep. She handed me tissues. I wiped my face and blew my nose, and after, Anna brought me to the bed she shares with Freddy.

"Did you want the belt?" she whispers now.

I stare at my smearing ocean.

"Was Doctor angry with you? I could see his skull bone, Finley," she whispers. "It's miraculous that he was speaking when we left."

I know I could brave the ocean now. I know I could.

"Finley...speak to me. I didn't mean to be unkind last night. I was— I suppose it was my own emotions. I felt...hurt, I suppose. That you hadn't confided. Finley...was he hurting you this morning? Doctor? You never speak of what you...of your life with him. The intimate life," she whispers.

I heard Mrs. Acton murmuring to Anna that the ship's waiting for Declan. If no one comes with word of him soon, I'll be forced to squeeze out Anna's bathroom window. I'll get to him. My Declan would never leave without me.

"Is he unkind to you...is Doctor? You can tell me. Finley," Anna whispers, "did he *know*? Perhaps from Father Russo? He's a nosy pillock..."

Kayti's cries draw Anna out into the hallway. Then it's Mrs. Acton with me. She sits gingerly on the bed's edge, smoothing her green skirt.

"Anna said your wrists were bound. Who tied them that way, my dear? Was it Doctor...or was it Mr. Carnegie?"

Her eyes flare as mine meet them. Then they gentle. "Tell me what prompted the ordeal, dearie. What happened?"

I roll on my side, away from her.

I need Declan!

I mustn't weep. I mustn't weep.

I turn back toward her.

"Marriage could keep me in my post. I could offer you some company. We would never have to consummate it. I'm too old for you, Fin. I know that."

It wasn't a love match. I can't find my voice to say the words.
"Finley...did he hurt you? Doctor? You can tell me if he did."
The bed creaks as she leans toward me. "You can talk to me."

"He's a good man on the inside."
   "Your father doesn't mean to be this way."
   "At times, a man can't help his temper."
   *"These are our secrets to keep. You understand now, darling?
Who are we to ask the others to concern themselves with our well-
being...just because your father drinks a bit. We get on well
enough here, don't we?"*

"Finley, you're so good."

*"You cannot truly believe I never meant to consummate it. When
I get back from Cape Town, I'll take what's mine. You are my wife.
And you'll enjoy it!"*

*"Yearning is when you want something, my darling...especially
something you can't have."*
   "So, when you want something forbidden?"
   "Yes, my dearest. It's a bit like forbidden."

*"There's no time for further correspondence. Hear me through
the stars."*

"Stay here, Finley! Do not move!"

A tear drips down my cheek, and Mrs. Acton scoots closer, to hug me. "You can tell me what happened. We want to see to you. So let me ask again, dearie. Did Doctor mean you harm?" Her hand comes up to my face, hovering. I flinch, and her green eyes widen. "Did he strike you?"

"Who are we to ask the others to concern themselves with our wellbeing..."

"If you can spread your legs for someone weak of spirit, someone lazy like him—someone who's not your husband, WHOM THE LORD HAS JOINED YOU TO!—then you can keep quiet as I take what's rightfully mine! In exchange for caring for you, I'm deserving of my marital rights."

"Who are we to ask the others to concern themselves with our wellbeing..."

I stare into Mrs. Acton's eyes. I'm overcome with powerful inertia. Profound apathy.

"I know myself. I'm loyal."

"Was it Doctor...or was it Mr. Carnegie?"

I inhale. The air in my lungs feels too large.

"Was it Doctor...or was it Mr. Carnegie?"

I try to tell her with my eyes, for my mouth resists moving. But Mrs. Acton cannot read my mind. Her face is searching.

Who has Declan? *I want Declan!*

"It was Doctor." Whispered words. Wobbly words. When they come from my throat, sickness follows, so I have to rush into the bathroom.

"Finley, you're so good. I love you."

I wash my face, taking my time. The water's cold. It stings my eyes and fingertips.

Perhaps I'll stay the night here. I'm so tired now. Declan wouldn't leave without me.

As I step woodenly into the bedroom, I hear voices in the hallway. I hear Father Russo. Before I can make out what's being said, the bedroom's door opens, and Anna walks in. She holds Kayti, but this time it's Anna weeping. Kayti blinks at me as Anna says, "They know."

How odd that, at first, I don't know what. Anna reads my face and mind.

"Father Russo arrived after Mayor. He told Mayor and Mrs. Acton you were having an affair."

My knees buckle. I grab the bed's post.

I croak, "And?"

"Mrs. Acton told them—she said Doctor hurt you. But..." She shakes her head. Her calm face speaks damnation. "Father means to take you. He says he'll sort this out in a God-like manner."

I'm shaking my head as she speaks. No. No, no, no. No.

"I'm well, sir. How are you?"

"I would be better if I understood why you ceased attending weekday masses."

"No." I grip the bed. "I don't trust Father Russo!"

"Well, why ever not?"

"He's friends with Doctor!"

"Finley, he's our *priest*. The Lord anoints all priests."

I dash into the bathroom. As Anna comes to stand in the doorway behind me, I push the window open.

"Please!" It's the only word I can get out as I hoist myself into the frigid air. As I drop to the ground, I'm stunned to see it's dusk. Perhaps I fell asleep. What if the ship's gone?

"I'm going to *my* house!" That's what I call Mum's house. It still stands, and Anna knows I sometimes visit it.

I take off down Middle Lane in that direction but cut back the other way, running so fast and hard that the twilight spins around me and gold stars bloom in my eyes. I run as I hear a car crank in the distance. Sobs wrench from my chest—sob-gasp, sob-gasp.

I'm not going to Mum's, I'm racing to reach Declan. I can reach him if I'm fast enough. He'll be at Gammy's; I know he will. He'll still be at Gammy's.

I burst through the door gasping, and there is Baby, happy to see me, but I don't pause.

"Where is he? DECLAN!" I run through the house, but I see nothing of him. "DECLAN! Declan, please! Declan! Please, please!" I run out the back door to check the ocean for the ship. That's when I hear the crunch of tires on gravel.

Declan! Please, oh please!

I peek around the house's side, and I see Doctor's white Land Rover.

* * *

Declan

As soon as I realize the priest is playing intermediary between that piece of shit doctor and the people who have Finley, I go crazy inside. That fucking priest knew about Finley and me last night. I could see it in his eyes—and he wanted me to know he knew. There's something about the man—something beyond your basic dick religious official. He's probably buddies with the doctor.

Pretty quickly after getting his ass kicked, the goddamn doctor's running his mouth, claiming Finley told him she'd been seeing me. I don't really see the point in saying "no," so I admit we sort of had a fling and then go full-on Homer, acting like I don't see what the big deal is, but also saying sorry. The mayor eats it right up, still acting a little deferent to my Carnegie status and the fact that I'm "Homer."

When I talk to Mayor Acton, Freddy, and the priest, I focus on what I saw when I walked into the clinic—"to get some Benadryl." How that sick fuck was holding her down, and Finley was crying. I point out I didn't break in or come seeking her out. (Oops, I'm lying). I just walked in, heard something that didn't seem right, and walked around the curtain to find the doctor holding her down, rubbing his dick against her underwear while Finley cried with her arms tied. I tell them I didn't lose my shit until I saw the bruises on her face.

"I've got a thing for men who hurt women—and you should, too. You want one of your women with a guy like that?" I ask the mayor. "Finley's sweet. She probably doesn't stand a chance around that motherfucker."

He bristles at my language, but he seems to think about it.

I tell Freddy, "That's your wife's friend, man. You want her getting knocked around? You gotta keep that guy away from her."

This whole act is last-ditch insurance in case they haul me off without me getting to see Finley. I guess I'm prescient, because in the end, that's what they do. When I can hear the doctor talking bullshit to the priest inside the clinic—meaning he's alive and undamaged enough to speak—the mayor tells me it's time for me to take a hike.

"We've radioed the *Celia*, and they've agreed to wait for you."

Yeah, because I booked a seat on the ship. The mayor clearly doesn't know that.

"Freddy here will take you to your place of residence and show you to the dock."

"What about Finley? I want to hear that you're doing everything you can to keep her safe. Sounds like that jackass she's married to is treating her badly. I don't want to hear about that happening again."

I give the mayor my best you-don't-want-to-piss-me-off-or-I'll-stop-sending-money look, and he nods.

"I'll see to her. Ensure she's healthy and safe."

"I'm going to want an update on that sometime."

Freddy takes me to the cottage, where I pack up and slide my passport into my pocket. He and I head to Mark Glass's place, where Freddy tells Mark I'm leaving sooner than planned. Family emergency. I guess they want to keep things discreet for Finley and the doctor.

Mark and I walk to the dock, and he points out his boat. It's pretty small, and made of wood. I'm pretty sure it's the same one I came in on. I watch him crank the motor, and I get a look around the dock, and at the *Celia*, anchored maybe three hundred yards out. Then I "remember" my forgotten passport.

"Want to meet me back here in an hour?" I ask.

"That will work."

I walk up the hill, then hurry toward the clinic. I come at it from the residence side and stand with my back against the wall outside the door. I spend a couple minutes listening to the women's voices as they talk inside while cleaning up our mess. Finley's at the church, one of them says. I try to make it over there discreetly, but I see some little kid and raise a hand to wave at him, then put my finger to my lips. *Don't tell, buddy.*

I check all the church's doors, finding there are three but the back two are locked. The church's big, wooden door—the one on the front—is ajar. My heart pounds as I stand outside it, listening to what's going on inside for what feels like a long time before I step silently into the back of the main room. That's when I hear her soft Hail Marys. I can't see her, so she must be kneeling in the front.

I start sweating as I spot that fucking Father Russo, dressed in all his priest shit, sitting on the third row from the front. I have to really work hard on my breathing so I don't lose my shit while I stand behind a partial wall and wait for...something. I'll know when I see it.

I try to keep track of the minutes. Five? Seven? Four hundred? Finally, I see her, and again, I go all sweaty. I watch as she approaches Father Fucker. I think she asks if she can use the women's room. My blood boils that she has to *ask.*

He must say "yes." I watch what hallway she goes down, and then I take a big breath and get going. There's only one option that I know of: I crawl down the far left aisle, moving fast and hiding behind church pews. My shoulder aches, and my head throbs where Freddy hit me with a metal surgical tray, but I'm still pretty agile. Father Russo seems distracted.

When I get into the hall, my head spins hard. Women's room. Fuck, I need the—

There it is. I open the door...step slowly inside. There are two stalls. As I lean down to look for her feet, I hear a sniffle.

"Finley?" I hiss. "It's Declan."

SEVENTEEN

FINLEY

I brace for the worst when I hear the door open. *Horror after horror*, I think, my body trembling. Then I hear him. I hear Declan. He's here or I've gone mad. Either way, I'm weeping as I rush from the stall.

He catches me and spins me slightly, with one arm around my back. His hand tunnels up through my hair, holding my head as his mouth presses over mine. He kisses me hard, and then I'm gasping. He's whispering something. My blood is booming in my ears.

"Hey there, sweet Siren. Are you okay?" He holds me tight enough to hurt, and I can feel the tremor in him as his ribs pump with his quick, quiet breaths.

I cling to him, my voice cracking on a sob. All I can say is, "Sailor."

"It's okay. I've got you now." We're leaned against the wall. I'm wrapped in his arms, scarcely standing on my weak legs as he holds me to him, his lips against my hair as he says, "Listen to me, Siren. He's still out there and we've gotta go. Are you hurt anywhere?" His hands stroke down my back and sides as he blinks down at me with warm, gentle eyes.

I shake my head as tears spill down my cheeks. It's not true, though. The answer is "my heart," but it feels better now.

"Okay—we're gonna have to find a different door. Is there a side door you could show me?"

"I can't leave with you! They won't let me!" A sob punches from my throat before his mouth seals over mine again.

"I know." He holds me tightly. "I know you can't without spousal consent. Somebody told me. Do you want to, though? You want to leave with me, Finny? I think I can get that ship to leave if we go right now, get some lead time."

"Yes. Yes, please! Don't leave me here, please!"

"Okay, baby. Where's that other door? You gotta show me where the other door is."

"The side door."

We steal through the darkened hall and past the lesson rooms and turn right. And there's the door. He pushes it open, and I rush into the frigid night, and then we're running through the semi-frozen dew that sparkles like diamonds in the grass. We're running so quickly, Declan's strong hands dragging me, and I suppose I'm too slow because then he's thrown me over his shoulder. With each bouncing step, his shoulder jabs me in the belly, so I shut my eyes. I can't see the places as we pass. I can't say goodbye. Perhaps it's better that way.

I feel when we reach the hill. The hill I walked up to look down and see him arriving. It's the last path that I walked with Mummy. When we reach the downslope where the grass rolls down to the dock, he sets me on my feet and grabs my hand, and we run down the path together. That's when raindrops start to hit me in the face.

"The queen pulls back up to the dock, and Prince Declan hops in, and he and the princess exchange smiles as best friends do. She

says, 'I'm glad you're here,' and he says, 'Oh, of course. I would never dream of missing rainbow glitter dolphins on your birthday.'"

Pain or something like it swells in my chest, but we're moving so quickly. I think of the coming ocean. I can see my mother's yellow flower halo. If I start to drown, can he save me? I'm aware as we approach the dock that the sea is choppy—like it was that day. Fear fills my lungs, spins my head. Declan's strong hand squeezes mine.

"Don't worry. I'm going to take care of you. You trust me, Siren?"

"Yes."

"I've spent a ton of time out on the ocean. And this ship's expecting me. Money can't buy everything, but I think it can buy a speedy departure for me and a plus one. If you're sure."

"I'm sure. Please!"

My legs shake awfully as we step into the boat. We're moving quickly, but he takes a moment to kneel in front of me and look into my eyes. "*Are* you sure?" He takes my hand in his and squeezes. "It's okay if you're not. I can stick around here with you. Try to work out something. I won't leave you, Siren."

Tears well in my eyes and spill down my cheeks. I nod once. "I'm sure."

It's a fact: nothing will ever be resolved here. Doctor would never absolve me of my vows. He'll never let me go, and Father Russo told me with his own lips just today that he'll never annul our charade of a marriage. After my four hours of Hail Marys, he'd been preparing to deliver me to Doctor for a consummation and re-dedication of our vows.

"I want to go with you, my Sailor. Even if we have to flee."

I think of Baby, and I wipe fresh tears to be leaving her behind. Then he's helping me into a life vest, and I can't stop my body shaking. It smells the same, the life vest does. I feel nearly just the same: so frightened.

Rain falls faster as he unties the boat from the dock. My eyes cling to the hill that keeps the dock hidden from the village. Any moment now, someone might come.

"You okay?"

When I nod, he pushes the boat away from the dock. We bob a bit, and I hold my head as he starts the motor.

"Really soon, we're at the ship, and you can go inside."

"Okay," I say between sobs.

I feel his foot against mine as the motor *whurrs*, and then the boat's front end tips up. I uncover my face and grip my bench. That's when I see the gold lights spilling down the hill —*flashlights*.

I gasp, and Declan glances back. After that, he revs the motor. The boat jolts up on the front end, and then it's planning off. We're flying over the dark water. I look back again. The lights are bobbing near the dock now.

I choke on a sob. "They're coming!"

He tries to gun it, but the motor is so old. It's weak and slow. As the flashlights bob—they're getting on a boat—and I gasp deep, salt-water breaths, I wonder if they're using the island's emergency vessel. I've heard tale of how fast it is.

I clutch my seat and shut my eyes.

God please. If you can hear me, please oh please! Help us! I'll do anything, endure anything, if you can make me safe—please!

I cross myself, and then the other motor's hum sends my heart racing. I open my eyes, and my body goes ice cold. They're perhaps a hundred meters behind. Declan's face is stoic, but I feel his fear.

What will we do?

I turn toward our boat's front, facing the for a view of the *Celia*. It's about the same distance away: perhaps a hundred meters. I can't stop weeping like a twit. Every bump over the waves throws my body back through time.

I cannot lose him, too! Please, Mummy!

"If we can't leave together, I'm not leaving you," he shouts over the wind. The rain tosses his words, needles my cheeks and forehead.

Sailor revs the motor again, and the boat seems to skip over the waves. Perhaps we could reach the ship in time. How long does it take to board? There must be some wait. I'm speculating on the logistics when I glance back up, finding the gold lights behind us have grown larger.

Stunningly quickly, they're beside us.

Declan swerves away. Our boat's front juts up. I shriek, and his eyes fly to mine as our motor makes a choking sound, and we're tip-up again. I'm weeping as I grip the bench. My final glimpse of Declan is his face bent in concentration as their flashlights beam over his shoulder.

And then there's a massive *BOOM!* It's so forceful, so ferociously ear-boxing, I feel as if it knocks me back. In fact, it's Declan who's thrown overboard. I watch in horror as he hurdles to the water headfirst, his legs flying up behind him.

In my bones, I understand the violent boom, its otherworldly echo. I'm a ghost as I step to the boat's side—terror caged in flesh and bones. At first glimpse, I see nothing but mad white caps. Then I hear his choking. It's not a human sound, but more a water gurgle.

I realize in that instant—*he's not wearing a life vest!* That's what jolts my frozen mind. I've this notion of the water taking him, and that's enough to help me clear the boat's side.

Gold light spills around me. I see my shadow flick over the water's surface milliseconds before impact. It's so cold—so horrid cold—my body and my brain lock for a moment. Then I'm grabbing at the water. My hand swipes his solid body, and I grasp a fistful of his hair.

"DECLAN!"

He pushes weakly at me as his gurgled moan rends my soul.

"Grab onto me!"

His groans morph into hoarse screams as his face tilts toward the moon. The water's swallowing him. I can only see his nose and upper lip as I grab for him frantically. My arm finds its away around his neck. I lock my elbow underneath his chin and lean back in my life jacket, pulling him onto me so we bob then sink a bit together. Declan's hoarse bellows blend with my own sobs.

I can feel his body shake as his breaths come faster, weaker...

"Siren." I'm aware of gold light as their boat idles up beside us, but all I see are his eyes, sagging half shut as he shakes so violently, and I realize *the warmth I'm feeling is his spilled blood.*

"I love you, Carnegie! I love you so very, very much!"

"Love...you." His teeth are chattering. His fingers grasp weakly at my leg. He's trembling so hard, near convulsing. "Worth it." The words give way to a groan that breaks into a whimper. "Siren—"

That's the moment I'm plucked from the water. I do my best to hold onto him, but the sea wins—again.

There's a splash, and spinning starlight.

As I feel the boat's hard surface beneath my back, another *BOOM* deafens my ears. Something heavy hits me. I smell blood before I'm taken by the darkness, and my last thought is a prayer: *save him, not me.*

EIGHTEEN
FINLEY
EIGHT DAYS LATER

His headstone means less than nothing to me. It's a slab of rock from...I don't know where, in fact. I don't even know who chose it. Someone fetched it in those days when I was bed-bound, sobbing beneath Anna's blankets, being spoon-fed soup and forced to swallow sips of water.

Now I feel as if I'll soon need my own resting place. I've cried so many tears for him—for everything that happened—that I've none remaining. I'm not the woman he knew any longer. I'm so very far from her.

I pull a letter from my pocket. Unfold it. I scan the simple message quickly, although I needn't do so to remember it. Its words are blazed into my memory. My hands are steady as I shred the letter into pieces. I watch them flutter in our Tristan breeze.

The sky is gray today, and cloudless. I approve. Let it be winter. It's winter in my heart, and I don't want to look at blue skies or wildflowers. One rogue tear stings my left eye. I wipe it before I start across the sloping hillside toward two other headstones.

These mean even less than his. Neither of them mark a body, for there are no bodies. There never were and never will be. Still, I kneel there by the left one—Mummy's—and I wipe my damp eyes.

"I never came here much to speak to you. Didn't feel I needed this place, I suppose. I know where you are." I swallow against the sobs that threaten. "When I arrive there, I'll be near the ocean. And you're there, right? Mummy, I don't ever want to leave you..."

I can't help my weeping as I recall what I realized that horrid night I lost Declan. As I awakened from fainting, I remembered something new to me: this vision of myself with my chin on the boat's side. No rain. Pale skies. Therefore it wasn't that night. I remembered myself floating over glassy waters. And I didn't want to leave her. I didn't want to return to the island without Mummy.

When Charles Carnegie arrived here before dawn this morning, and I looked upon his face, I remembered those old feelings with even greater clarity. Perhaps it's because I haven't seen him in the flesh since that time. But seeing him made me remember.

I don't want to be here. I won't tell our secrets. A mighty promise from a small girl. And one I kept it for so long—never speaking—for Mummy.

I stroke my palm over her grass one last time before standing. I cast my gaze to the man standing over by the gate. His head is down. I believe he doesn't want to make me feel as if I'm running short on time.

I walk to Gammy next. Despite how much I abhor weeping, I can't stop my tears. I sink down to my knees and hold my face as helpless sobs rack me.

"I'm sorry," I mouth.

"Never settle for an unkind man. That is the only thing I ask of you."

"I'm sorry, Gammy! Now I have to go, and I don't want to leave you! I don't want to leave our Hobbit house." I wipe my eyes and nose. "But...that's not true." Perhaps I'm really weeping because it's *not* true. I *do* want to leave our island. I must.

"Gammy, I wish you were with me. I know you're elsewhere now, but I so hate to leave you and your sea glass." I touch a bit of what adorns her stone. That's when I hear the footsteps behind me. I turn slowly and smile at wee Baby. She's standing with her head raised, as if she's posed for Gammy's inspection.

"Come here, wee rascallian." She bounds over to me, and I hug her warm body. "Are you ready, darling dearest?"

I cling to her, breathing deeply until I feel I can trust my eyes. Then I walk toward Charles, taking my time as I allow my gaze to explore the island from one of its highest slopes. I try to memorize each note of the scent here: the slight sweetness of the grass; the brisk, salty air; the smell of wet rock.

I look down at the village, with its colorful tin roofs. This is my home. I was born here on these rocky shores. No matter where I go, a part of me will always remain. I wipe a few stray tears. And then I'm near enough that his gaze touches my face. His mouth tilts slightly at the corners, making my heart ache as it reminds me of Declan's.

Charles's hair is peppered with gray and his face is leaner, slightly less feline than my Sailor's. But he's a handsome man. He's still broad about the shoulders, and he shares his son's kind eyes.

I imagine him before grief and worry etched their mark upon his heart, and I imagine my sweet Mum at his side. Then I force myself to quit. It makes me too sad.

I try to offer him a small smile.

He returns it. "Ready?"

I nod.

We walk the winding dirt trail to the village slowly. Baby

runs out front. When we reach the lanes, I find each porch and lawn are empty. I take my time memorizing details: Mr. Button's purple porch, Bill and Sarah Green's collection of six rocking chairs, the mermaid bench on Holly's porch—carved by her father. Then we're near the café. I think perhaps all the island's shown up for my farewell.

Inside, Charles and I are met with a crowd and a feast. I can't eat a single bite.

I step into the kitchen, and Mrs. Alice hugs me tightly. I break down, and she takes me outside through the kitchen door, into the foggy morning.

"Let me tell you something, my dear. Something I don't believe you know about me."

"What?" I whisper.

Her eyes twinkle. "This old lady, lifelong Tristanian, wanted to stay back in England. More than anything." She smiles gently. "Oh, yes. I was listening to Elvis Presley on the neighbor lady's records. I'd walk down the way and get a cut of steak from the butcher. All that was lovely. But my Harold didn't care for it. So we came back here to the island." She looks wistful.

My throat knots, so tightly I can't speak. I swallow hard.

"I didn't know," I whisper.

"I've had a lovely life here. I'll be buried by my Harold, glad to have these bitter winds whistle over my headstone. But..." She lifts her eyebrows. "But." She hugs me once more. "There's so much for you to see, my dear. Your grandmother would be dizzy with pride. I'll tell you a secret."

"What?" I murmur.

"Your Gammy—I believe she wanted your mum to go. She liked that Mr. Carnegie. In fact, I helped her stitch your mother's wedding gown. We designed it secretly to be befitting of a New York lady."

I start sobbing then and never do quite get a handle on

myself. Anna comes to fetch me from the kitchen sometime later, taking me to bid farewell to...well, to everyone I know.

Dot hugs my neck a long time. "I wish you the very best, my friend. No one deserves happiness more than you do."

Holly says, "I'm green with envy." She gives me a red-lipsticked smile. "Have the grandest time. And do send postcards."

Rachel's eyes fill with tears. "It's my dream as well," she whispers, so softly no one but I can hear her.

I'm standing for hours as I hug everyone I've ever known.

Mrs. Petunia White assures me, "I'll manage nicely till the next physician arrives. Mike Green has agreed to help me."

Mrs. Dillon presses something into my hand. A bank note. I frown, and she smiles kindly. "Some of us pitched in for you, dearie. Give it to that Mr. Carnegie. He'll turn it to the proper currency."

"The dollar." I note the amount and nearly pass out. "Nine hundred pounds! That's a fortune."

"Oh, that's pocket money. In America, you'll sell your gorgeous pottery. This is just a token of our well wishes. After all you've been through, my dear..." She hugs me close. "You know I adored your mum. She'd be so proud."

There's one person I haven't seen, and he appears as I stand near the coat rack, wincing at my aching feet.

"Father Russo."

At first I think he's looking at my feet as well. When he finally lifts his eyes to mine, I realize he'd been avoiding my gaze. I'm near stunned when his arms wrap around me. "Finley Evans —I'm so very sorry!"

For a moment, I fear perhaps he's weeping, but he pulls away, his eyes squeezed shut, shaking his head as if he's quite disgusted. When he opens them, they're brimming with tears.

"I am...so remorseful." He covers his face with a kerchief,

shaking his head before pulling it away, revealing a grooved frown. "I'm not sure what to say. I was blind to what was there before my eyes. So foolish. And so arrogant in my assessments. You have suffered greatly for my errors. And now what I've done..." He rubs his lips together, shaking his head once more. "Simply devastated over the young Mr. Carnegie. And...what happened with Daniels...it's on my soul."

I can't find the proper words. Father Russo hugs me again, and I pat his back. I find as we embrace that my heart feels... softer. As if something's shaken loose.

"What happened in the boat was merely tragic, Father. Not intentional nor your fault. Thank you," I say softly. "I forgive you."

And I do. I find I truly do.

Later in the afternoon, Mr. Carnegie comes to me and gives me his small smile, and offers me a plastic water bottle.

"We'll need to be leaving soon."

I nod.

"I'm told by the crew that the waves are picking up again."

"I understand."

And still...it's near impossible to imagine what fate awaits me.

At half past three, nearly the entire village gathers outside the café to shout goodbye. I'm fighting tears and losing as Anna and Kayti, Freddy, Holly, and Dot walk Charles Carnegie and I to the dock, where we find Mark Glass waiting with three trunks of my belongings—and dear Baby. She's wearing a lappy, her bow collar, and a leash. I'm not sure I've ever seen a sight more beautiful.

I can't help weeping as I squish wee Kayti and inhale her lovely baby scent. I was there when she was born. Now I'll miss most of her life. Anna's eyes well as I pass sweet Kayti back into her arms.

I hug Holly again. "Don't forget to write me," she says.

"I'll send all sorts of trinkets," I promise.

Freddy and Mark Glass load my trunks into the largest of the island's fishing boats. Anna steps in, followed by Dot and Charles Carnegie. He holds his arms out for Baby, and I smile a bit as I hand her over. Then I'm in a padded seat. I'm holding Baby as Mark fires the motors up, and soon we're off.

It's a large boat. Perfectly safe, I tell myself. I stroke Baby's soft head as my belly quivers with each swell that lifts the boat up toward the white sky. Dot rubs my back, and Anna smiles like a doting mum. After all that's happened, she seems genuinely pleased for me—which brings me enormous peace.

My eyes well again as my yellow and blue chariot comes into clearer view.

"Someday I'll come get you in a plane and take you to get tacos."

"You can't land a plane here. There's no air strip."

"Not all planes need landing strips."

"I want a glimpse inside," Dot says to Anna.

The odd contraption's called an Albatross. I'm told it floats like a boat and flies like a plane. When I first spoke to Mr. Carnegie by phone last week, he explained we won't be making any stops en route to Cape Town. We'll be airborne for some four hours and twenty minutes. I don't think of what will occur after. One thing at a time for me, beginning with the tethering of our fishing boat to the sleek Albatross.

A door on the plane's side opens, and, with great care, we file inside. It smells like leather and fine things and flowers, and it looks like something from a magazine. I spot bunk beds carved into one of the walls, a table sporting a yellow bouquet with an anchored vase, and a sleek screen displaying urban images as crisp as those on Declan's phone. The floor is short, tan carpet. Hanging from the ceiling is a lamp that looks as if it's made of crystal.

Two female crewmembers emerge from a dark hall-like

space. They're wearing crisp, navy blue uniforms and high-heels that draw Dot's eye.

"Welcome aboard," one says.

"Which one of you is Finley?"

I raise my hand, and from there they're fussing over Baby and me, and I'm saying more goodbyes.

"Call immediately—the moment you land in America," Dot murmurs.

"I demand a call tonight," Anna says. "The very moment you reach Cape Town. I know you'll fly out again nearly immediately, but please do call." Anna's face crumples, and that's all it takes. I'm weeping as I cling to Baby, and slowly—and too quickly—the Albatross clears out.

Mr. Carnegie—Charles, he keeps insisting—offers me a tissue, and I wipe my eyes and try to smile kindly at the crewmembers. He shows me to the bottom bunk bed, and I find it's piled high with pink pillows and soft-looking blankets. There's a glossy screen in the wall beside it and a bucket of what's perhaps snacks perched in a corner. I sit on the bed's edge, and he hands me a bottle of water and a small pill.

I frown at it, and he gives me Declan's smile, sans dimples. "It will only last a few hours. He wouldn't hear of you being uncomfortable."

Charles tells me how to work the TV and what movies it plays, but I don't start a show. After we're finished talking—he's assured me I'm safe and the pill will only make me sleepy—I swallow it and curl over on my side. Baby hunkers down beside me. I cross myself, pull the soft covers over my shoulders, and before the plane leaves the water, my eyes close.

NINETEEN

FINLEY

I awaken feeling...soft. And a bit thirsty. When I blink around the small, pastel-colored space, I feel a muted jolt of shock. I note the dull sound of an engine, and the way my bed bumps a small bit, and my belly clenches with fear.

Oh, what have I done?

Something presses at my ankles, and I realize with relief that it's Baby.

"Hi there..." I sit up and rub her head and check her lappy—all well—and one of the plane's employees appears.

She has long, brown hair and looks perhaps ten years my senior. "Hey there, Finley. How are you feeling?"

I yawn. Still quite tired, although I say, "Quite well." I look around the luxuriously appointed space, but I don't see an uncovered window. "May I ask...where are we?"

"We're approaching Cape Town."

I laugh in disbelief. "Are we?"

She nods, smiling. "You slept through most of the flight. Completely understandable, by the way. Would you like some dinner? We've got everything from all-American cheeseburgers to Wagyu ribeye."

When I frown, her eyes widen solicitously. "I can do an all-green smoothie...every kind of sandwich." She reaches behind her, turning to me with a booklet. "Here you are. This is our menu."

In the end, I have a peanut butter and jelly sandwich, one small orange, and water that's been flavored slightly minty, and watch out a window as the glittering carpet of South Africa begins to creep across the dark landscape below us. The lights are so numerous, I can't begin to count them. I believe I'm seeing lanes between them—large, dark veins of no light. Some of them look red and white. Perhaps from hundreds or even thousands of automobiles?

I ask Mr. Carnegie—Charles, he reminds me—and he confirms it. Those lights are from automobiles.

Unbelievable.

He sits by me as the plane descends, explaining what to do to fix my ears, and telling me about the sounds the plane is making so I won't be frightened.

I sweat a bit as the plane's wheels come down, making a grinding sound, and we bump onto the airstrip, but then I feel a rush because we made it. We step off the plane, and I smell... something odd. I catch Charles looking at me. He smiles as I meet his eye.

"What does it smell like to you?"

"Automobile exhaust...bread..." I sniff again, laughing myself now. "Dirt, I do believe. It's...an absence of water."

From then on, I can feel Charles watching me for my reactions, though I don't have time for many as two large men and one of the women shuttle us into a sort of wall-less car—a golf cart, Charles offers—and we're ridden across a smooth, paved road to a new plane. This one is bigger.

I forego the bed and sit in a seat by a window. Baby frolics all about as I watch all the people. Through the window, I see people servicing the other planes, and some at our plane. I've been counting since we exited the Albatross; I've counted no fewer than twenty-nine people—all here moving about the airplanes! Oh, and that doesn't count our crew.

Before we take off, the men—Steven and Hans—introduce themselves as bodyguards.

Like that movie, I wonder, but I don't ask.

"We're just here to help get you and Charlie make it to Seattle without any trouble."

I chew my lip. "There could be trouble?"

They laugh, but it's not unkind. "Some people use a bodyguard to clear the way for them when they go somewhere. Sometimes we'll drive for Charlie or get him breakfast. Not because there's trouble."

"We're just gophers, basically," says the one called Hans.

I smile, though I'm a bit puzzled. "That sounds lovely then."

Charles appears, raising his brows. It tugs at my heart, for he looks so much like Declan. "What are you two saying about me?"

"Just explaining what we do, boss man."

Soon we're all in seats and buckled. Baby's in my lap again, and I'm experiencing my first coherent liftoff. It's...quite frightening. But then it's better as we stabilize. I realize after we're in the sky that I never called Anna, but Charles says he spoke with Mayor Acton and he'd promised to update the entire island. My eyes tear a bit at that, and Charles passes me a tissue.

When it's seatbelts-off time and our wee crew has dispersed about the cabin, Charles invites me over to a table, and the woman with the brown hair serves us eggs, bacon, and toast.

"It's ten-thirty your time," he says. "Maybe after this, you'll want to sleep."

I nod. *Unlikely.*

After a brief silence, he looks at me cautiously, and I can sense he's working out a way to say something.

"You know...I hope this doesn't seem presumptuous. But I'm hoping you might see me as a father figure...over time. Someone who wants to look out for you. Help you when I can." He glances down briefly before meeting my eyes. "Your mother was the best thing in my life. Brief though it was."

As it turns out, I don't sleep until after we stop for a re-fueling in Amsterdam.

I listen with a tissue pressed perpetually to my eyes as he talks about his time with Mummy, answering my questions frankly—when at last I'm bold enough to ask them—and with tact and kindness. I learn they kissed beneath the arches that trapped Declan and I in the burrow. He begged her daily to return to New York with him.

"So...why didn't she?" It's perhaps my biggest question.

He smiles sadly. "I think she was scared. Too scared to leave her mother. And then the more we talked about it, through letters—" I arch my brows at that, because I've got them in my crates— "she felt more comfortable. But by then she knew I had a family setup for marriage. Like being promised to someone." He adds, "To Declan's mother, Katherine."

"Oh." I nod slowly.

I see him swallow. It's a brief thing, but I know the contours of his face so oddly well, for they're so like my Declan's. It's a bit of pain leftover...lasted decades.

He lifts his brows. "Your mom didn't want to interfere." After a moment of silence, he says, "I think she was too aware of the differences...in our economic situations. It was probably my fault. I talked so much about what I could give her. Trying to court her, you know?" He smiles wistfully. "I think it intimidated her."

He's so kind, talking through the entire situation with me

when we both should be sleeping. I confess I read some of the letters.

"You were coming for us, weren't you? You and Declan."

He hesitates before he confirms what I knew to be true. "We were going to take the two of you back to New York. Whether the powers that be agreed with it or not. Your mom was married, but that shouldn't make someone a prisoner."

"The laws are archaic. They've been changed now. I think they were never meant to be a chain. Or so I was told...after."

He nods. "That's good."

We drink tea and talk until my throat is tired. We talk of Declan...of his mother. How she left when he was four, and nannies cared for him while his father worked long hours, pining for my mum. I ask how Declan's mum passed and am floored to learn she died by suicide. She jumped off a building in Manhattan following years of alcoholism and addiction struggles.

All the things he didn't tell me...

"I'm so sorry."

His lips press together. "Declan was at Carogue. It was New Year's Eve. She texted him before. It was 2005. Newly 2005. After that..." He shakes his head. "Everything was harder for him after."

Charles says Declan wouldn't speak of it with him—not ever.

"He wanted to pretend that he was...less affected than he really was. I don't know why. Sending him to Carogue was a mistake, I think now. We left Tristan and I never even took him back home." His face twists, and for a moment, his hand tunnels into his hair. He meets my eyes, and I see his are desolate. "I couldn't go home without—" He shakes his head, and I know he means my mum. "So I took him to Carogue. I told myself at the time that he'd be better off there."

"Perhaps he was."

He shakes his head. "The staff there ignored a lot of problems. With the kids. Drugs...and drinking. One of Declan's friends—he died, and I think Declan found him. Actually, I know he did." I think of Nate. "That was after I found out he had been having problems himself. Using...downers, for anxiety—or partying. Who knows. But I think it really affected him...what happened to his friend. After Nathan passed away, I don't think he was the same kid. Declan. And I didn't do a good enough job after his mom died. I was flying over when they told him—someone at the school. So he didn't even hear it from me."

"That wasn't your fault."

He throws his head back laughing, and chills prickle my arms. "You don't need to reassure me. I should be alleviating your fears. What can I tell you about America?"

"He would always do that same thing," I say softly. "The surprised laugh." I add, "I don't want to hear about America. I want to hear about Declan."

And so he tells me. Things I don't know, like how my Carnegie potty-trained in two days— "That kid was determined. I think it was the superhero underwear. " How he fared quite decently when his mum left because already, he was mostly watched by nannies anyway.

"She loved him," Charles tells me. "She just had her problems. As he got a little older, I think he knew that."

Somehow, he mentions Declan's favorite restaurant in New York.

"Is it tacos?"

He laughs and shakes his head. "Un Romance Con Tacos."

A romance—or a love affair, perhaps—with tacos.

Every shred of information he doles out, I snap up and file away. Declan's favorites: tacos, motorcycles, fast cars, swimming, learning to fly airplanes, scaling massive mountains, baseball, soccer (football), parties with his thousands of dear friends (I was correct—it seems he's obnoxiously well-liked), roller coasters at "theme" parks, reading, foot rubs, saunas, yachts, Scotch whiskey...and, from his father's perspective, anything that can be snorted, swallowed, or injected.

I'm pleased to see that Charles seems to understand it, though—that addiction is a sickness much more than a choice.

"I could tell he was really trying," he says. "For a long time."

"I think that's true."

By the time I fall asleep a wee bit later, watching the screen by my bed as it shows the European light grid below us, I feel as if I've gained a friend—someone to help me through this odd new life. And my heart bleeds with wanting Declan.

TWENTY

FINLEY

TWO DAYS LATER

My pulse begins to gallop as the line that inches down the road depicted on the GPS screen nears the red dot.

102 Infinity Cir., Leavenworth, WA

.5 miles

Stone the cows!

It's Charles driving our rented sport utility vehicle. I'm in the middle row with Baby, who's got her nose toward the window, which is rolled partway down. The smell is heaven—like sunlight, if sunlight had a scent. There's a certain richness about it: a blend of dirt, water, clean air, and a lovely, slightly spicy, earthen aroma I believe must be the smell of all the tall, green-needled trees. It's like nothing I've experienced.

I'm not sure why I didn't realize this would be the case, but when our plane landed in New York, and I felt the warm, soft air, I realized—it's summer here. We're in the northern hemisphere. It's lovely summer, and I'm in America. Baby is in America. Last night for dinner after having my vaccines and physical in New York, I ate a hot dog. It was lovely. Everything has been so lovely.

New York was lovely, but I think Washington is quite a bit

more so. Charles thought the trees might make me feel a bit odd or perhaps out of place, but I adore them. I adore their canopy, the hiddenness of this pine-needle-paved lane. I'll confess I don't adore the asphalt, but I see its practicality. And all the same, I quite like this softer road.

When Charles turns the wheel and we start down the short driveway, I can scarcely draw a breath. We're rolling toward a green and yellow cabin in a clearing with tall trees above it, bending in the wind.

"You good back there?"

I nod, but that's not quite true. Everything is glittery and wobbling in the prism of my unshed tears. I squeeze my eyes shut, wipe them.

Then the car has stopped. We've parked. Charles says, "I'll take Baby for a look around."

I nod slowly, understanding. And I'm opening the heavy door. I'm passing Baby off then stepping out onto the spongy, needle-covered ground with its impossibly thick grass. I notice two red rockers on the cabin's porch. The entire front wall, where it's not door, is windows.

Knowing that he bought this property for my mum—for both of us, I suppose—hoping we might come here to adjust to American life bit by bit, these trees protecting us from people and their foreign germs while we adjusted to this vast, more modern world...it gives me chills. And fills me with such gratitude. And yet it's all so odd, because I realize now...if we had made it here I was seven, I'd be doing something very different now.

I try the knob and find it gives. I turn it slowly with my trembling hand and push the door open. I notice the room's vastness first. The roof's rafters, all the polished cedar. It smells...earthen. Like wood. The space is flawlessly appointed with fluffy couches, leather chairs and—

Him.

I see his tired eyes first. At first glance, I think they're bruised below, so dark are the circles there. I see the horrid paleness of his face—what of it isn't covered by his beard. I see the shock of white gauze all about his chest and shoulders. Both his arms are tucked against his chest in dark slings. He's propped up in a recliner with a pillow around his neck and a red blanket over his lap.

And then he's spotted me. I can tell the moment he does. His mouth trembles and tugs sharply downward at the corners as his eyes squeeze shut. Tears stream down his face as I walk to him.

Then I'm there beside him, and I don't know how to hug him, so I simply touch his hair. He breathes deeply, and then he groans, as I suppose the movement hurts his shoulders.

"Oh...my darling..." He groans again, more a bark of pain, and I take his face in my hands and lean down, pressing my cheek to his.

He's breathing deeply and shaking so terribly. "My sweet love..."

"Sorry." It's groaned.

"No. We won't be sorry...remember?" It shreds my heart that he can merely press his cheek against mine as he nods. He takes a few deep breaths, and then a low sob shakes his shoulders. I cling to his neck and hold his forehead against my throat. After each sob, he makes an awful, pained gasp, and I'm wrenched with worry.

"Cover my mouth." It's a low rasp.

I realize what he means, but my lips can't help a gentle kiss before I do as he asked. I hold his head and cover his mouth and stroke his hair and forehead and his neck. His hair is damp, and I'm stricken by his new fragility—the way he trembles and his tears drip down his face.

When he's breathing fast and shallow, but a bit more steady, I wipe his cheeks with my shirt. I wipe his lovely welling eyes, and when more tears fall, I kiss his temples and his forehead and his soft, tremulous lips.

I'm half atop him now, one of my knees up on his chair and my right arm around his neck, my hand in his hair.

"I don't want to hurt you," I murmur.

I lean back a bit, so I can see his sweet Carnegie face.

His eye shut. "Don't...stop touching me," he rasps. "Please."

I tuck his head against me, his forehead to my throat. "Never will. I promise." I kiss his hair. Then I kneel at his feet. I meld myself against his legs and lay my cheek against his thigh and wrap my arms around his waist and hug him.

"Sweet Carnegie." I rub his warm, damp back and then lean down to stroke his calves through his cotton pants. He swallows as he watches me with sad eyes.

"What can I do for you, love?"

He shuts his eyes, shakes his head.

* * *

For a second, I'm worried I'm gonna fucking cry again. I can't think straight—I just know that I don't want it. Any of this. I don't want the searing pain, and I don't want her seeing me lose it again. I grit my teeth and suck some deep breaths back, and finally, the feeling passes.

"Talk to me...if you can, darling." Her hand runs through my hair, and I'm back to square one. The gentle movement makes my throat sting. I squeeze my eyes shut, trying not to think about how good it feels. How fucking great it is to have her hands on me again.

Jesus...

I just know I'm gonna lose control again. Siren can tell, too, because she leans back down and moves in close and presses her cheek to mine. Her hand strokes up into my hair again. It feels so good.

She kisses my cheek and my temple, whispers sweet things in my ear.

I can't even hug her. I just want to hold her. I don't want to be in the chair by myself...without her.

I'm gonna cry, so I take deep breaths, but it hurts my left side. It hurts so bad I can't help but groan...and then I'm sort of halfway crying.

"Oh, I'm so, so sorry... Take some deep breaths."

"I can't." My voice is raspy. I can't even say more without breaking down.

I've got some hurt stuff up around my left shoulder, and every time I breathe, it hurts. Finley covers my mouth with hers again. I'm so used to touching her, I go to raise my right arm, and my newly repaired shoulder responds with a bolt of pain that leaves me panting.

Her hands stroke my cheeks. "What are you taking, sweet love?"

It takes me a second to process what she means. "Tylenol... and Advil." My teeth start to chatter from how much it hurts. "Had to...take a break from Toradol."

"But...that can't be all. Can it?"

Tears well in my eyes again. I shut them, and I feel one dripping down my cheek. *Get it together, Carnegie.* I can't even wipe my face. So I know she sees the way I'm struggling to keep myself in check. I don't want to tell her...but I know I have to.

"I...got Dilaudid...at the hospital."

"Do you want more? I can get you something. Your father and I will get you anything and everything you need, my darling. Just tell me what."

I close my eyes. She doesn't get it. I shake my head. I don't want that shit again. Why does she think I'm shaking and sweating?

"I had...the RC surgery..." I stop to get a careful breath. "On my throwing side...to *avoid*..." To having to take that fucking stuff again, in a few more months. I grit my teeth. Even talking hurts me where the bullet did its damage.

"You had the surgery sooner to avoid requiring Dilaudid again...so soon after they fixed the gunshot damage?" I watch her perfect Siren face as she realizes fully what I mean. "I think I see," she says softly. Her fingertip traces my eyebrow. It feels really good. My eyelids shut.

"You didn't want to recover from this—" her hand hovers over my left side— "and then go in again for surgery on your right shoulder that's been hurting for a while. I remember you said in the burrow that you'd have to get it sorted. So you convinced them to do both. They fixed up your left side, of course, and then turned right around and did the other surgery on the right shoulder—for the rotator cuff—the day you arrived in Boston from Cape Town. So...I believe that would be four days ago. Is that right? And time from the...gunshot itself...has been ten days."

I nod slowly, and she strokes my hair back off my forehead. "Your father told me some of that. I've missed quite a lot," she says hoarsely. "Now you're wrapped up like a mummy." Her hand waves to my chest. "You're in ghastly pain. And I think perhaps you're disappointed over the Dilaudid, even though no doubt you required it to keep from going mad, as you are now. Sailor...what must we do with you? Hopelessly stubborn."

I shake my head. I can't think straight enough—talk straight enough—to make her understand. I'm craving it again, so fucking bad now. Even more so because I feel so shitty. Even my skin and hair hurt from withdrawing again...since surgery.

"It's not...supposed to be this bad." The words are whispered, half delirious.

"What isn't? The *gunshot* wound with these two ribs fractured?" She points to where I'm hurt, up near the collar bone. "Your father said the bone in back is cracked as well—your scapula. I suppose that's why you can't take deep breaths. I'm sorry for that bit of horrid advice."

I shake my head. *Don't be sorry.*

"Is that supposed to be less painful, or the repaired shoulder on the other side? And I've heard that craving what you formerly relied upon daily for years and were re-introduced to in a dire emergency is quite the cake walk. Clearly going back off opiates won't hurt at all..."

My lips crack as they tuck up. Such a fucking wise-ass, Siren.

"Where the devil is your nurse? Who on earth has been here with you?"

"I had him go...before you got here."

"Wrong choice. But let's now take stock." My eyelids feel weighted as she looks at the pill bottles on the table by the chair. "Antibiotics and the empty Toradol." She lifts a brown bottle and frowns at it. "What's this then? CBD and THC...what's that?"

I swallow against my dry throat. "Marijuana."

"It's been legalized here, correct? It can be a powerful painkiller."

"I don't need it...if I don't move much."

"Why would you forego it? It's not an opiate."

I lift my shoulder out of habit and grunt as I realize the mistake.

"Can one become addicted to this?"

"Psychologically," I rasp.

"Okay, so as one could become addicted to chewing fingernails, or not eating...or over-eating...or melatonin. Psychological or mildly physiological. On television yesterday, I heard of the term 'nothingburger.'" She smirks, and I lick my dry lips.

"Yes," she says, unscrewing the bottle's top. "There's even a dropper, my favorite way to dose my wayward Sailor. What's this other bit, this wee canister?"

"It's marijuana," I whisper. "For vaporizing."

"Let's do all of the above."

I swallow the tincture, and she gives me some water.

"There now."

I'm half asleep as she rubs something on my lips. I want to ask her how she's feeling. Did she get all the vaccines my dad told me she'd need so something like the measles doesn't take her out? Dad said he made her take a Xanax when the Albatross left Tristan.

It was the same plane that got me from the *Celia* about twelve hours after the ship departed from the island with my gunshot ass. Ten days ago, like Finley said. Because of the special plane my agent's friend owned, I got to Cape Town within a day of what happened. It was a late debridement, but there wasn't much left in me anyway. The good doctor had a .22, so it was a small bullet. Probably the ricochet through the muscle is what snapped my top two little ribs and nicked my shoulder blade as the bullet blew out my back.

One of the scientists on board the *Celia* was an MD doing cancer research based on fish. I owe that guy my life. He packed my wound in a way that kept it from fucking up my lungs. The ship had oxygen for divers and a couple bags of saline for emergencies. The MD saved my life by keeping me warm and pumping me full of saline when my blood pressure would drop... which was a lot, I think. Dude even rode the Albatross with me and helped me till I got to Cape Town. I wish I could tell Finley about it.

But I feel so fucking weak. Even breathing takes a lot of energy.

Next time I open my eyes, my dad is here, and I smile because he's playing with Baby. "Hey, Baby," I whisper.

Dad's hand ruffles my hair. Then Finley is hovering all around me, checking my pulse...doing some other stuff. I think I'm drinking water. I don't know. It's kind of funny really. I'm just laughing.

"You make me feel...a whole lot better."

"Is that so?" She kisses my cheek. "I think that's not my doing. But I love you, darling."

I'm falling asleep, but I want to tell her... When I was trying to hold on between Tristan and Cape Town, I kept seeing those gold waves—my death dream waves; the waves that brought me to the island with the thought of drowning myself—and I finally knew what they meant.

I lived through overdosing just to fight again to kick up from below those flashlight-brightened waves at Tristan. When I was trying to hang on until Cape Town, I latched onto the thought that I'd never told Siren how much I really loved her. That's what I told myself to find the strength to hold on, even when it felt so fucking hard.

TWENTY-ONE

DECLAN

"When the plane—" My voice gives out. I swallow, and Finley holds a sports bottle to my mouth.

"There you go..."

"When the Albatross landed in Cape Town," I rasp, "I don't know. I kind of came to more, I guess. Realized...I didn't know what happened with you. I thought you might be dead. I don't remember, but they told me later that I flipped my shit." I almost raise my arm to run a hand through my hair, but I stop myself in time and shut my eyes a second instead. "They said I demanded to be taken back to Tristan. I was fucking furious that you weren't with me."

It's nighttime now. She and I are lying in the adjustable bed Dad set up before he left. Finley's got her arms around my waist and her legs threaded through mine. She's craning her neck back so she can see me over all my bandages.

"After the debridement—that's when they clean a bullet wound...my nurse told me later that I made someone call Tristan." I smile. "Ask about you. I don't know who they got, but they found out you weren't dead."

"And Doctor was," she whispers slowly. "It was Mrs. Acton who took that call. I found out the next day." She rubs her eyes, and I realize they're wet again. "Can you imagine? No one thought to tell me you survived until the morning after that call came." She shakes her head as her eyes glimmer with more tears.

"For two days, I didn't move from Anna's bed—Anna and Freddy's." Her lip tucks up a little on one side, but it's not a smile. "I tried to get an update, but that took another twelve hours. That time, I was told I couldn't have details, but your father called me back quite quickly. He listed your injuries, and I wept. I was passed out when they got you into the boat. From hearing when Father tried to grab the gun and it went off. Doctor fell on me," she whispers.

"Dammit. I think that's why I thought you might have gotten shot, too. I must have had some kind of memory of not seeing you...when they pulled me in."

"Yes..." Her mouth trembles before she presses it into a frown. "I wasn't conscious when Mark pulled you from the sea. I came to about the time the *Celia* departed. I screamed and raged to go, but Freddy wouldn't let me."

"Freddy. I think he was talking to me on the boat."

She smiles sadly. "He told me when they got you out of the water, he took care of you for me." She wipes her eyes. "It didn't make me feel much better."

"It's okay, though. I'm okay."

"You will be, because I'm not letting you come down from the marijuana cloud—not for...however long it's necessary." She smiles.

"Siren?" She kisses my lower abs, and my dick twitches.

"Yes?"

I swallow hard, because my throat's gone tight again. I have to whisper so my voice won't crack as I tell her, "I want to touch your hair."

She spreads it over my chest. I squeeze my eyelids shut. She's watching close enough to see my tears in the dark, I guess, because she wipes them. "What's on your mind, Sailor darling?"

"I wanted to tell you something," I whisper.

"I'm all yours." She kisses my ribs, and I close my eyes again.

* * *

Finley

"I couldn't say I love you...when I wanted to say it," he murmurs. "I didn't say it how I should have at the island."

"That's all right. I always knew you loved me."

He shakes his head. Tucks his chin to his chest, shuts his eyes. And then he looks at me. It's quiet in the bedroom, the darkness broken only by beams of milky moonlight. Baby's in the hallway. I can hear her moving around.

"There's something I want to tell you, Finny," he rasps. "Before you stay here a long time..."

"What do you mean?" I can tell he's feeling the effects of the marijuana. His eyelids are heavy and sometimes he speaks a bit strangely.

"I don't know if I can tell you." He sounds pained, which makes my chest ache.

"You don't have to tell me anything, my darling. All I need is to lie here with you. You elevate those shoulders, and I'll keep you warm and watered." I drop a kiss below his pec. It's been a game of loving him up without teasing him. Because I'm not sure he can be pleasured yet without the movement bringing pain.

"Finley...you remember how you told me...that first time... about your parents?" His voice shakes. "Inside the burrow?"

I nod as my throat tightens.

"You said you like ume candy...and phones with cords...that have colors?"

I nod, smiling a bit that he remembers.

"I like tacos," he whispers, "and airplanes that can land on water. And I really, really love you. In college one time...I auctioned myself off...and this old lady got a date with me. And we went swing dancing." He gets a breath, and smiles a bit despite his heavy eyelids. "I liked it. It was really fun." His face is relaxed, and his eyes look sleepy. So I'm utterly unprepared for what he says next.

"When I was in seventh grade, my mom died. And this man... who worked for my school," he whispers, "came to tell me. It was at night." His voice cracks there. "And my mom...she died from suicide."

He shuts his eyes and swallows hard and takes a deep breath, wincing after. "I was so...fucked up." He licks his lips. Inhales. "He gave me Xanax. Laurent was his name." His jaw clenches. "I wish I could hold you."

I scoot up by him, and I guide his face so that his cheek's against my chest. I stroke his hair. He's panting.

I lean down to put my mouth over his—do the breathing thing I do when he's having anxiety—but I don't make it before he says, "He raped me. It was just that one time. I was thirteen, but...I didn't fight him off. I think because of the Xanax. And I was so... surprised. I was so surprised he did it. He came back another time, and I attacked him. After that, I couldn't sleep, so I needed the Xanax." He swallows, and I press my lips against his hair. "I blackmailed him...with that secret. So he'd keep getting me the Xanax. I...wouldn't let him...so he started going to my friend. Nate."

He weeps as he speaks about Nate. He tells me all of what

happened, of finding Nate's body. Weeping hurts him, so I give him more tincture. As it begins to work, he whispers, "Usually...I try not to. I like pain...because it evens up the score."

And I realize there's so much here. There's so much for us to talk about: a lifetime's worth of secrets and the healing from them. I hold him as well as I can, and I kiss his cheeks and forehead. "Thank you for trusting me."

"That's all?" His voice is soft—so soft I scarcely hear it. "You don't think it's...fucking weird? And sick?"

"Weird is not even the second or third thing that comes to mind. I think I love you. And you've kept this secret for so long. And now you don't have to, because I'll help you. I'll carry it with you."

Tears roll down his cheeks. "I knew you'd say that."

"Then that means you know I love you endlessly. Insensibly. All I want is happiness—for both of us. The Sailor and Siren. I know you're bothered you were given the Dilaudid. I can feel it haunting you." He wouldn't look at me when he told me about it. "But...I trust you, Carnegie. I know how strong you are. Everything is different this time."

He squeezes his eyes shut, and I wipe his tears. "I can't believe you're here," he whispers.

"I knew I would follow you. If you made it, I knew I'd be on the ship behind you. What I didn't figure was your father's offer to come sooner."

"I wanted you. If you wanted to come." He whispers, "Needed you."

"I want to say something."

His eyes lift open to meet mine.

"Declan...I'm so sorry for what happened the night Doctor returned. I'm so sorry that you didn't know. At first..." I shake my head. "After the burrow, I thought someone would tell you. So I kept away. Out of shame, I suppose, and perhaps a bit of practicality. And then, when by chance no one did—when no one spilled my secret...I suppose I saw a way into the light. Just for a moment." I swallow.

I choose not to reveal more about Doctor that night. What Declan just told me should remain center-stage.

Doctor doesn't come up until the next morning, when Sailor awakens just before his NSAID dose and starts to tremble. He is radiating pain. He grits his teeth and whispers, "I know that fucker hurt you. More than once. Tell me he didn't...but don't lie to me."

I nearly laugh at that. As he holds the tincture under his tongue, I rub my cheek against his. "Don't worry about that. He's gone and we're still here."

"You were scared of him."

I rub his hair. "Carnegie," I murmur.

"I scared you," he groans, "that night. I'm sorry I scared you."

I abandoned him there on the floor when Doctor appeared, and it's he who's sorry. I realize something more in that moment: It must have bothered him...to see me that way, beneath Doctor. Given his own background...

"It makes sense, though, your reaction. Please, let's not dwell there. I want to be here with you. Only here, and nowhere else."

His tired eyes well. "You do?"

"Yes." I wipe his eyes and brush a kiss over his lips.

"I might not play again."

"What do you mean?"

"I don't know about my shoulder..."

"You still have to endure rehab with it, yes?"

"It might not come back...good enough, though." He looks anguished.

"I'll be praying it does, if that's what you want."

"You still pray?" His voice cracks, and I stroke his damp cheek.

"I'll always pray."

I help him swallow some Advil and feed him a bit of bread and more tincture.

"I don't see the point." His eyes are shut now. I can't read his face.

"It's okay if you don't." I mean it sincerely.

I wrap myself around his lower body, hugging him about the waist, and Declan groans. "I wanna touch you."

"I know, love." I kiss his side, and he groans...and I realize I can see him straining at his pants.

"Touch me."

My hands hover above him. "Are you sure?" My eyes search his. "What if it hurts?"

"*Please*. If you want to," he rasps.

Relief fills me as I realize the tincture is working a bit now. I can scarcely stand to see him hurting.

"I want to make you feel good." I start stroking him, and he groans, lifting his hips. "Does that hurt?" I murmur.

"Fuck, no. It's been ten days."

"You can't touch it yourself."

He shakes his head, and I realize...I'm in for fun. I tease him wickedly—taking breaks to check how he's enduring. When he spends deep in my throat, I suck his sex until he groans harshly.

"Do it again."

I realize over the next few days that he's back in the burrow... with respect to how he feels. His body hurts beyond his wounds due to the hiccup with the Dilaudid, and he craves sex.

"We'll do it all again," I reassure him one afternoon. I stroke his hands, which I've realized he likes, and kiss his cheeks. "And you'll progress again. And you'll feel better again."

That night, I straddle his lap, and we make love with his sex sporting one of the condoms I ordered online at his direction.

Afterward, we shower, and I change his bandages. I see the round hole in his shoulder and the corresponding one at his back, and I can't help weeping at the sight of it.

"It barely even hurts," he whispers. "The worst part is not moving the arm. Because I want to hold you."

That tincture is a bit like truth serum.

"Do you?"

He nods as I re-wrap the area.

"When I was on the boat..."

"Mm?"

"The *Celia*. I remember...I just...wanted you."

"I'm so sorry that I wasn't there."

"I'm sorry I missed what happened with the doctor."

"I passed out as Father Russo tried to get the gun from him. I believe I remember the gunshot sound, but that's it." I swallow. "I never saw him."

I get his arm back in its sling, and change the dressing on his right shoulder—the one that had the surgery. Before I get it back into the sling, he strokes my hip with his fingers, presses his cheek against my belly. It's one of his hugs.

"Don't feel sorry," I say. "Not for that."

I get him settled with his two slings, and he shakes his head at the mirror.

I quirk a brow at his reflection. "Isn't he that famous baseball player?"

He smiles sadly. "I don't think so."

"He's sure easy on the eyes."

We wander back into the bedroom, and I stop by my bedside table.

He whispers, "Get down on your knees Finley."

And *that* is how he finds some equilibrium those first two weeks...until he's able to move his arms more, bit by bit.

"Sit on my face, Siren. And stuff your fingers into your cunt."

I do as he demands, and he licks me till I'm screaming.

Every day, it's, "Suck me harder. I just need to...fucking come."

So every day, I help him come.

And in the mornings, we walk slowly underneath the lovely trees, with my arm wrapped about his waist.

"I'm sorry I can't hold you."

"I'm sorry my husband shot you."

It's the first time such things have been said. We laugh so hard, it brings him pain, and we're forced back inside. I tease his scalp with my nails and feed him an Orange Creamsicle. He likes eating them. I think somehow it must distract from the sensations of withdrawal. I kiss his cold, orange lips, and he whispers, "Turn around."

I do, and there's a strange man at the door.

"Who is that?"

He smiles.

It's the kiln he had his father promise me when he called Tristan to invite me here.

Declan watches me at the pottery wheel in afternoons. Our precious days together stretch into weeks. His left arm heals enough so he can push his fingers into me. We shower together, eat food a truck delivers, and tuck in close at night.

Some weekends, his father visits, and we'll drive down to Seattle. Sailor's grown so very lean, but when we go into the city, he eats. After some time passes and he's hurting less, we roam all about the downtown, gorging ourselves.

It's a slow road, with his shoulders. Dutifully, with the discipline of a teetotaler, he cuts the marijuana tincture back for use for PT only. He's healing physically, but he still has his Laurent nightmares. He holds me against him in the night and breathes into my hair.

"You're the only thing that's ever made me feel better. At rehab, they say it can't be someone else. But I don't know how to do it any other way."

TWENTY-TWO

DECLAN

Living in the woods of Washington with Finley is a revelation.

For the first few weeks, I'm so fucked up. Withdrawal, and pain. I'm worried that she's here...with me. There's so much I want to say to her, but I can't get my head on straight. I feel like a little kid—helpless. I can't even hold her when we sleep. Can't squeeze her back and kiss her hair. I can barely use the bathroom by myself. And when they did my shoulder, the right shoulder, the surgeon said that pitchers hardly ever come back from it.

I'm so fucking sad and tired. But Finley is a miracle-worker. She helps me get a leg up on my pain and figures out a way for us to sleep. She cooks some, and my dad helps her get a bunch of other shit delivered.

At night, she helps me get showers and re-wrap all the bandages. She's never watched real TV, and it's kind of funny because she likes all the things that everybody likes. HGTV. *House Hunters*. We lie in bed with the top part tilted up and Finley snuggled up against my side, and she watches these motherfuckers pick out houses for hours.

In the mornings, when I wake up hard, she teases me—but

not too much. She seems to understand how much I like, and how much feels like too much in those days when I can't touch her.

In the moments when I'm sick of this shit, she takes all my orders. When I tell her that she better ride my face or shove some fingers into her cunt, she lets me be a bastard—and she smiles while doing what I tell her to.

I'll never forget the rhythm of those early days together. After we get out of bed, we eat some breakfast. I eat whatever she gives me, if I think I can keep it down, and when we're done, we head into the woods. Finley wraps her arm around my waist, and I watch as she *oohs* and *aahs* over the nature shit. It's all new to her, this terrain. The critters. We see a deer one day, and Finley squeals so loud, the damn thing flees in terror, and she's sad.

"You want a deer?" I can't help laughing. "I think we can lay some feed out, and they'll all come."

"Will they really?"

"Could bring deer. Could bring out the unicorns."

She elbows me and then gasps in alarm, but it's funny. "C'mon, you think you can hurt me with your little elbows?"

She gaps again, this time in mock offense. Her mouth curves into a playful grin. "I think they're more threatening than yours are, tough guy." She jumps out ahead of me and strikes a karate pose, chopping her arms in my direction. "Eh, eh, eh?"

I whoop. "Below the belt!"

"I do believe you mean in the slings." She snickers, and somehow we're kissing. I can't hold her, but I want to. I'm so fucking hard. She looks around—as if someone's hiding out here on our eighteen acres. Then she leads me over to a tree. I lean my back against it, and she goes down on me, blows me till my fists are balled up with the need to pull her hair. I come so hard, the sky between the pine needles seems to pulse.

And then I'm laughing, and she's smiling.

"This is so fucked up," I mumble.

She pulls my underwear and pants up, and she stops to kiss my fingers, hanging from each sling. "That you're T-Rexing it here in the wilderness?"

I snort in laughter when stretches up to kiss my mouth. I bite at her lips. "Who's sucking dick in the woods, mm?"

"These are memories to cherish."

"Are they? Is this everything you'd hoped for when you thought of leaving Tristan?"

"Actually, it's everything, yes. Do you know what it was like for me—with him?" Her eyes glitter with tears, and I grit my teeth as my arm reaches for her automatically.

She kisses my side and the back side of my shoulder. I can hear her get a deep breath.

"He was horrid...like my father. When I first knew him, he wasn't so. He was more like...someone older. I suppose perhaps a father figure. When he proposed the idea of marriage, it was more so he could remain on the island. You can't do that, you know—unless you marry in. Not even doctors can become true residents."

I feel her breathing against me, and I try to turn so I can see her. But she's got her face pressed against the area behind my right shoulder. I realize I don't think she wants me looking at her, so I try to get a hold of myself.

"He said it would be companionship—and only that. And then he broke his promise." Her voice cracks. "He wanted...more of me...and when I didn't give it—" She sighs loudly. "I'd like to remind you what a good cook I am. And how fashionably I plan decorate my own home one day. Please don't see me this way... but...he hit me," she whispers. "More than once. So I grew terrified of him."

She's back in front of me, wiping her eyes, clenching her jaw and looking pissed as hell. "The bar's quite low—yes, you could make that point. But I enjoy it here because *you're* here. I have a T-Rex fetish and a bona fide addiction to *this*."

She gives me a teary smile as her hand covers my bulge, and I shut my eyes, trying not to get hard when I can't do what I want with her. Christ, I want to carry her back home and fuck her till she can't think of anything, but especially not that fuck.

As it is, she rides me later that night. That weekend, my dad brings some deer feed out, and we spend the next week sitting in rocking chairs on the back porch, waiting for the deer to come. I'm doing a little bit of PT on both arms—not much, though—and she's practicing pilates.

On a Sunday night, as Finley's pulling homemade cinnamon rolls out of the oven, I see them through he window.

"Hey, come here. Look at this," I whisper, pointing. "That's a buck, and that's a doe. See how he has the antlers?"

We don't move as we watch them eat what we left. When they're gone, Finley is laughing, and she's wiping her eyes.

"What?" I chuckle. "We're crying over deer now?" I lean up against her, kissing her shoulder and then her hair. "It's okay if you wanna cry." I kiss her hair back from her forehead—just this funny little move I learned to do with my mouth—and Finley's soft lips catch mine.

She kisses me deeply, and then she pulls away and whispers, "No, you lout. I'm crying because I'm happy to be here with you...and you moved your arms so much today. The right one in particular pleases me," she clarifies. "And I'm crying because I'm late with my cycle."

My stomach feels like I just swallowed a brick. "How late are you?"

"Only a day...but I'm frightened," she whispers.

I've never been so grateful for a little bit of range of motion in my arm. I hold her just a little and wrap one of my legs around hers. And I know we're still okay, because that makes her laugh.

"You ever been a day late, Siren?"

"No." She wipes her eyes, and more tears fall.

"What bothers you about it? Just...the baby thing?"

"I adore babies." Behind her, Baby hears her name and raises her head. "I don't have a home, though. I know not a single soul here in America but you...and your father. Everything is gotten with money. Your money. More than anything, I don't want to be a burden to you."

Now she's sobbing, and oh shit, somehow I've fucked up with this.

"Shit, Finley. This is your home. Wherever I am, that's your home. You want a card with your name on it? We can go get one at the bank tomorrow."

She's shaking her head.

"You don't?"

"My name is Finley Daniels," she sobs.

"Jesus. I didn't think about it."

"Why would you? I lied to you!" She pulls away, still crying. "It's been lovely, but perhaps I should go back if I'm not—if I'm not pregnant. Just give you a bit of time, now that your arms are moving a bit more and everything."

My stomach flips so hard, I almost think I'm gonna be sick. "What do you mean? You want to leave?"

"No." She steps closer. She's still crying as she strokes my hair back. "Don't go losing color in your face. We just got it back, you'll recall."

"I don't get it."

"It's all right." She's wiping at her eyes. "I'm just...a bit afraid. And I don't want to be a burden, ever."

More tears streak down her cheeks, and she wipes them. "I adore it here. It seems too good to be true. I think I'm waiting for the other shoe to fall."

I feel her tremble, and I realize—God, she's gotta be so shaken up. I got shot, yeah, and it was hell worrying about her on the trip to Cape Town. Then I got worked up over the Dilaudid, and got kind of fucked up by withdrawing again right around the time she got here. But I'm American, and I'm back in America with Finley—who I love more than the world. If I can't play ball again, I know I'll do something. Staying here and making babies with her seems like a damn good backup plan to me.

For Finley, though, her whole life changed. "I'm so fucking self-involved, I didn't realize." She's so sweet and strong, a guy could take advantage of it without even meaning to. "I'm sorry, baby. I don't want to be like that. I want to know what's on your mind." I kiss her temple. "Don't keep this stuff to yourself, okay? Being a moody prick and not talking about shit is my job."

We make up with sex. The next morning, I wake up before her. I can raise my hands up to my ears now, if I'm careful, so I call around and make an appointment. The next day, a Tuesday, I get us an Uber and we go to tiny downtown Leavenworth.

We eat cheeseburgers at a picnic table by the creek, and Finley grins as I feed myself...slowly. Then I've got my first official PT session. I'm so sore after that Finley gives me tincture from her purse, so I'm a little fuzzy as I try to explain to her about the therapist.

"You did what?"

"I booked us in...to talk to this lady. She's older...like mom-aged. If we had a mom."

"It wouldn't be the same mum." Her eyes are huge. She looks completely confused. I start laughing, and I can't stop till it hurts.

"Carnegie. Calm yourself."

"Sorry."

"We're doing what?"

"I thought we could talk to this lady—her name is Rachel Meyer—about what happened."

"What happened? Oh right," she whispers. "You got shot,

and I'm a widowed, hell-bound liar. I don't want to tell this person about it. She'll say you should never speak to me again. Who do you think has got the raw deal? It's not me!"

"Siren. Dammit. Where's your sense of self-love. Isn't that the big thing? Like on Instagram? I see it all over the fucking place...you need self-love."

"Do I?"

"Yeah, you gotta love yourself like I do."

"Like you love yourself?" She crooks a brow, and I laugh. "No —like *I* love you."

"And you love yourself like I love *you*?"

"I don't know. There's goals and there's reality." I laugh at myself. She sighs loudly and kisses me before we start to walk.

"How do you know where to go?" I ask.

"I'm following your walking GPS." She holds my phone up. "Put her name in just now. Keep up, Rexie."

"I'll show you up when we get home."

She smiles, but it's not her normal smile. It seems tighter. I can't figure out what about that tense smile bothers me so much until after the meet and greet with Rachel, our new sort-through-all-your-deepest-feelings-ologist.

I look down at Finley as we wait for our Uber, and it hits me: here is Siren on a street in Washington, her red hair blowing in a summer breeze. She's been ripped off the map as she knows it, flung into a different fucking hemisphere...because of me. She's here with *me*.

I introduced her as my girlfriend to Rachel, but Jesus— Finley's not my girlfriend. What the fuck is wrong with me?

"Hey...walk with me." I bump her lightly with my elbow. When she blinks at me but seems a little lost, I ease my arm out of its sling and hold my hand out for hers.

"What are you doing?"

"Just walk with me."

I can tell she doesn't want to hold my hand. She won't thread her fingers through mine. Then wraps her hand around mine, and she tries to keep my arm from moving. That makes me laugh.

"Have you gone quite mad?" she asks me. "I thought there's a car called?"

"No." I stop and cancel it. There's a fountain right between these two clusters of shops. I lead her over to it. Get her to sit down on the bench. "Would it bother you to wait right here for me, for just a few minutes? I need to go do something."

"It can be the first step in my being social routine." She smiles. Rachel recommended she get out more, which is a good fucking point.

"I'll be right back, okay?"

She smiles. "I'm not worried."

Three doors down, there's this little jewelry store we walked by earlier. I get some looks when I walk in, but I don't know if it's because I'm me or because of the two slings. The woman who comes over to help me is older, and she looks kind of fancy in a dress; I'm hoping that means she's not a baseball fan.

I tell her that I need a ring and ask about the January birthstone. It's red. I don't want it to be red.

"Does she have a favorite stone?" the woman asks.

I swallow. "I don't really know."

"That's okay. What about the month you met?"

"April."

"April's stone is the diamond."

My head spins a little. "Is it?"

"Yes, but you don't have to use that if it's not your intention."

"If what's not?"

"Well, if you're not wanting to get married." She gives me an understanding smile.

"I am."

Her eyebrows arch up. I clarify. "That *is* what I want to do."

"Well why didn't you say so?"

I try to think of Finley's style, of what she wears. But I realize I don't know. I realize Finley probably doesn't know. She's never had a lot of options. I think of what she said about her name, and how I want her to have my name. I think of what just happened with the doctor—her abusive husband just now died—and I'm not sure what to do.

"I recognize your cap," the woman says softly. She smiles as she leads me to a case with bigger gem stones, and I realize she means she knows who I am.

"Keep it kinda quiet for me, okay? I'm here under the radar."

"Absolutely. I just wanted you to know that I'm a fan."

She doesn't pry as I pick out a vintage sapphire—almost three carats—set in a platinum, oval-shaped, kind of antique-looking frame. I don't know why, but it looks like Finley to me.

When I get back to the fountain, I think of kneeling down right then, but there are people all around. Every time we're out, I see Finley glancing around with this look of what I think is disbelief. So we go home.

There, we eat pizza, which she's gone full-on, frat-boy crazy for. She feeds mine to me with a fork, but I don't mind. In two more weeks, both of the slings can come off a lot more frequently. I think in three or four weeks, I'll be able to fuck her like I want to.

That night, we start on the *Harry Potter* movies. As we're heading to bed, Finley spots our deer couple outside again. We watch them for a long time, and I think about the ring inside my pocket. Maybe this is a good time. But I don't do it. I don't know... maybe I'm nervous.

We climb into bed, and Siren blows me long and hard.

"I don't think I am pregnant, in fact," she says after I come. "I hope you're not too disappointed."

"Only because I can't ditch the condom." I laugh. "Come here...I want to taste that pussy."

She smiles slyly. "I want to feel you in me."

"What does it feel like?" I'm trying to head her toward some dirty talk, but Finley rolls the condom onto me and looks up with a smile. "It feels like I'm yours."

Earlier, as we rode home, I asked the universe to send me a sign. Something. Anything—to let me know what I should do. If it's too soon. If it's too much right now.

It feels like I'm yours. I replay her words in my head all night. They seem like as good a sign as any.

TWENTY-THREE

FINLEY

If you had told me years ago that my Prince Declan would take me deep into a magic forest on a warm, radiant day, and he would kneel before me in a grove while our pet lamb frolicked nearby... or that a gentle breeze would ruffle his dark hair, and overhead, the sky would match the blue of his eyes...I'd have said you were spinning fairy tales. And fairy tales are not for people like me.

It's late August now. I've learned how to work the high-tech kiln; I've made three pieces. If Declan holds his arms still, he can knit, and as it turns out, knitting is his favorite takeaway from island life. He says it quiets his mind. I've three scarves now, and Kayti has a baby blanket.

He's started PT four times weekly—two appointments per week for each shoulder, poor Sailor—and while he's doing that, I speak with Rachel or attend a yoga class. I tried pilates, but I've found yoga to be more my speed—which is to say, quite leisurely.

We spoke with Rachel together a few times, though all that entailed was Declan trying to wink-wink with her about subjects she's unclear on, such as urging her to urge *me* to tell him if I'm unhappy. Which I'm not. After two sessions of such madness,

Rachel said she'd like to see Declan alone, as she's seeing me. So we're each seeing her privately now.

"I don't know what I'll tell her," he said as he grilled me my first steak. Flipping the steaks is actually helpful for his PT, so there we stood beside the cabin in the cooling evening air.

"Oh, well how would you? You've had the perfect life with absolutely nothing awry. You feel lovely at all times, and never scared or sad or worried. Surely nothing from the past could linger in your heart. Let us hope you're good at spinning tales."

That made him laugh. The truth is, though, he's doing terribly well. His father has visited us three times now, and he likes that. A few days past, some of his teammates visited, and though they were shocked to meet Baby and me and hear what happened, they were all lovely. And he obviously cares for them as well.

He never speaks of what he'll do if his right shoulder doesn't return to its former power, so I'm not sure. He rides the stationary bike each day as if he's trying to "get fit," as people here say, and I do as well. We say we're preparing for a race, although I hope that isn't true.

Each morning, we spend nearly an hour in bed—often longer. Afterward, we lie and listen to the birds chirp through our open window, with its lovely screen that keeps the bugs out. In the evenings, he holds me just a bit, being careful what position, and I think that helps him feel...more abled.

This morning, he woke me and suggested we take Baby for a hike. And over time, via a winding trail, he brought us here, to this bright grove that overlooks the river. He kneels down to pet Baby, and I watch him reach into his pocket for an apple.

But it's not an apple.

I gape down at what he's holding till my eyes well, and it's blurry. Blue and sparkling and blurry.

Declan's eyes are warm on mine. He smiles softly, revealing

dimples. "I don't want to push you into anything...but Finley, I want you to change your name. I don't want to be the Carnegie." He flashes me a tight grin. "I want to be *your* Carnegie. And I want you to be mine. I want you to live with me forever. I want to give you everything I have...and I want you to give me what you have." He laughs, quite wickedly, and then I'm laughing as well. "You're my favorite thing that ever happened to me. And you make me so much better. I realized the other day it's been less than two months...since the Dilaudid," he whispers. "But I never think about it." He presses his lips together, and his eyes squeeze shut. I touch his hair, and his hand lifts to wipe his eyes.

"Don't do that." I run my fingers underneath his eyes. "Let me, so you don't have to lift your arm."

"I don't want to go back to Boston," he rasps. "Yesterday I asked if maybe I could be traded. If my arm comes back."

I nod.

"I think they're willing do it." He blows a breath out. "If it doesn't...I don't know. But I'll find something else. Finley, I just want to wake up with you every day and give you those babies you want. If I play again, I want you there for every game you want to come to. I won't ever use again. I wouldn't do that to you. I don't want to do it to me, either."

"If you do, I'll bring you here and break your arms." I smile. "In seriousness, though, I'm not letting you go off the wagon without me. If you struggle with it again, I want to go where you go."

I crouch beside him, press my cheek to his, because I know if he could hug me fully, he would. I hug him and whisper near his ear. "Of course, my answer is yes. And no, it's not too soon."

I feel him breathing faster—the old withdrawal bit. He shuts his eyes, shakes his head. "I won't be like this forever."

I kiss him, and then we're on the ground together. Baby's

there, poking her head into his pocket, looking for apples, and we can't stop laughing.

"Actually," I whisper between kisses, "it's the only thing I need, that. You must be like this forever. Or who will I be married to?"

He shuts his eyes and shakes his head, and I hug him. He kisses my neck.

"Can I see it?" I whisper.

Declan laughs. His eyes are so hung up on mine, he nearly slides the ring on the wrong finger.

I can't stop laughing. I can't stop hugging him. I can't stop hugging Baby. I have to help him get up, and we laugh about that.

When we're standing face to face, he looks into my eyes. "I know it's a gamble for you, but I swear I'll make it worth your while."

"I'm aware I'm getting T-Rex and his issues. You're getting a former mute who's responsible for getting you shot."

His face goes serious. "Don't say that. I mean it. You were not responsible."

I look down, and he nuzzles my face with his. That makes me smile.

"Dinos in love."

"Which one are you?" he teases.

"I'm the one that was afraid of water."

"No, I think you're a water dinosaur. You're from the water."

"I'll be looking that up on the Google."

He laughs.

"What?"

He's grinning as he shakes his head.

"Tell me."

"Just Google."

"Just Google?" I repeat.

"Yeah. Like it's just called Google."

"*The* Google is more official. They should change the name."

The sun glints on my ring then. I lift my hand.

"Hey, now you're just bragging," he jokes.

I pull my arms up to my breasts and fold my hands down, teasing him.

He shakes his head. "Just a few more weeks, and someone's getting T-Rexed."

"What's that?" I giggle.

"You'll see."

"I'm still calling you *the* Carnegie."

"You know what I'll call you?"

I shake my head, and he grins. "My wife."

* * *

Declan

It's good. It's really fucking good. I'm surprised how good it is—and also kind of not, because...it's Finley. Finley is the embodiment of good. She's where good goes to learn to be better and where bad goes to shrivel in the light.

It's been three months and two weeks now since she joined me in Washington. Today, we closed on a house in Seattle. Because I'm getting traded to the Mariners. I don't know how. I don't know why. But I'm already throwing almost just like last season. I can't do it too much yet, and the Mariners don't want to see me throw for at least four or five more months...but they agreed to take me, take the risk. If the contract's any indication, they even wanted me.

After we close on the house, we eat at a sushi place, and Finley fucking loves it.

"Water dino's all about the fish, huh?"

She laughs, and I watch her while I eat. She hasn't changed hardly at all since getting to the States and meeting people, making friends. I'm surprised at how relieved I am. She still wears her red hair long, down past her shoulders. The only difference is, here in Seattle, it sticks out more—because it's so damn beautiful. She's not into makeup, although she did buy some; she wore the lipstick once to make red rings around my cock. She is pretty into clothes, but I'm not shocked at that. She likes the flowy dresses and those wooden bead bracelets and big straw hats. She got her first cell phone recently, and she's obsessed with the camera. Yesterday she said she wants to start an Instagram.

I can tell I'm getting stronger on the laundry list of supplements and witchery Finley's got me taking, because when we go out, I've started getting recognized. A lot. I've bulked up enough now so I look like Homer again.

People keep asking why I'm not playing this season. I got suspended for the first few games for being in a "sex tape" that also showed me with a syringe, but I think everybody thought I'd be back after. I tell them I'm taking some time with my new wife.

Yeah. We did that. Right after we put the offer in on the house, we stopped by the courthouse. Finley wore a floppy hat. I'm stuck in button-ups because of my shoulders...but she says she likes that. We got a wedding picture with her new phone, and afterward, we went for a walk down by the waterfront.

That's when I caught her looking at the ocean.

"What do you think about the city? You like it?" I asked her.

"I adore it. It's so...fun. And busy. Happy."

"You think you could feel relaxed here?"

She grinned. "Beneath the covers with you."

But...I don't know. It's awfully busy here, and I don't know if I want to live in town fulltime. The cabin's too far to be used for more than a weekend getaway once ball starts. So I've got a surprise for her.

After we finish up our sushi and we climb into Finley's new Lexus, I give her a grin, and she knows something's up.

"What are you smiling that way for?"

"What way?"

"Like you've got wicked plans."

I laugh. "I'm surprised you have to ask."

She shakes her head and covers her face, and I start us up I-5.

"Where are you taking me?"

"Where do you want to go?"

She laughs. "You're insufferable."

I for her hand, and she laces her fingers through mine. "You like me."

"I do," she murmurs. "I'm afraid how much."

"Still worried about the other shoe falling?"

She nods, biting her lip. "Rachel says it's not abnormal...with my history."

"She told me the same thing."

"Let's be a one-shoe family, shall we?" she asks.

I nod. "One shoe forever."

I think maybe she knows when we pass the lighthouse park and start across the bridge. She sits up in her seat and looks out at the sound with her eyebrows notched together. "Is this an island, then?"

"I don't know." I'm trying hard not to laugh. "What do you think?"

She squeezes my hand, and I'm grinning like a fool. Finley's giving me the kind of smile that makes my stomach do a barrel roll.

"Welcome to Whidbey Island, Siren."

"Are you giving me a party?"

"You want a party? I can do that for you."

She draws her legs up into her seat, and I can tell her pretty face is getting red.

"It's not a bad surprise. And it's just gonna be us at the party."

We're on this side of the island—closer to the city. It's a little cottage—just three bedrooms—but it's right there on the sound, where she can dip her toes into the water half a step outside our bedroom's deck door.

It's white brick, but kind of mossy, with two red brick chimneys and a dark roof that's got some ivy spilling off one side of it. Finley peers out her window as we drive through the low-key little neighborhood. I hang a right beside its wrought-iron mailbox, and we roll down the long, tree-shaded driveway. Her eyes widen as I park outside the garage. When I hand her the key, she starts crying.

I laugh as she hugs me. "I can't believe you tried to bill yourself as a woman who doesn't cry."

Her mouth meets mine. It's hard, then softer...gentle and then fierce again—like Finley herself.

"No one ever made me cry like you do, Sailor."

I pull her up against me, and I hug her hard. I'll never take that for granted, being able to hug her.

Her hand runs down my chest. I grit my teeth as her palm cups me through my pants.

"You have an erection now?" She sounds accusing.

I laugh. "What's wrong with right now?"

"Is this our house?"

"It's your house. Well, I guess it's mine, too, but it's got your name on it. What do you think?"

She whispers, "I adore it." She opens her car door. "Let's go inside."

We get in, and she cries some more. "Who put in the furniture? The fire is lit!"

I laugh.

"Did you pay someone to light the fire?"

"Would you be mad if I did?"

"I'd be devastated. If you did, that means you didn't apparate here and then flash yourself magically back to me, which means you can't teach *me* your magic."

"I think I could teach you some magic."

I take her to our room, on the house's back side, right up by the water.

"Sorry that it's just a mattress and some sheets. I thought you'd want to choose the bed and all the blankets and that stuff."

I laugh as she starts unbuttoning my shirt. "You don't want to see the rest?"

"I want to see you," she whispers. "My home is with you... remember what you said?"

"I do remember." She kisses my neck, and then I'm groaning. "Who am I to turn a lady down in her hour of need?"

I make Finley come until her need has been met, and we both agree I've shown her magic.

Outside, we sit on a swing I don't even remember seeing when I looked at the house with a realtor, and Finley rests her head against my arm.

"Does it hurt much today?"

"No. Hardly at all."

"The other?"

"They both feel pretty good."

"It's the green smoothies."

"Oh yeah. Love those things."

"They're very good! You said so."

"They are. I mean it. You've taken good care of me, and I feel better for it."

She wraps her arms around me, and I wrap her up, too. She

sighs, the sound a little wistful. "Why are you so good to me, Carnegie?"

"That's easy. Because I love you so damn much."

Her grip on me tightens. "It's so strange to be here. And feel this way."

"What way?"

She's quiet for a minute before she whispers, "Happy."

"Yeah, it's kind of like that for me, too. But let's not question it, okay?"

She nods. "You really are my prince. You know you are, right?"

"I'm not sure I'm much of a prince. But I love you more than anything. I would give you anything I could."

"Well, all I really want is you."

"That works out pretty well. Because all I want is you." I look around. "What do you think? You wanna live here when we can? When we don't have to be in the city?"

"Yes." She laughs. "But can we still live in the cabin, too?"

"I thought we'd stay there for a while longer."

"It seems mad to have three homes."

I grin. Probably better to wait to tell her about the other ones. "We'll spend some time in all of them."

Her foot hooks around my leg. "Could we go walk in the water?"

"Yeah. Sure."

We take our shoes off, and we step down off the porch, over the sand, into the cool, blue water.

"I love it. Even though I was afraid of it," she says, catching my hand again. "I missed it. How did you know?"

"I don't know. Because I know my wife."

"Say it again," she whispers.

"My wife."

She smiles. "My husband. Does it give you a thrill?"

"Every time."

"It really does?"

"Of course." I pull her close and lean my cheek against her head. "Being your husband is the most important thing to me. It's the only thing."

"I feel the same," she murmurs.

"We're a team here."

"Team one shoe."

We stand there for the longest time with our feet submerged and our arms wrapped around each other. I rub her back in circles, the way I know she likes, and Finley kisses my chest. When I'm hard enough to hurt, and Finley's leaning on me, moaning, as my hand delves into her pants, we stretch out on our new mattress and spend the night there, christening the master bedroom and eating what my shopper stashed in the pantry: Pop-Tarts and wedding cookies.

In the morning, we drive back to Baby. To our cabin. It's our secret place, where nothing else can touch us. Even after we move fulltime to Seattle, I think the cabin will remain my favorite.

When we pull up in the driveway, there's our doe and buck. They're in the front yard this time. When they see the car, they don't move; they don't even freeze up. "I guess they just like us now."

"They're always together," Finley murmurs. "Never any other deer." She looks down, and then back at me. "Do you think they'll have a baby one day?"

"I don't know." I laugh. "Do you think they will?"

"Perhaps." Her cheeks color.

And that's how I know.

EPILOGUE

FINLEY

April 1, 2019

Mummy,

It's been a bit of a stretch, hasn't it? We were talking quite a lot as I would wander through the forest or along the shore last summer and I suppose into the fall...but now things are so busy. I suppose I felt like writing again on a day like today, when it's rainy and the sky is milk white.

Also, last night I dreamed of you. It was almost frightfully vivid. We were in a boat, just you and I, and everything was sepia —but a bit warmer and a great deal brighter. You were rowing our boat. After a while, you got out on the shore and went to walk, and you told me to come back any time. Declan had a game I was worried I'd be late for, so...I left you there. I didn't wake up crying, though. I felt at peace about it. As if you belonged there. That was a change, I suppose.

I know you know already...but I'd like to formally let you know I got the surname you chose for me. Yes, I'm smiling as I write this. It is a bit funny, isn't it? It was going to happen one way or the other, so I've carried out the family mission. I'm Finley Carnegie now...and Mum, it's simply glorious.

Sometimes when I watch him play, or we walk together in the woods with Baby, or I look across a table as we're at a restaurant, I feel so...happy. Really just joyous. I love him so much. He's simply perfect for me, despite the odd timing and the tragedy we went through. It's so wonderful, at times I don't quite trust it. I'm not sure it's supposed to feel this good all the time.

I'm told it can take a bit of time in the light to feel that it's not odd to be away from darkness. If I feel that way, can you imagine how my prince feels? Oh, but he's so healthy now. So well and, honestly, I feel he might be happier than I am! I've got swollen ankles, after all, while my Sailor is in tip-top condition, strengthening his physique so he looks more demigod than mortal. He just got the starting job, and I can't tell you how pleased he is. He adores playing. He said he didn't even know how much until being in full health.

He played his first game for the Mariners in March. I watched from the family spot, and after, we went out with other players and their families.

I have friends here. Really, five acquaintances and three dear friends thus far. One is the wife of another player, one a woman I met at yoga, and the third is my astronomy professor. Yes, I'm taking classes at a local college. Just a few for now, to satiate my interest in a few areas.

I have a business now. As of last week, I've got the business license they require here in America. I'm selling pottery to local stores and occupying sales space in some others. It's called The Siren's Fin. I've got an online shop as well, at Etsy.

I think you'd love it in Seattle, Mum. Actually, I know you would. It's so lovely all the time. Even when it's not, if that makes sense. There can be a lot of traffic, and sometimes it smells like automobile exhaust, but there are petits fours and tacos. Grocery delivery. I buy trinkets for myself when I like: earrings and nail polishes, sleek pens with ink that sparkles. Small things for my Sailor and items for friends at Tristan. There are so many people here, and an absurd percentage of them are lovely. And also... Declan is here. I see why you loved his father. He is so much like his father.

And he's getting better. I'm sure you heard me when I talked of that with you. And I do feel it's better now. He so rarely has the dreams, and sometimes now I sleep behind him, with one arm about his waist. He's not meeting with Rachel anymore. We've both had to find new people in the city. In fact, he's found someone who specializes a bit in what he needs. It's gone rather well. One day, all that will pass like gray clouds, leaving only sunshine. But it's sunny now, in this moment, so who's complaining?

Mostly, I suppose I wrote today because I feel more confident than ever in letting you know that I'm okay now. If you're watching over me, as I know you must be, please know how well I am, and that perhaps you need not watch with any worry.

Mummy...our baby is a girl. When she's born—any day now!—she'll be named Isla Katherine.

I never went to the stars, Mummy, but you did. I'm so sorry that you didn't get away in time; you never got the happy ending you deserved. It still makes me weep sometimes. But I don't weep as much now. Now I try to simply think of you, and hold you very dear, and live exactly as I feel you'd want me to. When I hold Declan, I know you'd adore him. (Would you be pleased to know his father is seeing someone, as of recently? She runs a charity Charles started with Declan. It's focused on helping people talk more about their mental health. They've been on three dates thus far!)

What more is there to say? I'm not sure. Baby! She's doing quite well. In fact, she's here by me now, prancing about the garden. She's a big girl now, but still our Baby.

I'm a bit nervous about the delivery, but not so much. Declan and I learned Lamaze, although I already had some practice from when Anna had Kayti. If I need to, I'll get the epidural...or I'll be grateful for the C-section. Serious risks are blessedly low here.

I pray our baby girl will look like you, and be like you and Gammy. Please tell Gammy I'm so well, and send my love. And please give all my love to Katherine as well. It's a bit unorthodox, but I know you're all happy there, as we are here. All this ends well. On our end, I promise it will. I can feel it now, that it's all going to be well.

I shriek as something touches my back. I whirl. "Declan!"

He's grinning as he looms over the bench where I'm sitting in our garden behind the city house. He's clad in practice clothes and sporting sweat-crazed hair.

"What are you doing here?" He's home nearly three hours early.

"I don't know." He moves around the bench to sit beside me and drapes his arm around my back. "I guess I just missed you."

"You think she's coming today!" He lifts his brows, and I laugh. "You've got no chill, Carnegie. Go play baseball." I hug him even as I say it. "Truly, I missed you, too." I sniff his shirt and giggle. "You need a shower."

"I think you mean *we* need a shower."

We're wicked as ever in the shower, despite my whale-like state. He's so ready to be in me, but I so dearly love denying him. He suckles at my swollen breasts and rubs his long, hard sex between my soapy thighs. Then it's early bedtime for us. How ironic that the best way for us now is with him thrusting from behind, and pillows propped beneath my belly.

He parts me with his fingers, dips one in and paints me with my slickness. When he pushes in, he's a bit gentle—and I know why. I giggle at the absurd reason why, and he slaps my backside.

"Don't be a naughty Siren, Finley."

"Oh, but naughty sirens have the most fun." I'm laughing till he thrusts, and then I'm gasping. I'm so swollen now, and he's ever so thick. He fills me so I moan, and drags himself out. Then he pushes back in, and I cry out.

"Ohh!"

"You like that?"

"Yes!"

He pushes in again, until I'm panting...and then slowly drags out. "You need more?" He rolls his head at my entrance.

"Oh, please! Don't tease me."

"But I love to tease you." His hand strokes my spine as I push back against him, urging his sex deeper.

"I love teasing you," I whisper.

"I just love you, Siren."

"I love you, my Sailor."

He groans. "Love you more."

I cry out. "You more."

Afterward, as I lie with my pillow propped between my legs, and Declan's hard, thick body pressed against my softness from behind, I hear the echo of our words.

I love you...

I love you more...

Several hours later, we're repeating them—through groans and tears—as we welcome our daughter into the world.

It's an easy birth. So easy, he has to remind me we're a one-shoe family.

"One shoe and one baby and one lamb."

"And you and me."

He grins, and it's my favorite kind of grin. A bit shy and a lot kind, keen and assessing and teasing and...just my love.

That night, we lie in my railed bed together, sniffing Isla's head and laughing as we ponder whether we should truly be allowed to take her home, I realize something: I am home. Right here with him. It's true what they say, that home is where the heart is. And my heart is joined to his heart.

"I love you more," I smile.

"You more."

It's raining softly outside. And that's how we fall asleep.

ACKNOWLEDGMENTS

I spent nearly twelve months writing Covet, and it was often not pretty. Without a great deal of support from my family and close friends, and a lot of kindness and generosity from my publishing team, this book would not be in your hands. Jamie, Kiezha, Mary, and Rebecca—thank you is not enough. I appreciate your love and friendship more than I can ever express. As you probably know, LOL, I would never have finished this book without you. But hey...I did finish it! Yay team! To Candi and the team at Candi Kane PR and Kylie and the team at Give Me Books, innumerable thank yous for your patience and kindness. Kiezha, my dear friend and editor at Librum Artis Editorial Services, read Covet in many pieces and in at least two different story incarnations, and never once failed to make time and energy for this mammoth project. Thank you for making my work shine and for being one of the best friends I've ever had. Jamie Davis, who also helped behind the scenes with her author management services, donated many hours of her time reading my randomly timed deluges of fifty-seven texts—often fifty-seven panicked, wailing texts—and listening to me babble on the phone while I tried to "find the plot." I could not do life without you. Mary, thank you for reading Covet in its early form and for your constant generosity and support. I'm so lucky to have you as a friend. Rebecca...no words. I'm so, so grateful to have you in my life! Thank you to Abby for formatting two versions of Covet in close proximity, at the last minute. I appreciate you! A thousand thank yous to the members of my author group, Ella's Elite, who faithfully read my Covet updates and cheered me on through many delays. You mean so much to me. Thank you to the bloggers who signed up for...oh, I think at least two blitzes. Maybe three? Thank you for your patience and kindness. To my author friends —a massive THANK YOU. It's impossible to successfully release a book without a community-wide effort, and I have so many kind friends who have supported me during the writing process and offered their support this week, too. There are too many of you to list, but you know who you are. Thank you for making this solitary path less lonely. Especially thank you to Harloe Rae for your non-stop generosity and kind texts. Thank you to Laurelin, Sunniva, Anna Paige, and whoever else ends up offering a blurb for Covet at the last minute. You guys are awesome. Last but not least, thank you to my husband and my kids. My work on Covet rearranged our lives, and I could not have finished without you guys' love, patience, and support.

If you read and enjoyed Covet, please consider leaving a review on Amazon. If you do review, consider refraining from mentioning "the big twists." Inevitably, someone will leave spoilers, but when fewer people do, the reading experience is more enjoyable for others.

If you loved Covet and want a signed Covet paperback, you can get one for a limited time here: http://bit.ly/EJCovet

There is a prequel scene in which Declan finds out about his "sex tape" in the Sox locker room. If you want to read that, sign up for my newsletter. I'll be sending it out sometime later this week, and also sending out my playlist.

https://www.subscribepage.com/EllaJamesNews

Want to keep in touch? I would love that! Follow me on Instagram, my favorite social media, at @authorellajames and join my wonderful reader group at https://www.facebook.com/groups/EllasEliteTeam.

Finally, if you're struggling with addiction or mental illness, please be gentle with yourself. In choosing to write about such sensitive topics, I acknowledge that my work could be triggering for some people. If I was reading this book, I would be one of those. Some of my favorite people in the world struggle with addiction, and I have struggled with mental illness. If you need a lifeline, consider calling the National Suicide Prevention Lifeline at 1-800-273-8255.

Thank you for reading. I hope you enjoyed Declan and Finley's love story as much as I did.

XO,

Ella

ALSO BY ELLA JAMES

Off-Limits Romance

Crown Jewels

The Boy Next Door

The Plan

Fractured Love

Off Limits Box-Set

Sinful Secrets Romance

Murder

Sloth

Erotic Fairy Tales: The Complete Box Set: Red & Wolf, Hansel, and Beast

The Love Inc. Series

Selling Scarlett

Taming Cross

Unmaking Marchant

Made in the USA
Middletown, DE
10 January 2022

58302503R00321